UNRULY OBSESSION

*For those who want a man who can protect and provide,
yet also forces you into submission, only to praise you for
being such a good girl,*

This one's for you.
(Even if you're a brat.)

WARNING

This book contains adult language and sexually explicit scenes and may be considered offensive. This book is intended for adults only.

Lily

I never thought I'd be involved with the Italian Mafia.

My association with them has made me a target, so they've appointed one of their most ruthless to be my bodyguard.

He pretends to be my boyfriend, but a man as cold-hearted as Lorenzo Moretti is not built for high society and will never receive my father's approval.

Worse, he's getting too close to my secrets, my heart, and the seemingly perfect life I've built.

Lorenzo

Lily Taylor is my most challenging mission yet.

She's spoiled, bratty, and intent on making my life a living hell.

But the temptation of her curves and sharp tongue is distracting, making it hard for me to focus.

Her safety is my priority.

And I'm willing to take out anyone who compromises that safety—even her father.

1

LILY

The sun kisses my skin, and my eyes close as I embrace the idea of momentary freedom. The ocean offers a refreshing scent, the sand and breeze prick my senses as I savor this moment along the Italian coastline, avoiding the chaos slowly creeping into my life back in Manhattan.

A heavy sigh gets trapped in my chest when I think about my father's recent pressure for me to close down my floral business and focus on finding the ideal suitor to marry. I'm expected to fall in line to accommodate his unspoken agenda.

Don't talk back.

Do as I'm told.

Be the good girl.

I've been conditioned to all of these things, but it's becoming harder to oblige, even for the sake of upholding my family's name and reputation.

It didn't go down well when I told my father I was spontaneously flying to Italy with Ara and her husband, Luca, leaving out the fact that I was crashing their "babymoon." It was Ara's suggestion, and I'm grateful for the temporary out so I can figure out how to convince my father to change his unreasonable expectations.

He'd forbidden me from going and called me a brat for not taking his "request" to close my business and get married seriously. I walked out and was on the private jet within two hours.

I should be able to marry the person of my choosing, someone I truly love. I'm not spoiled goods just because I don't have any prospects at twenty-eight years old.

I've done everything I can to stay out of my friends' way since we landed two days ago. But there's one person I haven't done much to avoid.

I crack open one eye and glance over at the larger-than-life Italian man sitting beside me, looking far too uncomfortable under the sun as he shifts ever so slightly in his black suit. Surely, he's sweating under that. He's been sitting at the edge of a fold-out chair that looks far too small for him for thirty minutes, staring at the beach with absolute disdain. Although I can't see his eyes through the black shades he wears, it's obvious in the way his lips tilt down, he'd rather not be here.

The few times I've encountered this man, I've never seen him smile.

He's beautiful, though, in a stoic, silent way.

He looks like he's been carved from stone, and part of me wants to reach out and check for his pulse just to see if he has one.

"Didn't your parents teach you it's rude to stare?" he says, and a chill runs down my spine from the gravel in his rough voice. It's so intimidating that my gaze immediately redirects to the beautiful ocean.

Heat rises to my cheeks, but I ignore it as much as possible, trying to push away my embarrassment at being caught.

"I was just making sure you're okay," I bluff.

I'm not shy around men, but there's always been something about *him* that makes me tense and nervous. I'm curious about his past, present, and what type of man he truly is. Maybe it's because he's the biggest person I've ever seen, or perhaps, it's because he has a dangerous vibe not often found among our inner circle of the wealthy, which makes it hard for me to look away.

There's just something about him that's different from anything I've known.

"Why wouldn't I be okay?" he scoffs, only making it more obvious he doesn't want to be spending his time with me.

So, why are you? I want to complain. I didn't ask him to join me.

The conversation he and my best friend's husband exchanged was short but loaded with so much tension, I thought better than to question why Luca had convinced him to join me on the beach. I don't know either of the men too well, but my impression was that under no circumstances did Lorenzo want to leave the vacation villa. Though it would probably be more correct to say he didn't want to leave their side.

He's been hanging around Ara a lot lately, and he definitely has the build of some kind of bodyguard, and he gives off that impression. It wouldn't surprise me if Luca Armani is the protective type, especially with his wife being pregnant. It's a little insulting, though, to know Lorenzo will only sit with me because he's been told to do it.

Life can't be that bad if we're on a private beach that the Armanis own. He even grumbled his complaint about the ten-minute walk down to the beach from the villa because I didn't want to take a car. He just shadowed me every step, his silence filled with enough tension to slice the air.

"Well, aren't you hot in that suit?" I ask as I bring the piña colada to my lips and take a sip. He hasn't so much as touched the bottled water the server offered him from the makeshift bar.

Trips like this are meant for winding down and taking it at a slower pace.

Lorenzo, however, seems to work on an entirely

different level. I wouldn't be surprised if the man runs on oil and diligence.

Lily, don't be so rude.

I don't know why I'm so anxious around him; maybe it has something to do with my obvious attraction to him. I'm certain it has to do with his six-foot-two height and the obnoxious amount of muscle that makes it hard not to imagine what he might look like without a shirt on. He has dark hair, brown eyes, thick eyelashes, and a perfectly shaved shadow of stubble along his jaw. He looks like he was molded by the gods themselves, but his aura warns not to get too close.

Damn it, I'm staring again. I take another harsh slurp of the drink, trying to drown out the heat rising to my cheeks.

"Is that how you usually hit on men?" he asks, his face turned in my direction for the first time since being here.

"Excuse me?" I whip my glasses off to glare at him.

"You're trying to get me to remove my shirt, no?" he asks, still with that grimace staining his face.

"I was being polite because I thought the temperature might be intense with your twenty layers of clothing." I huff out a breath. "You know what, I think I've had enough sun for today," I say, snapping my book shut and moving to sit on the side of my lounge chair. I push to my feet, wrap my sarong around myself, and begin walking away, immediately regretting it as the sand scorches my feet, but too proud to go back for my shoes.

"You forgot your shoes," he calls out behind me, as if I'm a nuisance more than anything.

I can't believe I was ever attracted to this guy, but maybe it's because I looked at him from a distance. I can appreciate beauty, but I can also categorize someone with a sour attitude.

"Another drink, miss?" the bartender asks as I storm toward him.

"No, thank you. Thank you for today. The piña colada was incredible." I attempt a bright smile, reminding myself it's not him who's ruined my peace.

Lorenzo is only a step behind, infuriating me even more because the guy just doesn't take a hint. I internally curse his name the moment I hit the coarse gravel of the road, but continue to charge on with a cool indifference.

"Would you at least put your shoes on," Lorenzo says dryly from behind me, as if he's speaking to a child.

My feet stop of their own accord, and I look over my shoulder to glare at him again. If anything, he's probably happy because he thinks he's getting his own way since we're returning to the villa. I don't entirely understand his relationship with Luca Armani, nor do I care to give in to his antics. I came here for me. And I'm not going to be pushed around; I get enough of that from my father.

I snatch my shoes out of his hands and put them on. His expression doesn't change, only infuriating me more.

Flipping my hair over my shoulder, I decide I'm not giving in to this brute of a man. Instead of walking up the grassy path that goes directly toward the villa, I continue along the gravelly road.

"Where are you going? The villa is in that direction," he says with a trickle of irritation in his tone. Good, at least I'm not the only one who's annoyed.

"Surely you don't need me to escort you there, do you?" I say, turning and popping my hand on my hip. It's rude, but I don't care for his attitude toward me. "I'm going to find a nice, quiet place to read my book. Please, leave me alone." I tighten my grip on the paperback.

He probably thinks it's stupid that I enjoy reading romance novels. He seems like the type, anyway.

Stop being judgmental. You don't know anything about this man.

What I do know is Lorenzo gets under my skin.

Exhaling a frustrated breath, I try to bring myself back to the polite and polished version of myself that people expect.

"You can read at the villa," he says matter-of-factly.

"I can read *wherever* I like."

He remains silent as he continues to walk a foot behind me, and I release a cleansing breath before I can face him once again. "You really don't have to join me. We're literally in the middle of nowhere, and I can make my way back to the villa. I'll even promise to be back before dark. So, please, don't feel obligated to be by my side because Luca said so."

"If only it were that easy," he grumbles.

"What's that supposed to mean?" I ask as a car comes speeding around the corner. My stomach drops, and I freeze as it lines up in my peripheral.

Oh my God, it's going to hit me.

I'm jerked to the side, the car narrowly missing me, as I watch everything unravel in slow motion. My body is already beginning to tremble as adrenaline pumps through my veins. Lorenzo pushes me behind a tree with ease, caging my body with his, and my mind goes blank as he pulls out a gun and aims.

My entire world spins as he pulls the trigger, and I realize with startling clarity that I've stepped into another world entirely.

2

LORENZO

Lily freezes like a deer in headlights, and I pull her behind me just before the car that was aiming for her gets to where she was standing. I pull out my gun and shoot once. I'm already running toward the car as the impact of the shot blows out the back tire, and the car fishtails before hooking the next corner and then rolling.

The car lands on its roof, and there's only a moment of silence before someone from the vehicle starts shooting. I dart for the closest tree, cursing as I look back toward Lily.

"Stay behind the tree!" I order her. She's terrified, in a daze, her face stricken. Fuck me, it's probably the first time a princess like her has ever seen a gun go off that isn't aimed at a flying plate. "Lily!" I yell again, trying to get her attention. Another shot barely misses my shoulder, and I pull in tighter behind the tree. I look toward the villa. *Fuck, I can't waste much time here. What if they've ambushed the Armanis as well? I need to get to the boss.*

When I look back at Lily, I'm relieved that she's tucked herself farther behind the tree. Her chest rises and falls in that blinding pink bikini. The moment she's out of harm's way, I round the tree and take two shots. The first is at the driver's hand, holding the gun aimed at us. He's hanging upside down from the seat belt, screaming as he drops the weapon and clutches at his now-useless hand. I aim the second shot at the back of the knee of the other asshole trying to run away from the car. He buckles, immediately hitting the ground.

The man who is trapped in the car continues to scream as he awkwardly tries to unbuckle himself. The other one, however, smiles like a crazed man, and I realize too late, as I point the gun at him, that I won't be taking anyone with me to interrogate. He shoots three times at the belly of the exposed car, hitting the fuel tank.

Suicide.

No evidence.

No survivors.

The car explodes, and I'm thrown back from its heated blaze, hitting a nearby tree. Hard. My back and head smack against it, and I drop, disoriented. Ringing pierces my ears as I shake my head once and then twice, trying to gather my bearings as quickly as possible. *Are there more? More cars? More intruders?*

My vision fades in and out as I stand, pushing through the inconvenience.

A faint voice in the distance creeps in through the fog in my brain, but I focus only on the threat that's evaporated into flames. Lily comes into my peripheral vision, and I realize it must've been her calling out to me. *Damn it, she was meant to stay exactly where I told her to hide.*

I immediately pull her in and behind me, adrenaline taking its course and surging me back to life. We need to get back to the villa. I grab her hand and begin to run toward the grassy path. I glance back over at the car; now it's nothing but a bonfire, with nearby trees catching fire. I stop at the second figure, the one who was thrown as far as I was from the explosion. When I flip him over, there's barely anything to identify. He's scorched and smells like melting flesh, and I know immediately without checking his pulse that he's dead.

Fuck.

We have to keep moving.

"Is he...?" Lily's small voice trails from behind me, and before I can even look at her, she's vomiting into the well-trimmed grass.

Fuck me. I don't have time for this.

I throw her over my shoulder, well aware she's still vomiting and uncomfortably trying to squirm off me, but I don't give a flying fuck. My objective is to reach

Luca and Ara. It's just good fortune that Lily weighs barely anything and doesn't hinder my speed.

Within only a few minutes, I'm pointing my gun at someone who approaches, until I realize it's one of our own men.

I'm quick to update him in our native Italian tongue. We don't have many men on the grounds, but fortunately, because of Ara's pregnancy, Luca has been more reasonable in my demand for heightening security. Two more members of the security team race down the hill as I run up and am greeted by Luca, who stands at the opening of the French doors that over-look the usually serene view of his private beach. Now it's in chaos, with flames spreading quickly.

"What the fuck happened?" Luca demands, the muscle in his jaw ticking. "One car did all of this?"

"Yes, sir," I inform him as I see Ara pacing behind him, two guards at her back.

"Lily!" Ara snaps into motion, and I'm reminded that Lily is still hanging over my shoulder like a sack of potatoes. I'm quick to put her down, but her legs go weak, still dependent on me to hold her up, seemingly nothing but an incoherent, pale-looking doll. Her sarong has long been lost, and she looks shell-shocked as she stares at nothing in particular, goose bumps all over her skin. She keels over and vomits again, this time right on my fucking shoes.

"What happened?!" Ara demands as she runs to her friend's side, and it's the first time I've seen the boss's wife reveal any form of panic. A woman like Lily Taylor isn't cut out for this type of world, and I'm not surprised whatsoever that within a split second, her world has been flipped upside down as she discovers that stories of boogeymen under her bed are, in fact, living and breathing things.

"There was a man..." Lily says quietly. "Am I dreaming right now?" she asks Ara, looking up almost pleadingly. My jaw tightens, because despite my being desensitized to these types of things happening, I pity her and feel guilty for not entirely being able to shield her from seeing the ugliness of a world she most likely didn't even know existed.

But the only thing that matters is my boss's safety and his next direct order. I report quickly, still holding the shivering woman up.

"We can't stay here, Luca," Ara insists. "Look at Lily."

Luca reluctantly turns his attention to Lily, and I can tell without him even saying it that he doesn't give a flying fuck about her—he only cares about his wife and unborn child. I'm also certain he doesn't want to elaborate that this "babymoon" was also meant to provide him time to check on business on his own turf. I think this is enough of an answer as to how his return has been received.

But who the fuck would be so bold? The Armanis own this territory. Anyone to attack him on his own property is idiotically audacious.

"The car definitely swerved for Lily, possibly mistaking her for Ara since they were attacking on Armani property. I'll gather information as to who is behind this. Give me more men, and we can flip every corner of the families and—"

"No," Luca says. "Have the jet readied immediately. We're returning to New York. I don't want Ara here."

"I don't care about me. Look at Lily!" Ara growls, hanging her head beside Lily, who looks like she's about to vomit again.

"*I* care," Luca warns her with a sharp tone. Either way, both women will be removed from harm's way.

The men behind Ara begin moving. She looks furious but doesn't argue again as she tries to peel her friend away from me, but I don't loosen my grip.

The poor fucking woman looks like she's been stripped of her cognitive functions. They say in situations like these, people discover what they're made of. And Lily doesn't appear to be a woman with the heart of a lion. She reminds me of something far softer than the jagged edges I've cut my own teeth on being in this world. I just simply can't put my finger on it, nor do I want to sympathize with it.

I remove my suit jacket and place it over her shoulders. At the very least, I don't like anyone seeing her half-naked while so exposed and vulnerable. She doesn't even seem to register it as I scoop her into my arms, Ara's hand remaining on her forearm. I briefly glance at Ara, who looks regretful for bringing her in the first place.

It's not that I like it when things like this happen, but I'm wired for anything to go worst-case scenario at any given time. It's a lesson that Ara will learn in time. Friends and family are weaknesses. When she chose to marry the Armani family boss, she should've cut all ties with anyone she loves.

I wouldn't blame anyone who has the sense to run away from a friendship that offers the calamity of being close to the Mafia. If Lily Taylor is as smart as she appears, then she'll run for the fucking hills.

"Where are you taking her?" Ara asks, the vulnerability that was there a moment ago blinked away, returning to the wife of a Mafia boss, all action now.

"To the jet, unless you want her taken another way?" I ask.

Ara grimaces, guilt clearly flooding her. "Thank you for keeping her safe."

"Those were my orders, were they not?"

"They were," Luca growls.

I pull Lily closer to my chest, her usual floral fragrance quickly being overtaken by the vile smell of her vomit.

She's too innocent for this world.

Too paralyzed to resurface into her own.

For now.

3

LILY

The night sky of Manhattan looks different when we land on the airstrip. I'd watched the sun dance along the clouds as we flew home, but much of it was a blur. Ara had tried to speak to me a few times, but I didn't have the capacity to reply. She'd settled for sitting outside the bathroom on the plane while I showered and put on a dress so I didn't feel so vulnerable, only wearing my bikini.

Vulnerable.

Life and death. I'd never seen a man die. Never had my life flash in front of my eyes either.

If I die today, would I be happy with my life? My accomplishments, my impact? *Have I lived a happy, authentic life?*

It's terrifying how silent everything becomes after that question. But then, when I try to pull away from that lingering insight, I fall into another abyss where I can't quite compartmentalize what I just witnessed, let alone process that my friends are clearly not who they claim to be.

Should I be scared of them?

Should I run away?

Yet I'm resistant to fearing her or feeling betrayed. Even if I don't know all of her secrets, does that change the person I thought she was? I should let her explain herself, because isn't she still my friend? But part of me is scared to hear her out, knowing it could change everything I thought I once knew about her. My thoughts continue to loop as I sit in a numbness that seeped into me after the explosion. I simply sit and stare, unable to come up with any answers.

"Lily?" Ara's voice breaks through my thoughts, and I blink once. Then twice. "You'll be safe here. Luca owns this hotel. We just need to sort out a few things, and then I'll be back so we can discuss this properly, okay? I'll explain everything."

I look outside the car window and up at the glamorous hotel positioned centrally in the city I love most. But somehow the city doesn't feel as radiant. I feel tarnished in some way, still praying that I wake up from this nightmare.

When did we even get here?

I look into the rearview mirror, where dark-brown eyes study me. Lorenzo is staring at me from the driver's seat. The moment we make eye contact, I avert my gaze.

Deadly.

This man is dangerous.

I want to be anywhere but here, and this time, I should listen to my instinct to run. I vaguely recall him hovering around me over the past few hours, hushed words being exchanged, then voices raised on the flight. Lorenzo was the one I had to block out the most, as I recalled multiple times the way he'd protected me. How at ease he is with a gun. Without thought, he'd come between me and the men who'd swerved to hit me. What if he'd been hurt or killed trying to protect me? What if they'd been successful in hitting me?

A chill runs over my skin, and I'm aware that his gaze still lingers on me. No, I have the distinct impression that a man like Lorenzo can't be killed. I don't know him well, but watching him in action in that situation, being pushed back by flames and standing as if it were no more than a scratch. This man was built for this kind of life... whatever this life is.

"Miss?" the valet says, and I blink back into the now as he offers his hand to help me out of the car.

"Lily," Ara calls out again from behind me. When I turn to face her, I can see the worry in her expression. "I'll be back, and I'll explain everything. I promise you. You're safe here."

Safe?

I nod numbly, because as of twelve hours ago, that was never something I even questioned. Who is Arabella Barone? I know she's been one of my best friends for almost three years now, and realizing I might not know her as well as I thought *hurts*. It's also confusing, and I just can't process any of it.

My legs carry me into the hotel lobby and to the reception desk, where I'm checked in and then escorted directly to a room on the top floor.

The concierge says something about calling upon him if I need anything, but right now, I just need to be alone. The moment he excuses himself from the room, I expect to feel a sense of relief, but it doesn't come.

I barely appreciate the chic suite that offers a plush king-size bed in shades of white and beige. I peel off my dress and throw it over the corner of the couch, then vacantly walk toward the bathroom. It's adorned with gleaming marble, a gold-framed floor-to-ceiling mirror, luxurious products, and a light that's too bright. Too polished. Too perfect.

Everything just feels too much.

I turn off the light and run the water into the claw-footed bathtub. It's barely an inch full of water as I sit and bend my legs to my chest. Goose bumps erupt over my skin as I wait for the water to rise, but I welcome the chill and bite of the air.

What ugly secret have I been exposed to? Like a coward, I didn't ask Ara any further questions.

I rest my head to the side, looking at myself in the mirror beside the basin. A streak of light from the bedroom seeps in, revealing a version of myself I don't like. I'm a mess. My hair, matted in some areas, usually has a glossy curl to it. Even in this predicament, in a time of uncertainty and fear, I startlingly realize I haven't even thought about calling my family.

I don't have anyone I can confide in. Maybe my other best friends, Romi or Sienna, but I don't want to drag them into any of this mess. Plus, they're friends with Ara as well. I can't involve anyone else until I know the truth.

I hate it here.

This reality.

This fear.

This isolation.

It's as if I'm waiting for something more powerful and courageous within me to click into place, to make sense of it all and handle the situation. But the further I delve into myself, the more I realize there isn't a deeper substance. It's chilling how empty I feel inside.

Am I truly this weak?

Is my existence truly this insubstantial?

Suddenly, that feels far scarier than almost being killed.

4

LORENZO

It never goes unnoticed when Ara touches her stomach. Luca's gaze immediately falls to the action as we step into his office at the Armani mansion. I try to focus on the crackling fire as Ara and Luca argue about the woman who isn't even here.

"We need to make sure Lily is protected. She has nothing to do with this!" Ara snaps. It's the continuation of their argument that started the moment we dropped Lily off at the hotel.

Lily's usual bright light dimmed the moment that car swerved for her, leaving behind only a shell. The few encounters I've had with her over the last two years have always left the impression that she's innocent and sincere. She's clearly terrified to the point she can't even function right now. And I can't even blame her.

After dropping Lily off, I drove Luca and Ara here

to the house, where only Luca's brother, Dario, lives. But for matters of business, Luca still uses this as the Armani home base. It's also a good way to make sure his brother's rehabilitation from drug and alcohol abuse is going well.

Dario's shadow casts across the doorframe, but for once, the fucker has better sense than to get involved and is quick to leave, much like the house attendants who always find themselves busy elsewhere the moment any voice rises. They're paid well, but efficiency isn't the only thing that keeps their jobs here; it's having better sense than to get involved or be around when Luca is in a particularly bad mood.

"Luca, don't pretend like I didn't just say anything!" Ara snaps, throwing her hands in the air.

"I don't think it's good for the baby if you—"

"Don't you dare start treating me like I'm some helpless, weak damsel or use the pregnancy as an asshole excuse to not listen to my demands!"

His jaw tics, and I silently stand to the side of the office, watching the two of them. It's always like this with them; they like to argue as much as they enjoy making up, but they're both especially tense tonight.

"Have you called the hounds?" Luca asks me, and I nod in response. The moment he gave the order, I called in his five most trusted men—those who are at his beck and call. Monsters who enjoy drawing blood, given any excuse. Very few know their identities; they always appear in white masks with a different colored gem on each, identifying them. Though I've worked with them long enough to differentiate them between voice, build, and irritation level. That, and those who work closest with them know what they look like without the mask, but only a few in the family receive that honor. They only ever take them off in the presence of those higher in hierarchy. Nothing is left to chance, even in the Armani mansion, where a staff member might see them.

"Ara, stop. Let me think," Luca demands as he walks to his polished wooden desk, positioned near the end of the room, to pour a glass of whiskey.

"There's nothing to think about when I'm telling you what you need to do," Ara says flatly, following him. "My friend was attacked because of us."

"This is why we don't *do* friends," Luca grits out.

"*I* do friends," she bites back. It's very different from the woman who first appeared almost two years ago, using people to get closer to the Armanis to seek her revenge. It's evident from the way her body is shaking that she fiercely wants to protect Lily Taylor, and I can see why, considering the woman is just... far too innocent to survive this world. Even if only dancing on the outskirts of it.

At this point, I don't even know if Lily realizes that Luca *is* involved with the Mafia or if it was simply a bad vacation incident.

I bring my thoughts back to the now. Thinking about Lily Taylor is nothing but a distraction, much like she has always been when she stands in any room with her blinding ray-of-fucking-sunshine light. The only thing I need to focus on is how we're going to eradicate this threat to Luca's empire.

"I've been here for too long without replacing my second in Italy. We need to reinstate our position there. It's also likely that this could be an attack from the Bratva." He gives me a pointed look. Assisting Dmitri Volkov months ago with his situation and killing his father, "The Lion," who was a high-ranking member in the Bratva, alongside a few of his men, might be leading to consequences now.

As for not replacing his second, Ivan, in Italy, that should've been managed sooner. By letting Ara have her revenge and kill Ivan, who used to do business on Luca's behalf, we've created a blind spot within the organization. But no one was daring enough to make a move until now. We had ample men in positions that deterred anyone from overstepping, so why now? Because Luca has a soon-to-be heir?

"We can deal with all that shit later, but if people are questioning your authority over there, we might have problems here," Ara says matter-of-factly. "Lily was targeted, whether they mistook her for me or not, and they might come for her again."

"Can you care more for your own safety, woman!" Luca snaps, fisting his hands. He looks like he's going to kill someone, but that deadly gaze is also his weakness, because it's nothing short of the love he has for his wife that makes him, at times, illogical.

Silence fills the air, and the tension in the room shifts. I'm not sure if Ara is about to throw the closest book at him or burst into tears. Not that she's usually capable of that, but her moods have been erratic during her pregnancy. Either way, she's about to explode.

I don't understand this. Never have from the moment my boss stepped into this turbulent relationship and decided on marriage. I do, however, know one thing: he'd do anything for her. Which, in my opinion, is stupid, since I'm the one tasked with his safety. But I also know, besides his insidious obsession and need to monopolize things, he loves her.

"Luca," she says carefully as she walks toward him and grabs his hand. "*Please.* She's my best friend. I can't have this come between us."

They stare at one another, and I look away, feeling like I'm intruding on the intimate exchange. These are the conversations he once conducted with me. He still does to an extent, but her influence impacts him far more than I'd like it to, especially when I have more logical, self-preserving suggestions.

"Hey, boss!" One of the hounds enters the office, the first of the group to arrive. Three more follow, each with different builds and colored gems on their masks.

Ara releases Luca's hand, and something I can't

understand transpires between them, now shut away from anyone else's view.

"I'm going to explain everything to Lily. Who we are. Who you are. What type of business is conducted by the family. Full transparency," she says carefully. "We'll sort this out, yes?" She peers up at him through thick eyelashes. How can a woman as small as her control our boss so easily? I couldn't possibly imagine myself giving that much power to someone other than Luca himself.

"Yes, my little viper," he agrees, sounding defeated. An obvious sense of relief washes over her, the tension in her muscles loosening as she kisses him on the lips, and he watches her as she heads toward the door to leave.

The hounds scatter around the office space, lounging lazily. Ara walks among them like a queen, and the men watch her with interest. They're the same as me, curious about the shift in dynamic, they have better judgment than to interfere. Ara is a strong woman, but in turn has a weakness for our boss. We can't see it any other way.

"Eyes on *me*," Luca grits. And then there's that, his immediate jealousy of anyone who looks at his woman.

"Something go boom to put you in a pissy mood?" Sky, the light-blue hound, goads.

"Watch yourself," I warn, kicking off the shelves and coming to stand beside Luca.

Each of the hounds is a thorough killer, but four out of the five are still in college, only in their early twenties. Luca gave them power, an outlet to express their bloodlust and curiosities, in exchange for loyalty. Doesn't mean they don't have to be trained like dogs, which is precisely where I come in.

"We had an issue arise in Italy. Explain it to them," Luca instructs as he pours another glass of whiskey, and I proceed to do exactly that.

I provide a detailed account of the incident and the limited information we have to go on. "We'll need to do a thorough investigation and shakedown. We're unsure if this planned attack was intended for Ara, considering she was the only woman expected to be at the villa, but our arrival was only known by a few. It doesn't change the fact that someone could've been waiting for their chance." I look at Luca. It doesn't comfort me to think of leaving him, but the sooner this threat is sorted, the better. "My first recommendation is to send me back. I'll get to the bottom of this matter and reinstate your authority, removing this adversary."

Luca shakes his head. "No, I need to return and deal with this myself. The only reason I came back was to make sure my wife was delivered here safely. I need you here."

My jaw tics. I don't like not being by his side. Although he's more than capable of protecting himself, I take my responsibility seriously. And the best way to have our boss protected is by using me as a shield.

"There's also the matter of Lily," Luca says, tapping his finger against the tumbler thoughtfully.

"Who?" Tyson, the green-gemmed hound, asks.

"Mrs. Armani's friend, Lily Taylor, was the woman caught in the crossfire. Ara's advocated that she wants her guarded until the matter is dealt with, in case anyone gets cocky on New York territory."

Tyson whistles. "Sounds like babysitting duty. Is she hot?"

"It's irrelevant," I scold quickly. The thought of any of these fuckers looking upon Lily makes my blood boil. She's too innocent to be around the likes of men like this. Men like *me*.

"Oh, come on, Lorenzo. Stop being so stiff," Sky teases, forever the shit-stirrer of the group.

"Or maybe that's the problem. He needs to be stiff so he can actually manage a release for once," Izak, the hound with the yellow gem, dryly says.

"Enough," I bite, and they're quick to shut their yapping mouths before I have to do it for them. Always pushing boundaries, these young smartasses. Even at their age, I wasn't so loose with my tongue, understanding the real threat of it being cut off.

The red-gemmed hound, Kage, remains quiet. The only thing that gets him engaged is the promise of bloodshed.

"Want us to follow her?" Tony, the oldest of the

group and the one with the brown gem, asks. For the most part, he can rein in their shitty attitudes as well.

"No," Luca says, considerately. "I want your identities to remain hidden. She's protected at the hotel now, but going forward, she'll need someone to remain with her at all times. The hounds are better suited to managing the current situation to make sure no one steps out of place. I want us to follow up on every person we conduct business with, reiterating our expectations. Our rates go up by ten percent, and anyone who revolts, show them that we mean business. As for her friend..." Luca's sharp blue gaze lands on me. "I want you to follow Lily Taylor."

All the suggestions and game plans circulating in my mind immediately halt. "Excuse me?"

Luca then looks to the leader of the hounds, Tony. "While I'm away, I want you guarding Ara day in and day out with your life. You're permitted to reveal your identity as her bodyguard. Lorenzo will watch her friend. The sooner this is dealt with, the sooner we go back to normal."

"I don't follow," I grit out, and I certainly don't condone it. But I'm cautious with my words, because when Luca is in a bad mood, it's poor timing to challenge his orders. I might get away with it sometimes, but I keep it to a minimum. I don't fear Luca; I respect him and the role I've been given. But lately, he seems comfortable with putting himself on a ledge, sticking out his neck. I'd struggled being put in charge of following his wife around the moment he found out about her pregnancy, but to then be demoted again to babysit her friend... There are only so many blows I can handle, and his clear lack of dependency on me is concerning.

"There's no way Ara will allow anyone she doesn't trust near her friend. You should be honored," Luca says dismissively.

"I regret to disagree," I say quickly.

"Luckily, I don't pay you to make opinions on the orders I give you."

My jaw tics as he continues addressing the hounds. "Tony, Ara knows who you are. The rest of the hounds are better suited elsewhere. I want you to follow her like the air she breathes. If she so much as spills a tear or drop of coffee in your vicinity, I'll have your head for it. You're all dismissed."

My hands curl into fists as I rein in my rising frustration. I don't like this plan at all. Luca begins to look over the paperwork that was gathered on his desk during the time we were in Italy. When everyone else is gone and the door closes behind us, he says, "You don't agree with the plan."

I understand I have to be made an example of; speaking against him is as good as a crime, especially in front of the others. He suggests I sit across from him and then pulls another glass out from the desk's top drawer to pour me a whiskey. We rarely share a drink together, having always kept our relationship mostly business. But it's times like this that I also realize, besides the new addition of his wife, I'm the only person he confides in because I'm willing to take his secrets to the grave.

"My expertise is better utilized elsewhere. Using me as a babysitter is a waste when I can better assist you in other areas. I'm even more surprised you're willing to prioritize me being by anyone else's side but yours or your wife's. Do you really think Tony can do a better job than I?"

Luca stares at me, his expression unreadable. I thought I once understood how his mind worked, but more than ever, I realize that as he steps further into his power, a greater distance grows between us because of the way he approaches things. He wants to do everything himself, willing to put his life on the line for personal satisfaction when he wins.

"This has nothing to do with who I think can do a better job at protecting my wife. Both you and Tony are skilled in that regard. Don't ever question my ability to make decisions to best protect my wife."

I dip my head. "Apologies, sir."

"There's another task I want to assign you while you look after the Taylor woman," Luca continues, and this does pique my interest. Despite his unhinged ways, Luca is very methodical. "I want to look into her father's affairs and estates. I've heard rumors of fractures within his company. The man's empire is worth a fortune."

Realization dawns on me. "Are you certain now is a good time to focus on expanding when we need to have the issue in Italy sorted first?"

Luca's lips tip up in an evil grin, the one that tells me he's up to no good and has found ample pathways to get precisely what he wants. "I'm always expanding my fortune and power, Lorenzo. You, of all people, should know that. After all, you benefit, do you not?"

I consider the amount of money that Mr. Taylor might be worth. Luca's wealth definitely impacts mine directly. When his expands, so does mine.

"This feels rather opportunistic, using Ara and her friend to get close to her father, doesn't it?"

"Some tactics never fail to work. Of course, my wife isn't to know about this. If she found out I was using her friend to exploit her father, she'd chop my balls off."

I want to ask him why he's willing to risk it, because I think if anyone is capable of doing precisely that, it's Ara. But I know better than to question his scheming mind and self-assurance that he can handle matters in Italy directly.

"It might be difficult to explain Lily Taylor suddenly having a bodyguard. Her father will surely become suspicious." I consider it, thinking carefully as to what the best angle of approach might be. Whether she agrees to my help or not isn't in question. What Luca wants, tends to happen, especially when being endorsed by Ara. From what I've seen of Lily so far, she's more than accommodating and easily agreeable, even when she doesn't want to be. In fact, it's always irritated me to watch her submit to the wants of others. Especially because I've seen another side of her—a woman who takes things for herself and comes to life, instead of bending to another's will. My mind drifts back to a memory of her lips on mine, but I'm quick to shove that thought away.

A distraction, that's all she has been and ever will be.

"That's why you're going to pretend to be her boyfriend."

A chill runs through my body, as I slowly glance up at Luca, who looks like the devil himself, all matter-of-fact with no falter in his scheme. "*Boyfriend?*"

The word feels like sand on my tongue, leaving a parched, bitter taste in my mouth.

Luca has the balls to laugh, and I realize I haven't so easily concealed my expression. "You look revolted by the idea. Come on, Lorenzo. Love might not look so bad on you."

I stare at him. No, I don't understand my boss at all anymore. Because *love* and *boyfriend* are not words that often appear in our vocabulary. We take, torture, scheme, and bury bodies to grow our power and wealth. Anything outside of that is not where my preferences or skill set lie.

"We've done plenty together over the years," Luca says, straightening his paperwork and placing it to the side. "But I've never seen you look like you're about to vomit at a given task. Even then, you will do as I say and follow the plan."

I swallow, trying my hardest to push away the volatile mix in my stomach. And suddenly, it tastes like sunshine and rainbows in a package of Lily fucking Taylor. It's not her fault. It's not her plan. But anything that seems to include her has caused me nothing but grief, and this is going to be my biggest trial of all.

5

LILY

"No." That's the first word that falls from my lips when Ara suggests that Lorenzo act as my boyfriend to be my personal security. I glance in his direction as he stands against the wall. When I meet his dark-brown eyes, which are already locked on me, I'm quick to avert my gaze, shutting down all the rising questions I have about this enigma of a man. I take another sip of the foul-tasting liquor. I don't know what it is. I asked the bartender to give me something that would make me forget.

He gave me an apologetic grimace and said, "I have just the stuff."

Ara scans the room, most likely seeing who else is in the hotel bar at three in the morning, but we're the only ones here. I don't know how long I've been sitting here or how many drinks I've had.

There was an array of dresses to choose from in the

suite, and I couldn't help but think about how prepared the Armanis are. Most likely because Ara and I are similar in size. The dark dress is so different from anything I'd ordinarily wear myself, yet it seems fitting for my mood.

When I finally broke through the surface and came back to some form of reality, Ara joined me to explain that not only does her husband run the Italian Mafia, but due to a case of mistaken identity, I might've been targeted instead of her. Now she's running through a contingency plan to keep me "safe" until they've dug up the person behind the attack.

Having Lorenzo be my bodyguard and fake boyfriend is the worst plan. Ever. In fact, I'm still not entirely sure how to process all of this. It's one thing to be targeted and almost killed. But then to be told that my best friend is not only involved with the Mafia but married to its leader, and I'm in danger by association and mistaken identity? No. That's something I can't comprehend right now. I take another harsh swallow of the vile drink.

I should have better sense to not want anything to do with this, with Ara and her involvement with the Mafia, but I naturally revolt against the idea. Maybe my loyalty is part of my stupidity, or maybe it doesn't change the fact that she's my friend.

I'm a positive person, but surely, even I have my limit as to how much I'm supposed to numbly believe or agree to. Suddenly, being told the best plan of action is to have a bodyguard and that my life might still be in danger all feels far-fetched. It's a reality I don't want to consider.

"It's the surest way to keep you safe if you want to continue with your normal day-to-day life," Ara pushes gently.

"My normal day-to-day life," I say, pondering what my usual life looked like before this. How do I even separate the two? She winces and makes a pointed look at the drink, and I'm quick to move it away so she can't reach it. It's snatched out of my hand from behind.

"Hey!" I yell, and when I turn, my face practically slams into a muscular chest because of how close Lorenzo stands behind me. His glare is challenging, those dark-brown eyes almost scolding, and I look away, unable to meet his gaze, too frightened by what I might find.

A killer?

Attraction?

Memories of flames catching on trees, and the smell of burning flesh?

I huff and flop back into my chair with my arms crossed over my chest, trying to push all of these bubbling thoughts away. Okay, I've had a lot to drink. I'm not handling any of this well. Maybe I'm even being unreasonable right now, but considering the circumstances, I don't care. "I never asked to be caught up in this," I grumble, and when I look at Ara, guilt floods me. I know she's never been one to openly express her feelings, but I never thought it was because of such a monumental secret.

"I'm sorry I didn't tell you about any of this sooner. I just..." She hesitates, a flicker of uncertainty marring her features. "I wasn't sure if you would want to remain my friend. And your friendship *is* important to me," she says earnestly. "It just became too difficult to ever bring up organically, and I thought if you did know this about me, maybe you'd be wise to walk away."

Her shoulders sag, almost in defeat. It's not often I see Ara vulnerable like this, and I can't help but sympathize with her. No matter what she's told me, she still appears the same to me, and I don't know if that makes me a fool or if this is what true friendship is about. You're together through thick and thin, right? But this is on a whole different level.

"It's a lot to take in," I admit as I glance at my feet. "I need to understand everything better before you ask this of me. It doesn't even sound like I have a choice."

She cringes at the last part because the reality is, I don't. I've wound up in a situation I can't get myself out of, and I still haven't had the time to process it. I'm trying to think straight, but the alcohol has me spinning in circles, doing exactly what it was supposed to. I just don't feel like myself right now.

"Luca is on a jet back to Italy now, to set everything back into place. But with that, we need to make sure we're safe here in New York. Depending on who is behind the attack, they could reach as far as here. And I'm not leaving your safety to chance. They know what you look like, that you're associated with me. I don't want anything to happen to you. Especially because of me," she adds quietly at the end.

The remaining bit of fight drains its way out of me as I sigh. I don't want to see Ara like this. I know I should be more concerned for my own safety, but I'm still in disbelief. This is just a security measure, right? Surely, no one is really coming for me?

At my very core, I don't want to lose my friendship with Ara. I absolutely adore our relationship, but finding out I may not know as much about her as I thought still hurts.

"How did you even end up marrying a Mafia boss?" I ask, still trying to come to terms with this revelation and dark secret. I knew Luca Armani had an air about him, but lethal and all underworld-like? Nope, I've definitely been living a sheltered life.

I look back at the empty bar, wishing my drink was still there. I throw a glare in Lorenzo's direction. He's returned to standing against the wall, the drink miraculously gone. He seems unfazed by my attempted stink eye as he watches us.

How did I ever find him attractive? Did I really think he was simply a business friend of Luca's? I'm such an idiot.

Ara seems conflicted as to how she should answer, and I remain silent, waiting. Usually, I'd say she doesn't have to tell me if she doesn't want to, or something to that effect, but this time I need answers. Ones that will probably need to be repeated tomorrow, because if I don't wake up from this nightmare, I'm certainly waking up with a hangover.

Ara sighs, and her hand goes to her stomach. "I don't know if you'll still want to be my friend if you know about all the awful things I've done."

There's more stuff?

Do I want to know? Will this change us going forward? But I'm sick of everyone tiptoeing around me. People only tell me what they want to, and everyone keeps each other at arm's length in the wealthy social circles I grew up in. I thought Ara and I were different than those people, but maybe her reasoning isn't what I think it is. Shouldn't I want to know more about someone I consider one of my best friends, even if it's not all flowery? Isn't that being real?

When she sees my determined expression, expecting her to continue, she uncomfortably shifts on her stool and nods.

"Right. Let me try to shorten it, but what I tell you, you can't tell anyone else. Please, Lily, I'm not saying that as some Mafia wife bullshit but as a friend. It's pretty damning."

"I would say so, given I was almost run down by a car, wearing nothing but a bikini. But, hey, if this still isn't a dream, then here we are," I say as I casually shrug. She seems a little shocked at first, and I sigh, defeated. Okay, maybe I crack a few unsolicited dry jokes when I've had a few drinks.

"That's a fair call," she says, thanking the bartender who walks over with two glasses of water.

Damn it. That's the last thing I want right now, even though I know I'm probably better for it.

She waits until the bartender is out of earshot. "When I was a child, my mother was murdered in front of me." My jaw drops, but I'm quick to bring the water to my lips to cover most of my shock. I didn't know her mother was killed in front of her. The incident of her mother being murdered in a home invasion was publicly known, but Ara never spoke about it.

"I made it my life's mission to find the person who did it. I discovered my father was involved in an underhanded business agreement. He *knowingly* allowed that night to happen. So, I played obedient daughter, slowly growing my influence to run one of his companies, Cleo, temporarily here in Manhattan. I put myself into a position where I worked the social circles during the day so I could stalk and monitor the Mafia family involved in that business transaction. I tried to avoid having direct involvement with Luca because I was aware of his... power. I also knew if I got too close, there was a high chance I'd be killed for it. But it became this *obsession*. I had to avenge my mother and free myself," she says, as if in a daydream, staring off at something I can't see. Then again, I can't comprehend the horror of what she saw as a child. Somehow, it puts what I witnessed in Italy into some twisted perspective.

She was all alone, and I couldn't even imagine the weight of knowing my father was involved with my mother's death. I have my issues with my father, but this is something on an entirely different level. My thoughts snag on one important detail.

"It wasn't Luca who killed your mother, was it?" I whisper, horrified at the thought.

"No," she's quick to say. "No, not Luca. It was his second-in-command at the time. He'd worked for Luca's father during the time of my mother's murder, so Luca ultimately gave him to me as a gift to get my revenge. Everything that happened between me and Luca during that time was real and certainly not with Lorenzo's permission or blessing," she half-heartedly jokes, and glances over my shoulder at him.

I don't look his way, still actively avoiding the fact that Ara has suggested we become inseparable for the coming weeks. I've barely been able to make eye contact with him in the past without the help of some liquid courage. But now, knowing how deadly he is, I need to squash my infatuation with him.

Then again, as I stare at Ara, who's slowly blurring in my vision with the influence of the alcohol, I'm simply trying to retain as much information as possible, not to mention focusing on the looming presence standing behind me. This all sounds so made up, something out of a terrible, traumatic drama. And there's something I'm almost too scared to clarify. But I'm in too deep now not to ask.

"When you say you got your revenge, do you mean you *hurt* him?" I ask in a voice much quieter than I anticipated.

"No, Lily. I killed him," she says matter-of-factly. Her answer hits me like a speeding train. Ara has *killed* someone.

"Oh." I drop my gaze to my lap, staring at my hands, which look fuzzy. It's not every day your best friend tells you she's murdered someone. But I can't understand what life must've been like for her to lead to so much hate. I momentarily imagine someone standing over the body of my mother, and a cruel dread hits me so deeply, I immediately shove it away.

I know she's most likely left out a lot of details, but it shifts the world I've been living in ever so slightly. What I've been taught about right and wrong.

The world of being nice, smiling, and dressing a certain way, seems so substantially small compared to this new world I've been exposed to.

"I understand if you no longer want to be my friend after this, but I really mean it when I say I want to make sure you're safe," Ara says, and I quickly look up and grab her hand desperately as she goes to stand.

"I don't want our friendship to end, Ara." And that's the truth. Despite all of this, I don't want to lose Ara. I have Romi and Sienna, but besides those two, no one else feels like a friend. Although I may not know this part of her, I want to understand her better. Maybe because deep down I want others to understand me better as well. I shove away that stifling thought.

She's a murderer, and yet I've only ever known her as my friend. Am I crazy for not letting it impact us like it should?

"It's just a lot to process right now, and I'm trying. I just need time. I don't think poorly of you for this. It's just..." *It's just what?*

Ara offers a remorseful smile as she leans over and wipes the tears I didn't even know were streaming down my face. "You know I've always admired you for how you wear your heart on your sleeve, Lily. You're loyal and empathetic, even when someone like me doesn't deserve it. And I promise I'll protect you. You were the first friend I made here, and I'd like to return the favor."

"Friendship isn't a favor," I say, because I don't want this to be something measurable. Everything in our world is measured—fame, wealth, dealings, opportunity. It's all so... fake. But Ara isn't. At least, I thought she wasn't.

"Nor is it always easy. And I know I'm asking a lot right now. You're a fierce friend, Lily. It's why I appreciate you the most," she says, and I'm surprised. No one has ever called me fierce before. I certainly wouldn't label myself as that. Her gaze drifts over my shoulder to Lorenzo. "He'll protect you until we figure this out."

"Please, there has to be someone else," I find myself saying.

Her eyebrows furrow, and she quietly whispers, "I promise he won't hurt you."

"I know that," I immediately say, and I'm shocked by the force of its truth. I'm not *scared* of Lorenzo, even when I know I should be. It's simply the thought of Lorenzo being around constantly that terrifies me. I can't imagine what he'll look like as part of my life, even if it's pretend.

I shake my head again. "It'll be bad if I bring him to parties or if my father so much as catches a whiff of any of this. Ara, he won't respond well to this. You know he's already been threatening me with match-making. This will push him over the edge."

"Do you really care more about what your father thinks than your own safety?" she asks, her gaze narrowing, and it's a sobering question. "I don't want to force this on you, Lily. But it's also non-negotiable. I'm not leaving you unguarded for something I've brought you into. You're more courageous than you give your-self credit for. You just need to tell your father to go fuck himself, or even better, set him up and put him behind bars like I did to mine."

My jaw drops. "Oh my gosh. That was all you?" I ask, shocked as well as mildly impressed.

She chuckles, dark and ruthless, a side of my friend I've never seen before. She brushes her hands along her black bangs, making sure each strand is still in place. "I'd had many years to plan his undoing. It seemed crueler than killing him. I simply put him in a cage, just as he had tried to do to me. Maybe you should start doing the same to your own father."

I bite down on my lower lip before I spill the first words that come to mind. *But I love my father.* However, the weight of that statement lodges in my throat. I do love my father. But we have a complicated relationship. Although nowhere near as messed up as Ara just described.

The truth of the matter is, I've been questioning the sincerity of my father's feelings for me for as long as I can remember. We come from generational wealth, and my father runs multiple businesses and hundreds of investments. The family image has always been first and foremost. When I was younger, I was convinced that's what family meant, but lately more than ever... it's feeling more like a cage.

Ara's phone lights up in her hand, Luca's name appearing on the screen, but she ignores it. She stares at me expectantly.

I feel like I'm being looked after like a child, but I'm also so out of my depth that I can't even comprehend what my daily life will look like going forward. A hiccup escapes me. Well, maybe I'm not supposed to, considering how drunk I am. I grudgingly sip the water.

"You said Luca should be able to fix this quickly, right? So, maybe no one will even notice a six-foot-two wall of muscle trailing me," I joke, but it falls flat. It all seems so unbelievable, but then memories of the gunshots, the car exploding, and the charred, dead body have a sobering effect.

An unfamiliar man appears from the shadows. He's not as imposing as Lorenzo, but from the way he moves and has his attention locked on Ara, I can tell he's some type of bodyguard. "This is Tony. He's taking over my security while you borrow Lorenzo."

My eyebrows dip as it suddenly dawns on me. "Hold up. If you said Lorenzo is Luca's best, and he's been basically trailing behind you since you announced your pregnancy, shouldn't you have him?"

Ara chuckles as she looks at Lorenzo. I can't tell what type of face he's making, but since I'm learning that his default expression of late is looking like he sucked on a lemon, I'm sure it's similar to that. "I insisted that you have Lorenzo. I thought it might be slightly easier since you're already acquainted." She leans in and whispers as she gives me an uncharacteristic hug, "I recommend not getting too close. I've never been able to warn you away from him directly, but he is dangerous, Lily, and I'm sure now you understand why."

I scoff as I hug her back. "Eww. I found him hot from a distance, but now that I know he's..." Rude? Obnoxious? Dismissive? Conceited? A criminal? A killer? When I pull back, though, I realize the silence might've been read wrong. *A part of the same world Ara lives in.* It looks like she took it personally, as she offers a tight smile and squeezes my arm.

"We'll figure this out and pretend like it never happened. For now, we should keep some distance. If they're targeting me, I'd rather keep it at that than—"

"No," I say quickly. "We have our breakfasts every week. Ara, if I really let this impact me, I'm going to lose my mind." I *need* my routine. She bites the inside of her cheek, obviously conflicted. I can tell she's most likely weighing the risks involved. "If these guys are as great as you say, surely, we can have at least that. *Please,*" I beg, now standing, and an immediate wave of dizziness sweeps in.

Ara reaches for me, but her hand remains extended as a firm grip closes around my arms from behind. My breath hitches as I look over my shoulder at Lorenzo, who's glaring down at me like I'm the bane of his existence.

"Still a lightweight, I see," he reprimands.

Heat surfaces to my cheeks as I step out of his hold. "I'm okay. I don't need to be bubble wrapped. I just need... time... and sleep."

Ara bites her bottom lip. "Okay, maybe we can have a better conversation about this tomorrow? Call me with whatever you need. Lily, I'm really sorry about all of this. I swear I was trying to help by bringing you to Italy."

I offer a sad smile. "I know. It just appears that my

luck wants to throw me from one shit basket to the next."

Ara laughs. "Did you just curse, Lily?"

I roll my eyes. "I'm not the quintessential perfect daughter all the time, you know."

Ara's still laughing as she says. "I don't know many drunk people who can still use the word *quintessential*, but sure. Go get some sleep."

Her bodyguard, Tony, whispers something into Ara's ear, and when she looks down, he's offering her his phone. Obviously, Luca wasn't impressed when she didn't answer his call, and he's using his man to force her to answer.

I think back to all the times we encouraged their relationship, even when Ara showed reluctance. We thought she was in denial about their chemistry, and I suppose to an extent she was, but had we known this about Luca Armani, would we have still encouraged it?

All I know is that right now, I want a hot shower to try to drown out this swirling uncertainty.

I mean, honestly, me involved with the Italian Mafia?

It's laughable.

Except I'm not laughing.

I collect my handbag from the bar and begin walking to the elevators. I can't help but look behind me twice as Lorenzo follows me. It's kind of creepy, but I'm sure he has to do it until I reach the elevator safely. Except he steps into the elevator with me.

"What are you doing?" I ask. He leans over, pushes the button for my floor, then leans against the mirrored wall, ever imposing. His six-foot-two frame buttoned up tight in his usual black suit. It's only been by chance that I've seen the hint of a tattoo around his neck, and it's made me wonder if he's riddled with tattoos. Having that visual in my mind right now makes me extremely frustrated.

The doors close, and I'm still staring at him expectantly as we stand in silence. I bite at my bottom lip as the tension devours me whole. It's not just his size that's imposing, but his simple presence. Right now, after a few drinks, I don't know where the mix of disgust, frustration, and need for a release begins or ends.

When the elevator door opens, Lorenzo holds a hand in front of me, and I'm shocked by his rudeness until I realize he's looking down either side of the hallway. Surely, there's not some assassin lurking on the top floor? Or maybe he's doing it intentionally to goad me.

"Is it always going to be like this?" I ask, irritated. There's being looked after and then there's excessive diligence. Surely, this is excessive, right?

"Just making sure there's no uneven floorboards so you don't have obstacles on already wobbly legs," he replies as he steps out, giving me space to walk through. Okay, so now he's sassing me, as if it's my fault we're stuck with each other for the foreseeable future.

"Ha ha, very funny. I think I preferred you when you didn't speak." I step over the elevator threshold. I'm squinting at each door number as I try to find mine. There are only four rooms on this level, but considering I don't even recall the first time coming up here because I was in such a daze, I'm left to embarrassingly play a guessing game.

I just want to be in my suite already.

I stop in front of the third door, hovering the gold key over the locking mechanism, when I realize Lorenzo is still behind me. "Um, coast is clear, sergeant. You can leave now."

He glares down at me. "I'm not going anywhere, and don't ever call me sergeant again."

Touchy.

"Well, you're not staying in my room." As if tonight couldn't get any worse, the last thing I need is an overbearing, brooding killer sitting in my room while I try to sleep. He shoves past me and steps into the suite, uninvited. "Hey!" I call out after him.

"Calm down, Sunshine. I don't want what you have to offer. But as of now, whatever room you step into, I'll be by your side. I've been ordered to protect you, and I will, even if you hate me for it."

I slam the door, infuriated. "So, what? My feelings don't matter in any of this?" I demand, and when he looks at me, deadpan, I realize this man doesn't have one emotion in his body. I want to wring his neck. I don't know how I could have ever found him attractive, even in the slightest. "Do you even know what feelings are? Or did they remove that in your default setting?"

In a matter of seconds, he's in my space, leaning over me. I hold on to the dresser as I lean away, the heat from him radiating and pressing against my acutely aware body without even touching me.

"Let's have an understanding. I didn't ask for this any more than you did. In fact, I was against it. Every second I'm left trailing after you removes me from what I'm supposed to be doing. Which is protecting my boss. So, no, I don't expect you to be comfortable with any of it. But I will warn you that how easy this is will depend on you and your attitude."

My heart is racing as a crazed laugh bubbles to the surface. Of all the reactions I could have right now, laughter is not what I was expecting. I should be scared, intimidated even, which is clearly what he's trying to make me feel, and yet I can't refrain from saying, "You don't scare me. You can try those feral tactics on others, but you don't use them on me. You speak to me like a lady, and you certainly treat me like one as well. If you want to act like a dog, I'll train you like one."

His dark-brown eyes narrow. I do my best to hold my ground, clinging to the fact that I know one thing about this man: He's on a leash. But I understand that doesn't mean much. Maybe I'm conceited or too drunk, but I know he won't hurt me.

No, instead he's willing to pull me to safety when

someone tries to run me over, and shield me when there's a gun pointed in my direction.

My hands act of their own accord as I grab him by the jaw and pull his lips to mine. In a matter of seconds, his body is fully pressed against mine, pinning me against the dresser, a pure wall of muscle. I moan as he dominates me entirely, forcing his tongue against mine and demanding more. I give him as much as he wants, feeling the tension leak out of me and twist into a completely different type of heated frustration.

I try to pull him even closer, but that's when his lips leave mine, and he pushes away, his hand going through his brown hair. "No. We're not playing this game of yours again," he's quick to say. "You're dangerous when you've been drinking."

I stare at him in disbelief. My mind is reeling from what I just did and his rejection.

Why did I do that?

Heat flushes my cheeks.

Again.

This isn't the first time I've forced myself on him after having a few too many drinks, and I'm not in the habit of throwing myself toward unfamiliar men. But the last time was almost two years ago. *Why? Why? Why?*

I despise this man, I remind myself. I'm a mix of embarrassment and muddled confusion.

I don't say anything. I simply hold my head high

and walk toward the bathroom because I don't know what else to do. I can't even trust myself around this man, let alone make sense of anything else.

Once I've showered, I try my hardest to ignore him as I make my way to the king-sized bed in my pink nightie. It's a relief when I notice him in my peripheral vision, sitting on the couch opposite the bed. Good, because he's certainly not sharing the bed with me.

I throw the blankets over my head and hide under the weight of them. My stomach starts swirling, and I curl into myself. No matter how small I feel, I can still feel his presence. Imposing, dooming, lingering on every inch of my body. I can't help but torture myself by reliving the kiss and the embarrassment that followed it.

It was hot, demanding, something I've only experienced once before—with him. Except by now I should know better, even while drunk.

I cut off those thoughts. I have more important issues to handle than worrying why a man doesn't want to kiss me back. Our worlds shouldn't mingle, so how on earth am I supposed to convince everyone he's my boyfriend, especially when we can barely tolerate one another?

Groaning, I turn to my other side, hoping that when I wake up, this is all a horrible nightmare.

Or at the very least, that I never see Lorenzo again.

6

LORENZO

She's pissed. Also, clearly nursing a hangover, but I'm not going to be the one to point that out especially when she's holding those giant-ass scissors. *Snip*. The bottom of the long stem falls to the counter. Lily isn't looking at me, but I know her intent was certainly more toward me than the flower she's trimming.

The iced tea I purchased for her goes untouched, even when I know it's her beverage of choice. When she woke, I insisted we go to her apartment so I could check the security measures already in place. It seemed to have only dawned on her then that I would be temporarily living with her, and instead, she adamantly advised I either drive her here, to her flower shop, or she'd call a driver. As if I were going to let her out of my fucking sight.

Fuck me. If I had known being a babysitter was

going to be this difficult, I would've put up more of a fight against the order. Not that it would have done any good.

"Are you just going to stand there all day and stare?" Lily grumbles, still refusing to make eye contact with me.

I stoically remain where I am, wondering how many people get to see this side of the polished high-society daughter. A woman who wears pinks, purples, and yellows like a fucking beam of sunshine but who has the tongue of a viper when hungover and the vocabulary of a woman who is ever demanding and seductive after a few drinks.

The vivid memory of her hips grinding against my cock and those needy little kisses last night comes to mind, and I clear my throat, avoiding the urge to readjust myself.

"Yes. That's my job," I say matter-of-factly.

Dangerous is what this woman is. She plays little Miss Goody Two-shoes through the day, and at night, after a few drinks, turns into a seductress. Ordinarily, I might be tempted to break something so precious, but even I know it's a line I can't cross. In truth, I resent her for the fact that I have to play babysitter instead of protecting my boss, even if it isn't her fault.

She sighs and places the scissors down.

"I didn't ask for you to be my bodyguard or play fake boyfriend." That scathing gaze finally lands on me. It's as if she can read my fucking mind, or maybe it's evident I don't want to be here.

Since the moment she woke up this morning, moaning about a headache, and her gaze landed on me, she's been scowling. I heard her whimper something about not being a nightmare after all as she drew the blankets back over her head. I didn't sleep a wink last night in that chair because of how loud her snoring was, and she had the audacity to look at me as if I were the problem for her shitty mood.

It took me the first hour to fight any temptation of forcing her to finish what she started last night with that desperate kiss.

She's always been a temptation for me. I might be a man of discipline, but fuck me, resisting her might be my breaking point.

"Then we share the same sentiment," I remind her. My skills are better utilized elsewhere, like helping my boss expand his empire. Hell, it would've even made more sense to send me to Italy to deal with the current situation there.

She bundles the flowers, maneuvering them in a way I don't entirely understand. I walked past the store once and was mesmerized by how at peace she seemed as I looked at her through the window.

"You don't have to be at my work. No one's going to do a drive-by while I'm selling flowers." She looks at me, then her eyes go wide. "Right? Like, that stuff only happens in movies."

My silence is answer enough as she mouths, *"holy shit,"* and then sits back in her chair with an *oomph*. It's the same way I found her last night, as if her world had just been cracked into a million pieces, and everything she once knew was unraveling. And maybe it is.

Not only has she realized her best friend married into the Italian Mafia, but now she's a target by association. It's Ara's guilt over the matter that has me here in the first place.

I don't dare probe the question looming in the air between us. Sure, she came on to me last night, but I concluded a long time ago that Lily is a good woman, and her world just got blown wide open. I rationalized that it's the only reason why she practically threw herself at me last night, and although I understand she needs comfort, I'm not the right person to give it.

And this is just business, I remind myself. An abnormal task I've been assigned and will take professionally, like all of the missions given to me.

However, it's hard not to notice what looks like her entire world being sucked into a vortex and her normally bright, sparkling blue eyes devoid of the life they usually brim with. If I had the choice, I would've protected her from this. Most people are better off not knowing about the scary monsters in the night. It tarnishes and changes them, just as it has her.

It's only then I realize my knuckles are whitening. I don't even know how long I've been fisting my hands, as if forcing myself to maintain the distance between us. I know better than to get emotionally entangled with the people I'm protecting, but watching her like this is... uncomfortable. It should be easy for me to avoid it; the only person's emotional welfare I'm attuned to is my boss's, and yet I find myself stepping toward her.

She doesn't look up. She's simply staring at her hands, appearing entirely vulnerable. Something everyone I associate myself with knows better than to do. There should be no opening, no weak spot, no moment of letting one's guard down. But hers is always down, exposing every sensitive part of her. Her neck still has a bruise from where she ran into a branch, and a knot of feral anger unravels in my stomach. She's too easy to break.

"Stop pitying me," she says, bringing her hand to her neck and massaging the spot, noticing precisely what I was staring at. It's only because I'm looking for it that I can see it through the makeup she's covered it with.

"I'm simply curious." I straighten my shoulders and come to a stop at her side as I redirect my attention toward the flowers.

She scoffs. "I doubt you've been curious about anything for a long time. Anything besides straight and narrow might give you an aneurysm. Wouldn't want you to defect now."

I try to keep my expression neutral, although the possibility of a smile breaking through threatens. She's the only woman I know who can so elegantly insult me. Even then, she still seems polite about it, which is a double-handed offense.

"I was curious about why you do this." I nod toward the bouquet she's working on. Her blue eyes glare up at me, and I immediately know I've hit a sore spot. Does she think I look down on her occupation? Who am I to judge someone else's pursuits when all I have on my resume is underhanded dealings and killing people?

"Because flowers make people happy," she says, not at all sounding like a ray of sunshine, but as if she's had to repeat this time and time again. "I know people don't understand it, and it doesn't turn over nearly as much profit as my family's companies, but it makes *me* happy. I like putting smiles on people's faces or being a part of healing in times of mourning. Flowers are appropriate for almost any occasion, and I like being creative, even if it seems stupid."

My eyebrows furrow slightly as I pick up one of the flowers and roll it in my fingers. Can this single rose do so much? I thought they were only used for funerals or courting a woman. Then again, what would I know about courting since I've never had any semblance of a relationship other than one-offs to meet my needs. I never looked at a single flower any differently until now.

Lily's phone screen lights up on the counter with *Dad* flashing on the screen, and she grumbles her complaint as she picks it up. I did a notable amount of research on her family last night while she slept. Her father is as money-hungry and ambitious as the next person in most wealthy social circles, and he recently pushed for his son to take over multiple companies.

"Hey, Dad, is everything okay?" she asks, her hungover self suddenly chipper, but I can see through it. There's obvious tension she holds toward him. I put the rose back down. "Yeah, we decided to come back from Italy early. That's all." Another long pause. "This Friday night? Oh, that's short notice." Silence. "I'll be there."

Just like that, he hangs up on her, and she stares down at her phone. She then looks back up at me, her face paling. "I have to go to a party. You can*not* come."

"That's not an option," I say matter-of-factly.

"My dad can't find out about this situation. If he does, he'll have me close up the store and sell me off to the highest bidder. He's already breathing down my neck about marriage now, but if he knows I'm somehow involved in Mafia misconduct, I'm epically screwed."

"Lucky you're not involved in any Mafia misconduct, simply introducing your boyfriend."

"You're not my—"

I encroach on her space, baring my teeth. "This is not up for discussion. If Luca has ordered me to be with you at all times, then I'll be with you at all times. I'm doing my best to play nice here, but I think you forgot I'm not some pup to be toyed with. I don't take orders from *you*."

Tears spring to her eyes, and my jaw grinds painfully. Fuck, I'm not cut out for this. Her floral scent infiltrates my nose, and it's so different from the usual smells of my day-to-day tasks that I want to deem it offensive, when it's anything but.

"You're such an asshole," she says quietly. "This is my life." It's better she realizes the truth of who I am sooner rather than later. I'm not her friend nor her confidant. If she's deluding herself that I'm kind, then I should clear her of that notion.

"Right now, your life is mine to protect, and I take that *very* seriously."

Noticing a silhouette approaching the front door, I end the discussion. The bell that dangles above the door chimes, and we look up in unison as a woman carries in two boxes. I step back, creating space between us, and slip into the back room, where I can still see her through the cut-out window but not interfere with the running of her business.

"Oh, you're early." Lily brightens and quickly wipes away the tears that sprang to her eyes, as if all is well and life is as it always has been.

The sooner we're both freed from this arrangement, the better, because I don't like the idea of playing boyfriend at some ludicrous party either. One of the hounds would've been far better suited for this role. I push away the thoughts because I don't often stray or question my boss's orders or plans. But this one is thrusting me too far out of my comfort zone. I don't have the expertise to pull this off. Two days in a row, I've made this woman cry without meaning to.

If I didn't know I was an asshole before, I certainly fucking do now.

7

LORENZO

This woman has a perfectly rehearsed stink eye, which she frequently trains on me.

"You can use the guest room downstairs, but my room is completely off limits," she says as she opens her apartment door. Her apartment building is prestigious and well known, as expected of anyone who carries the Taylor name.

It seems to infuriate her more that I don't give in to her threats, which, dare I say, might even be *cute* if she thinks they have any genuine weight against me.

When we first walk in, I scan the main living area. It's ridiculously spacious, yet it has a nice flow to it. It's contemporary in feel, with small splashes of beige and light pinks. But mismatched colored vases sprinkle the room with various flowers that have already begun to wilt.

On my left is a large island counter with barstools

framing a polished kitchen. In front is a living space that, instead of a TV, has a large wooden library filled with books and a fireplace. I curiously walk over, ignoring the plush couches and cushions, grimacing as I look over the titles, which are all romance.

"Don't come in here and judge what I read," she says defensively as she removes her heels and leaves them at the door, stacked with another ten pairs. Then she begins removing her jewelry, starting with the earrings.

I'm not judging her choice of reading, but more so the fact that I don't understand the appeal of romance.

The floor-to-ceiling windows let the night spill in. It's busy, bright, irritating—and dangerous. "The blinds are to be closed at all times."

She snorts, and I turn to face her, her hands on her hips. "I like the nightlife and the city. The blinds stay open."

My temple pulses as I lick my lips, trying my hardest to play nice. "Have you ever seen a movie where the target gets a bullet through the head because they've been sniped through a window?"

She immediately pales. A cold, palpable tension drifts between us. "You're so obnoxious. If you're as good at this security thing as you say, then you'll figure out another way. They stay open. I'll remind you that you're a guest in *my* home. Actually, not even that—you're lucky I'm giving you a room at all. I could very well just make you sleep on the floor outside the apartment door."

I casually shrug. "I've slept on worse. But, no, whatever room you're in, I'm in."

She raises her finger to silence me, and my temple pulses again.

I can already tell this woman is going to drive me insane.

"Ground rules. You don't go into my room. I need my privacy, especially if I have to entertain this fake boyfriend bodyguard bullshit. If you come to my shop, you stay in the back and out of my way. No, inviting any weird cold-blooded killer friends into my home. Most importantly, you're not going to parties or events with me. The sooner this is over, the better, and we'll pretend like it never happened."

"I go wherever you go." I fold my arms in front of my chest. For such a tiny woman, she's very defiant.

"No."

"Yes."

"I need my privacy. You're not coming into my room." She stands her ground. "And no parties where gossip will definitely spread."

"I think you misunderstand the point of using the cover of being in a relationship. I'm with you everywhere, unless you're daring enough to create a believable excuse as to why you suddenly have a bodyguard. It's your choice, Sunshine."

She doesn't seem to like that as her cheeks turn a shade of furious red.

"Do you even know what a relationship looks like?" she berates.

I shrug. "I get the gist of it."

"No to you being in my room."

"Then you close the blinds in your bedroom," I challenge.

"No."

"Yes."

She waves her hands in the air. "You're so insufferable."

"Your attempt last night to seduce me would say otherwise," I say matter-of-factly.

Her cheeks flush a deeper red.

"I actually hate you." She turns toward the staircase that, from what I can see, leads to a private room. Her bedroom, I'm assuming. She points to the room beside the living space. "That's your room. Don't speak to me." She hovers at the middle point of the stairs and looks over her shoulder. Despite the upheaval she's gone through in the past few days, she appears regal as she looks down her nose at me. "And the blinds stay open," she adds defiantly, then continues storming up the stairs.

"You still haven't eaten today," I call out. The door slams behind her. This woman is going to be unbearable to deal with. She's bratty, which only complicates my role. Sure, I can understand how this might inconvenience her, but I'm not letting that jeopardize her safety.

I search the home, which has hardly any security. I send a text message to Sky, one of the hounds, with an immediate request. I then call Izak, the hound whose strength most certainly lies behind a computer screen.

He answers on the second ring. "Quite the extensive security list you want installed in her apartment."

"Get it done tomorrow while we're working in her shop."

He chuckles. "While *we're* working at her shop. You already sound domesticated, brother."

"Need I remind you that I can easily have you removed?" I grit out, sick of these little punks and their attitudes.

"Touchy. Of course, I can get it done. Wouldn't it be easier to have her at your property, though? Why go to all of this effort?"

I cut the call. I'd already considered that myself, but as I look up at her closed door, I would've had to drag her kicking and screaming. At least being in her own space might offer her some type of comfort, and she should be grateful that I'm being so fucking accommodating.

I continue investigating the apartment. Her preferences, her art, the lack of food in the fridge—soaking in everything I need to know about Lily Taylor. Of course, I already know more about her than I should, since I looked into her right after she first piqued my interest almost two years ago.

A memory I've tried countless times to forget, but one that has lingered far more than any other, pushes its way into the front of my mind.

Luca had stormed the club, Telltale, where Ara and her friends were dancing, to take his woman home. After I'd driven Luca and Ara back to his apartment, he'd ordered me to return to make sure her friends were okay. I'm never particularly agreeable when it comes to leaving his side, but much like now, I had no choice.

By the time I'd arrived, two of her friends were preoccupied with the men they'd chosen for the night. Lily had been shining brightly as she'd danced and drank herself into a stupor, and the moment a guy approached her on the dance floor, and she'd stumbled back to kindly say "no, thank you," I'd already been moving through the crowd. The little fucker had stopped persisting after I'd loomed over her back, staring at him like the Grim Reaper.

I'd thought she'd be the easiest to return home safely. From what I'd observed in our few previous interactions, she was quiet and agreeable. That night, Lily had been a reminder to never let my guard down or underestimate anyone, even if they came in such a petite package.

The memory of her soft skin pressed against me

that night lives in my mind and resurfaces more frequently than it should.

———

Two years ago…

"You don't really talk much, do you?" Lily asks from the back seat of my car. "How do I know you're not kidnapping me? He wasn't that bad looking." She sulks, crossing her arms over her chest.

"I was definitely doing you a favor," I reply dryly, looking through the rearview mirror. Objectively, I suppose he was handsome, but not nearly enough to match her in any regard. "Also, don't you think you should ask that question before getting into my car?"

She casually shrugs. "I just assumed since you came with Luca, that you're his friend. Why? Are you going to hurt me?" Her blue eyes slice to mine through the mirror, and there's a gentle challenge there. My cock twitches at the temptation of all the ways it'd like to break something so precious. But that's the thing with this little one—she would shatter. Crumble within seconds, even at the thought of my depravities.

"No, I'm not," I say.

She looks down at her phone with a sigh and then turns to gaze out the window. I can't gauge what she's thinking, nor do I care. Drop her off at home—that's all I have to do, and then I can return to Luca. I don't trust Ara Barone alone with him. He might say it's for his own entertainment and gathering intel on her, but I know there's far more to it. I'm uncomfortable when he doesn't disclose all of his motivations to me. It makes outcomes unpredictable, something I prefer to limit. I'm the keeper of his secrets and his first weapon. When he doesn't depend on me... it makes me feel useless.

"I think I'm going to be sick," Lily suddenly says.

I hook a sharp turn against the curb and am out of the car in seconds, opening the back door for her. Her eyes widen at the sight of my offered hand. I'm not letting this car stink of whatever concoction of alcohol she consumed tonight.

Skeptically, she takes my hand and steps out of the car. She looks pale... but isn't she always pale? Her hand is small and cold compared to mine. As if noticing the same thing, she's quick to remove it, a blush blossoming on her cheeks. *Shit. Too innocent. If hand-holding is taboo for this little princess, then she has no right to even step out into the real world.*

"Are you a virgin?" I blurt.

"*Excuse me?!*" she says in a shrill voice. "No, don't be ridiculous. I'm twenty-six, not sixteen." Lily removes the elastic that's holding her long hair in a high pony-tail and then shakes out her loose blonde curls to hide her obvious embarrassment as she walks toward the park. I look back at the open car door and internally growl as I chase after her. This is taking up too much time.

"I need to drop you off at home," I say, following her.

"And I told you I need fresh air," she replies flatly.

"No, you said you feel sick." I scan the area, noting no one else is out here at this time of night, but it doesn't make it any less exposed.

She runs her hands over her thighs before sitting on the lip of the fountain in the middle of the small park. Her outfit is distraction enough—tight-fitting pink pants, a matching pink bralette, and a pair of black heels—and I'm tempted to cover her, if only for my sake, so my gaze isn't tempted to rake over her, *again*.

"You're a weird friend. Do you know that?" she says, ignoring my previous comment.

Friend. Is that what she really thinks I am to Luca? Fuck me, the poor girl doesn't have very good instincts about people.

A few dim lights dot the park, creating a contrast against her porcelain shoulders, which seem to shine, compared to her face, which is hidden in the shadows as she gazes at her feet.

"I've been called worse, I suppose," I admit as I reluctantly take a seat beside her, because as much as I want to hasten this, I have a feeling that she might not be out here because she feels sick. She looks more like a girl who's avoiding going home. But she's not a girl. She's a beautiful woman. Precious perhaps... but she's not at all like the others in the circles Luca mingles with. And maybe that's what makes her appear so breakable—because she's so transparent.

We sit in an easy silence. I watch her as she stares at her feet, and it irritates me. Someone as beautiful as her shouldn't be staring at the ground, but I don't care to ask about the demons she may be fighting.

"Are you just friends with Luca, or is there something else to it?" she asks.

"We have business together," I say vaguely. *Friend* is definitely not the right word to describe Luca's and my relationship. This little rabbit would shake in her boots if she knew the depths of darkness we conducted *business* in.

She's studying me now. I don't know what she's looking for or why she stares so intently with those big blue eyes. But she certainly doesn't seem sick. When I'm about to suggest we walk back to the car, she moves with lightning speed. I grab her arm tightly on reflex, but am surprised when her soft lips press against mine.

For the first time in a long time, I'm momentarily shocked into inaction. Startled by the gentle neediness of a woman I shouldn't touch. Yet my firm grip pulls her closer into me, her breasts pressing against my chest. I force my tongue harder against hers, exploring the depths of what this woman is willing to give me.

I wait for her to pull back and run away scared, but the more I demand, the more she opens up to me. She swiftly adjusts herself, getting on her knees, and uses my hold on her to ensure she doesn't fall into the fountain as she straddles me. Her knees barely fit on either side of me from the size difference, but then she rubs herself against me, those delicate hips grinding on my hardening cock. The moment she feels me through my pants, a little whimper escapes her throat.

Fucking hell, this woman might be my undoing.

When I come back to my senses, I gently ease her away from me. I can't fuck this woman. I've never had concerns about who I fuck before, but I can't cross that line with this one. She is completely off-limits and will only complicate matters with Arabella Barone as it is.

Lily's eyes widen in shock. "I, um—" She looks confused. "I'm sorry. I—" She throws back her head and laughs, then slowly climbs off my lap. "Can't say I've been rejected before," she says, sounding somewhat refreshed.

I'm intently watching her every move, the dip of her curves, the shimmer of her skin as the water hits it. I'd be a fiend to touch something so unintended for bloody hands such as my own.

"Trust me when I say you can't handle me, Sunshine."

She laughs again, the sound light and freeing, an entirely different version of what I thought I knew about her. She's still the agreeable, doe-like woman, but there's something more confident in her peeking out. She holds out her hand expectantly. "Give me your phone."

My eyebrows dip. "I'm not giving you my phone."

"Interesting that you thought I was asking. If you're going to reject me, the least you can do is take my number."

"Why do I need your number?"

"So you can message me later to make sure I got home safely after I call my driver to pick me up from here." She wiggles her fingers expectantly. "Come on, you've already rejected me once, help a girl's ego out. Surely, a phone number isn't going to hurt you."

I stand. "There's no need for any text messages because I'll be taking you home."

She holds her ground, placing a hand on her hip. "I'll let you take me home if you give me your phone."

"No."

"Yes."

"This is not a negotiation," I growl, then throw her over my shoulder and stride back toward the car. She squeals as I lift her with an *oomph*. Fuck me, she barely weighs anything. There's nothing to her, yet I can't help but have already noticed the perfection of her figure. How smooth her ass feels under my hand, and her tits, which press against my back. A fucking temptation I don't need.

"Put me down! This *is* kidnapping."

"Trust me, Sunshine, you'd know if I kidnapped you." I slowly place her down on her tiptoes when we reach the car. "For starters, I'd gag that running little mouth of yours," I say as I rub my thumb against her bottom lip, mesmerized. "I'd tie your hands behind your back and then lash your legs together so you couldn't run away."

A physical shudder runs through her, and my cock twitches at her transparent response.

She's off-limits, I remind myself.

It's enough to pull me out of the trance, and I look back into the depths of her blue eyes. Her smile stretches as she brings my phone to eye level and steps back with a smirk as I go to grab it out of her hand.

When and how did she manage to steal my phone?

Fuck, was I really only thinking with my cock?

This woman *cannot* be underestimated.

"What's your passcode? Luca's birthday?" she jokes over her shoulder with a smirk. "Oh, goodness, it isn't, right? Not that I'm judging, but even I'm not that close to my—"

I snatch the phone out of her hand. "I'm dropping you off for the night. You and I will not see each other in the future, and even if we do, let me make this very clear—you should keep as much distance from me as possible."

This woman is slightly infuriating. Or maybe it's because I don't like the fact that she was able to so swiftly steal my phone without me realizing.

The corner of her mouth tilts up. "It's just a number, Lorenzo. Stop being such a scaredy cat."

Lorenzo. My cock twitches, enticed by the way my name rolls off her tongue.

Lily Taylor is somewhat unassuming. She probably knows she's beautiful, but I doubt she understands the true force of her magnetism, and I'm unnerved at how it's working on me. Seduction never works on me. Especially when it can be used as a weapon. But she's so sincere, and far more daring tonight than I ever thought she could be.

Considering I still want to adjust my cock, and need to return to Luca's side, I realize the easiest route is giving her my phone. Especially if I don't want to technically kidnap her just to return her home. I offer my phone. "I won't text you."

She smirks as she enters her phone number and then hands it back. When I look down, my eye twitches. She put her name in my contacts with a flower emoji behind it. And she's sent herself a message. *New friend.*

Before I can respond, she slides into the back of the car and closes the door behind her. What the fuck just happened?

I pocket my phone, trying to shake off the bizarre exchange. When I get back into the car, she's preoccupied with her phone and doesn't speak to me for the rest of the drive. It's unsurprising that her apartment building is one of the most expensive ones in Manhattan.

Lily Taylor is the type of woman I usually despise most. And yet, when she climbs out of the car and then dips her head back in through the back door, she smiles at me. "Thanks, new friend. Maybe I'll see you around."

"I doubt it," I deadpan.

She shrugs. "If not, thanks for the humbling rejection." She laughs, but a small blush tinges her cheeks before she slams the door. I watch her hips sway from side to side, baffled by the contradicting version of her brought out by some liquid courage. I thought she was a shy, doe-eyed daddy's girl. But now I'm certain there's something more to be explored. I immediately shut the thought down, sending a message to Luca.

I turned into a babysitter tonight.

———

LILY TAYLOR IS a distraction I don't need in my life. I can have any woman I want, and I choose to keep it at that. Lily is a woman I have no interest in entertaining, but I'd be lying if I didn't admit I want to taste her.

But I know even one taste will be damning.

A soft knock on the door breaks me out of my thoughts, and I once again try to forget the memory, infuriated that I became consumed by it.

When I open the door, Sky stands there, wearing his bike helmet, the visor down so no one can see his face.

"Since when did I turn into some food delivery guy?" he demands, opening the visor with a scowl as he holds out a brown bag.

"Where's the iced tea?" I demand, and he holds it up in the other hand.

I take both. "You tried the salad?"

He rolls his light-blue eyes. "Yes, not poisoned. And if you ever make me eat kale again, I'll fucking kill you."

"Watch your tone," I growl, irritated by the little shit. "No onion?"

He huffs. "No onion."

He shrugs and pockets his gloved hands. "Seem to be going out of your way for the new girlfriend, huh?" he says with an arrogant smirk.

I close the door in his face, then I open the brown bag and inspect the contents. It's her usual order from one of her favorite restaurants. She can hate me all she likes, but while I'm in charge of her safety, I'm not going to let her wilt away into nothing.

I hover outside her door, thinking better of barging in. Instead, I place my offering on the floor and then knock before walking down the stairs. I've got a lot of work to do, investigating her father, and I can't help but think Lily Taylor might be my most turbulent mission yet.

8

LILY

Ridiculous. That's what this situation is. And I can't do anything about it. I don't want to end my friendship with Ara, but I also don't want to be stuck with a brute of a man whose default setting seems to be broody and annoyed.

I don't know what I ever saw in him.

This thought repeats in my mind as Lorenzo drives us to the party, and he hasn't even so much as spoken to me since practically forcing me into the car. I've never met someone with the skills to irritate me so spectacularly. He's beyond offensive, and I can't see myself getting used to this arrangement any time soon. The sooner Luca gets his shit together, the better. For all our sakes.

I've done my best to ignore him all week, despite him never being far from my side, but my curiosity has limits. I side-eye him, betraying myself as my gaze trails over his immaculate suit and freshly trimmed facial hair. Strong wafts of cedar roll off him, and I despise every intricate detail I notice.

He looks good.

Too good.

He always has, and that's certainly part of the problem.

Shouldn't killers give some indication of the danger they pose? Shouldn't they look scary or repulsive?

"You're staring," he says. *Damn it.* I immediately divert my gaze out the window. Of course, he notices everything.

I swear I can sense his gaze shift to me, which unfurls an uncomfortable unease in my stomach. Something that flutters before it's washed over with the cold reminder of exactly how my father is going to react when he sees me at this party with Lorenzo.

I don't know what to do. I'm trapped, because even if I run from Lorenzo, I know he'll find me. I'm a fool for romanticizing him before. I always thought he was attractive, and I would sneak glances whenever he was around Luca and Ara. But now I wish I had never gotten too close, because I've only found a closet full of demons.

Perhaps my taste in men is worse than I imagined. Maybe I really should let my friend Elanee matchmake for me.

A startling thought hits me, and I can't help but look back over at Lorenzo. I don't know much about

Dmitri and Elanee's relationship, but there was a lot of weird tension going around when they got together.

"Is Elanee a part of the Mafia?" I ask quickly, too scared I'll lose my nerve if I don't throw it out there. Oh my gosh, are all of my friends actually part of some underworld scene? Am I so sheltered that I even lack the natural instincts to warn me when I'm around dangerous people?

Lorenzo's gaze meets mine. "I don't share other people's secrets."

A cold dread washes over me, and I'm once again quick to divert my gaze, too scared that he'll see every little pebble of fear piling up inside me. The small flutters in my stomach become heavier. I focus on my breathing as I try to push through the sheer panic washing over me. *Holy fuck.* What have I gotten myself into? I don't know right from wrong anymore. I don't know who my friends really are. I mean, I know they're my friends, but as evidenced by my current situation, it's obviously dangerous just to be associated with them. But I can't seem to blame Ara for any of it. Nothing has happened all week, and I'm starting to believe it's all an exaggeration.

My mind begins to spiral as it becomes harder to breathe.

I try to control my thoughts. *Let's just focus on the issue at hand.* Fuck, my father's going to lose his shit when Lorenzo, an unknown bachelor with no money or connections, comes in, declaring himself as my boyfriend. But I can't tell him I'm best friends with a Mafia boss's wife or... or... Fuck!

The car comes to an abrupt halt at the curb, and the back of my head hits the seat hard, stunning me for a moment. Adrenaline pumps through my veins as I look up, expecting an accident. Or worse: will there be men pointing guns at us?

People are yelling and screaming at us, but there's no accident or ambush; we're simply parked halfway over the curb onto the sidewalk.

What the—?

"Breathe." Lorenzo's voice carries hypnotically through the car. It's only then that I notice the rough pads of his fingers that prickle along the back of my neck. It pushes a fresh dose of adrenaline through my veins as his feather-light grip redirects my face to look in his direction. Those dark-brown eyes pin me, bringing me back into myself. "Breathe," he says again, and I trail the word to his lips, following his lead. Slowly in and slowly out.

In and out.

In and out.

Oh shit. Was I having a panic attack? *In and out.* I haven't had one of those since childhood. *In and out.* The jitters slowly recede, and I welcome the sweep of calm that slowly but surely begins to push through. *In and out.*

I don't know how long we remain like that, but it's enough to bring my racing thoughts to a startling ease.

The spike of adrenaline quickly recedes into embarrassment.

Lorenzo must think I'm a joke. A coddled princess. I'm not as strong as my friends. They're daring and bold in their own unique ways, and I live in a glass house, trying to appease my family. My only outlet, the only part of me I give myself space for, is the florist shop. But how insignificant is that to a man who most likely sees blood daily? Hell, he's probably the executioner. I must seem like an embarrassment to someone like him. I haven't been able to keep my emotions in check since everything that transpired in Italy. I guess I'm learning what I'm really made of, and it's pathetic. Especially because the person who's soothing my inner storm is a man I very much think lacks emotion or empathy.

"You're a dangerous person, aren't you?" I ask quietly, staring into his eyes. Despite already knowing this, it's the first thing I can think of blurting out to distract me from my spiraling thoughts that I've often had to fight through this past week.

I know his answer before he gives it.

"I am a dangerous man," Lorenzo says each word slowly, as if letting me absorb their weight and magnitude. If anything, I'm grateful he didn't make a comment like, "Finally talking to me now, Sunshine?"

"Fearing me is the smart thing to do. But know that I will never hurt *you*. However, don't ever confuse me for a hero or knight in shining armor. I'm only here because I was ordered to be."

A mocking laugh bubbles from my throat, and I sound unhinged. Maybe I really am losing it, but it's enough to exorcise more of this unsettling energy. "No, a hero you certainly are not," I say, gliding my hands down the silk of my light-yellow dress. It does nothing to distract me from the heat emanating from his hand still cupped around my nape. He says he won't hurt me, but these hands could easily break my neck. "If you could remove your hand, please."

His eyebrows furrow slightly, and he looks at his hand, as if only just realizing he's still touching me. He clears his throat, grips the wheel with both hands, and pulls back out onto the road, unfazed by the onlookers.

I pull down the vanity mirror so I can assess my appearance. Whatever that panic attack was, I don't want it controlling my life. I don't want to be that scared girl anymore. Then again, it's been a long time since I've feared anything besides my family's judgment. Perhaps this is what they call a rude awakening. I adjust the curls that frame my face and ensure my hair is still neatly positioned in a bun. I touch the pearls on my ears and necklace, as if trying to harden my confidence. I have to, if I'm going to survive tonight.

"My father will do a thorough background check on you. You're hardly someone he would consider a proper suitor."

"'Proper suitor.' Jesus Christ, who even speaks like that?" he sneers.

That little tickle of irritation begins to stir in my stomach again. "Excuse me, sergeant, but some of us have to abide by the rules of high society. You might dip your toe in it now and then because your boss tells you to, but I have obligations to my family." The corners of his mouth tip up, and I realize he's purposefully winding me up, and I too easily bite at his taunts. I don't even know why I'm justifying myself, because he doesn't care one ounce about how his appearance will impact my family's reputation.

"Must be tiresome being a good girl all the time," he says, not the least bit apologetic.

"Don't pretend like you know me," I bite back, glancing up at the tall buildings that glitter against the night sky. I've always loved this city's splendor and constant busyness. Sometimes, I wish I could just get swept out into the sea of people and truly live amongst them, instead of caring what everyone thinks or how it might impact the Taylor name.

"I know enough to call a spoiled princess a brat when I see one."

I chuckle darkly, and I don't know where it's coming from. "Ironic coming from a man whose master says 'jump,' and you ask, 'how high?'. Maybe we're not as different as you think."

"The difference is, I enjoy my position, Sunshine, while you're clearly begging to run away from yours."

It hurts. The amount of truth in that statement. Not that I'd ever give him the satisfaction of letting him know it. I don't want him to see any more of my weaknesses.

"Most people would thank the person who's protecting them," Lorenzo continues.

We're only a few blocks away from the party, and the only thing I'm grateful about is the fresh air blowing in my partially open window, because laughing and smiling through the night is going to be a challenge, even for me.

And yet, he has a point. Maybe I'm picking a fight with the wrong person.

"I will assume your silence is a thank you."

"Then you assume incorrectly," I snap. What is it about this man that pisses me off? Is it because I'm still bitter from his rejection? Most likely. Despite having a million other concerns, I seem to come back to that minor detail.

"Yet, you're not begging me not to go anymore," he says, and I can't stand his smug tone.

"Would you listen?" I ask dryly as I survey the upcoming building when the car slows down. A black carpet leads to the grand front doors, where two cameramen wait. This event is nothing more than a breeding ground for rumors and a showcase of wealth. These events are all the same, no matter who hosts them or what the occasion is for.

"No," Lorenzo says flatly as he brings the car to a

stop in front of the building. I scan over my hair once more as he gets out of the car, walks around it, and hands the keys to the waiting valet. I'm actually shocked when Lorenzo opens the door for me and offers his hand. Does he actually know etiquette?

I glare at his outstretched palm, and the corner of his mouth tilts up ever so slightly. My eyebrows furrow because surely, I'm hallucinating for me to actually think I saw the ghost of a smile on his lips.

"Come on, Sunshine, we're only here because of you," he says blandly. I don't understand this man. He goes from completely cold to the tiniest touch of warmth, but I'm certain that's only because of the cameras on us right now. The act begins now, and maybe Lorenzo knows how to play the part, after all.

I slide my hand into his, allowing him to lead me out of the car. My heels hit the pavement, and I adjust my dress accordingly. "You didn't even tell me I look nice tonight."

"I don't need to. You already know that you do," he says matter-of-factly.

A warmth floods my core, and I reprimand myself for getting fluttery over something so small.

"If you actually want anyone to believe this charade, you'd better compliment me more like a real boyfriend would, and *please,* be friendly with others," I grit through a smile as I make a point to look at him lovingly.

"Despite what you might think of me, I haven't

lived in a cave all of these years," he says, sliding my hand into the crook of his elbow.

My breath hitches at the gentleness of his gesture. It's embarrassing how acutely aware I am of his every touch. Even when I shouldn't be. Even as I beg for it not to be the case.

The flutters of nervousness creep back in as concerns about how tonight might play out begin to pile up. I know Ara said it was necessary, but right now I'm thinking I'd rather risk the idea of a hitman at my back than my father's disappointment. That in itself is all sorts of messed-up.

"It'll be fine. We're just going to go in and be seen for a bit. Unless you want to leave right now. And if that's the case, we can get back in the car and go. I really want to leave," Lorenzo says, and it brings me back to the now. I realize how torturous this is for him, and a feral smugness ripples through me. If I have to be stuck with him in this fucked-up situation, then I'm sure as hell going to do my best to make him as uncomfortable as I am.

"No. I'm ready." I straighten my shoulders, and I can see him die a little more inside. He expects me to crumble so easily, and I refuse to give him that satisfaction. Even if he's still attempting to soften his features to be friendly as we're approached by a photographer, I can see right through him.

He's dressed as a gentleman, yet still looks like a wolf stepping through a herd of sheep. No matter what mask Lorenzo is wearing, I'm certain that will never change about him. The threat of danger simply oozes off of him. He knows who he is; it's deeply ingrained in his DNA. I might not know yet exactly what kind of man he is, but I know he's as beautiful as he is deadly.

I also know that right now, I have my part to play. And so, I resort to what I've been trained to do.

I push down my emotions and... I smile.

9

———

LORENZO

I can't stand the people in this room. They have an air of entitlement and a conceited existence. I was raised to serve the Armani family, and I chose to stay because there is one thing I appreciate about the shadows we live in. Everything is black and white. Respect is earned, business is direct, and consequences are harsh. People here stand behind fake smiles and facades.

I know almost a quarter of the room's deepest, darkest secrets, thanks to the side deals they've made with Luca and his "unconventional" connections.

I don't have the patience for these circles, and although I understand why Luca slithers throughout them, I don't have to. A perk of being the monster in the dark, which far better suits my role of being the one to hand out the consequences.

"Everyone is staring at you," Lily says under her

breath. "Can you at least try to remember what a smile feels like?"

I finally look at her. It's a habit of mine to survey for threats in the room, which I've been doing since we walked in. But unless someone is dying from an overindulgence of champagne, the only threat seems to be me. Lily clicks her tongue when I don't adjust my expression. Smiling and pleasantries are not something I excel at; I only use them when it's necessary. Right now, my preference is to keep the number of people approaching us to a minimum.

"My God, who told you too soon in life that Santa Claus, the Easter Bunny, and the Tooth Fairy don't exist?" she grumbles, frustrated.

I refrain from smiling. She's a brat, but when she's not holding in her thoughts, she can be a funny brat.

"They don't?" I ask, feigning surprise. Her eyes grow wide, as if she realizes she just broke a child's heart. The corner of my mouth twitches.

She lets out a shaky breath. "Please, don't mess with me right now." She reaches for a glass of champagne as a server walks past with a tray full of them. I'm inclined to steal it away from her because every time this sweet little vixen gets a little alcohol in her, she turns into a temptation I don't have the strength to fight tonight.

"It's you who's messing with me by bringing me to this party. What's it for again?"

"Charity," she says as she scopes out the room.

"And don't pretend like you're interested in what charity."

"Didn't expect to see your kind here," Dmitri Volkov says, coming to a stop in front of me. His fiancée, Elanee, pulls Lily in for a hug, but Dmitri's attention is only on me. We've worked together in the past, and his hands are no cleaner than mine. That doesn't make us friends, though. After all, it could be because of our part in ruining his father that we might be being attacked now.

His gaze slides to Lily, and although they're familiar with one another, and I know he only has eyes for Elanee, I don't like that he's looking at her. Maybe it's because I'm hypervigilant about keeping her away from any threat, and Dmitri himself is capable of being a threat.

"You look beautiful as always, Lily, but care to explain why you've arrived with Luca's bodyguard? It's unlike you to bring a date," Dmitri says, his gaze then sliding to me, most likely searching for a reaction. Even after having a tumor dug out of his head, he seems to have kept his unpleasant humor.

"Does everyone know about this but me?" Lily whisper-shouts, and Elanee gives her a sympathetic smile before pulling her away. I go to follow them, but Dmitri purposefully blocks me.

"Want to explain why you're in this neck of the woods?" Dmitri asks, holding a glass of water. He no longer drinks alcohol after having the tumor removed.

If anything, his attending events such as these might already be too soon, but despite the shaved head and glaring scar, Dmitri looks no different than before he went under the knife. I guess some rotten things can't entirely be cut out.

He acts as if nothing has happened, like only months ago, we weren't allied in assisting him against the Bratva and his father. Despite his overconfident personality and shit-stirring capabilities, he's one of the few I might actually hold respect for, but it doesn't make me any less pissed that he's so deliberately stepping in the way of my mission of protecting Lily.

"Business" is all I say.

A devilish smirk pricks at his features. "I understand Luca having business here, but you... are not meant for a place like this."

"We share the same sentiment. But business is business."

"I can see that." Dmitri tries not to laugh as he looks over his shoulder at Lily, which further irritates me. If I didn't already know he was obsessed with his fiancée and willing to die for her, I'd physically remove the former playboy's gaze from Lily.

Another two women join them in light conversation, and it would appear that Lily is her usual self. It's almost terrifying how easily her mask slips on in a setting like this. I could never understand how someone genuinely finds joy in a superficial life like this. Don't get me wrong, I like nice things, but these circles are toxic.

"Does this have something to do with the incident in Italy?" Dmitri quietly asks. My lethal gaze sweeps back to him, and he chuckles as he takes a sip of water.

"I thought we were friends. And don't be so surprised that I know; I have my sources."

"We aren't the type to do friends," I remind him. "And I'm here as Lily Taylor's date."

Dmitri chokes on his water, and I step back from him, brushing over my sleeve. A nearby couple stares at him, indignant.

"Her date? Not for real, though, surely?" he asks incredulously. I don't respond. "Listen, I don't know what you and Luca are up to, but tread carefully around her father. It's well known that he coddles his daughter. He might be someone who plays by the rules, but he can get messy when he becomes focused on taking somebody out."

"You think I'm scared of her father?" I could almost laugh.

"No, I'm just warning if you're trying to go under the radar, then *dating* Lily Taylor is the brightest fucking sunbeam you could be standing in."

"I suggest you don't look into my business unless you want me involved in yours," I warn Dmitri, and the asshole has the audacity to chuckle and shrug as if to say, *Don't say I didn't warn you.*

When I look back at Lily, I realize we're being surveyed by the group of women.

"Oh boy, looks like you've officially made it into the gossip circle." He places his hand on my shoulder. "Welcome to high society, my friend. Good luck."

My jaw tics because I shouldn't have to be the one to remind him that I deal with far worse than these chimpanzees.

I brush his hand off my shoulder and then make my way toward Lily, uncomfortable by the distance between us. With Luca, at least I know he can look after himself in the event of an assault or ambush, at least until I can get to him. Lily is as vulnerable as they come, which causes an unnerving need to be by her side at all times.

"Wow, never thought you'd be daring enough to introduce someone to your father, especially at a party," I overhear one of the women say. I don't look at her, only focusing on Lily, who still hasn't looked back at me.

She lets out a small laugh, eloquently brushing off the underhanded dig.

"Well, you know how he's been pressuring me to date more seriously lately," she says lightheartedly, and I'm surprised when she pulls me in by the lapel of my suit jacket. "I suppose everything comes down to timing. Right, dear?"

My entire body locks up with the foreign endearment and the way she so desperately uses me as a decoy. I'm used to being used as a shield against bullets, not bitchy comments. She might consider them friends, but she so clearly wants to be anywhere but here. I force my body to soften as I pull her in by the waist and slam her back to my chest possessively, my hand resting on her hip.

"I don't care too much for the timing of things, but if it led me to my Lily, then I have someone to give my thanks to," I say as I loom behind her, peering down at the women who would so openly mock her.

The two women's mouths open. I can feel Lily stiffen under my touch, but I hold her in place. I don't give a shit if she reprimands me later for my tone or intimidation tactics. These women are nothing.

In my periphery, I notice Elanee trying to hide a smile. I don't know what exactly Lily told her, but I doubt it's the truth. Even then, it's less of a hindrance that she's not one I have to pretend around, since we've had dealings before.

"Wow, we've never seen you attend any of these events. Are you new to the area?" the blonde woman asks flirtatiously, suddenly recovered.

"I'd like to know the same thing." The voice carries over their shoulders, and they immediately part to give a direct view of Lily's father, Henrith Taylor, dressed in an expensive tailored suit.

Meeting his gaze, I see where Lily gets her bright blue eyes from. But where she is soft and kind, he's cynical and cold. And not in the way I like. I know men like him aren't forthcoming in their business affairs. He's as slimy as they come. And I always stand by my first impressions because my instincts have never failed me.

"Father. It's good to see you," Lily greets, stepping out of my hold, basically shoving my hands off of her, like I've scorched her skin. She leans in to kiss her father's cheek. She then does the same to her mother, Isabella, who stands beside him, a frailer-looking version of Lily. Her mother's gaze falls to my shoes and trails all the way up, curiously. Her father, however, looks at me with complete disdain.

"Care to introduce yourself, or will you hide behind my daughter the entirety of tonight?" Henrith asks haughtily.

As expected, a patronizing elitist.

"I'm not the type to hide," I reply as I hold out my hand. "Lorenzo Moretti."

He looks down at my hand for a beat, as if it's covered in dirt, but slowly places his hand in mine as others watch on. I squeeze a fraction too tightly.

"Quite the firm handshake," he comments as he quickly pulls back.

"My father always told me that a firm handshake is the start of good business," I tell him. I give the man credit; even when I'm playing nice, most men would have averted their gaze by now.

"Yes, and who precisely is your father?"

"Dad, can we talk about this later?" Lily quickly

interrupts, making a point to glance to her left, where two men are shamelessly eavesdropping on us.

He turns his attention back to me, giving me the once-over, and makes no attempt to hide the fact that he thinks I'm less than gum on the bottom of his shoe.

"This conversation isn't over. It seems I've allowed you to have too much fun if you're bringing peculiar types of guests to these events," he says dismissively.

Lily turns two shades paler, and as she goes to speak, her father pins her with a narrow-eyed gaze, causing her to snap her mouth shut without saying a word.

"Peculiar?" Dmitri says, inviting himself into the group. "I've done plenty of business with Lorenzo. He's a little brazen and rough around the edges, if you ask me, but he's not a businessman who should be looked down upon." He throws an arm over my shoulder. "I always considered you an opportunist, Henrith."

Henrith scowls, an awkward tension rippling through the circle.

This fucker is actually inserting himself just so he can piss me off again, but I have the good sense not to brush off his arm just yet.

But I grab Lily's hand and tug her closer to me to make a point. She seems taken aback, but I don't give her the chance to pull away again. Her size makes it easy to tuck her against me, as if physically shielding her from her own father while spitefully making my claim.

Her father's gaze snaps back to mine. Vivid images of all the ways I could easily end his life right now flash through my mind.

"Henrith, we should say hello to the others," Lily's mother says as she offers us a tight smile. "It was a pleasure meeting you, Lorenzo. My, how the youth are thriving today. Isn't that so, Henrith?" she says, practically pulling him away.

"So it seems," Henrith grumbles, glaring at his daughter once more before adjusting his jacket and walking between the two young women who are obviously uncomfortable in his presence.

"Oh, we should say hello to Maria. We'll talk soon, Lily," the blonde says, and is quick to scuttle away, dragging the other women behind her.

"It's harder to keep the fangs retracted here, isn't it?" Dmitri says as he lowers his arm from my shoulder with an arrogant smile.

"Not at all." It goes without saying, I didn't need his help in the first place. I might not be a charismatic playboy like most of the men here, but silence is something respected and feared, no matter the company you're in.

"A word of advice—you might want to learn how to soften around the edges for whatever this 'business' is. Or your girl isn't going to make it through." Dmitri side-eyes Lily, who stares after her father, and I notice the slight tremble of the hand holding her drink. She's terrified of him.

It's all the more reason why he should be removed. Permanently.

"It doesn't start with killing your girl's father either," Dmitri says quietly, with a shit-eating grin.

Lily overhears the last comment and looks up at me, horrified.

"You can't"—she tightens her jaw, as if suddenly coming back into the room—"*kill* my father."

I say nothing because I don't make promises I can't keep. If I want Henrith Taylor dead, it's only a matter of time until it can be done.

She scowls just as someone new approaches us, but she recovers quickly.

"Good luck, friend," Dmitri says as he clasps his hand with Elanee and pulls her away.

I'd really like to kill him right now.

"Just don't speak. That's what you're good at, right?" Lily bites out, then turns and smiles as another woman comes to hug her. And just like the other two who approached Lily, her gaze immediately drifts to me, curious and judgmental.

I've done a lot of bloody deeds. And I would choose to do each of them again rather than stand in this room like a spectacle for these people.

I'll definitely be asking for a bonus after this ridiculous mission.

The sooner we're done here, the better, because I'm struggling to rein it in after only one event.

10

LILY

"This is a mistake," I bite out the moment Ara picks up my call. I don't usually raise my voice. Don't usually instigate any type of confrontation. I don't usually crack from my perfectly polished facade because I learned from a young age that it's not only unattractive but a weakness.

But the six-foot-two looming presence trailing behind me through the busy crowds of Manhattan might've single-handedly ruined everything tonight— worse than I could've imagined. And it wasn't even what he said, because that's the problem. He doesn't need to speak to get his point across. And his murderous intent toward my father was loud and clear. Which is terrifying because he wouldn't flinch at the idea, let alone the execution, of killing someone.

"What did he do?" Ara asks, which only highlights

how bad a matchup Lorenzo and I are if those are the first words that fall from her lips. "I'm so sorry, Lily. I know I've put you in a shitty situation. I swear, Luca is working tirelessly to get to the bottom of this." The sincerity in her voice makes me feel somewhat guilty for calling her. I look down at my phone. It's almost nine in the evening. It's not late, but it's not a time I'd usually call her.

Is it okay for me to be selfish in this? I mean, they were after Ara, not me. Shouldn't I be more concerned about her safety than my own entitlement? But the look in my father's gaze told me otherwise.

This is my life, and while I already thought it was spiraling to a grim place, this has only hardened my father's resolve to marry me off to a man of his choosing. I'm sure of that much.

Compared to her safety, though, it seems immeasurable.

Have I always been this selfish?

"Lily?" Ara says. "Talk to me. I don't know what's happening unless you tell me, and I'm certain if I ask Lorenzo directly, he'll give me nothing but a few grunts in response."

A small bubble of mirth rises in my chest because there couldn't be a more accurate statement. It seems like the only times he chooses to speak is to intentionally infuriate me or argue with me. Or when he surprises me with possessive hands and slips into a "doting boyfriend" role.

I push away the thoughts and lingering presence of his touch. He's been nothing but cold to me all week. Then again, that's Sergeant Lorenzo Moretti for you. And it's royally ruined me.

"My father looked like he was about to blow a gasket when I introduced Lorenzo. I think this will only make my situation worse. I know you think this is"—I look around and whisper into the phone—"protecting me, but I should be fine now that I'm back in New York, shouldn't I? It's been a week, and I'm more worried about you."

"You need to put yourself first for once, Lily," she quickly reprimands. "I want to say that we're safer here, but I can't guarantee that. I'm so sorry for involving you in this. It should only be a few weeks at most until Luca has sorted everything out. I just... these types of people are unpredictable."

Flashes from that day appear. I've been trying to push the memories away ever since it happened. Cars swerving, shooting, blood, explosions. It's all like a movie, except it lacks the entertainment. My heart kicks up in pace, and my stomach rolls uneasily with the graphic images that reappear. I try to drown them out again, always shocked by the impactful hold they have over me.

My bottom lip wobbles, and my eyes begin to burn. I'm not going to cry. I have a complete and utter overwhelming feeling of being useless and not at all in control of my life. I've always been told how to act, speak, and present myself. My father has been very vocal about my needing to find a suitable partner soon. And presenting him with Lorenzo? He'll most likely conclude I'm going through a rebellious stage. My feet come to a standstill.

Rebellious?

I've always done as I'm told.

I look over my shoulder at Lorenzo, who's stopped two feet behind me. And although this is an attractive rebellion to have, should I use him in the process? Do I really think using Lorenzo might help me in any capacity with my father? No. If anything, it'll make it worse. But, suddenly, I don't feel like doing everything I've been told to do.

I'm tired.

I'm scared.

I want to live.

"Lily?" Ara repeats.

"It's just a lot. I'm scared," I confess quietly, hoping Lorenzo doesn't overhear. I've tried my hardest to run my store and spend time at my apartment like I usually would, ignoring the threat that I don't want to believe in. Yet I still can't help but worry about how this will impact my life going forward. What happens after all of this? Am I still forced to eventually sell my shop and date whoever my father chooses for me?

My father's judgment seems so insignificant compared to this real threat, and yet, I'm so scared of it. Of being pushed out of the family if I don't oblige. "I'm just not built like you are," I tell her. Ara is strong and always seems like she has her life together. She was able to choose herself over her family, but I don't have the same courage.

I don't want to leave my mother behind.

"Which is precisely why I've always admired you," Ara is quick to say. "It's okay to be scared. Most people should be in this situation. You're safe as long as Lorenzo is with you. He's Luca's best. He might not be the greatest conversationalist, but I swear he will keep you safe while we fix this."

Unfortunately, Lorenzo can't fix what my actual worries revolve around, which is my father. But even I can't confess those secrets to Ara.

I let out a shaky breath.

"Sorry to call you so late," I finally say. I'd be lying if I put all of this down to only recent events, and although Lorenzo's influence might exacerbate the situation I was trying to run away from, it's only forcing me to face it.

I can't be angry at him for that, although there's plenty more I can be irritated by—his personality to start with.

"Don't apologize, Lily. Do you want me to come to you right now?" she asks.

"No, it's fine. I just need to walk for a bit and think. But we're still on for breakfast, right?" Because I refuse to lose my friendship over this.

Ara's quiet for a moment. I've known from our first

meeting that she isn't forthcoming with her emotions. I can see how she's opened up little by little through our friendship, but it's like I'm learning about her all over again. I don't want this to come between us, so I need to show her at the very least that I can handle myself in this situation.

"I'll be there. Are you sure, Lily?"

I bite down on a bitter smile. I need to be brave. I need to figure my shit out and sort out these mixed emotions I've suppressed for so long, the ones that have nothing to do with her and this circumstance. "I'm sure. Thank you, Ara, for being my friend."

I hang up the phone and look to the sky, exhaling, feeling something within me shift. I let the sound of the busy street take over. It's why I've always loved this city. It's chaotic, forever moving, and when it all feels like too much, I allow its noises to drown out all the bad.

And it was working, until Lorenzo speaks. "If I could make a suggestion... Perhaps we should retrieve the car and—"

"No," I say, turning on him and placing a hand on my hip.

His gaze narrows on me, as if I'm no more than an insignificant bug. "No?"

"No. You can go get the car, but I'm going to walk." I finger one of the curls framing my face, the action always making me feel more put together, and then I continue walking.

"Are you simply saying no to be defiant?" Lorenzo asks, coming up beside me. I hate how my long strides don't affect him whatsoever or create the space I clearly need.

"No. I'm living my life as I usually would. You might have orders to follow, but I don't." I have no idea where I'm going, but I don't care. I just need to walk. Do something I wouldn't normally do. Be free, no matter how small the action.

His exasperated sigh brings me comfort enough to know he's as inconvenienced by this as I am, which I can't help but feel smug about.

We walk past multiple shops before he steps in front of me. "How about a little retail therapy? Doesn't that usually make women feel better?"

I scoff. "You think I'm just a pretty little thing that likes to buy stuff?"

His eyebrows furrow. He's obviously confused by my response. *Oh my God, he actually thinks that's what being a woman entails.* I step around him, shaking my head.

"What planet did you come from, Lorenzo? Did you not have women in your life to show you that they are complicated creatures with thoughts of their own, not simply something pretty to look at?" I feel like a hypocrite saying it, considering that's exactly how I was raised. I don't agree with it, and it pisses me off to know that *he*, of all people, has this same belief.

"You seem to project a lot," he says, like he's simply making an observation.

I snap, spinning toward him. "Are you *fucking* kidding me?" The curse hits me tenfold, having more of an effect on me than him. But it also felt *good*. His expression shifts.

It's menacing.

Dangerous.

All too provocative.

"Did you just curse at me, Lily Taylor? The elegant, sheltered dove knows how to cuss after all," he drawls sensually, eliciting goose bumps to raise on my skin because it not only entices me but feels like a threat all the same. I don't know how to react or be around Lorenzo. He throws me off entirely.

One thing holds true: He undeniably infuriates me simply by his existence. Us being in the same room together turns into a disaster the moment he speaks, and it's becoming more difficult for me to refrain from vocalizing my scathing thoughts.

"Okay, Mr. I-Think-I'm-Better-Than-Everyone-Else. What is it about the wealthy you don't like? Are you jealous? Have some weird notion that rich people are bad? Whatever preconceptions you have, stop applying them to me. Maybe you're mad because your boss won't give you a pay rise, but don't project that onto me." I stand my ground because I don't often take jabs at people, but if it's the only way he might leave me alone, if only for a second, so I can breathe and think, then I'll pave the way to damaging whatever part of his armor I can.

His face reverts back to his usual broody, I'm-miserable-with-the-world expression. "The ins and outs of my business have nothing to do with you, Sunshine. The people at that event, who you've been circulating with your entire life, are like a pack of wolves. They will tear you to pieces the moment you show a weakness. They're predatory. All of them. And that's coming from a man who seeks opportunities and exploits them. It's not the wealthy I hate. It's the high society you circulate in that I loathe. At least I admit to being a monster, instead of parading around like a prestigious show dog."

I'm taken aback. Is that how he views me? As some show dog? He thinks he knows me. Thinks because of my upbringing that I should be lumped in with them. If I'd known this man's personality when we first met, I would've never once thought him beautiful.

"You seem to be on a high horse for someone who literally kills for profit. Is your moral compass that far gone?" I ask, leaning in, refusing to let his looming presence intimidate me. "I'm almost curious about how you view yourself differently." I offer a condescending smile as he glares down at me, folding his arms across his chest. "What sweet little stories do you tell yourself at night so you can fall asleep? Or are you so certain that monsters have nothing to fear, that your actions won't catch up with you?"

He mirrors my vicious smile, and the palpable tension between us sparks like wildfire. I refuse to back down. Refuse to be this precious little doll he thinks I am, even if there's truth in it. With Lorenzo, I can be anything I want. If it's only for a few weeks, why not give him hell and bring him to his knees? Take out all of my frustration on a man who won't be in my life forever. And if I push him too far, then he leaves early. It's a win-win.

Lorenzo forces a smile. "I'm honest about who I am, Sunshine. I certainly don't walk around pretending to be a saint," he says cruelly. "And call me a monster again, I'll think you're coming on to me. That didn't work out so well for you last time, now, did it?"

The dig hits its mark, and heat burns my cheeks. *This absolute asshole.*

"You seem to bring that up more than I do. Maybe it's on *your* mind more than mine. I've never even given it a second thought."

"Which time?" he purrs as his fingers twist around the curl that frames my face. Flashes from two years ago surface, and I shove them down quickly as I slap his hand away.

I can't believe I was ever attracted to this man.

I turn away from him, smoothing over my hair once more. His words cut exactly where they were meant to, slicing my female pride in two. But I absolutely refuse to let him have the last word or think I'll back down because he thinks my self-worth hinges on whether he's attracted to me or not.

A rage I've never known fires in my blood. I can't stand this guy. I want to make him eat his words.

I walk down half a block, and a big pink neon sign shines like it has all my answers.

Fine. If he wants to play, then let's play.

I walk down the staircase, ignoring Lorenzo calling after me. When I reach the door, a man, who is clearly high, chomps on his gum as he looks up from his magazine. His smile feels slimy, but I return it with one of my own. "Just yourself tonight, sweetheart?"

"She's not by herself." Lorenzo steps so close behind me that I can feel his hot breath feathering against the back of my neck. The man's smile falters, but he seems too high to acknowledge the extent of Lorenzo's intimidation, which seems to further piss off the Italian giant behind me. *Good. This is the perfect place.*

"Two tickets, please," I say, and walk toward the entrance.

"The show's already started," the man calls out behind me.

"That's okay. He'll pay," I tell him, not looking back at either him or Lorenzo.

I open the door and walk into the peculiar-looking bar. It's dimly lit with red neon signs behind the bar and stage. The selection from the bar is underwhelming, but the musky-smelling room gives me a strange electric buzz. It's different from any other place I've been.

I would've never come to a comedy club on my own. Not that I'm by myself, but it's not the first choice for most of my friends for a night out, and if anyone saw me in here, there would be rumors going around that I'm having a midlife crisis at only twenty-eight.

But that's what makes it exciting.

It's different.

Not at all what's expected of me.

More importantly, it's undoubtedly going to piss Lorenzo off. I look over my shoulder at him and find him scanning the establishment, something I noticed he does upon entering every room. He looks disgusted to be in such a place, and that only makes this all the sweeter. Hopefully, it's enough to make him break and give up on playing bodyguard.

I walk up to the bar and order myself a drink. The bartender looks over me appreciatively, but his smile falters when Lorenzo looms behind me.

"Don't you have some shady corner to stand in and watch from a distance?" I berate under my breath.

"I need to make sure he doesn't slip anything into your drink, because this is certainly the type of place where that would happen," he says loud enough for the bartender, who looks utterly terrified, to hear.

I release a frustrated sigh. This man is insufferable. When the bartender hands over the drink, I grab it and then point at Lorenzo. "You can pay. It's the least you can do since you're such an outstanding boyfriend, right?"

I push past him, not waiting for a response, and look through the crowd, spotting a man sitting by himself in the back row. I head in his direction. I'm not someone who's in the habit of playing games, but tonight I don't give a shit.

"Oh, look, latecomers. Thanks for finally showing up!" the man slurring on the stage says. I awkwardly wave in apology as I come to a stop beside the vacant chair.

"Is this seat taken?" I ask. He removes his baseball cap and brushes over his dark-blond hair while pointing to the seat. He seems uncertain as he looks over my shoulder, where I'm assuming Lorenzo has materialized, but I offer him a smile.

"I'm Lily."

The man's eyes light up as he smiles, confused. "And you're too good for a place like this." But he holds out his hand. "I'm Aaron."

"Oh, looks like we have a bodyguard in the building, folks. Jesus, man, what do you press?" the comedian asks, and part of the crowd turns to Lorenzo. I try to hide my smile as I peek through my eyelashes.

"Is that your boyfriend?" the comedian asks.

I take a sip of the drink, immediately regretting it because it doesn't taste anything like what I ordered. I slide the glass to the side, with no intention of finishing the drink.

"No," I reply, not able to keep the venom from that singular word.

"Ah, the quiet type, eh? I suppose focus either has to go to the brawn or the brain, yeah?" the comedian shouts back at Lorenzo. My bottom lip wobbles, and I try my hardest not to laugh. It's so ridiculous that it's hilarious.

Lorenzo leans against the wall, folding his arms over his chest and glaring between Aaron and me. His irritation gives me satisfaction. "Ooooh, too good for the shitty chairs, right?" the comedian calls out. "I mean, there are more than enough of them available. Thanks for not selling out tonight!" A few waves of laughter rumble through the crowd. "But what can you do?" He casually shrugs. "We don't all have muscles like Mr. Terminator. This is the only way I get laid! Something about the funny man, you know? But it's a hit or miss. Sometimes I get my dick out, and they're unimpressed. To be fair, I get it. I've got a small dick, but I make up for it in enthusiasm. On a good night, though, they're just as drunk as I am and think it's a good idea to suck it. Well, you know, for the thirty seconds it lasts."

My nose scrunches up. The comedian is crude, but I embrace it for the experience it is. It might be a little dusty and, well... tacky, but I think about all the people who come here simply to laugh. To feel free from the pressures of their day-to-day life. And I laugh at the next joke. Not because I think it's particularly funny, but because I need to get rid of all of this nervous, pent-up frustration and uncertainty.

Because if I don't, I'll cry.

But already, being in this run-down room with a bunch of strangers, I feel lighter. I laugh harder at the next joke.

I'm conscious of Lorenzo behind me. It's hard not to be affected by his presence, but eventually, I fall into an ease with the crowd, laughing on cue and talking with Aaron. Instead of thinking about what or who I have to be tomorrow, I imagine what it's like to simply be a stranger in Manhattan, losing myself amongst the crowd, and Aaron seems like the perfect distraction. He's reasonably attractive and seems nice so far.

I'm not a little bubble-wrapped princess, and I certainly won't let Lorenzo keep jabbing me over the fact that he rejected me, because the reality is, as they say, there's plenty of fish in the sea. And that asshole, no matter how beautiful, needs to be reminded that he's not God's gift to women. Even when it looks like he was carved by the gods themselves.

11

LORENZO

Exercising restraint is not easy for me, but I'll do so when it's necessary. So it's certainly hard not killing the man who's sitting beside Lily, laughing with her and stealing small pockets of conversation between sets. Every time he glances her way, I think of all the creative ways I can remove this motherfucker permanently, then his gaze naturally gravitates to me, and he sits upright, staring at the front, terrified. Good. He's no more than a fucking weasel.

I'm a reasonable man, perhaps even more so than my boss, but while she's under my care, I take any threat or leering gaze seriously.

The problem with someone like Lily Taylor in a place like this is she attracts attention, even when she thinks she's shrinking into the shadows. She's not made for the darkness—she shines too fucking brightly.

Everyone sees her and feels her light as she walks into a room, and in a sad, sorry place like this, she is undoubtedly attracting attention. Two bartenders whisper to one another, looking in her direction. Not that she notices. I step into their line of sight, and the moment they see me, their conversation dies and they make themselves busy. My jaw tics. She's too fucking beautiful for a run-down joint full of riffraff and people who are beneath her.

I move back into position against the wall, arms crossed, unimpressed. Then I glare at every fucker who dares to even glance at her.

Then there's the matter of dealing with *her* after this little stunt. I know she's doing it intentionally, trying to make a point.

Lily's laugh grabs my attention as she wipes away tears, chuckling to herself.

She's too beautiful.

Too innocent.

I don't often empathize with those involved in my missions, and it's not like I've been a bodyguard for many other than Luca, but I meant everything I said to her. Her safety *is* my priority. She might think this little stunt of bringing me in here is cute, but she'll learn the hard way what my persistence looks like. She'll only wear herself out with these antics.

The comedian makes another joke, I'm certain at

my expense, but I don't acknowledge him, continuing to watch Lily as her shoulders ever so slightly loosen over the evening. It increases my vigilance because I want her to enjoy this moment, and if she lets her guard down, then I'll be the fangs at her back.

That is, until the little fucker sitting beside her has the audacity to place his hand on her arm. I'm across the room in two long strides.

"Get up," I growl at him, and I'm certain the fucker shits his pants on the spot.

Lily's mouth drops open before she grits out, "It's fine, Lorenzo."

"It's not *fine,*" I reply as I stare down at the man I'm two seconds away from aiming my gun at. Bouncers hover at the door, but they seem to have the good sense not to fuck with me. It's highly likely one of them might even know who I am.

"There are literally so many other chairs," the dickhead is ballsy enough to say.

"Are you sure that's the answer you want to go with?"

"Lorenzo, people are staring," Lily chastises, but I don't look up. I don't give a flying fuck. The only thing I care about is this pipsqueak moving his sorry ass away from Lily immediately.

Suddenly, the seriousness of his situation seems to hit him, and he stands up, avoiding eye contact with Lily, and leaves entirely.

She huffs as I take his seat.

"Looks like we have a lovers' quarrel here," the comedian awkwardly says, drawing the attention of the room back to the stage. For anyone who continues to stare, I scowl in their direction, and they're quick to look away.

"You can't be serious," Lily bites out as she flops back into her chair, arms folded over her chest. "You don't own me."

"I'm in charge of your safety," I snap, fucking furious at the fact that she'd even entertain some fucker like that.

"That guy was completely harmless. You're being obnoxious. If I want to bring a guy home—"

"You will not be bringing any man anywhere."

"I can—"

"No."

She throws her hands up in the air, and I can sense those closest to us are listening more to our conversation than the comedian's final bit.

My temple pulses, and my jaw grinds as I steal a glance at the gorgeous woman beside me, who is biting her bottom lip into a shade of red and oozing with pure rage.

I've never had to deal with someone like Lily before. Everyone listens to my commands, but she has to fight me every step of the way. I can't train her or force her into obedience like I do the hounds, and the longer this bratty attitude persists, the more difficult my life and the mission become.

She's lucky I don't bend her over my fucking knee right here and now, and spank the brat out of her. My cock twitches, and I internally groan, wanting to readjust myself.

Of course, I'm attracted to the little vixen, but she's completely off-limits.

Then again, if I don't fuck her, but just simply force her into submission, isn't that a form of training as well?

My jaw tightens painfully hard.

No.

Off. Limits.

My gaze narrows on her phone screen as she scrolls through what appears to be some kind of dating app. *Absolutely fucking not.*

I pluck the phone out of her hand.

"Hey!" she whisper-shouts.

"You wanted to be a brat and come in to watch some comedy show because you thought it'd make me uncomfortable? Well then, enjoy the show, Sunshine."

"So now theft is part of your crime list as well?" she seethes through her teeth.

I level her with a glare, my cock twitching uncomfortably at the thought of all the ways I can stop that little mouth of hers from running. I have to stop myself from trailing my thumb along her bottom lip.

I look away, infuriated to acknowledge that resisting Lily Taylor is my personal hell, and that if I act on it, I'm done for.

But one thing is certain: She's going to have to be trained on how this little arrangement between us is going to work.

12

LILY

I've never imagined what it might be like to murder someone, but if I ever did, it would feature Lorenzo Moretti.

I throw my clutch onto the side table when we step inside my apartment. I then slip off my heels and set them alongside my other favorite pairs.

Lorenzo follows me, as quiet as he has been since we left the comedy show. I'm so furious I can't even speak.

He's right behind me, and every step feels more insufferable than the next. Sure, he gave me my phone back when we were in the car, but that wasn't the point. He's overbearing, arrogant, and rude.

One minute I was looking at a picture Romi sent me of an outfit option for an upcoming date she has, the next he'd stolen my phone and refused to give it back.

Pulling the pins from my hair, I turn to face him because I'm not done tearing into him, not even close. I've never known this kind of frustration, but I have to purge it. The only way to do that seems to be giving this asshole a piece of my mind, and I hope it pushes him away. I pray he thinks I'm so bratty, he won't be able to stand another moment with me because the tension between us is becoming too palpable.

"You were out of line tonight," I accuse, pointing a hairpin at him. My hair spills over my shoulders with stiff curls after being so tightly restrained.

He takes a few steps back and sits on the armrest of one of the living room chairs. "You were a brat tonight."

"*Excuse me*?" I run my hands through my hair. Does this man truly have the audacity to flip my world upside down—with no regard to the impact he's having—and still have the confidence to reprimand *me*? "I don't know what you think this agreement is, but it goes along the lines of *silently* protecting me. You're not to judge what I do with in spare time, and you certainly don't get any say in who I take home."

He slowly removes his suit jacket, then places it carefully over the back of the chair. "I'm sick of discussing that little fucker. He's lucky he didn't wind up dead in the alley."

My eyes bulge. This guy is out of his fucking mind. I click my tongue. He's so infuriating. He thinks he's the smartest one in the room; better than everyone around him. I've met confident men, but none of them hold a candle to this enigma of a man.

"Is that the wisdom coming from a fifty-year-old man?" I dig.

His gaze narrows. "I'm only ten years older than you, Sunshine. And as for wisdom, it's simply that I have two eyes and the knowledge that he's not good enough to touch you."

I huff out a breath as I begin to pace, ready to rip out my hair.

"I can see what you're doing, Sunshine. Your tactics don't work on me. Little games like these won't push me away from being by your side. The sooner you understand that, the smoother the next few weeks will be... for *your* sake."

I shake my head as I move toward him. I should know better than to provoke a man like this, but I can't help myself. "Today was a total disaster, in case you didn't realize. My father is going to look into you. And he's most likely going to start forcing me into dates with men I don't even know. So, don't you dare accuse me of *anything.* I'm just living my life, and you were ordered to follow me."

Silence settles heavily between us. My words were harsh and unfair, but I refuse to be the "nice girl" with Lorenzo. I don't owe him anything. And if he's determined to make my life a living hell, then for the first time, I'm stepping up to the challenge.

The way he watches me, as if he's assessing an

enemy, is unnerving. The lights from the city shine brightly through the windows, flashing across his features. I hold his gaze, unsure as to whether it's out of defiance or something else. But I take another step toward him and then another, frustrated by the fact that he's remaining so quiet. I'm desperate for him to speak, wanting to shove at him or something so we can continue this fiery dance we seem to be caught up in. It doesn't make sense, but I'm just so *angry*.

"Come here," he says, his voice gravelly. He points to the space between his knees and then begins to roll up his sleeves, as if preparing for something. A shot of adrenaline pumps through me. *He said he wouldn't hurt me. So why does he look like he's about to get his hands bloody?*

"Why?" I try to say it with an even tone, but the tremble in it isn't missed by either of us.

Lowering my gaze from his, I notice the tattoos on his forearm. A snake head, a rose, and a Renaissance angel with a bow and arrow that looks similar to Cupid. My eyebrows furrow. I certainly wasn't expecting something so delicate and beautiful inked on his skin. Further evidence that I have no idea who this man truly is.

"We need to work on that mouth of yours; it seems to be in the habit of talking back," he says, watching me expectantly.

Warmth floods my core, and the fury coursing

through me turns into a wired tension buzzing along my skin.

My mouth opens to speak, then immediately closes because I don't know how to respond.

"We can take all night, Sunshine, but we're not leaving this room until you've received your punishment."

"My *punishment*?" I squeak, and I hate how pitchy my voice is.

He doesn't reply. No, a man like Lorenzo doesn't feel the need to repeat himself or give explanations.

I can ignore his command—walk away and go upstairs—but I feel naturally drawn to him. I know I shouldn't be tempted. It's ridiculous and makes no logical sense. I'd be willingly stepping straight into the lion's den, and yet... my feet quietly pad across the wooden floor toward him, accepting his challenge.

"That type of stunt you pulled at the comedy show isn't to happen again. Do you understand?" Lorenzo says as I come to a stop in front of him.

I swallow hard, still unsure about what's happening, but my core is throbbing for something, anything to bring me to life. Maybe it's the chance to experience his world, to get a little dirty before we part ways that tempts me—when logically I know it shouldn't. Maybe I'm quietly praying that this pent-up anger will only dissipate with a release that my treacherous body tells me only he can provide.

But it still doesn't mean I'll comply with his demands.

"I can do what I want in my life. You don't own me," I reply.

The corners of his mouth twitch as he grabs my hand and slowly tugs me until I'm standing beside his knee. Even when he's sitting, his size is imposing, and we're almost at eye level with each other.

"You can, but there are consequences when you're being a brat," he says, his thumb stroking over the delicate bone of my wrist, as if reminding me how small I am compared to him. I should be scared, but it thrills me in ways it shouldn't. "Bend over," he orders.

My brain short-circuits.

"S-sorry?" I stutter.

"It's too late for apologies. Bend over my knee so I can slap the brat out of you."

Liquid warmth floods to my core, and my pussy begins to quietly throb at the thought. Surely, I can't be into this. I've never done anything like this before, and it feels foolish to give in. Yet there's a spark of excitement flashing inside me.

"I wasn't apologizing."

"That'll be five strikes. Do you want to continue adding to your punishment? Or are you demanding the belt instead?"

"What? No, I don't want a belt," I'm quick to say. That seems too extreme, doesn't it?

What is happening?

"We need to establish some rules," he says as he threads his fingers through my hair and arches my neck back slightly. My pulse kicks up, and my breath hitches at the thought of what he might do next. "In public, I'll play the part of doting boyfriend. But when you make my life a living hell, you will be punished in private. Do you understand?"

I'm consumed by the gaze of a predator who's ready to leave his mark. I can't think rationally as my body begins to flood with a desire I've never known.

This is a choice, even if he doesn't make it sound like one. I can easily walk away from this. But as I stare into his molten brown eyes that dance with light from the outside world, I don't see malice or cruelty in them.

I see something I've never experienced before.

Desire.

Danger.

Dare I say... trust?

That last thought catches me off guard because how many others have I trusted who have disappointed me? But whatever *this* is, it defies all logic.

"You don't get to tell me what to do," I say breathily.

The corner of his mouth twitches, and I find myself staring, praying to see what he might look like with a full-blown smile. "Part of me thinks you like it, Sunshine. Now, have you come to play?" He looks pointedly at his knee.

My heart is hammering in my chest. This man is dangerous. Still...

I find myself willingly lowering, bending over his knee, my ass up in the air as I brace my elbows on his other knee.

"She does listen after all," he purrs appreciatively.

I go to speak, but his callused hand, slowly grazing along the back of my leg and up my bare thigh, has me snapping my mouth shut. Goose bumps erupt everywhere he touches. My breath hitches with the slow and painful anticipation for... what? Everything? Anything? It's been almost a year since I've slept with a guy, but Lorenzo is different. He is a man whose touch I shouldn't want. Yet I yearn for it like my next breath.

He shifts my dress over my hips, and a low, guttural growl escapes him. I peek at him from over my shoulder, mesmerized by his eyes, which seem to have darkened to almost black as he stares at my ass.

"This is a perfect ass to punish," he growls.

I bite down on my bottom lip as I watch him with bewilderment, his hand pulling back and then coming down hard on my ass cheek. I yelp, the taste of blood bursting into my mouth from where I was biting down on my lip. It stings, and black spots dance across my vision. When I can refocus, he's staring at me, the raw burn of his handprint on my skin feeling like a brand.

I realize he's pushing me. I shouldn't want this, but my body hums with anticipation. I want more. More from *him*. It hurts, the pulsing of his mark on me, and yet my body naturally arches into him, a silent request for him to continue.

I've lost my fucking mind.

I've never liked pain, but this feels completely different. It's not to hurt me; it's being completely dominated in a way I've never known, and testing my limits.

And I fucking *like* it.

His other hand brushes my hair from my face, his thumb rubbing over my bottom lip. When he pulls his hand back, he looks down at the small smear of blood. It's embarrassing. I should be mortified, and yet, when his fingers slowly wrap around my throat, my body is arching farther into him, a victim to his touch.

"That just won't do," he says as he readjusts my head, angling my neck into the position he wants. "You like the pain."

"No," I say defiantly, because I can't be into this depravity. Shouldn't I be ashamed?

His hand that rests on my ass skims lightly over my panties, and I bite down on my lip to stifle the moan.

"You're soaking wet for me, Sunshine," he says matter-of-factly. "Let's see how you like this on your cunt."

I gasp at the vulgar word. But I don't have time to dwell on it, because he pulls back his hand and then smacks my pussy.

A moan escapes me as I buck against him, still held by the throat. My pussy pounds angrily. It hurts so damn much, but then a wave of pleasure flows through my core as he circles my clit through my underwear. Fuck, what is he doing to me?

"Do you understand you're being punished for being a brat today?" he growls. I can feel the hard press of his erection against my ribs. Another flood of liquid rushes to my core, and I can't help thinking about that cock.

Wanting that cock.

Crack! I buck as he slaps my pussy again, eliciting goose bumps and a new threshold of pain. It's too much... isn't it? A more treacherous pulsing begins.

I want this.

"Every time you step out of line, you will be punished. Do you understand?" He tightens his grip around my throat to the point I can barely breathe, and angles my head to face him. "Answer me, Sunshine."

But all I can think about is his cock pressing against me. This is turning him on, right? He wants this, too, doesn't he?

But more importantly, he's still waiting for my answer.

"You will never own me" is the most truthful answer I can give, because I don't understand what the fuck is happening. All I know is my body loves it, but I'm not going to give in to his every demand.

That almost-grin teases his lips, and his hand

comes down, hard, this time on my ass. I buck as his fingers press tighter around my windpipe, and I can't even squeak. A shudder of fear runs through me for the first time. *Have I bitten off more than I can chew? This isn't who I am, so what—*

My thoughts cut off, and my eyes roll into the back of my head as his thumb circles my clit again, and his grip around my throat loosens.

"So fucking beautiful, how wet you are for me. Fucking perfect in every way," Lorenzo praises, seemingly enthralled by my ass. A different warmth floods my chest, and I bat it away. This isn't normal. I shouldn't feel anything for this man. But I'm not used to a man whispering such sweet nothings to me. If anything, it infuriates me. *Sure, you've won this time. I find you attractive. But don't say unnecessary things, like I'm beautiful and perfect, when you don't mean them.*

All of a sudden, I want this to be over. I want to go to my room.

"Do you usually talk so much to all your torture victims?" I grit, now all fire. One more smack and then I'm gone. Hell, I know I don't even have to stay for it, but there's a sense of sheer determination and rebellion that fuels me now. I try to ignore the throbbing of my pussy, which wants more, and cling to my self-preservation instead.

His gaze slides to mine, the fire previously burning in them gone. "I only torture if I want something from it."

Slap. I'm blinded by the pain that sears my flesh. It's so strong that tears spring to my eyes. My body tingles everywhere, something new and dark unfurling within me. Something I don't want to greet.

I open my eyes and scowl. "Are you done now?" I ask, as if unaffected by the thrumming of my body, which wants to sit up until I'm straddling his cock.

He's too beautiful. I've become disarmed around him.

His eyebrows furrow slightly as he says, "Yes." His hand gently caresses my ass, as if soothing it, then he gives me the space to stand. His hand is still resting on my hips as he helps me to my feet.

I don't understand him, nor do I have to.

"Good night," I say as I pull my dress down and walk away with my head held high. My body aches, the subtle friction of my dress shifting back and forth over my skin irritating every step. But I pretend to be unfazed as my inner world spirals, awoken by some-thing new I'm not entirely ready to address.

I don't look over the railing of the spiral stairs to my bedroom, but I can feel his gaze follow me as I slam the door shut. The moment I'm in my room, I rest my head against the door.

What am I doing?

I bite my bottom lip, the small split apparent, but the taste of my own blood isn't off-putting. In fact, I feel alive. The throbbing in my pussy lingers, and I can't help but stretch my hand farther down.

I'm irritated and frustrated, imagining his rock-hard cock pressing against my ribs, curious as to what it would feel like inside of me.

Fuck him and whatever game he's playing at. But it doesn't take away the hum of the mark he left. And although I might not have given him permission to finish the job, I'll certainly finish it myself. I walk to my bathroom, stripping away my clothes before turning the shower on. I look over my shoulder through the mirror, staring at the large handprints branding my ass. The mark is so big, almost covering my entire ass cheek.

Dark-brown eyes appear in my mind. I try to blink them away as I step into the shower, embracing the pulsing heat from his punishment. My pussy is still thumping wildly, and I try my hardest to let the day go down the drain with the running water. I don't want to think about it. I just want...

My hand lowers, and I begin to circle my clit, looking for a release. Yes, that's exactly what I need.

Fuck him for leaving me like this.

Every thought continues revolving around Lorenzo—the last person I want to be thinking about. Though, honestly, it's not the first time I've used him as inspiration. I rub more vigorously, cursing him.

I can't stand him.

I shouldn't be into these types of things.

He treats me like a child.

The angrier I get, the more I assault my clit, thinking about him, expressing my rage.

Fuck him and those callused hands.

I replay the strike on my ass. The shock and pain. The pleasure that's quick to follow.

Warmth floods my core, and I moan. My other hand comes up to grab my breast and twist. It hurts, but it acts as a tug at my core.

A delayed response, but well rewarded.

Fuck me, that feels good.

I relive each and every slap, squeezing my breast mercilessly.

A steady build begins to grow, and I chase it like I'm running away from the very man who put me in this situation. *Fuck me.* Why does he have to be so...

The climb continues, and my breathing comes in shallow pants as I swallow steamy air.

Infuriating!

I break apart, crumbling into my own touch as I ride the wave of bliss. I'm shocked and confused.

I've never been able to please myself like that. Not without a toy. I've never truly understood how to satisfy myself, and I've been too shy to explore self-gratification further.

But what happened tonight felt incredible. Empowering even. The dull throb where he spanked me continues as I take a deep breath, realizing that perhaps the pain might be the gateway to my pleasure. That makes no sense, though. I've always been scared of a raised hand. I've heard women talk about it over cocktails, but never thought I'd be into it.

Because... I'm a good girl? Right?

I hate that I even think that. I've been conditioned even in my sexual exploration, and I only have myself to blame.

Low, consistent knocks on my door rip me out of my thoughts, and I turn the shower off. "Don't come in!" I shout as I reach for the nearest towel. I step out of my bathroom, surprised that my bedroom door remains closed.

When I open the door, no one's there. I furrow my brow as I look over the railing to see him working on his laptop beside a crackling fire.

I go to step back into my bedroom, and that's when I see it. A plastic bag. I expect it to be one of my favorite meals—something he's been in the habit of leaving for me every night. But instead it's filled with ointment, bath salts, and cream.

"For the marks. It'll help with the swelling." His voice drifts up to me, and if I had to guess, he's not even looking in my direction.

My heart skips a beat, and I hate how easily it betrays me. It's silly. And I still don't know what to make of the entire situation, let alone what happened earlier. What I do know is that Lorenzo is a man like no other I've met. And my curiosity might be leading me into a world of depravity, but I can't let my heart get involved because I know where this ends.

The same place it always does—in disappointment, my heart shattered into a million pieces.

Because men don't want me, and if they do, it's only about what my father can provide them.

I doubt Lorenzo has any interest in that, but only a few moments ago, I was also certain he had no interest in *me*.

13

LILY

I'm furious. There's a difference between pretending to be a doting boyfriend and being an overbearing, embarrassing brute. Lorenzo stands beside the entrance of the Cappa Café. It's certainly not the first time he's stood there, but usually it's for Ara's sake. Now there's another unexpectedly large man, Tony, who sits closest to the door, enjoying a coffee and reading something on his phone. The two men attempt to be discreet, but they still stand out.

Sienna takes her seat, arriving late as usual, and looks over at them. "So, like, security is the new trend?" she asks, flicking her hair over her shoulder.

"Well, if you look at recent tabloids, one might suggest Lorenzo is an overbearing date," Romi says, smirking at me. I kick her under the table, which only intensifies her laughter.

She's wearing a shirt with a cat on it that reads *I'm*

purrfect. She's been wearing these types of shirts since junior high. The moment someone teased her for it, she made it her daily mission to wear a shirt with some kind of humorous message. "Well, am I wrong?" she asks, rubbing her shin.

I shift uncomfortably, trying to hide a wince as a dull pain pulses in my bruised ass cheeks. It remains as a reminder of what happened between Lorenzo and me.

Ara seems unfazed by their jabs, and I try to use her as an example not to give too much away. But it's easier for her because even if they don't know who Luca Armani truly is, his being overprotective of his wife, who is carrying his child, doesn't come as a surprise. But that leaves me out in the cold, trying to find a reasonable excuse for Lorenzo being here.

"He's been helping me in the store. I told him to meet me there, but he decided to come here instead," I say, settling on a partial truth. Because I had begged Lorenzo to give me space and let me enjoy my time with the girls, but he adamantly refused.

We've been living in each other's pockets. I have no privacy. Though the last few nights he's given me a bit of distance after the intensity of the night of my "punishment."

Both Romi and Sienna stare at me, most likely not believing the lie, but Romi smirks and casually shrugs. A shudder runs over me because nothing good ever comes from that smirk.

"Hey, Big Daddy," she shouts at Lorenzo.

"Romi!" I chastise, immediately embarrassed.

Sienna chuckles and looks over to see his reaction.

"Why don't you come and join us if you're going to sit there looking all glum? You don't exactly match the wallpaper."

Warmth leaves my body as I look into the icy gaze of Lorenzo.

I told him he couldn't be inconspicuous.

Despite the awkwardness, Lorenzo does come over. He drags a chair with him and sits at the end of the table closest to me. Part of me is grateful we meet so early in the morning, when the cafe isn't yet flooded with customers, because I'm certain he'd create a blockage for people being able to get past him to pay.

I glance at him only once. His gaze is devouring me, and I quickly look away, heat flushing my cheeks. It's so difficult to ignore him because he's so damn imposing. And I'm still furious with... well, the entire situation, and the fact that my body is still acutely aware of his every move and lingering look.

"Soo..." Romi says, staring between us. I know I should grab his hand or place mine on his knee or something that looks remotely couple-like, but I'm not good at pretending. "Want to explain what happened on that trip to Italy?"

"What do you mean?" I ask. Surely, Ara didn't tell them about the drive-by or her involvement with the Mafia.

Romi raises a brow and then darts her gaze between Lorenzo and me, and I suddenly realize what she's talking about. "Oh."

"Oh?" Sienna, the gossip hound of the group, says. She's usually the first in the know, and I'm certain her finding out from some blog or social media photo about me taking Lorenzo to the charity event has wounded her ego. "You go to Italy with Ara for a short time and then come back with a boyfriend?"

"It was one date," I reply.

Sienna rolls her eyes. "Because you've taken so many dates of your own choosing to a public event. Weren't you dreading last time we met here that you'd have to have Elanee potentially matchmake for you because your father has been pressuring you on the matter?"

Elanee, the most recent addition to our morning coffee meet-ups, remains quiet. As a professional matchmaker, she's the obvious choice, but I refuse to give in to my father's pressure or threats. If anything, I'm surprised I haven't heard anything from him yet regarding the charity event, and it looms over me dauntingly.

"We're just..." I look up at Lorenzo for support and realize the mistake immediately. A man of few words is not going to embellish a lie if he doesn't need to. "Seeing how it goes. You know... casual."

"Casual?" Romi repeats as she plays with the rim of

her chai latte, staring at us skeptically. "When have you ever done casual?"

"Lighten up, Romi." Sienna nudges her shoulder. "Our little girl is growing up. I still think you should tell Daddy to shove his expectations up his ass."

Romi scoffs, then asks Sienna, "Are you willing to do the same with your father?"

Sienna rolls her eyes, and the table settles into silence. Because the reality is, we were all raised with particular expectations. Sienna is no exception. She, however, is now engaged to someone her father at least approves of, but he hasn't appreciated the long two-year engagement.

"Any progress on a wedding date?"

Sienna sighs at my careful nudge, trying to hide it with a smile. "Michael is just really busy with his acting career. And it's fine. It doesn't change the fact that we love each other and plan on having a family. It might be a few years later than I'd hoped, but relation-ships are give and take, aren't they?" she says, almost desperately.

My heart sinks for my friend, because I know how much she adores Michael, but it feels like the last six months she's pulled back on her modeling career simply so she can cater to him and the demands of his career.

"When was the last time you saw him in person?" Romi gently asks.

Sienna offers another tight smile. "Two months

ago. But we FaceTime almost every week. He's busy with projects, you know. I plan on seeing him soon, though. We're just going through a stage, you know?" She looks up at us with hope in her eyes. It was a quick engagement, and as time passes, I wonder if the relationship is already coming to an end before they truly had the chance to start.

But who am I to judge the ins and outs of someone else's relationship when my alleged one is fake?

My phone buzzes, and when I look down, a cold dread washes over me. It's my father's assistant. I answer it because I know better than to ignore her calls.

"Good morning, Tania," I say, faking a bubbly tone.

"Good morning, Miss Taylor. I'm calling to inform you that your father expects you for dinner tonight at six."

My stomach drops.

This dinner invite has to be about Lorenzo. And, as usual, my father can't even be bothered to call personally. Even if I had plans, I'd be expected to drop them.

My fingers curl into my palms as I stare down at the holey jeans I decided to wear today instead of a dress. Nausea swirls in my stomach as I brace myself for what always feels like impending doom, but I do my best to muster my strength. It's humiliating to be this crippled by my own treacherous mind.

Warmth fills my hand as my fingers are slowly pried open to make room for Lorenzo's fingers. The others remain talking amongst themselves, and it takes me two blinks to realize Lorenzo has entwined his hand with mine. I don't look up to see his expression. Instead, I bite my bottom lip, appreciating his gesture.

He might be a domineering robot, but he's an observant one. Confusion fogs my brain as I'm torn between wondering if he's doing this to genuinely support me or if it's all for show in front of my friends.

"I'll be there. Thank you for taking the time to call, Tania."

"Of course, I'll try to make time sometime soon to drop by the flower shop," she says, and instead of grimacing, I relax further into Lorenzo's touch. I know Tania only ever stops by to report back to my father, but instead of feeling that usual sense of apprehension, I take courage in the subtle support Lorenzo offers.

"I look forward to it," I say, sounding chipper even when I feel anything but. I hang up and turn to Lorenzo. He's not looking at me. He's staring toward the door, as if expecting at any moment something might happen. Always on guard, ready to fight.

I can't help the small smile as I uncurl my fingers from his, thankful for the kindness he was willing to offer, even when he's made it abundantly clear he can't stand me.

I rejoin the conversation, but not before noting that Ara's gaze is bouncing between Lorenzo and me. I wonder if she's questioning the same thing I am. If anything, I should know better than to think his gesture was more than just being part of the act. I offer her a tight smile, though she says nothing, her hand moving to rest on her belly. Nothing goes unnoticed by Ara, but even if she asked for an explanation, I couldn't give her one. Lorenzo's kindness is an abnormality, but one I'm grateful for right now.

Whatever my father wishes to discuss isn't good, but I harden my resolve. I'm not the same woman I was before the trip to Italy. I can't be after the experience I went through there. If I were unchanged by that, then there'd be no hope for me. I have to show him that I can make my own decisions and I am my own person.

He has to know.

But the fear of being discarded by my family is very real, like a noose around my neck, because no one has ever defied my father, or at least no one has and come out unscathed.

14

LORENZO

Lily sits beside me in the car, her floral scent wafting over and making my nostrils flare. We've been arguing all day regarding her family dinner. It wasn't even a question as to whether I was going. I take my mission very seriously. But then she had the nerve to call Ara, who intervened and told me I'll have to wait outside.

We haven't spoken a word to one another since. I don't like the idea of having her out of my sight, not even for a minute. Anything could happen, and I don't trust her family's security for shit, unless I'm there by her side.

I'm not someone who casually comforts another, but the moment she took that call this morning, I knew something was wrong. Watching her withdraw into herself was awful. A woman like her shouldn't crumble in any way, especially not because of someone else. Before I knew it, my hand was reaching out to hers. The action wasn't missed by Ara, but I don't give a shit. She was the one who encouraged this whole fake dating thing anyway, and I'm certain hand-holding is what people do in relationships.

But the moment our hands touched, it brought memories to the surface that I've pushed away for over half my lifetime. A time when I was barely a teenager, reaching out to the hands of a small, frightened girl who would never make it past the age of five.

Lily reminds me of my younger sister, whom I wasn't able to save, and it slowly unravels something uncomfortable within me. I shouldn't be having flashbacks of the life I left behind so many years ago. I fucking hate it.

Watching Lily bow to her father's whim is something else I fucking can't stand. She could flourish more than she knows if she'd just free herself from the shackles he's chained her in. I find it infuriating that it's affecting even me. I just want to shake her, but after this morning, when my hand seemed to move of its own accord, I need to remind myself that I'm not here to save Lily Taylor.

Well, technically I am, but only if she's in physical danger.

I glance at her from the corner of my eye. Her arms are folded over her chest, and her expression is set in a pout. And she has the balls to be furious with me, telling me I'm overbearing, when it's literally my job.

She doesn't even know to what extent I could be over-bearing. And besides, I prefer the term *diligent*.

As I pull up to the Taylor estate, I can tell by the way she stares at the thick metal gates that she doesn't want to be here. But she takes a deep breath and then places her hand on the door handle with an air of indifference.

If she doesn't want to be here, she should just say no, instead of trying to please every fucker.

"I don't like it," I growl.

She doesn't even bother looking over her shoulder at me. Instead, her nose points higher, and she says, "I told you, my family, my rules."

"You could still be in danger there," I grit out.

She rolls her eyes. "From choking on a lettuce leaf? Stop being ridiculous, Lorenzo," she scoffs. Then she opens the door, climbs out, and slams the door behind her. I glare at her back as she waits for the grand gates to open upon her arrival. She won't even let me drive her up to the house. And as soon as the gates close behind her, I curse under my breath, hating the physical barrier that comes between us.

I check my phone and then bring it to my ear. I can hear the small stones of the driveway crunching under her feet. *Good.*

She might not let me join her for family dinners, but it doesn't mean I'm above bugging her to make sure I'm alerted to any shift in the household.

Nothing will come between me and my job, not even Lily Taylor herself.

My phone buzzes, and I answer on the first ring.

"Any update?" Luca requests. "I've just been on the phone with Tony, and nothing seems out of the ordinary so far."

My jaw tics because I don't like the idea of him consulting with anyone before talking to me. But considering his top priority is Ara's safety, I can rationalize it.

"No, boss. No signs of anything out of the ordinary. What have you discovered on your end?" I continue watching Lily until she walks into the house. Not being able to see her puts me even more on edge.

"Let's just say I've given a bloody reminder to the families here of why they conduct business with me in the first place. But so far, no names. Only a few know about the attack, and that's because one of my guards at the house got too loose with his tongue. It's fair to say he doesn't have a tongue anymore."

As expected.

"What have you found out about the Taylor Empire?" he asks, and in the background I can hear the muffled cries of someone who is most likely bound to a chair, ready for "questioning." It fills me with unease that I'm not there beside him. I'd give anything to be torturing someone right now, as opposed to dealing with a woman who goes out of her way to argue with me on everything.

Even punishing her hasn't seemed to train her the way I thought it might, and it seemed to have more of an effect on my cock than her.

My dick twitches at the memory. My jaw tics as I try to push away the visual of her bent over my knee. She's fucking perfect in every way. And that temptation is the fucking problem, and why I've tried as best as I can to keep her at arm's length since that night.

Fuck. I readjust myself.

Telling Luca Mr. Taylor is a dirty player in business wouldn't be news, but I have dug deeper into his transactions. "In the past two years, he hasn't expanded the business, and his profit has gone down significantly. However, in the past six months, the companies his son has taken over have boomed. The others Henrith runs himself plateaued after declining at an alarming rate."

"Do you think his son is that much of a capable little shit to revive the companies he took over?"

"Or a fairy godmother is financially assisting them," I suggest. It's not uncommon for families like the Taylors to look into alternative loans when they can't flourish in the current economy.

"Find out who's supporting them. We'll offer them a better deal," Luca says.

"Yes, boss." Crippling Henrith Taylor's business and waiting to force him into a position to sell to us shouldn't take long.

"Good. Keep me updated. I want this all sorted

quickly. I don't want any loose ends when I return. I only want to focus on my wife and unborn baby."

"Yes, boss."

The line cuts out, and I listen in on Lily greeting someone who sounds like a butler.

My screen lights up again, and my eyebrows furrow.

It's been a while since I spoke to my younger brother, Dante, and for good reason. I'm ready to kill the little fucker myself. Our last phone conversation didn't go so well. Or the ones before that with years in between them.

"You have a lot of nerve calling me," I grit out. "Can I assume you've reconsidered?"

His arrogant laugh comes through the phone, and I feel my temple pulse. I know he does it on purpose. He's always known how to irk me.

"Do you really think I'm going to change my mind because you stopped sending me money? I never realized you thought I was so cheap."

My jaw grinds as I keep tabs on Lily during the conversation. "We had an agreement. You'd go all the way through with your studies, and I'd fund it. I wanted a better life for you."

The humor drops from his tone. "It was you who wanted me to become a hero, not me, and I dedicated the last twelve years to becoming a surgeon. Don't pretend like I haven't put in my time while you commit petty crimes."

Petty crimes. This smug little asshole knows exactly what I do and what I've been up to, considering he was trained for the same thing by our father from the day we could both fucking walk.

It was because I wanted to give him a better life that I encouraged him to do something useful with his hands—helping and saving people instead of following in my footsteps and hurting them.

"I just called to remind you I don't need your money, Lorenzo. I never really have. And I wanted to let you know that the guy you sent to follow me? Well, he's not exactly able to work anymore. Don't send anyone else, or I'll start sending body parts as gifts."

This little fucker. "Might take some time coming from London, don't you think?"

He chuckles. "Who said I'm still in London?"

I listen in as Lily excuses herself to the bathroom.

"So, what will you do now?" I question.

"Oh, you know me. I'm an opportunist, looking to see what work might be around."

That's never a good thing. The reason I forced him to agree to study something with a noble cause is because of his unfavorable personality. And whenever he decides to go rogue, it's never a good thing.

But I have bigger fucking problems right now.

"I'm not bailing your ass out when you get into trouble," I warn.

His patronizing chuckle comes through the phone

again. "Stay out of my business, Lorenzo. Playing hero has never looked good on you, has it, big bro?"

The ghostly sound of my little sister's scream immediately echoes in my head, and I hate how his jab hits the mark. The memory of my outstretched hand trying to grab hers in time, knowing it was already too late.

That day changed everything.

It changed both of us, and I'm furious that he uses it as a weapon.

I hang up the phone, only now noticing how my knuckles turned white from gripping the steering wheel.

Fucker.

I refocus on the task right in front of me.

Except when I try to hear Lily, I realize the receiver isn't working anymore.

Only silence greets me. And a beat of dread—much like on the day I lost my little sister—pumps through my veins.

15

LILY

My palms are sweaty. It's never a good thing when I've been called to the family estate. It's why I prefer staying in my own apartment and focusing on my store. When my father summons a family gathering, memories flood back that are best left forgotten. I hate returning to this house. I look up at the three-story white mansion. It's magnificent, often hosting grand parties that only the most exclusive of guests are invited to.

Despite arguing for Lorenzo not to come, I'm suddenly aware of his absence. Undoubtedly, having Lorenzo join a family dinner will only worsen the pressure my father is putting on me to find what he deems a suitable partner.

I feel like I'm just being passed around between powerful men. But I'm actually scared of my father, which is not at all how I feel about Lorenzo. It pains me to admit it, but as much as I try to center myself and prepare for what's to come, I can't help but be frightened.

I walk around the fountain positioned at the front of the French-style home. A butler holds the two grand wooden doors open for me, and farther past that, I can see one of the housemaids reorganizing the fresh flowers in the corridor.

My legs grow heavier with each step I take up the stairs as impending doom looms over me, so I try to focus on the long, light-pink satin dress with white heels I decided to wear. I often wear cheerful colors because they serve as a reminder to look at the brighter things. My hair is done up, and I'm wearing the pearl earrings and necklace my mother gifted me on my last birthday.

"Welcome back, Miss Taylor," Bentley, the family's longtime butler, says.

"Thank you, Bentley," I reply sweetly. I only say his first name when no one else is around because my father reprimands me for being friendly with the house staff, which never felt right to me to be so formal. He barely contains a small smile as he removes my white coat.

"They're in the drawing room if you'd like to join them before dinner. Your brother has already arrived."

"Thank you. I might quickly excuse myself to the bathroom, first," I say with a polite smile. I see the shift in his gaze, the remorseful expression, as if he senses my unsaid words. Then again, Bentley has seen more than he should in the years serving our household, and his loyalty and silence have not necessarily been rewarded.

My brother's and father's voices raised in discussion come from the drawing room, but I hook a left to the closest powder room. The moment the door is shut, I run my sweaty palms over my dress.

It's fine. Everything is going to be fine.

I assess my makeup, already exhausted by my parents' expectations. There's always something I have out of place or haven't touched up enough. I sigh as I play with the pearl necklace at my throat.

I fidget with the hairpin I've tightly wound my hair through. I pause momentarily as I smooth my fingers over it once again. I was in such a hurry to look presentable I didn't notice earlier that there seems to be something different about it.

Removing it from my hair, I study it carefully. It's not the same white pearl color, but an off-yellow. My eyebrows furrow. It also looks slightly bigger. What the—?

I fiddle with it, an ominous feeling running over me. This isn't my hairpin, and I didn't think twice about using it because I always have it on my bathroom basin, often wearing my hair up.

Snap! The stick breaks away from the small ball. I look at the edge of the ball that certainly isn't a pearl. Is that... some kind of chip?

Realization dawns on me... I might not know how Mafia business works, but I've seen enough crime documentaries to know that this is some kind of tracking or listening device.

"Are you fucking kidding me?" I whisper to myself, an unyielding rage running through me. That *asshole* has no concept of personal space. Especially after I made him promise not to go into my room, and now he's *bugging* me.

I shake my hair out, then open the toilet seat and flush the device. It's only by chance I found it, but how do I know he hasn't done that to other pieces of my jewelry?

What an overbearing fucking asshole.

I release a harsh breath. It doesn't matter. I'll deal with him after I've dealt with my family.

One mountain at a time.

Bentley waits for my arrival outside the drawing room. He opens the door but doesn't dare enter himself.

Three sets of eyes look up as I step into the room, and my father immediately clicks his tongue. "Lily, your hair looks like a mess today. Did you put any effort in at all?"

"Now, now, Father, be nice," my brother, Vince, says as he approaches me with a smirk, scooping me into a big hug. I cling to his warmth, not often getting to see him since he took over my father's businesses in the London office. But even as a child, he was in many ways my safe space. I've missed him since he left over a year ago.

"You look beautiful as always," my brother says, pressing a kiss on top of my head.

"You spoil her," my mother says with a small smile.

"Don't be jealous, Mother," Vince replies teasingly. He's always been charming, and most certainly the child my father favors. I've never despised him for it, though. If anything, I felt sorry for the amount of pressure put on him when we were younger. But over the last year, he seems to be thriving.

The fireplace crackles at the end of the room, my father stoking the flames with a glass of whiskey in his hand. My gaze slides to the half-empty bottle beside him. At least it's not an empty bottle. *Yet.*

"It's not often we're all here together," my mother says as she glances over her shoulder toward my father. When he doesn't reply, she turns back to us. "It's nice."

My heart sinks ever so slightly because none of us in this room, except perhaps my father, ever feels happy or comfortable being in this house. There are too many haunting memories lingering in every corner. No matter how good the others are at pretending that some things never happened, I'm unable to forget, even when I try to.

"Yes, well, I thought a meeting was in order so we can make sure everyone is on the same page," my father finally says, and his gaze lands on me. A shudder runs over me, and I can't help but look at the fireplace poker in his hand that glows red-hot on one end. He follows my gaze and makes a point to put it down.

"Your brother is doing well with the business—profits are up," he begins as he throws back the rest of his drink, then walks over to my mother. He presses a kiss on top of her head and then pours himself another glass.

My brother is sitting on the couch adjacent to my mother, looking between my father and me. It's very obvious a "but" is coming, and who it's about.

"Lily, I've organized a meeting between you and Riley Timber," my father begins. "He comes from old money and recently divorced his second wife. He has two children, but they remain with the mother, so serve as no real hindrance."

"Riley Timber is in his late forties," Vince interjects, and receives a scathing glare from my father because of it. I haven't been in the room for more than five minutes, and he's already orchestrating my life. It's precisely what I thought would happen, but it doesn't take away the bubbling anger or sting of having my rights once again taken away.

"This isn't a request. Lily, you will be going on this date when he's in town two weeks from now. You need to grow up."

"I should get to choose who I do and don't date," I grit out angrily, still wary of how close he stands to the fire poker.

He scoffs. "So you can bring another barbarian to a party to humiliate me? I think not."

My nails curl into my palms as he insults Lorenzo. Even if the situation itself is a facade, it gives him no right to look down on him with such contempt.

"Lily," my mother says, giving me a small shake of her head, a signal to not object to my father's wishes. She looks so small compared to him, and the reminder of how we're all under his thumb makes me so angry. But the anger quickly rolls into sadness. I know too well that my mother is the one who fears him the most. At least my brother and I can escape.

Why has she chosen to remain by his side all these years?

The door swings open. "Sir, you can't!" Bentley yells as the larger-than-life form of Lorenzo steps into the room.

"Sorry, I'm late, sweetheart. Parking the car took me longer than I expected," Lorenzo says as he places his hand on my hip, pulls me in, and presses a kiss on my head. I'm too stunned to speak.

"What's the meaning of this?" my father grits out, and my brother stands from his chair, obviously intervening as he holds out his hand to Lorenzo.

"Vince Taylor. You must be the date from the charity event I've heard so much about."

Lorenzo holds out his hand, as if the most pleasant of gentlemen, his other hand still gripping my hip tightly.

"Lorenzo Moretti. And it's boyfriend, actually."

I freeze under the scrutiny of my father's gaze. I want to hide as much as I want to wring the neck of this insufferable man who can't take a hint.

"Boyfriend? Isn't that something?" Vince says, looking between us both, and I turn to him, trying to brighten with a smile as best as I can.

"Yep" is all I can manage to get out, because a million other things run through my mind. The room fills with palpable tension as my mother and I stare at my father, unsure of his reaction. Forever treading on broken glass around him.

"Well, I can't wait to hear how you two met." Vince claps his hands and rubs them together. "Shall we go in to dinner?" He hooks his arm around my shoulder, pulling me in. It's the same as when we were kids, except now we know opposing my father is anything but a game. "This is going to get interesting," he whispers into my ear with a mischievous grin, and my skin tightens as I recall the many times that smirk has gotten us into trouble.

Yet, there's an odd sense of security as I look over my shoulder at Lorenzo, who only watches me, blocking my parents' view, and begins to follow us. The feeling of safety is short-lived, though, as I recall the listening device he planted on me. I aim a scowl at the asshole who disregards my boundaries, has stalker tendencies, and went and did the one thing I said was strictly forbidden: inserting himself into my family.

"Bentley, bring out our finest bottle of whiskey!" my brother yells, slipping ahead of me. The moment he does, I drop back to Lorenzo.

"You shouldn't be here," I whisper angrily.

"You shouldn't have tried to be clever," he replies, glaring down at me.

"Clever? I—" I stop my outburst, looking back at where my parents now argue. A harrowing thought because I don't know how much my father has had to drink. "You shouldn't have *bugged* me."

A slow smirk stretches his lips, and I want to slap him stupid for it. "And you thought you're not cut out for this world. More observant than you thought."

"Is this just a game to you?" I ask. "You had no right—"

He gets in my face, forcing me to lean back, as he sneers at me. "I have every right when it comes to your safety. You wanted space. I tried to give it to you in the best capacity that I could. There are consequences when you think you can cut me off."

"You're insane," I say on a shaky breath, bewildered at how persistent this man is in ruining my life.

My parents walk out of the drawing room at the same time Lorenzo kisses the tip of my nose. I'm stunned by the show he's putting on. I stare at my mother, whose gaze softens ever so slightly, and I'm led by the man who's single-handedly trying to destroy my life at a family dinner he was never invited to.

16

LORENZO

Her father sits at the head of the table, attempting to glare a hole into my head as he throws back another glass of liquor. Unfortunately for him, he's trying that bullshit on the wrong person. His wife stares at the ridiculous amount of food in front of us, the table ornamented with fresh flowers. She takes a long sip of her champagne, as if her life depends on it.

I make a point to entwine my fingers with Lily's and bring our hands above the table. She pales as she stares at them, almost disbelieving my boldness.

I'm not a man familiar with affection, but I am someone who takes my missions seriously. And I've observed enough lovesick fools to understand the foundations of public displays of affection. I don't know what conversation I'd walked in on, but the room was tense. Whether Lily was aware of it or not, the moment her gaze landed on me, a spark of relief washed over her before her expression morphed into that scowl she's adopted lately when dealing with me.

"Perhaps I've been too busy internationally, but I'm not familiar with you or your family," her brother says as a conversation starter. I've done my research on Vince Taylor. He's three years older than Lily, and from what I can gather, the two have a good relationship. I'm especially interested in his recent business success, though. He doesn't look like a man who could flip a company's profits overnight. He's seemingly the most carefree one at the table.

"Lorenzo and his family dabble in a lot of different businesses," Lily rushes to say, her voice high-pitched. I squeeze her hand reassuringly. Whether Lily believes it or not, I can act the gentleman when it's required of me.

"I thought you were just a friend of the Armanis," her father interjects. "Bring an Armani son here, and I might be inclined to offer my approval."

"Dad!" Lily says with a gasp.

I chuckle, and it seems to unnerve the table. Ignoring their reactions, I take Lily's plate and fill it with some of her favorites.

"I prefer to keep my dealings private and mostly focus on my portfolio throughout Europe," I tell them.

"Real estate?" Vince asks, seemingly interested.

"Amongst other things," I reply, keeping things vague.

"I don't trust a man who hides things," Henrith says.

"Henrith," Lily's mother says under her breath, but avoids his gaze. It's obvious she fears her own husband, and I briefly study Lily, her body language giving away more than she'll ever realize. She fears for her mother, because she continuously looks between her parents like a well-trained child, noticing the subtle shifts when something is about to go awry.

I place Lily's plate in front of her, knowing she often doesn't eat when stressed, which has basically been the entire time I've been staying with her. I usually have to force her to sit and have a meal.

"I agree entirely," I say matter-of-factly, and I can see from the tiny shift in Lily's posture that she's trying not to overtly react. I don't like pretending to be something I'm not, but for the sake of the mission, and at my boss's demand, I'll get in their good fucking graces. Whether Henrith likes me or not.

Men like Henrith Taylor are used to people kissing their ass and giving them anything they ask for, if only for the chance to be offered a favor.

"I've recently gotten into real estate myself," Vince declares. "I'd be interested to hear about your investments after dinner."

"We'll be leaving after dinner, unfortunately," Lily is quick to say.

I offer a small smile and slide my hand onto her knee. Her body jerks ever so slightly, but she doesn't push away my hand. "I've promised Lily an evening for just us. Work has been busy lately, so I hope you don't hold it against me for prioritizing my time with her."

Henrith glares scathingly across the table. Although Vince seems like the welcoming party of the family, I can read the underlying tension that skirts amongst the table. It isn't only to do with my presence; there's something that runs deeper. I watch as her father takes another gulp of his drink.

I have no doubt that it has something to do with that.

The next thirty minutes are underwhelming as I probe about their own business dealings. Lily and Isabella remain quiet, which is concerning. I didn't come from a happy eat-at-the-table type of family, but even I know this is uncomfortable at best, and I'm far from welcome.

Staff begin clearing the table before I've even finished my meal, certainly prompted by her father, who only has to shoot a few malicious glares to get them in motion—*such a self-important man.*

Her mother is the first to leave the dining room, and Lily is quick to shake my hand off her knee to follow her. I stand to go after her, but Vince asks me about my properties in Italy. I entertain him only for a few more minutes before tracking down my woman.

It makes me uneasy when she's out of my sight. A female staff member offers me a small smile and simply points to a set of open French doors. I follow her direction and come to a stop at the threshold. Rows of flowers are highlighted under soft lighting. Beyond that is what appears to be a rose field that's swallowed into the night.

Lily and Isabella look deep in conversation. Lily seems tense, and her mother waves her off and points to a few of the flowers, as if brushing off the conversation. It dawns on me then that perhaps Lily's interest in the florist shop isn't due to her own love of flowers.

"Oh, yeah, Mom's hobby got a bit out of control," Vince says as he comes to stand beside me and lights a cigar. He offers me one, but I decline.

"Has your mother always been this way?" I ask curiously. It doesn't serve me any purpose to have this knowledge. There's nothing about it that could really offer me any help in bringing Henrith Taylor's business to its knees. But it's the way I watch Lily with her mother, both of their admiration for the flowers as they're deep in discussion about something. I can tell from the way Lily's eyebrows dip and she touches Isabella's elbow that she's now comforting her in some way.

"For as long as I can remember," Vince replies. "Most likely how Lily got her name." Vince chuckles. "Not that I think my father really cared what she was called since she wasn't a boy."

I slice a glare in his direction, and Vince casually shrugs his shoulder. "Come on, everyone knows my father's a dick."

"Yet you still work for him," I state.

"Better the devil you know than the one you don't, right? Besides, it's not like I don't like the lifestyle it provides me. So maybe I'm a bastard for it, but if all I have to do is run a few companies, then so be it. At least I'm not stuck here in New York anymore."

It's not news to me that Vince works internationally, but there's something he's leaving unsaid. Now I'm even more interested in the dynamic between Vince and Henrith and their business dealings.

"I said I didn't like this scotch anymore!" Henrith's voice explodes from the dining room. A woman screams, followed by the sound of something smashing. Vince and I stride toward the chaos. The woman who only moments ago pointed me in Lily's direction is on her knees, picking up pieces of glass from what once was a bottle. "Why is everyone so useless around here?" Henrith demands as he slicks back his hair. The moment he sees us, his eyes narrow on me, and he adjusts his suit jacket. "You're still here."

"Henrith." Isabella's voice sounds small as she pushes past me and into the room. "Let's take this to our rooms. You're obviously not feeling well."

"Not *feeling* well?"

Lily's hand grabs my wrist, as if to hold me back. I hadn't even noticed she was next to me.

This little display has me realizing with startling clarity that Henrith isn't only an asshole, but he clearly has violent outbursts after drinking.

My fingers curl into my palm, memories coming back of my own father. I might not have been able to stop him then, but men like this...

Observe, I remind myself.

Find his weakness. Take down his business.

That was the mission I was given.

Me beating the shit out of this man wouldn't even feed my personal satisfaction, so why was I so quick to move, and Lily just as quick to stop me?

"We have guests," Isabella reminds him quietly.

Henrith shoots a disgusted glance at me and scoffs. "No guest of mine."

"Come on, Dad, let's go get you another drink," Vince says cheerily as he walks around the mess.

"We should leave," Lily says quietly, and pulls me away from the scene. I follow her, scowling and confused as to why she's in such a rush to leave. It's as if she's in denial of what just happened. But I know better than anyone what it's like to live with an alcoholic's outbursts and the monster that it can bring forth.

I let her lead me out to the car before I grab her wrist and spin her toward me.

"Has he ever hurt you?" I growl out. Right now, it's the only thing I seem to care about. Of all the leads I might've gained tonight, the only thing I want to know is if at any point he's ever laid a hand on her. Because if he has, I'll burn this fucking mansion to the ground with him inside.

She gapes at me. "How dare you?"

"Answer the question."

"How dare you come into my home, uninvited, and accuse my family of what... violence?"

"I only care about your safety."

She scoffs, tears brimming in her eyes, and I don't entirely believe her act. Suddenly, I'm realizing that the woman I thought was so sweet might be harboring her own dark secrets and demons.

"I loathe you so fucking much. You stepped over a line tonight."

"There's no line that I won't cross to remain by your side."

She shakes her head furiously. "You're such a tyrant! I hate you so much!"

"I never asked to be friends," I deadpan. Lily is gravely mistaken if she thinks I'm anything close to friendly. In a matter of weeks, this arrangement will feel as if it never happened. She'll forget about me, and I'll continue with my work.

Doesn't mean I won't do everything I can for her now.

And she still hasn't answered my fucking question, and the deflection eats me alive.

There's so much unknown to me about this family, and the closer I get to answers, the farther she pushes me away. I'm not entirely sure if it's self-preservation or to protect her family.

She's already storming toward the car, ignoring me as I call out for her.

For fuck's sake. This woman is so painful to deal with, and somehow those little legs pick up speed whenever I'm asking her for an honest answer.

I wonder if Lily's ever really taken the time to thoroughly dissect her family dynamic and look at it through an honest lens. Or if, much like tonight, she's used to running.

17

LORENZO

She's been silent the entire car trip. I've been grinding my jaw and trying my best not to snap the fucking steering wheel in two. I'm pissed about her not answering my question, but also at the fact that she removed the listening device I bugged her with.

A crackle of tension runs between us like a physical barrier, and I try not to laugh, because she's playing the wrong fucking game with me.

This is why working with men is easier. Women have emotional highs and lows that I can't regulate. They are complicated beings, and I have no experience in reading their emotions or caring about their feelings, because I've never had to.

"Stop here," Lily commands.

"Why?" I growl. We're in one of the busiest areas of Manhattan. Thousands of people scamper throughout the night. There's nothing but restaurants and luxury stores surrounding us.

I'm forced to come to a stop at a traffic light, and she goes to open the door, discovering it's locked. She looks over her shoulder furiously. "You've seriously locked me in here?"

"It's a safety lock meant for children," I deadpan.

Her eyes narrow. "Then I'll just have to break it."

I bury the smirk wanting to form on my lips, knowing it'll piss her off even more. Still, when she looks at my suit, directly at where I holster my gun, I say, "The glass is bulletproof, sweetheart, so even if you do find the courage to attempt to steal my gun and take a shot, you'll only be damning us instead."

"You're so infuriating. Unlock the door right now. I need out." It's the dangerous edge to her tone that has me watching her cautiously. I have enough sense to know that something definitely happened tonight, and it's not simply because I bugged her and asked about her father's vice.

I know better than to poke too much in a time like this, even if my curiosity is piqued. I've seen Luca do it enough to Ara to know the wrath that follows isn't worth it.

I round the corner and pull over.

The moment the engine switches off, Lily all but throws herself out of the car.

"Lily," I call out after her. For fuck's sake, this woman drives me insane. I lock the car, then catch up to her, but come to a stop as I look up at the store she's beelined for. Cartier. My entire body tenses as I look at the stores on either side. Fuck me, she really is going to drag me through the perils of retail therapy.

I adjust my belt and suit jacket, then push through the door after her, accepting the challenge head-on. A staff member near the door gives me an insincere greeting and a suspicious once-over as I follow Lily. If I didn't know she was pissed off, I would've thought that bright fucking smile on her face meant she was the happiest person alive right now.

A woman behind the counter is already talking with her, agreeing with her quick choices. I come to a stop behind her, but am treated like I don't exist as Lily slides a ring on her finger and admires it. She then shifts to a pair of earrings, and we stop at every fucking display as she coos enthusiastically with the sales clerk over every piece.

"You have good taste as usual, Miss Taylor," the clerk encourages as she continues putting items to the side. "Will that be all for today?"

She's chosen several items in the span of five minutes. I'm actually impressed. I'm not one for jewelry personally, but I can appreciate the classical style Lily prefers.

"That comes to one hundred and twenty-two thousand," the woman says with a smile.

"Wonderful," Lily replies, then suddenly turns to

me and slides her hand over my chest. "My *boyfriend* here is buying them for me as a little apology gift."

"Excuse me?" I glare down at her.

She's smiling sweetly now and batting her thick eyelashes. "Thanks, honey." Lifting on her tiptoes, she presses a kiss to my cheek before heading for the exit.

That. Little. Brat.

"How will payment be made, sir?" the woman asks, grabbing my attention before I storm after Lily. I don't have to pay. I know that. But Lily is challenging me, and I'm not one to ever back down, even if she's being a pain in my ass. One that needs to be placed over my knee and punished again. My cock jumps at the thought.

And so, I find myself handing over my card, hurrying the woman along because Lily is already gone. I take the bag and head for the door. By the time I'm out of the store, she's already on to the next.

What the fuck is this hell?

By the time I enter the second store, she's somehow magically racked up three garments to try on.

I spot the back of her as she enters the changing room. I beeline for it, ignoring the woman who asks me to remain in the waiting area. The store itself looks like the lobby of a luxury hotel.

I never go shopping; everything is ordered for me and delivered to my home. And although I understand having expensive taste, she's lashing out.

I open the red velvet curtain and freeze. She's

wearing only a white G-string, exposing perfect tits ample enough to fill my hands. Her gaze flies to mine, but instead of the skittish, shy Lily I'm used to, a different version of her stands in front of me; this one furious, raging, looking for somewhere to release all that pent-up anger.

"Want to explain this?" I say, lifting the Cartier bag.

She turns, ignoring me, and steps into a dress.

My jaw grinds as my gaze drops to her ass, and I step into the tiny space, pulling the curtain closed. Fine. If she wants to play this game, I'll goad her into giving me a reaction. "What's with the pissy mood?"

Her head whips in my direction, and I feel smug, assuming it was that easy to draw her attention. Because I'd rather have her wrath than her cold shoulder.

"You ignored my rule about not going into my room and *bugged* me," she accuses.

We're still stuck on that, eh? "That's it?"

"*That's it?*" she says in disbelief, throwing her hands in the air. "Oh, I forgot I'm talking with a criminal."

"Don't lump me with petty crooks," I growl. This can't be all she's upset about. There has to be more.

"I can't breathe with you around, Lorenzo. You need to give me space," she bites. "I don't need you within five feet of me all the time."

"Your safety is my priority. So until I'm released from this mission, you're stuck with me being your constant shadow."

She sucks in a sharp breath and then scowls as she turns toward the mirror. *Fuck me, I can't say anything right with this woman.*

She admires her reflection. The dress is beautiful, but only because she's wearing it. The back of it gapes open, the zipper not zipped. She infuriates me, and yet, I find myself stepping closer, closing my fingers around the tiny zipper, and slowly pulling it up for her.

She watches me through the mirror, her breath hitching as I reach the top. It's a tight dress. Different from the usual free-flowing ones she wears. It accentuates her curves in all the right places, and now that I've seen her bare tits, I can't unsee them. Suddenly, I hate this dress because it's showing too much cleavage.

After a moment, she says, "You can unzip me. I want to try the next one."

I remain standing behind her, looking down at the small scar between her shoulder blades. I trail it with my finger. "How did you get this scar?" It's the only blemish or imperfection I've discovered on her smooth skin so far.

Lily pulls her long, wavy hair over her shoulder, blocking my view of it. "Just being a reckless kid. Can you unzip me now?"

"Hmmm," I hum, not at all liking the vague answer, but who am I to ask for her secrets? I unzip the dress, my gaze roaming over her exposed skin. My cock twitches, and I swallow hard.

She's so incredibly smooth, so opposite to me in every way. So polished and yet perfectly cracked.

"Lorenzo," she says quietly, and it brings me out of my fixation. "Stop looking at me like that."

"Like what?" I ask, my voice gravelly. I hate the restraint I have to impose on myself around this woman.

She's too tempting.

She turns, facing me again as she swallows and looks up at me through her eyelashes. "Like you want to break me."

I chuckle because wanting to break her is an understatement. "Well, you've been a brat. You should be punished in some way." Her gaze dips down to where my cock is pressing against my pants. "Why are you really upset tonight?"

"I told you. It's because—"

"You told me only part of the reason," I say, placing my hands up against the mirror on either side of her and leaning into her space. "I know I'm not the only one you're angry with." My shoulders bunch. It's the only way I can make sure I don't put my hands on her.

To feel her curves.

Tempted to taste her.

Curious how tight she'll be around my cock.

My jaw tics. This woman and her fucking floral scent are slowly undoing me. I'm no better than a starved man begging for his next meal. But I can't submit.

Something soft and vulnerable shifts in her gaze. The flicker of the sweet Lily I've come to know. "My father set me up on a date in two weeks. I have no choice but to go."

"You always have a choice."

"No, I don't." She looks away, but I grip her chin to force her to look back up at me.

"You're not wearing this fucking dress on a date," I warn her.

Her eyebrows furrow. "You don't own me."

"No, I don't, because you'd know if I did," I growl, irritated by her defiance.

"Is everything okay in there?" a saleswoman calls from the other side of the curtain.

"We're fine," I bark, not breaking eye contact with Lily.

"O-okay. Just let me know if you need anything," the woman replies before leaving.

Lily bites her bottom lip, and I can't help but track the movement. I want to be biting those fucking lips. Tension crackles between us. I know I should step back, leave the room, and wait until she's done. But I can't move. I'm trying my fucking hardest right now to restrain my own demons, because if I don't, I might reach out for her instead.

"I'm stressed," she admits quietly, "and just need a release." A guttural sound comes from my core. "Or maybe... I need to be... *punished*?" She says the last word uncertainly. She doesn't know what she's asking of me. Has no idea the thousands of ways I can make her break apart and never come back the same.

And yet I'm reminded that I'm only a man. No matter how much I've tried to rid myself of my need for her, I want to taste her at least once.

"You don't know what you're asking," I grit out as my cock strains painfully against my pants.

A spark lights in her gaze, probably surprise that I haven't berated her for trying to tempt me. She raises her hand and cups my cheek.

The gentle touch is so foreign, I pull back from it. I can see the shift in her demeanor the moment she takes it as rejection, so I quickly say, "I don't do sweet, Sunshine. But if you need a release, how about I help you with that instead of you taking it out on my bank account? You've been a terror tonight."

"I—" Before she can spout any excuses, I grab her delicate throat. She's stunned into silence as I press her back against the mirror and encroach farther into her space.

I rub my thumb over her neck thoughtfully. It'd be so easy to break. She's so small. Meek at times. But I know the truth about her. I see the woman beneath waiting to break free. Both are beautiful. Both are temptations.

I wonder if Lily truly comprehends how much blood stains my hands. If she did, I doubt she'd so freely invite me into her space like this. Or maybe little Miss Perfect is rebelling, and if she wants to use me as some kind of distraction, then I'll gladly oblige.

If she's already on the descent to ruin, then why shouldn't I get on my knees and show her how good it can taste?

It's not like she'll be in this darkness with me forever.

It's only a matter of time until she gasps for air and returns to the world she's meant for.

I slowly guide my other hand down the dress.

Her gaze lowers as heat infuses her skin, and I tighten my hold on her throat, forcing her eyes to spring to life.

"Don't look away from what I'm about to do to you. You're going to take your punishment in full. Do you understand?" I say as my hand curls beneath the dress and pulls it up over her hips.

She swallows but nods as I begin to circle her clit. I look down at the white lace underwear as I slip a finger under it and rub against her wet cunt.

"Already soaking for me, Sunshine," I praise, my cock twitching at the sight of her reddening cheeks. "Not used to dirty talk, huh?"

"You're just... a lot," she whispers.

"And to think I was about to sit down on that stool, bend you over my knee, and spank the brat out of you for that shit you pulled in the jewelry store."

"It's Cartier," she corrects.

I thrust a finger inside her, and she gasps as I

tighten the grip around her throat. "I don't give a fuck what it's called. You were being a brat."

She's fucking soaking my hand. So fucking perfect and tight. My cock painfully strains against my zipper, wanting to be inside her, forcing her into submission, but I know I'm too much for this little princess.

"Now what do you say?" I croon as I slip a second finger into her.

"Oh my God," she says on a moan as her head falls back to hit the mirror. Her hips begin to rock back and forth against my hand—such a needy little creature. I lean into her, my hot breath brushing against her neck as I get high from her floral scent.

"What do you say when someone gets you a gift, Sunshine?"

"Oh fuck," she says quietly, and I can't help the smug smile that tugs at my lips at making her curse. Her hands wrap around my neck as she pulls me in closer. "Thank you," she whispers, half dazed.

There's a gentleness she embraces me with that I don't entirely feel comfortable with, so I focus on what I can do for her instead. Probably what most men can't.

I pick up my pace as I whisper into her ear, "You're going to soak my hand like a good girl, aren't you?"

"Yes," she breathes.

I want to force her tight little cunt around my cock, but this isn't about my gratification. No, it's about her release. Her pleasure. Because I've never seen this woman light up like she does when she's being set free.

"Stain this dress from the inside out."

"Yes." Her breathing becomes heavier.

Fuck it. I can't wait any longer. I drop to my knees, withdrawing my fingers and hooking her leg over my shoulder, widening her hips. Finally, I get to taste her. I've been imagining what she tastes like ever since the night she straddled me in that park almost two years ago.

"I want... I want you," she pants.

My cock twitches at the soft neediness of her request.

Maybe I'm a masochist, but right now I only care about her pleasure. It's not a line I can cross.

"You're being punished, remember? You don't get my cock tonight, sweetheart," I tell her before dipping my head between her thighs. Her nails immediately curl into my shoulders as I feast on her. Fuck me, she's the sweetest thing I've ever tasted. I grip her ass, eating her out like a starved man.

I suck at her clit, rewarded with tiny whimpers as her breathing chops in and out. Her body is so responsive to my touch, teetering on the edge. I want to see her come undone. My cock throbs painfully as I devour her; sucking, tugging, and teasing.

So fucking beautiful.

Too fucking perfect.

I insert two fingers again, stretching her as I continue to suck and pump into her. She clings to me, her perfectly manicured nails digging in as a slight tremor begins in her hooked leg.

"I'm going to—to—"

Her sweet cunt squeezes around my fingers as she floods my hand, her entire body bending toward me, but I hold her upright. Now it's about my reward as I take everything she's willing to offer me.

She shudders, her fingers loosening their grip, and a small hand begins to feather through my hair, as if petting me. When I look up, she has a small smile on her face. A contented expression that is far more beautiful than any other I've seen on her face.

This is what she should be walking around looking like. Then again, I don't want any other fucker seeing her like this.

My hold on her hips tightens, and I rein in that dangerous thought.

I'm losing myself to her. An abnormality that I don't entirely understand.

"Don't be too cruel to my card in this shop," I tell her as I unhook her leg from my shoulder and then stand. Her eyebrows crowd in confusion as she reaches out for my cock, which is pressing painfully against my pants. A low, guttural warning growl escapes me.

"I want to please you as well," she says quietly.

I'm not willing to tarnish her any further.

I need to make sure she doesn't become attached.

I'm not a hero or knight in shining armor. But

when she looks at me like that, it makes me wish I were a better man, if only for a second.

I've never once thought about the blood on my hands or the deeds that I've committed. But all of them make me irrevocably unworthy of touching this woman.

I kick up an arrogant smirk. "This was your punishment, Sunshine. At least now, when you're on that date, wearing this dress, your own cum smeared on the inside from where I ate you out, you'll be thinking of me."

Her jaw drops, that scowl reappearing.

I step out of her grip and pick up the Cartier bag, knowing more than likely she's about to rain hell on my card. So be it if that's what will make her feel better about me being an ass. I can't offer her what she clearly wants.

It's not just sex for Lily Taylor. No, she's a woman who wears her heart on her sleeve.

For once, I can't be the monster, especially when I can't be what she needs most.

A good man.

18

LILY

I continue arranging the flowers, ignoring Lorenzo as he places the iced tea at the edge of the counter. He hasn't commented on my silence. I don't think clearly around him. Whenever we interact, I lose all common sense. I'm still furious with him for bugging my hairpin and barging into my family's dinner last week. And yet that same night, I let him get me off, and he paid for all the stuff I bought. It doesn't make any sense.

I watch him from the corner of my eye as he walks into the back of the shop. I have no understanding of his financial circumstances, but he's obviously got more money than the average bodyguard if he can purchase those items for me without batting an eye. It only further confuses me as to who he actually is. And it's not something I should be showing any interest in.

We've fallen into a weird pattern. He comes to the shop with me, silently helping me when I haven't asked him, then goes in the back, often taking phone calls or working on his laptop. He looks more like a receptionist than a man involved with the Mafia.

I haven't heard from either of my parents since the night of the dinner, and it's got me concerned. I wish Lorenzo hadn't seen any of that. I don't have any loyalty to my father to cover up his secret, but for my mother's sake, I remain quiet.

She practically denied everything I said to her in the garden that night, the memory infuriating me.

"Has he had any... outbursts lately?" I asked her, and her eyebrows furrowed as she looked at me as if I'd gone mad. Using the word "outburst" seems easier for her to comprehend what I'm really asking.

"Don't be silly, Lily." She tried to laugh it off. "Everything is fine."

"Don't do that to me," I gritted out. "Don't pretend like it's okay when it's not. Leave him, Mom. I'll help you."

She looked abashed as she pulled me closer. "I don't want to leave your father." She hushed me as if we were being spied on. When I looked up at the door, I noticed Vince and Lorenzo watching us. It was unnerving to see Lorenzo fill the doorframe to the home I'd forsaken for so long. He seemed out of place, and it was unsettling because I'm sure he saw more than he let on—more than I'd willingly let anyone see before.

"Everything is fine," my mother lied. "Your father is stressed with work as usual, but we're okay. Nothing to worry about here. Though you really should visit me more often. I miss you," she said, placing her hand on my cheek.

A lump lodged in my throat. Her denial hurt, but the way I so willingly compromised myself so I could remain close to her, even if at a distance, cut deeper. It's not my role as the child to look after her. I know that, but I worry that something will happen to her, and so I've always abided by my father's rules, too scared of the consequences, not only forced on me but on my mother as well. That and he'll cut all contact between my mother and me if I ever do decide to leave.

"They're blooming beautifully, aren't they?" she said, admiring the flowers.

"Mom, Dad's going crazy. He can't seriously expect me to date and marry some stranger just because he says so."

Her hand froze on the flower, and she tried to smile. "You know how determined your father can be. He only wants the best for you, Lily."

I scoffed. "You can't seriously believe that, can you?" I hate how it hurts, that her denial and unwillingness to face the truth unintentionally slice deeper than anything my father might ever say to me.

"Maybe Lorenzo will win him over," she said with a smirk.

"You know Dad hates him." That was when I saw the twinkle of mischief in my mother's eyes—something I hadn't seen for quite some time.

"But isn't that why you brought him? Don't worry about me, Lily. Make your own choices and embrace them with conviction. I'm okay, really," she said, squeezing my arm.

But I know better than anyone else that she's not.

The bell above the door tinkles, and I jump, brought back to the now in my store. "Welcome." The greeting falls flat as Tania, my father's assistant, walks in with a smile. "Tania. Wow, it's good to see you," I lie. I have nothing against her personally, but I know she's here on my father's orders. I haven't heard from him since the dinner. My brother, however, sent me a text saying he liked Lorenzo.

"I thought I'd drop by and see how things are going with the shop," she says, looking around. "Oh, and I have this to drop off as well." She rummages through her handbag and pulls out a red velvet box, holding it out to me.

"What's this for?" I ask, confused.

"It's a gift from Riley Timber. He looks forward to your meeting. I encourage you to wear it."

My blood runs cold. I didn't think my father would have given up, but to have received something directly from a man I don't even know creeps me out.

"Aren't you going to open it?"

I glance over my shoulder in Lorenzo's direction. He's on the phone, looking furious at whoever he's speaking with. Tania waves her hand. "I wouldn't worry about that. Although I can understand why you went there," she says, her gaze roaming him appreciatively. "It never hurts to have a side piece in place. Marriage isn't for everyone, but it certainly offers security." She winks.

Precisely the reason why she's been my father's assistant for more than twenty years. She's in her mid-forties now, but I'm positive they were having an affair at some point. When I was a child, they spent many evenings together. I'm sure my mother knows too, which saddens me. So many secrets swept under the rug. I wonder how many times my father had to pay people off just to keep their mouths closed.

I open the red box to reveal a beautiful silver necklace encrusted with diamonds. It's not to my liking. I prefer simple elegance over something so... flashy.

"It's stunning!" Tania gushes, looking over my shoulder. I pull out the small note hidden inside—a location and time for Friday night. "Wow, he's very interested. How lovely for you."

When I glance up, she's looking through the bouquets. "I can take any one I want, right?"

"No, you'll pay," Lorenzo says.

I turn, not even noticing when he'd finished on the phone.

Tania's stunned as she turns to face him. "Oh, I understand you're new here, but we have an arrangement—"

"This is a business. Her time and expertise are to be paid for," Lorenzo says in that no-nonsense tone.

On reflex, I go to say it's okay, but I look back down at the red velvet box in my hand instead, realizing I'm getting pushed further into a corner.

"Lily?" Tania says, smiling in disbelief.

I put the red box to the side. "They all have their price tags on them," I say simply.

She chokes on a laugh until she realizes I'm serious. "Well, I'm rather busy today. So, I'll come in another time," she says dismissively, turning to walk away. I'm not surprised she's not willing to pay for the flowers, but it only makes my blood boil hotter.

Once she's gone, I glare at Lorenzo. "You don't need to intervene."

He shakes his head. "Stop fighting me, Sunshine. You'll only exhaust yourself. What's in the box?" he asks.

I hide it behind my back, raising my nose in the air. "Stop asking questions. You'll only exhaust yourself," I bite back. For some reason, I'm nervous about how Lorenzo will react. Or maybe I'm more scared of the fact that he won't react at all, which lacks any logical sense.

"Are you hiding something from me?" A devilish smile appears, and I'm too stunned to move because it's breathtaking. It's the first time I've seen him with a full smile, and warmth floods my core, though I know too well nothing good will come from it. He's in my space within seconds, and I squeal as I try to hold the box away from him.

He pins me between his body and the counter, and we freeze as the vase on the corner crashes to the floor, exploding into pieces, water splashing everywhere, with a heap of flowers spilling out.

"Now look what you've done. You've—" The words die on my lips as I look up at him, acutely aware of everywhere our bodies touch. My chest rises and falls faster at the way he's staring at me. The way his dark gaze devours me.

It's been a week since he last touched me, and the way he's looking at me, it's as if he's thinking the same.

The bell chimes, and Romi walks through the front door, holding an iced tea in one hand and her roommate's long-haired terrier in the other. "Can you believe this little shit gave up on his walk two blocks up?" She huffs and freezes when she sees us. I shove Lorenzo away, as if I've been caught doing something inappropriate.

"Oh, did I walk in on some hanky-panky time?" She raises an eyebrow. "Didn't think you'd have it in you to fuck in the middle of your shop while still open."

"Stop!" I raise my hand to her, not wanting to hear any more, and noticing the distinct heat that blooms over my cheeks. I slide the red velvet box under the counter as Lorenzo heads into the back room and then comes back with a dust pan and broom.

"Don't pick up the pieces. I'll get those." He practically pushes me out of the way. I don't know where to look as Romi smirks at me. She then hooks a thumb over her shoulder.

"The evil assistant that just walked out of here? We don't like her, Borris. She's a bit of a bitch," she says to the dog.

"Borris?" Lorenzo questions, finishing picking up most of the pieces and scraping them into the nearby trash can.

"Yeah. This is Borris." Romi dumps the dog in Lorenzo's hands. He looks like he doesn't know what to do with it as she throws the red leash over his shoulder. I bite my bottom lip and try not to laugh at the awkward-looking scene.

"Lorraine's traveling at the moment?" I ask, taking the dustpan and broom to clean the remains of the mess.

"Yeah, she's visiting her mother for the week, don't even get me started on that situation, so it's just me and this little guy in the apartment," she says with a smile, scratching under his chin. She's been living with her roommate now for almost two years, and Borris is the terrier Lorraine allegedly adopted after working at an animal shelter for only a week.

"Do you mind taking him out to pee? He became

skittish in the last two blocks, but I'm certain he needs to tinkle." Romi looks pointedly at Lorenzo.

Lorenzo and Borris stare at one another. "You want me to walk him?"

"Just around the block." Romi does a circle with her finger. "While we have some girl chat. I get there's a honeymoon smoochy period and all, but you don't want to be clingy or toxic, right?" she says with her hand on her hip. "Don't want us getting bored with you so quickly. Looks don't hold up as much as you would think."

Lorenzo's eyebrows rise. "You certainly don't care about what you say, do you?"

Romi casually shrugs as she leans over the counter, her shirt stating, *No. You do it.*

"No," she says flatly. "Oh, I got you an iced tea," she says, noticing the one already on the counter. "But I guess this will be mine then." She takes a large slurp as she looks at Lorenzo expectantly.

He's not going to leave.

He never does.

No matter how much we argue or fight, he's forever at my side.

He leans in, and every hair on my arms rises, an immediate flashback of the night in the changing room comes to mind. "I'm locking the door behind me. I won't be long. Call me if you need anything."

My jaw drops as I watch him leave. Is he actually giving me... a moment of space?

"Wow. I don't want to know what dirty talk he was whispering in your ear to make your jaw drop like that," Romi comments as we watch him leave.

He does exactly as he stated, except I'm not surprised when he only walks back and forth in front of the store, seemingly encouraging the small terrier to urinate.

Romi blows out a whistle. "I didn't realize he was helping you around the store as well. Remind me what he does for work again." She leans in as I bend over to finish cleaning the mess we'd created.

Guilt slices through me. Romi's been my best friend since childhood. She knows most of my secrets, but this is one I can't share with her, especially when it's not mine to tell.

"Investments and a lot of real estate. Nothing exciting," I say, trying to sound as calm as possible.

Her gaze narrows. "You're not pregnant, are you?"

"Wh-what? No!" I stammer. My God, we haven't even had sex yet.

Yet.

That ominous word has me shaking my head.

"Not pregnant, just taking things slow. My father's not too happy about it. He doesn't think Lorenzo is the best candidate to date a Taylor, and has organized for me to meet with some guy on Friday for a date."

Romi pulls a face. "And you're actually going to go? You can't be serious, Lily. Lorenzo is clearly besotted with you. And to be honest, I haven't seen you this *lively* for a while. What does Lorenzo think of it?"

"This was your punishment, Sunshine. At least now, when you're on that date, wearing this dress, your own cum smeared on the inside from where I ate you out, you'll be thinking of me." Liquid warmth trickles into my core at the memory of his words.

"He hasn't said much about it," I lie.

"Hmmm. He doesn't strike me as the laid-back type."

"Well, I hardly think it'll be a forever thing," I reply quietly. Ara said it'd be easier to be under the pretense of a fake relationship, but it's me who will have to have the awkward conversations explaining why we suppos- edly didn't work out when all of this passes.

"You never know. I like his vibe. Maybe he'll give you the courage to seriously step up to your father. I know it's hard," she says softly as she places her hand on top of mine, her silent insinuation tangible.

There are so many things Romi knows about my family, yet so many things I keep to myself. But despite her quirky, aloof demeanor, she's always been very observant. Must be the artist in her.

"You've been acting strange lately," she notes.

My shoulders sag because I don't like lying to her, but I don't even know how to articulate half of what's happening. If I say it out loud, I'll sound like a crazy person. "There's just a lot happening. That's all." I'm trying to cover for lies upon lies. Tired of their weight and how sticky they feel, as if they're keeping me stuck in place.

"You always used to talk to me," she says, sounding concerned. "So, when you need me, you let me know, yeah? Promise me." The ends of her deep-red hair brush her shoulders, and I think about all the ways she's growing while I feel left behind. Her paintings are getting notice, and she's often traveling for her artistic pursuits. And I've remained here in my store, creating a safe haven, but perhaps I've become too reliant on its comfort.

"Promise. But you don't have to worry about me. If anything, I'm worried about Sienna. Has she spoken to you lately?"

"Nice deflection, not," she says, but lets it go, shrugging. "No, she hasn't spoken to me, but something is definitely up with her and Michael."

I throw the paper towels into the trash after soaking up the water on the floor. "Maybe I should do something for her. I want to make sure she's okay and—"

"Or you can focus on yourself for once," Romi cuts in. "You're always doing that. Offering to help others first and putting yourself on the back burner. Don't pretend like this last year hasn't been weighing on you as well."

I don't know what to say to that. It's what I've always done, and I never thought it was necessarily a bad thing. Well, not until as of late.

"Maybe this is good for you." She hooks a thumb in Lorenzo's direction. "It's time you focus on yourself, Lily. We're all old enough now. If Sienna needs us, she'll come to us. So for now, focus on yourself."

The bell jingles, and Lorenzo looks unimpressed as the tiny terrier gazes up at him. "For such a tiny dog, he certainly shits a lot, and he got some on my shoe." He points at his shoe.

Romi bites her bottom lip and turns, and we both burst into laughter.

"Oh, that's so weird. I thought he just needed to pee. Anyway, I'd better leave you two love birds. But just so you know, I'll be stealing her away for a night out soon, and to make it clear, you're not invited," she says, poking her tongue at him and taking Borris.

I wonder if Romi knew who Lorenzo truly was, if she'd be as bold to poke her tongue out at him. Most likely. She's always been fearless in her own way. It's why I was always drawn to her.

"Bye, kids, and don't be in a mad rush to have any babies soon. It's bad enough we have to deal with Luca's mood swings while Ara's pregnant, let alone yours, as well." She gives Lorenzo a pointed look, and his gaze narrows.

She chuckles as she closes the door behind her. "What's this about babies?" he demands the moment she's gone.

I shake my head because it's just like Romi to leave such a lasting impression. But she also doesn't joke with those she doesn't like, which means that for whatever reason, Romi approves of Lorenzo.

But it doesn't shift the reality that none of this is real. "It's nothing," I say, refocusing on the bouquet in front of me. "She likes to joke a lot."

I can sense the intensity of his gaze, a feeling I still haven't gotten used to. I don't think I ever will. And even if I did, he'll be long gone by then. Soon, they'll get to the bottom of this threat that I'm starting to believe isn't even real. As the weeks have passed, the memory of that day has slowly receded, and it doesn't hold as much of its terrifying power over me anymore.

"Any news on the hitmen?" I ask curiously.

"No leads yet," Lorenzo replies.

I steal a glance at him as he stares down at his phone. I haven't seen him sleep, even when I've peeked in on him at all hours of the night and morning. He seems to be forever working, and I wonder if it's all for my safety or if there's something else to it entirely.

He looks up, those dark-brown eyes freezing me in place, and I'm taken back to the changing room.

I want him.

Can feel him all over my body, even when he's not touching me.

His gaze drops to my lips, and I know he's thinking the same. But when he steps forward, he bypasses me, heading into the back room instead, and I feel the icy rejection in his wake.

My jaw clenches. It's infuriating that I'm longing

for a man that I shouldn't be. The sexual tension is insufferable. But even worse than that is the constant rejection and acute realization that this will never be anything more.

The red velvet box catches my eye, and I'm yet again reminded I'm facing bigger issues than Lorenzo Moretti, even if he takes up more space in my mind than I've willingly given him.

19

LORENZO

"You're not going on that date," I say as we walk into her apartment.

She slips her heels off, then her earrings, and removes the tie from her hair. It's routine. So is her fucking scowl that is begging to be punished.

"You still seem not to understand that you don't get to tell me what to do." Lily's been particularly hard-headed since we had dinner at her family's estate. Something about overstepping boundaries, but I don't give a fuck about any of that when it comes to keeping her safe.

"I don't have time for your games tonight." I follow her to the bottom of the stairs. She's making a good show of ignoring me lately, but when she does speak to me, it's rapid fire until she eventually slams a door in my face. Her hips sway from side to side as she walks up to her bedroom.

"We're done with this discussion, and don't you dare follow me. My room is off-limits," she reminds me.

She even put a lock on her bedroom door this week, following our disagreement over her "personal space" after I replaced a few of her things with listening devices. I didn't tell her there are more than the ones she found, even when she asked me. I will lie, cheat, and get my hands dirty to keep her safe.

It will also only take me a matter of seconds to break into her room, but I'll let her believe the lock will keep me out if it makes her feel better.

"I'm serious, Lily," I call after her.

She flips me off over her shoulder, and my eyebrows shoot up in surprise. Definitely brattier this week. Women are hard work. It's like stepping on land mine after land mine, yet I find myself still catering to her. Making sure she's eaten for the day, has her iced tea, and is attentive to her daily clothing choices. I was even aware of when she changed her perfume for one day, for fuck's sake.

I slip into the guest room, peeling off my suit jacket and unbuttoning my shirt. I place my gun on the end of the bed, then pull my phone out of my pocket and make a call.

My mood sours the moment Dmitri Volkov's voice comes through the speaker.

"Never thought I'd receive a call from you personally. You're either in deep shit or have decided to pull the pole out of your ass to have some fun," the asshole has the balls to greet me with.

"It's shocking that God gave you a second chance in this life," I reply.

"Let's not pretend either of us prays to a particular god. Need I remind you that *you* called *me*?"

I make a habit of searching my room to make sure nothing has been shifted or seems out of the ordinary. It's a modern, beautiful apartment, but it never feels right, not that I've used the bed much. Instead choosing to stay in the living room where I have the easiest access to her, taking only a few hours of sleep when necessary.

"Vince Taylor. What do you know about him?" I ask. I've seen the two engaged in discussions before. There's something off about Lily's brother, but I can't place it, and digging into their affairs is taking longer than I'd like.

Dmitri lets out a low whistle. "Why? Trying to win over the new brother-in-law?"

"Do you still like your pretty face?" I bite back.

Dmitri chuckles again, and I can hear shuffling in the background. "You know I'll always be indebted to you and Luca for protecting Elanee. Vince is a party boy. Or was. Of course, we circulated in similar crowds, but since he took over a few of his father's businesses in London, he doesn't come back to New York often, or at least I haven't seen him for a while."

"Well, he's back in town now." I undo my belt as I

look out at the bustling city beneath me. I don't like being in the middle of everything like this. It's too busy and noisy for my personal preference.

"What are you hoping to get from this phone call?" Dmitri asks diplomatically.

"Can you organize a meeting with him tonight? Something... *organic*, perhaps?"

"Shouldn't be a problem. What if I *organically* invite both of you to my club? However, this time when you show up, don't point a gun at my head."

"Then don't be a dickhead."

"No can do. It's all part of my charm." His tone grows more serious when he says, "Is this about Lily? You know, Elanee gave me a word of warning that if you were to hurt her, she'd be extremely pissed. She's her friend now, so with my own personal agenda of keeping my woman happy, I warn you not to do anything underhanded."

I hang up the phone. The last person I need advice from is Dmitri, especially considering he most likely has suspicions already about our involvement with Lily in the first place.

I don't entirely understand Lily's friendship circle, but they're all protective of each other, almost as much as I am when it comes to Luca. The difference being, of course, that I doubt they're willing to die for one another's secrets. Then again, as I'm learning, a woman's wrath is definitely something to be feared.

I send through a text to one of the hounds. Luca

won't be thrilled that I used one of them, but I need someone here in my stead while I personally handle matters elsewhere. If I'm slipping out for the night, I need to make sure Lily is still protected. I'm certain there's something about Vince that might give me insight into their father's business. Often, his type becomes looser with their tongue, and shares what they consider bragging rights, after a couple of good rounds of whiskey.

I strip down to nothing, then turn on the shower at an ice-cold temperature. I'm not comfortable with leaving Lily's side, but remind myself that the mission comes first. I'm here for her protection, yes, but I'm also tasked with unraveling the inner workings of her father's business. If Luca makes a profit from it, he won't care as much if I use one of the hounds as a resource in the process.

It's unnerving that we aren't any closer to figuring out who was behind the attack in Italy. Top of the suspect list is still the Bratva, but we have no evidence yet.

It's definitely part of the reason Dmitri is willing to help, considering we were in that mess because of him. I never understood why he was willing to go so far for his woman, in the same way that Luca obeys and alters plans, all because of what Ara demands.

I notice the small shift within myself. Lily is bad for me in so many ways. I'm no longer focused on her presence because it's my job, even when I try to convince myself that's the reason. There's an under-lying need to know what she's doing and thinking, which goes beyond my mission. Even the thought of being away from her for a few hours tonight has me uneasy.

Especially if she discovers I'm digging into her family affairs for my boss's gain.

I embrace the frosty spray of water, doing every-thing I can to cool my temperament. Being around Lily is testing my patience in a way I didn't think it would.

My shoulders bunch as I hunch against the wall tiles, looking down at my straining cock. And that vulgar mouth of hers does things to my cock that it shouldn't. I remind myself that in a matter of weeks, I'll be back by Luca's and Ara's sides, and it'll be as if this time never existed.

Don't get involved.

It's been the same brutal reminder circling in my head since the moment I was tasked with this role, and I'm doing a terrible fucking job at it.

Lily's scream splits the air, and a cold weight of dread sinks in my stomach. I'm running for the door, grabbing my gun with a speed I've never known, and praying to whatever God might listen that I make it in time.

20

LILY

"**B**rutish asshole," I grumble under my breath. It's not like I want to go on the date, and it's been a constant back-and-forth argument between Lorenzo and me since I admitted my father's demand. If anything, it's the only topic of conversation we've really circled over the last week.

What Lorenzo doesn't know about is the gift Riley Timber sent me or the time and date I'm supposed to meet with him.

It's tonight, and as I peel off the dress I wore to work, I consider my options. I could suck it up and go on the date. Or... I could not go. That will definitely be defying my father.

I bite at my bottom lip, tight knots twisting in my stomach as I think about finally disobeying him, but it's quickly followed by the thought of losing my mother and brother, or how he might lash out at them as well.

I pick up my phone and call my brother. He's tried to call a few times since the disastrous dinner with my parents, but I've been avoiding him, selfishly considering he won't be in town for much longer.

"She finally calls back. Hold up, give me one second." I can hear him lower the phone and say to someone, "I'm stepping out for five minutes. You take over the meeting." A few more words are exchanged and then he's back on. "About time you returned my call."

"You shouldn't be leaving meetings. I can call back."

"No. You're more important than any meeting. I wanted to talk to you anyway. You looked stressed at dinner. Is everything okay? Is it Dad?"

That final question prickles at the unsaid words. Vince had reservations about leaving me behind in Manhattan when he left for London. But if I cut ties with the family, then Mom will be stuck in that house with Dad, and I just don't have it in me to do that to her. Even the thought of it terrifies me.

"No, I hardly visit them," I admit as I put on a silk robe and sit at the end of my bed. I pick up a pink pillow and hug it to my chest. "I've been thinking about not going on this date tonight with this Timber guy."

There's a beat of silence, then he says, "I don't think that's a good idea."

I curl further into myself. I've always looked up to Vince; he's the only voice of reason I can depend on in our family. I half expected him to agree with me, as if I were seeking his permission.

"I know you don't like it. I don't like it either. But you know how he'll react. Dad's really good friends with Riley Timber's father. Just go on the date, entertain the idea. You never know, you might hit it off."

Hit it off? I doubt that. In the past, Vince has told me to ghost the men Dad pushes at me. And last week, he seemed happy about me being with Lorenzo. I know it's not a real relationship, but the idea that not even my family acknowledges someone of my own choosing hurts.

"Lily?"

"I thought you liked Lorenzo," I find myself quietly saying, dejected.

"I do. Look, he seems nice, but we have to be real for a second about your future," he begins, and my heart shatters. He was the last person I expected to hear this from. "I know it's hard right now, but it will get better. I promise. You know I didn't want to take over the companies, and now look at me. I'm thriving."

"But you're not being sent around like a bargaining tool," I retort angrily.

Silence again.

"I know I don't understand, because I'm not his daughter, but I'm certain that although he doesn't show it, he's doing this out of a sense of caring somewhere in that diabolical heart of his. It's just a date."

It's not just a date.

It's a lifetime of control and abuse.

We're all conditioned to work around him, programmed to step on eggshells around him, and I'm just too tired to dance for him anymore.

"I've been thinking about distancing myself from the family," I confess.

"What do you mean by that?" he says sharply. "Lily, you can't do that. What will you do? There's no way you can support yourself without the family money and—"

"I have my shop and—"

"I thought that was a cute passion project you were doing." Tears well in my eyes the moment I hear *passion project.* It was Vince who supported the idea, so my heart breaks realizing not even he truly believed in it. "Shit, Lily, that surely can't pay for your lifestyle. No, you absolutely cannot do that. You know he'll cut all ties with you. Hell, he'll make me and Mom cut all ties. Look, I know sometimes it feels a little restrictive, but we have everything we could ever ask for. What more could you want?"

Tears trail down my cheeks. I've squirreled away money for years now, in case my father ever did freeze my accounts. I'm self-sufficient and haven't depended on family money for a long time, other than the wardrobe my parents expect me to have for all the grand events I'm forced to attend.

I've done everything for my family, and yet, what has it ever done for me? But the ache in my chest intensifies at the thought of my mother and how my father might retaliate against her if I leave.

I thought my brother was my ally, but in truth, I have nobody.

"Lily?"

I wipe at my tears and break out into a maddening smile. "It was just a thought. Anyway, I need to get ready for a date. Talk soon!" I hang up the phone and take a shaky breath as I stare up at the ceiling.

Maybe I should run away. But the moment I do, I know the guilt will eat me alive.

I stand, adjusting my robe, then descend the stairs to grab a glass of wine. If I'm doing this, I need to have some liquid courage so I don't say the things that are truly on my mind.

I glance in the direction of Lorenzo's usual spot when I reach the bottom of the stairs. But instead of my overprotective fake boyfriend, I find a man wearing a white mask with a light-blue gem staring at me.

"Hi there, sweetheart."

I scream, pure dread running through my veins as memories of what happened in Italy assault me.

The guest bedroom door bursts open. Lorenzo and the intruder whip their guns at one another in unison.

The two stare at one another only for a moment before Lorenzo grits out, "You're early."

All thoughts of blood and fire evaporate as my heart pounds, but my focus drifts to something entirely different. My mouth dries as Lorenzo steps toward me, butt-ass naked, water dripping down his muscles as he leaves small puddles of water in his wake.

He doesn't look away from the man as he prowls toward me and comes to a stop as if blocking the man's view of me. My gaze dips down to his ass.

That's a good fucking ass.

The man in the mask chuckles as he lowers his own gun. "Since when have you ever been disappointed by punctuality? But if you want me to join you in the shower to help loosen you up a little, I'm not opposed."

His gaze drops to Lorenzo's cock, and I can't help but angle my head slightly to do the same. I swallow. Hard.

It's only semi-hard, and I'm terrified by the sheer size.

I don't even think that would fit inside me.

Tattoos mark his back and chest. They're random yet elegant, and I'm surprised by the renegade style. There's one that sticks out, the one on his arm that looks like a childlike angel with a bow. *Cupid maybe?*

"Quit being a smartass and remove your mask," Lorenzo instructs.

I lean into Lorenzo, my heart loudly beating as I find safety in hiding behind his size.

"Are you sure about that? Boss is pretty clear he doesn't want anyone seeing this pretty face. Aren't you scared your woman might fall for me?" the man asks.

"That's an order. Remove your mask. Don't make me regret this, you little shit," Lorenzo bites out. "I'll deal with the boss's punishment. I'm ordering you to remove the mask because… it's unsettling for her," he says, looking over his shoulder, his dark-brown gaze scanning over me, as if to make sure I'm okay.

The man seems hesitant to remove his mask.

"What's going on here?" I quietly ask. Nothing feels like mine anymore. Not my apartment. Not my life. Why am I doing everything to keep my shit together when everything is being imposed on me from the outside in? This, of all places, was meant to be my sanctuary, and now I don't even have that.

Another rule broken. I told him specifically not to invite his weirdo friends, and here we are, with some guy wearing a fucking mask, casually leaning against the couch in my living room, as if it's the most normal thing in the world.

The man removes his mask. I expect to see jagged scars or burns or something terrifying, not bright-blue eyes set in a youthful face. He's younger than I would've guessed; perhaps a few years younger than me. But there's an edge to him that definitely has me taking a step back. He smiles, and it's perfect yet malicious at the same time. This is not a good man. And although I know the same holds for Lorenzo, he feels different.

"I need to do some work tonight," Lorenzo says, turning to face me. My gaze immediately drops to his cock, and that palpable tension crackles between us. I hate how I naturally lean into him, and I have to force myself to step back. Because no matter how attractive he is, this constant invasion of my privacy is not okay.

Lorenzo snaps his fingers, and without any further communication, the other man throws a cushion toward him. He snatches it from the air and holds it in front of his cock. And I know it's for my sake.

"What the fuck is happening?" I find myself asking.

"The Armani household conducts a lot of underhanded business. When it gets messy, he calls on his hounds. Despite this guy being a total pain in my ass, I trust him to protect you in my absence," Lorenzo states. "The hounds, however, aren't usually allowed to show their faces, but I'll take the consequence in making an exception for you."

A breath whooshes out of me. "Are you kidding me? I'm not some object to be passed around. What, you didn't think I'm worth even a conversation when you're inviting murderers into my home?"

He frowns, almost as if confused. I don't know why he's shocked; we've been having constant arguments about boundaries, and he's disregarded them every step of the way.

"Murderer is such an ugly word. I prefer professional killer because I do get paid for it," the newcomer says.

"Shut up!" I snap at him before Lorenzo has the chance. I fold my arms over my chest. "I'm not some package to be handed off. This is my home, and you yourself are not even a guest. I'm sick of all of this shit! No one is coming for me, Lorenzo, so you need to pack your shit and get the fuck out of here!"

Silence fills the air as he stares at me, those brown eyes darkening.

The newcomer whistles. "I think I like her."

"You don't touch her," Lorenzo barks.

He throws his hands in the air. "Okay, Daddy, don't need to get all territorial with me."

Fuck this.

This is just a game to these people.

I shove past Lorenzo, but he grabs my wrist. "We're not done here."

I fling my arm out of his grasp. "No, we're very done here. It's funny how you tell me to have some backbone, to stand up against everyone, and yet you're no different than any of them! If anything, you're the worst! You can shove your duty right up your ass. Don't even speak to me. We're done!"

I walk to the kitchen, my head held high as I reach for the wine.

Fuck this and everyone involved.

I'll go on this stupid date like a good girl, performing as expected, but I'll be calling Ara tomorrow. I don't care about the circumstances anymore. I need Lorenzo gone and to figure out what I want for myself.

Because this is not it.

21

———

LORENZO

Despite only being eight in the evening, the line to enter Dmitri's club, Lev, is already wrapped around the corner. Most of those lined up are wearing bold outfits and masks. I'm not a fan of wearing the fuckers, but considering it's a themed club where everyone is expected to do so, I wear a simple black wolf-shaped one.

The bouncer at the front, wearing a bull mask, stops me. "Name?"

"Lorenzo Moretti."

He doesn't have a list to look at, but permits me inside.

The heavy beat of music oozes from the esteemed establishment. Stairs trail up three levels on either side, but most who enter never make it past the first floor. Bright lights flash stripes across the dance floor, and the booths along the walls are crammed with people.

Manhattan truly is the place that never sleeps. I wonder at what time some of these people began partying and when they'll finish. Or maybe this is only a continuation from the night before, since most of them purchase drugs that are being circulated by the staff wearing bunny masks. They offer trays of alcohol and suspicious bags for sale. This is the place one goes if they never want the party to end; concoctions of drugs and euphoria that will keep them awake, dancing, and fucking for days.

Heading toward the staircase on the right, I don't need a guided tour of Dmitri's club. I've been here plenty of times before. When I reach the second floor, I briefly scan the lit-up red rooms on either side. Admittance into these rooms is for VIPs who purchase the service of whomever might be inside, depending on their preferred theme. Two of the rooms are already blocked out, meaning they're occupied.

I can't help but wonder what Lily might think if she knew places like this existed. I wonder if she's been at Lev herself. If she has, she's certainly not ventured past the ground floor. The upper levels are where temptation and sin are catered to and encouraged.

This club is based on fantasy and animalistic pleasure. However, more often than not, those who enter vaguely know each other. In fact, most of them want to be known, though some prefer to slip under the radar so they can enjoy personal affairs, the mystery, or often the sexual fantasies they might not ordinarily get elsewhere.

The two bouncers who stand at the next staircase size me up but say nothing as I proceed to the third level, where business is conducted or private parties are held.

It's different from when I first met Dmitri here, and he had women dressed in leather and rabbit masks all over him. Now they fixate on other powerful men partaking in the depravity on offer.

Two men have removed their masks, and I'm not surprised to see they're well-known businessmen within the wealthy circle of Dmitri's professional dealings.

Dmitri, however, sits in the center, his legs crossed, his horned skull-like mask resting on a table beside him. The third floor is the only one where masks are permitted to be removed. His blue gaze follows me expectantly as he nurses a drink that won't be finished by the end of the night. I imagine he holds one to feign a recovery he hasn't yet truly reached since his brain surgery. I've heard he's become less active with regard to his club; however, I think that has more to do with who's waiting at home for him. It's strange to know that even a playboy like Dmitri can settle for one woman.

A figure stumbles from the private bathroom on the left, still pulling up his fly, and walks straight into me.

"Sorry, my dude," Vince says, looking up, his own mask already removed. His eyes are dilated, and he squints, as if trying to make out who I am. I make it easier by removing my mask.

Vince's eyes widen. "My man!" He jumps joyfully. "I should've known you two were friends!" He points at Dmitri, shaking his finger as if he were holding out on some secret. I don't know what similarities Dmitri and I could possibly have for him to conclude we're friendly toward one another.

Then again, Vince is also shitfaced on fuck knows what, so in his world, perhaps everyone is good friends.

Vince staggers toward the table, drops to his knees at the edge, and snorts a line of coke. I briefly glance at Dmitri, who says nothing. The other two men cheer Vince on like he's some kind of legend.

"Come on, do a line with me, man!" Vince looks to me, wide-eyed, his smile just as big.

"It's not my thing." I look down at the poker chips and cards in front of us. Most of the chips are piled in front of Dmitri. Doesn't seem like much of a challenge, since everyone else at the table is off their fucking faces and more fascinated with the women's tits on display.

"Hey, handsome," one of them purrs, walking up behind me, her nails grazing across my shoulder. "You seem tense," she says as she grabs either side of my neck as if to start massaging.

I place my hand on hers. "I recommend you don't

touch me. I'll only say it once." I give her hand a forceful enough squeeze to make my point, but not hard enough to hurt.

She's quick to recoil, and I have the sudden urge to shower all over again because of her presumptuous touch.

Lily's blue eyes flash in my mind, and I readjust my suit, uncomfortable. I don't know why I think of her when another woman touches me. All I know is I hate the smell of this woman because it isn't the sweet floral scent to which I've become accustomed.

Dmitri chuckles, and I don't like how he looks at me, as if knowing something I don't. "Should we play another hand?"

"Yes, let's!" Vince slams his palms on the table excitedly. He shoves his hands in his pockets and then looks up at me with a smile. "Fuck, I don't have any more cash on me."

I raise an eyebrow but dip into my inside pocket. Money is only a tool; if it creates favor in a situation like tonight, then so be it. I throw some on the table, and Vince's eyes widen as the dealer offers us chips. This is by no means a professional game. Those who enjoy gambling know to go to the Balmere club, which Luca owns, for that purpose.

Vince sits beside me, grabbing one of the women, who squeals as he places her on his lap. He licks his lips excitedly, and the difference between the man I met at the Taylors' house and the one sitting here now is like day and night. I wonder what Lily would think if she saw her brother in this state. I don't usually care for what others do in their spare time, but I imagine this is very different from the respectful man she's built him up to be.

"Vince was telling me he's only in town for another week," Dmitri begins as our cards are dealt. Two cards are placed in front of me, and I take a peek—Queen of Hearts and Queen of Spades.

Not a bad start.

I'm not usually a gambling man, but I've played my fair share of poker.

"Oh, helping your father with business here?" I ask, pretending to deliberate on whether to check or fold. I call.

"Yeah, something like that," Vince says, still licking his lips and raising with a quarter of his chips. Interesting. If this is how he plays, I can see how Dmitri bled him dry already.

"Yeah, well, if you weren't fucking it up, you'd be back in London already," one of the other men says.

"I'm not fucking it up," Vince says defensively, and his gaze sheepishly moves between Dmitri and me as he shrugs. "My old man and I have different views on how things should be run. That's all. Every business has highs and lows. Surely, you've experienced it as well."

"As if my dad would ever let me run his business," one of the others scoffs. "As long as he keeps putting money into my account, I'll stay out of his hair and be on my best behavior. Well, at least I won't be caught. I fold."

Vince's knee starts bouncing, even when he tries to distract himself with the woman on his other one.

"It's never easy when a deal goes wrong," I say sympathetically, and Vince looks at me like I'm a beacon of hope.

"Yeah. Like, shit happens all the time. It's a shame my father's so hung up on Lily dating Riley because I actually like you, Lorenzo. You're not a bad guy," he says, watching as the next three cards are turned over. Another queen sits amongst them.

Ironically, he's wrong about both. The idea that I'm not a bad guy is laughable, because on the wrong night or if I'm in a bad mood, I can be the worst. And Lily certainly is not going on a date with that Riley dickhead.

"I certainly don't intend on handing Lily over to any man, whether your father approves of it or not. Why is he so hell-bent on the idea that I'm not the right guy?" I question carefully, making it sound like it's coming from a place of insecurity, when the true question is why her father is suddenly so insistent on her marrying.

Vince shrugs as he raises two-thirds of his remaining chips with a cocky grin.

Dmitri doesn't say anything as he folds, silently watching us.

"Fuck it, I fold," the guy sitting across from me says. "I need to take a piss anyway."

"Fold," the next man says as he grins and shoves his face into the tits of the woman on his lap. Like the others, she's wearing a rabbit mask, and she giggles beneath the mask. "I could drown in these all day," he says, his voice muffled.

Vince is staring with a shit-eating grin as he only half answers me. "My father's old school. You know, gaining reputation and favor through family connections. Even when it bites him in the ass, and he wants me to clean up after his mess. He never fucking changes," he says, distracted by the woman on his knee as he squeezes the inside of her thigh, his gaze raking over her body appreciatively.

"Is that why you're stressed? Has a deal recently gone sour?" I ask, feigning sympathy and concern. I need something more tangible. It's obvious he despises his father, and for good reason. His dad's a dick, but this offers me nothing to go on.

The dealer flips the next card. Queen.

I don't raise, sensing that Vince is a cocky hotshot who will most likely go all-in. I don't care about the outcome of this game. The only thing that interests me is the next answer Vince offers me.

He glances between his cards and the ones on the table. "I mean, deals are always stressful, aren't they?

They're always a gamble. I just wish he wouldn't bring me into his shit, then expect me to roll over like a good boy and do as I'm told. Like, you either want me to take over the business completely or you don't, right?" He looks up at me then, hopeful, and when I nod, he seems satisfied by the validation.

"All in," he says with a smile.

"If there's anything I can do to help, let me know. I care deeply about your sister. I'd rather take away as many stresses as I can," I say, matching his chips.

He watches me do so, a small swallow making his throat bob. He's definitely bluffing.

The woman across from us squeals as Vince's friend leaves the table, leading her by the hand to the second floor. Vince watches them with a wide grin, easily distracted in his current state.

"Thanks, dude, but unless you can dig my dad out of a financial pickle, I still don't think he'll accept you. You know, you kind of look like a criminal." Vince chuckles as he reveals his hand. A pair of kings, giving him three in total, including the one on the table.

"If that's what your father needs, then perhaps you should set up a meeting. I could be inclined to invest in something other than real estate," I say, revealing my own hand, and he pales.

I see the corner of Dmitri's mouth kick up.

"Fuck, that's some wild luck," Vince says, licking his lips. "And, nah, don't worry, I've got my dad's back.

Just more work for me, you know. You're good if I pay you back when I see you next, right? For now, I kind of want to enjoy the second floor." He turns his attention back to the woman on his lap and asks, "Care to join me?" She giggles flirtatiously, playing into the fantasy that's expected of Lev.

He doesn't wait for a response as he stands and takes her with him. We watch him stumble down the stairs.

"You're just going to let him leave without paying you?" Dmitri asks curiously.

I have the distinct feeling that the other guy passed out in the bathroom. I pick up my glass of whiskey and take a sip, still noticing Dmitri hasn't touched any of his.

"I don't care about the money. What I want to know is what trouble his father's gotten himself into." It's not uncommon for deals to go wrong, but the consequence always depends on the kind of people you've been dealing with.

"Have you noticed any Bratva dealings since you killed the lion?" I ask Dmitri. Something definitely feels underhanded here, and if it's not by Luca's or my hand, then we've got ourselves a problem.

"Not that I've heard. I'm assuming you haven't seen anything out of sorts in the city either. You think they're involved in the attack on Luca's vacation villa?"

I'm still watching as the woman helps Vince down

the stairs. This is precisely what type of guy I thought he might be. Someone like him couldn't run a business effortlessly, not to mention showing such an increased profit in the way that he has.

The dealer starts converting my chips to cash, offering me the amount I started with plus some. I leave it on the table as I stand. My business here is done. "Keep the money. Think of it as payment for your assistance here."

Dmitri chuckles as he leans back. "Always business, aren't you, Lorenzo. I would consider this a favor between friends."

I turn on him then, pulling my wolf mask back on. "I don't do friends."

He shakes his head and raises an eyebrow. "You also don't smile, but I hear Lily Taylor can make you do that."

An icy tension runs between us. I don't like her name coming from his lips or what he might be trying to imply. I turn my back as I begin texting Tyson, one of the hounds. Despite his hot-shot temperament, he's the best for a slow hunt. He likes to take his time. So I specifically request that until Vince leaves Manhattan, he follow his every move and update me on anything peculiar.

When I reach the second level, Vince is being pulled into one of the red rooms.

I'm not even out of the club doors before I hit call.

"Did you miss me, Lorenzo?" Sky asks with amusement in his tone.

"Don't fuck with me," I growl, irritated.

He chuckles, and I want to wring his fucking neck. It's that cocky laugh that pisses me off so much. Most likely because it reminds me so much of my younger brother.

"Calling to see if your princess is all tucked up in bed?" he asks in a sing-song way. When I don't reply, he continues. "I don't know how to break it to you, buddy, but she's on a date."

My blood runs cold, and my hand closes into a fist. "*What?*"

"I tried to stop her, but damn, she's a little spitfire when she wants to be, and who am I to get in between someone and potential love? Don't worry, I'm keeping close to make sure she's safe." He's intentionally winding me up, and although I trust him with her safety, I know for a fucking fact he probably didn't even try to detain her in any way. If anything, his mischievous little mind probably encouraged it. "I mean, it's not like anything's happening between you two, right? It's just a little security gig and all."

I can imagine the fucking grin splitting his face right now, and I carefully bite out each word. "I'm. Going. To. Fucking. Kill. You."

He laughs. "Not before you kill this guy, I hope. He looks like the handsy type."

I'm seeing red, especially after I specifically told her she wasn't going on any date.

Over my dead fucking body.

I hang up, bringing up the tracker on her phone.

And she wanted me to give her privacy, I internally scoff.

This woman is driving me fucking insane.

22

LILY

An awkward silence fills the space as I sit across from Riley Timber. Despite my original preconception of a man in his late forties, he's objectively attractive. However, as he smiles and charms the server, I'm left to fidget with my hands beneath the table. I can now see why he's already had two wives.

I gulp down half my champagne, trying my best to eat away the nerves. I'm not nervous about being on the date, just about everything this entails. I can see the domino effect. My father will try to pressure us into a quick engagement, ship me off into a loveless marriage, and force me to leave New York for Los Angeles, where Riley is based.

The restaurant has been entirely booked out, and we sit alone in the dining room, a clear show of his money. My only small comfort is the hound who sits outside in front of the neighboring restaurant.

I came here under my brother's recommendation, but I hate being here. It's not easy to shove it down anymore when all I want is to be heard. I feel my world shrinking, and even if I wanted to ask for help, who would I turn to?

The first person who comes to mind is Lorenzo, and I quickly try to shake away the idea of that. Lorenzo isn't someone who can quietly help me wipe away my problems. No, he'll burn them to the ground in a devastating manner. There is no in-between or balance with someone like Lorenzo. And even then, it's presumptuous to think he'd even care to help when he'll so easily reject me and remind me it's not part of his "job" or "mission."

"That'll be all, honey," he says charismatically to the server. She bites her bottom lip, avoiding my gaze as she saunters off. I take a sip of my drink, needing all the help I can get tonight.

Considering my father is addicted to alcohol, I've never overtly liked it, but I do enjoy the freedom it gives me, even if it's temporary.

"So, I hear you have a cute hobby selling flowers," Riley says. "Do you plan on selling the shop soon?"

I offer a polite smile that I know doesn't reach my eyes. "Cute is an interesting word to describe my business."

"Well, it is. And surely you don't make that much

money with it. Considering you went to Harvard, surely your skills are better utilized elsewhere. Not that you'll have to use them if this date goes well."

My manicured nails dig into my thighs as I bite my tongue. "And if this date doesn't go well?"

His harsh gaze meets mine. He's just like my father, sharing the same mentality toward women. I braced myself for it, half expected it. But I don't have it in me to pretend or even hide my distaste.

Why am I even here?

I tried so hard to prepare myself for this, but it's like all that energy of pretending has finally reached its limit.

The only person I can still care for is my mother. Because if I don't have the fight in me anymore to pretend I'm the good daughter, and I'm cut from the family... what will happen to her?

Riley scoffs. "Do you desire more than simply a dinner at the restaurant I own for this date? Name your price. A helicopter ride over the city? Diamonds? Tell me what it is that impresses Henrith Taylor's daughter on a first date? No amount of money is too much."

"The problem is she's already taken," a rough voice says from behind me.

Dread runs through me at the lethalness that hangs off each word. I slowly turn and face Lorenzo, who is dressed immaculately in his usual suit that doesn't entirely hide the danger he exudes.

"And who are you?" Riley scoffs at Lorenzo. My

heart starts pounding, and it's the first burst of adrenaline I've felt this entire evening. I shouldn't be surprised he's here, but I didn't expect him to get here so soon. I thought I'd at least have until the end of the night. I briefly glance in the direction where the hound was sitting, realizing he's no longer there.

"Who I am is irrelevant. This woman belongs to me. Look at her again or try to contact her, and we'll have a problem," Lorenzo growls. "Get up, we're leaving," he orders me.

I'm torn. I don't want to be here, but I don't want another man telling me what to do, treating me like property.

That's when Lorenzo's dark-brown gaze slices over to me expectantly, and I can see the rage unfurling there. I'm out of my mind for choosing to leave with the most dangerous man I've ever met, and yet, I find myself standing, as if charmed, a part of me almost grateful that *someone* came for me at all.

"You will sit down, Lily. Henrith promised me—"

With lightning speed, Lorenzo steps into Riley's space, and I jump at the sound of something being slammed into the table. Riley's eyes and mouth widen, and as he goes to scream, Lorenzo covers his mouth with his hand, staring him dead in the eye, his back blocking my view of whatever just happened.

"You can tell whoever you want about this night, but know I will find you, and it won't be pretty when I do. You don't come anywhere near her ever again. You tell Henrith the date was pleasant enough, but that you can't continue seeing her because you've chosen to pursue the stripper you knocked up months ago. Do you understand?"

Riley's eyes bulge as tears stream down his reddening face, and he shakes his head frantically.

It's not until Lorenzo steps back that I see the fork embedded in Riley's hand and the blood spreading across the white table cloth.

My mouth gapes at the sight, and I'm reminded of the men in Italy. Flashbacks of other memories I try to shove back down. My mother's face bleeding. My own cut hands...

"We're leaving," Lorenzo says, grabbing my hand and dragging me out.

"I'm not—" I'm swept from my feet and thrown over his shoulder. The shock of his gentle force shakes away the memories I struggle to force away.

"Not up for discussion," he growls. I look up, facing Riley for the first time, but he's not even looking at me. He's weeping as he stares at his hand in shock.

A slight sense of satisfaction unfurls in my stomach, and I'm disgusted with myself for even having the feeling.

Lorenzo is a bad person.

I know this, and yet... I don't fight him as he takes me away, tears welling in my eyes as an exuberant amount of relief washes through me.

It's selfish, and quickly taken over by the reality of

the situation. We're already halfway up the street as the shock subsides and sheer horror about what's to come creeps in.

My father is going to lose his mind.

"Put me down, Lorenzo," I demand. He ignores me. "Put me down!" I knee him in the stomach and then curse as I hurt myself on his ridiculously hard abs. But he puts me down gently, and I'm humiliated at the few people who walk past us, staring.

"You have no idea what you've done," I tell him, eyes wide. But it's not just his fault. I'm just as responsible, because I found relief in the fact that he came for me.

My mother's face comes to mind, and I'm terrified of how my father might respond to what happened tonight. I'm petrified that my mother lives in that house with him. If he has an outburst over this, she's the one who will face the wrath for my selfish actions. Even if I wanted to be taken away, it's still only Lorenzo who has the courage to do it, and it only serves to remind me of how weak I am.

I can't stand it. He's everything I'm not.

"I'm scared." I can hear my eight-year-old self as a memory hits me.

"It's okay. Everything will be okay," my mother says as she hugs me.

"Can't we run away?" I beg, terrified of the monster my father has become.

"No, Lily, we have to stay."

And stay we did.

I push away the painful memories bubbling to the surface, and it only ignites the fire in my stomach. Anger toward my father. Toward Lorenzo. But mostly at myself. I push through the crowd, furiously trying to run away from my own self-loathing.

I'm still such a coward.

Like I'm hiding again with my mother, covering my ears and wishing for it all to go away.

Every step I take, I'm aware of Lorenzo's that follow. I can't breathe with or without him, but I don't want him to see this part of me. I don't need to be reminded of how much of a coward I am by facing a man who is anything but.

He takes what he wants. When he wants. Unapologetically.

And now I'm comparing myself to a killer.

I really am losing my mind.

Everything was perfectly set into routine. If I were the good daughter, then the monster was less likely to appear. But I can't run away from it anymore.

"I've had enough of this, Lorenzo!" I swing around to face him, my eyes brimming with tears. It's too much. I can't keep fighting everyone as the walls continue to close in around me. "You just don't get it, do you? My father is going to lose his fucking mind when he finds out what happened in there."

"Why don't you make a decision for yourself for once?" he asks simply, and his gaze narrows when I scoff at him. "Don't scoff at me like that. You can't stand it when I tell you that because you know it's the truth. You're so scared to break out of your safety net, to explore the real world on your own. Who would Lily Taylor be if she weren't under her father's thumb?"

I flinch and then lock my body into place because all I want to do is shove him. Hate him. Curse him for being so imposing and pretending like he knows anything about me.

I turn and continue walking, ignoring anything he calls out behind me. Droplets of rain begin to fall on my face, but I don't care as I continue through the sea of people that begin to sprout umbrellas.

The rain is refreshing as I charge on, no idea where I'm going. Will I go home to repeat the same routine?

I bump into someone, and immediately apologize to the teenage boy who's dragging a sign.

"Sorry. Did you want in?" he asks, almost embarrassed. "The movie started ten minutes ago, and no one else showed up, but I can reopen it if you want?"

I look from him to the sign. A cinema? I look down at the board that showcases the old-school romantic film playing. Lorenzo will hate a black and white romantic film.

"I know exactly what you're thinking, Sunshine," he growls behind me. "We're not done with this conversation."

"Yes, please," I say to the teenager and then make a

beeline for the cinema. I hear Lorenzo curse behind me as he handles paying for tickets.

"Theater three," the teenager calls out from behind as I step into the small cinema. A popcorn machine sits empty, a few snacks behind the counter. The woman behind it seems surprised to see a customer but points in the direction of the screening room.

The first two theaters are closed, and I walk into the third. There are rows of empty seats, the black and white film already playing. I can't even remember the last time I went out to see a movie. I step into the middle row, skirting across numerous seats until I get to one that feels central to the screen.

I fold my arms over my chest as Lorenzo comes to sit beside me, his imposing size filling his seat, his arm pressing against mine.

"There's literally a roomful of seats," I growl.

"The only seat I ever need is the one beside yours," he says, making himself more comfortable. I hate how my heart skips a beat, longing for what? A confession? Something deeper with Lorenzo?

My scowl returns. There's just no reasoning with this man. And unlike the other times I took him to a place I knew he'd hate, he's pretending to actually *enjoy* this.

The man infuriates me. More than words can even express. He's an asshole. Demanding. Rude. Arrogant in every way. Just once, I want him to look at me as more than a pitiful woman trapped in her own life.

I hate how he shoves it in my face.

I know I can't keep living like this. I need to stand up to my father, but the last time I tried that... I hide away from the memory, the scar between my shoulder blades acting as a cruel reminder.

I just want to live for me. What I want. When I want. How I want.

I side-eye Lorenzo, who pays me no attention. He looks stoic as he watches the screen, even when I know he's interested in anything but the film. I uncross my arms, exhausted by myself, and rest my hand beside his. It's so much bigger than mine.

My gaze roams down his suit jacket and lower. He's always well-dressed. In fact, I haven't seen him wear anything other than a full suit. It's as if he never stops, constantly in impeccable shape. But he's only human, right? Surely, he has some kind of weakness.

My lips part when I notice the bulge in his pants. When I look back up, he's staring at me, and I swallow. "I didn't think the movie was that exciting," I jab.

"Your bratty attitude seems to excite my cock. It's becoming a problem," he says matter-of-factly.

My eyebrows furrow. I never know how to read Lorenzo. I don't understand this magnetic pull and tension between us, but I know my body yearns for his in ways I've never felt with anyone else. He infuriates me, yet it seems to wreak havoc on my body.

"You'd better stop biting that bottom lip, Sunshine,

before I do something about it myself," he growls, trying to focus on the film.

I take a harsh swallow, that bundle of fury and anxiety needing a release. I'm tired of fighting the tension that runs between us.

"What will you do about it?" I daringly ask, pushing him as much as he's been pushing me. "Will I be *punished*?"

23

LORENZO

"Will I be *punished*?" she asks.

This woman is dangerous. I shouldn't want her. Should definitely punish her for her bratty attitude, but even my patience and self-control are fraying.

She's too sweet.

Too innocent.

I know all of these things, but I'm still sitting beside her. Not because I've been ordered to, but because I *want* to.

"You can't handle me, Sunshine. I told you that the night we met, and it remains the truth now," I tell her honestly.

Being with her day in and day out has become a living hell beyond the means of simply babysitting. I've been profusely looking into her family affairs, betraying her in some ways and trying to set her free in others.

It all comes back to her.

This delicious temptation.

"Yet you're the one telling me to make my own choices," she says daringly, and slowly drops to her knees in front of me.

I put a finger under her chin, forcing her to look up at me. "Careful, little one. I'm not someone to be messed with."

"So you keep saying. I'm starting to think your dick has a defect with how shy you are about bringing it out around me."

I gently wrap my fingers around her throat, and a slow smile blossoms across her face. "Careful, sweetheart."

Her body always tells me everything I need to know. She loves being forced into submission. She especially loves the pain.

Her fingers skirt up the inside of my leg and land on my belt. My jaw tics as I consider stopping her. I know I should, but dear God, she looks stunning on her knees. The black and white movie flashes on the screen behind her, silhouetting her like some kind of fucking angel.

But that sassy mouth of hers is all sin. And so, I let her undo my belt and zipper. When she frees my cock from my boxers, she gulps, and I can't help the arrogant smirk.

"Is size a defect for you, sweetheart? Bitten off more than you can chew?"

She stares, dazed for a moment, and then she begins to laugh. I frown immediately.

"My dick doesn't often get laughed at," I growl.

She leans back, staring at it in disbelief. "I just, I don't know if that will fit."

"I'll make sure it fits."

Those bright-blue eyes blink innocently. I expect her to run. In fact, I pray she does because I don't have it in me to fight temptation anymore. My other hand remains fastened to the armrest, ensuring I don't grab her and allow whatever she's willing to give me.

Her small hand wraps around my cock, and I hiss at her cool touch. My cock jumps at the slow strokes, and she stares into my eyes, as if looking for some weakness in my armor. Little does she realize, it's slowly becoming her.

"I want your mouth wrapped around my cock, Sunshine. You've been particularly bratty lately, and we need to put that attitude to good use." I barely recognize the deep rumble of my voice.

Her breath hitches, but she leans up on her knees, and just as she's about to lower her mouth over my cock, she glances around, as if suddenly remembering where we are. "That wasn't a question," I growl.

Her sharp gaze snaps back to my face, and I can see the determination in her eyes. Her desire to please me, even when I know she can't fucking stand me.

Her tongue slides up the underside of my shaft, following the vein, before she widens her mouth to take me in.

"Fuck." She's so fucking perfect. I grip the armrest tighter, my other hand threading through her loose golden curls. I take everything she's willing to give as my cock hits the back of her throat over and over again. "Such a good girl."

So. Fucking. Perfect.

Never would I have imagined that this woman would impact me the way she does. Her tenacity in continuously talking back to me when I thought she'd be my easiest mission yet. But she surprises me at every turn, those lips far more suited to other things than running her mouth.

Fuck. I lean back. It's been so long. I haven't touched another woman since being given this mission, and the wait... It all feels worth it now.

Her small hands palm my shaft, her mouth unable to take all of me.

I want to see her break around my cock.

I'm an asshole. The worst for taking something so pure and beautiful and wanting to dirty it up, but my cock throbs with every stroke of her tongue. Every depraved thought that she's about to come undone in front of me.

My fingers curl, and I curse under my breath as I blow into her mouth, shoving my cock in farther than she's taken it yet. But like a good girl, she swallows.

She sucks and slurps, coaxing more out of my sensitive cock. Maybe not such a good girl. She seems pleased with herself as she pulls her head back, licking at the tip of my cock, all while never breaking our eye contact.

The tension that bunched her shoulders only moments ago seems to recede as she licks her lips, and I can't help but trail my thumb over the bottom one, making sure not one drop goes to waste, and wishing I were stuffing her cunt with my cock instead.

But I'm not ready to tarnish her in that way because a small part of me understands it'll change our relationship entirely.

I shove my cock back into my pants and zip them up before redoing the belt. "Such a good fucking girl."

She straightens ever so slightly, and I try not to smirk at her immediate reaction to being praised. It's as if she were built just for me.

A subtle movement in my peripheral vision grabs my attention, and I push Lily to the ground, covering her with my body as a gunshot goes off. Pain explodes against my arm, but I'm pulling out my gun, countering with two shots of my own.

The figure takes off, and I give chase, bursting through the cinema doors and looking toward the entrance where the intruder bolts out onto the street.

"Lorenzo!" Lily screams. Adrenaline courses through my veins. I can't give chase, because if I do, she'll be on her own.

I pull out my phone and call Sky as I stride over to her. "We've just been shot at. I need you and the other hounds to find the culprit."

"Got it." Sky shouldn't be too far from the restaurant where he was watching over Lily, so with any luck, we'll find the asshole quickly.

Lily's ghostly white as I gently grab her arm. "We're going to my place."

"You're bleeding," she says, concerned, and I look down at my arm for the first time, adrenaline still coursing through me. I've had worse, but I don't care about any of that. The moment I heard that gun go off, the gripping terror of the bullet hitting Lily was like an arrow to my heart.

Without a doubt, mission aside, I'm not willing to lose her.

24

LILY

"It's fine. It's just a graze," Lorenzo says as we pull into the driveway of a house on the water.

"It's not fine if you're bleeding," I grit out, becoming more irritated by his lunacy than anything else. It's dark, so I can't see much of the property from the outside, but when he leads me through the garage, I'm momentarily stunned by the beauty of the home.

It's all dark woods and black leather in the living space, leading to an open kitchen with a long, black marble island. Skylights stretch across the ceiling, and large windows line the back wall, giving a spectacular view of the dock and city lights sparkling from across the water.

Lorenzo throws his car keys onto the counter, then turns, realizing I've stopped dead in my tracks. I don't know what I expected his home to look like, but this wasn't it. His eyebrows dip slightly, and I refocus on our argument.

"If you weren't so hell-bent on not going to the hospital, I might not worry." I come to a stop in front of him. "Don't you have an underworld doctor or something?"

He raises an eyebrow, seemingly indifferent about the wound. I know he wants to chase whoever shot at us. He's been firing off commands over the phone ever since we left the cinema. I'm still in complete shock that someone would actually shoot at us in a movie theater, of all places.

Yet, all I cared about was *him*.

"Unfortunately, it's too early in the night to sneak into the veterinary clinic to see the doc," he deadpans. My jaw drops. I don't even know how to respond to that, then I see the slightest twitch of his lips.

"Are you seriously making a joke right now?"

"Well, I assumed when you said underworld doctor, you had some inspiration from some TV show."

I throw my hands in the air. "You're such an asshole sometimes."

"Only sometimes?"

"Sit." I point to the barstool. "Do you have a first aid kit here?"

"I told you it's fine," he insists, and I pin him with a deadly glare.

"I said *sit.*"

The asshole's lips twitch again, but he does as he's told, pointing to a bottom drawer in the kitchen.

I round the counter to the drawer he indicated. It's strange. Despite the circumstances, for the first time, I feel like instead of falling into chaos or a nauseating swirl of uncertainty and despair—I'm calm.

Maybe it's because of the indifference that Lorenzo shows for his wound, or perhaps I'm just so sick of being frightened. So tired of circling around other people's expectations. Tonight, the reality finally hit that I'm not guaranteed tomorrow. This is the second time I've been shot at... and I'm fucking done with not having that power in my own hands.

Lorenzo's phone buzzes, and he picks up immediately. Whoever is on the line is rapidly speaking in a language I can't understand, most likely Italian.

"Yes, boss. I'll update you," he says as I stop in front of him with the kit.

I don't know how to accomplish it, but I want to protect him as well.

Ridiculous, considering how self-sufficient he is, even if he's also reckless at the same time.

"The hounds are searching for him now. They'll find the fucker who shot at us today, and when they do, I'll make sure he pays for what he did," he promises.

"Good" is all I say as I open the kit.

Lorenzo's eyebrows dip slightly, as if he's surprised by my response. I cross my arms in front of me.

"It can't be that surprising, can it? He hurt you. Now, take your shirt off."

"So bossy tonight."

"Can you please take this seriously?" I bite back. "Just for once, work with me."

A slow smirk appears on his expression. "I thought we always worked well together."

I pin him with another glare, and he actually has the audacity to chuckle. I'm so stunned by the foreign sound that my hands are on my hips as he peels back his suit jacket, then removes his shirt.

"Have you ever stitched up a wound?" he asks, nodding to the kit.

I pause, memories resurfacing of times I had to tend to small wounds my mother endured. But I can't confess that out loud. It's always been our secret.

It's so fucked-up.

"I had to tend to some of Vince's small cuts when he was a kid. You know, boys being boys. I'm sure I can figure it out."

"Hmm" is all he says, and I don't like the way he watches me, as if seeing straight through my lie.

"How are you so calm about this?" I question, wanting to shift the subject. It's confusing that not only is he calm, but that he almost seems to find the situation amusing.

"I'm anything but. I'm doing everything I can so you don't see the violence roiling beneath the surface," he replies.

I stare for a moment at the tattoos scattered over his arms and stomach. Then I inhale a sharp breath when I see the deep red wound across his bicep. Our eyes lock, and that ever-present tension between us flares. His jaw tics, and I can almost sense that we're both holding back.

Unsaid confessions.

Wavering emotions.

Because if I delve any deeper with Lorenzo, I know there's no coming back from it. Yet the invisible thread that pulls us together is a palpable and sensational thing.

And for once, I don't want to play by the rules.

I don't want to hold myself back.

I don't care what others might think is good or bad for me.

Lorenzo is a devil in disguise, but he's bleeding for me because he took a bullet in my place.

I tentatively step forward. I almost expect him to push me away or tell me he's fine. I'm here for his wound, and yet, I can't tear my gaze from his as I step between his knees and bring my hand to cup his stubbly jaw.

A spark ignites when I touch him, that undercurrent that's always smoldering between us, erupting and feeding me adrenaline. My heart begins to race as I offer a comfort and vulnerability I've never known before.

He may be a killer, but I know this man will never

hurt me.

And I want to protect him. In whatever way I might be able to.

His gaze drops to my lips as I gently stroke his jaw.

Guilt floods me for taking my wrath out on him tonight, when he once again gave me his strength to walk away from a situation I didn't fully have the courage to remove myself from.

As if knowing my inner thoughts and addressing my demons, he slowly touches his forehead to mine. I'm surrounded by his dominating presence. This man, whom I don't entirely understand, calls to me on a primal level.

"We're okay," I breathe, stroking his jaw once again and pressing my other hand to his chest.

Those words feel like our undoing as I inhale his breath, as if fueling my own lungs. His nose brushes against mine, and I close my eyes, simply to be in this moment, to feel him cocooning me in the enigma that is Lorenzo Moretti.

"Are we?" Lorenzo's voice is soft, and my eyelids spring open, surprised by the gentle tone of a man who is usually cruel and guarded. There's a softness in his expression I haven't seen before, something I want to drink in before it vanishes.

Lorenzo scoops me into his arms, barely wincing from his still-bleeding wound, and I hook my legs around his waist. He pushes back the loose strands of my hair, his callused hand cupping my jaw in the same manner I had him only moments ago.

He walks us toward a bedroom, his cock straining between us.

Slowly, as if he's still fighting the magnetism between us, his head dips to mine. So I embrace courage and bring my lips to his in a gentle kiss. A confirmation of our safety. His hand slides from my jaw to the back of my neck, deepening the kiss, demanding more. I open to him, offering everything and anything he needs from me as I desperately feed from him.

He lowers us to the bed, his cock pressing against the material directly over my pussy. My legs are still wrapped around him, as if I'm scared he might pull away at any moment. He guides my hands above my head, his fingers threading through mine as he holds me in place. I feel exposed, despite still being fully dressed.

I pull his bottom lip between my teeth, eliciting a low, carnal growl I want to draw from him again.

Lorenzo might be a monster, but he still bleeds.

He bleeds for me, and I'm too tired to fight my attraction to him.

Too scared to not explore this chemistry—when I don't know if it might very well be the last chance I have to do so.

25

LORENZO

ine.

I need to explore, to mark every inch of her as mine. To ensure no part of her is harmed after tonight, just so I can damage it myself.

Her small whimper destroys the last of any restraint I might have had. But her readiness for me, her neediness and demand for the same thing... I can't deny either of us any longer.

My hand slides up her smooth leg, pushing the silk dress over her hips. I match her feisty, insistent kisses. She's quick to undo my belt and zipper, freeing my cock from its painful confines, and I straighten up to step out of my pants. Lily sits up on her knees and bunches the bottom of her dress, trying to pull it up and over her shoulders.

"Let me," I growl, wanting nothing more than to unwrap my own present. She pouts but does as she's told. She always has in the bedroom; it's the only time I can get the little brat to obey.

I replace her hands with mine, pulling the dress over her head, appreciating every inch of her I uncover. So fucking perfect. Tits that are just the right fit for my palms. Hips that demand my grip.

She reaches for my cock, but I let a disapproving grunt escape. Her pouty expression remains, but she leans back, sitting on her heels.

"Such a fucking good girl." I twist her dress to create a makeshift rope. "But this will ensure you're going to do as you're told."

"I—" Her mouth snaps shut, and I smirk, looming over her.

"I'm unsure if I should use this to tie your hands or use it as a gag so you're not so tempted to talk." I consider it. "Then again, I want to hear you screaming my name."

She sucks in a sharp breath.

"Hands up, sweetheart."

I can tell she's nervous. I doubt any man has brought her to life in all the ways I want to acquaint her with.

I wrap the twisted silk of her dress around her wrists above her head, then trail my hand with a feather-light touch over her ribs and farther down, satisfied by her sharp, unsteady breaths. "That's my good girl," I praise as I run my fingers down her perfectly smooth body until I'm rubbing against her folds. She's already needy for me, and I hook a finger into her pussy, satisfied with the way she wriggles around and accepts me.

I insert a second finger as I stretch out over her, kissing and worshiping her throat, reveling in the small noises that escape her. She's already soaking wet for me, but I don't know if it's enough for her to accommodate the size of my cock.

"Fuck." Her panted breaths sound as if she's riding a high. "I want— You."

I remove my fingers from her pussy and bring them around her throat. Her eyes widen, and I love the element of surprise, the split second of uncertainty that is then taken over by an unspoken trust.

A small squeal escapes her as I jerk her up by the silk restraint, bringing her to her feet next to the bed. My cock presses against her stomach as I look down on her, deciding what I want to do. A boat passing by on the water draws my attention to the patio outside my bedroom. Her gaze follows mine.

My cock strains, ready to be inside her. But I'm a disciplined man. My imaginings of what she feels like have been the only things to get me through these torturous weeks with her.

"Stay," I command. Her nostrils flare, and I raise an eyebrow at her silent challenge. She nibbles at the inside of her cheek but doesn't make a move. *Good.*

After rounding the bed, I open the top drawer of the nightstand to pull a condom out. I offer it to her, and those perfectly manicured fingers curl around it. She looks confused but doesn't say anything.

I walk to the sliding glass doors and open them, stepping out onto the patio that overlooks the lapping water. The city lights twinkle in the distance, and the chilly air prickles against my skin as I turn to face her.

I lean against the waist-high glass railing. "Crawl to me, Sunshine."

"E-excuse me?" she stutters.

A cruel smile stretches over my lips as I lean farther back, stretching my arms along the top of the railing. Will this be what pushes her too far?

"I—" She looks shocked. "You've tied my hands. I can't—"

"Are your knees broken?" I ask, watching her expectantly.

She scoffs. "What if someone sees us?"

I offer a casual shrug. Only she cares if she's seen. Ironic, considering I'm the one who hides in the shadows, but the moment the spotlight might be on her, she wants to hide away from it. I fist my cock and begin to stroke myself as I admire her. Standing only a few feet away, perfect hips and tits, her hands bound in front of her like a good fucking girl.

Slowly and elegantly, Lily drops to her knees, and like a moth to a flame, she shifts toward me, her bound hands in front of her. When she comes to a stop in front of me, I reach out and twist her nipple. She hisses under the intensity, but those blue eyes gleam with something a little more feral, something very unbefitting of my princess, and it's a warm welcome compared to what I'd usually expect from my woman.

"Do you want this cock stuffing your cunt?" I ask, stroking myself. She bites the inside of her cheek as she nods eagerly, almost greedily. I squeeze my cock hard, reminding myself I want to last throughout the night. That's the thing with this woman; my cock wants her more than any other pussy it's been inside of. And I know I'll undoubtedly be fucked the moment I thrust into her, certain I'll never be able to come back from it.

"Yes," she says breathlessly, and I reward her with a twist and pinch to the other nipple, forcing a curse out of her normally polite mouth.

"Then put the condom on so I can bend you over this railing and destroy that cunt of yours."

"Do you have to be so vulgar?"

My smile stretches wider as I bend enough to cup her pussy. She inhales sharply, and I rub between her folds. "But you're so fucking wet for me, sweetheart. You love it. Remove that posh little attitude when you're on your knees in front of me, because the only thing your mouth is good for is sucking my cock."

"And kissing," she adds.

She's still defiant, but I realize that more than anything, my Sunshine needs a connection. I might not be a *real* boyfriend, but I can give and take a little, if only to coax out the brightest version of her. I wrap my hand around her throat and kiss her, ever so slowly cutting off her air supply. But she still eats away at me hungrily, letting me take and take like the good girl she is.

I bite her bottom lip and drag it through my teeth as I break the kiss and stare at her expectantly. She brings her bound wrists to her mouth and rips at the condom wrapper, making quick work of it. Then she kisses the tip of my cock, her tongue darting out to lick up the pre-cum. I hiss because this "innocent" woman knows exactly how to drive a man insane. The thought of her with anyone else brings a feral part of me to the surface, mixing with the fear of losing her tonight.

Once she slides the condom on, I grab her by her restraints, jerking her up. I spin her around, pressing her hips to the railing, forcing her to look out at the city she claims to love so much, the possibility of someone seeing us as I fuck her within an inch of her life only enhancing the encounter.

I sweep her hair to the side and then gently kiss down her neck, smirking with satisfaction as her pulse picks up when I line my cock with her wet little cunt. Her breath hitches, and I slowly nudge inside her, stretching her.

Her body stiffens, and I rest a hand on her hip, pulling her into me. I murmur encouraging words into her ear, doing everything in my power to restrain myself, giving her time to adjust before I turn into a madman.

I can't explain why I'm offering her this mercy; she's the only woman I've treated this way.

I jerk her backward, slamming her into me until I'm buried to the hilt, her tight walls squeezing my cock painfully hard.

"Fuck," she curses.

"Does it hurt, sweetheart?" I ask as I slowly pull back out.

"Yes, but keep going," she pleads as I use her hips to pull her back into me, our bodies slapping together.

I chuckle. "I never had any intention of stopping."

I fuck her from behind, her bound hands coming to wrap around the back of my neck as she arches into me, as if using me as an anchor.

I pound into her, cursing silently at how incredible she feels. I pinch her nipple and then bring my hand down lower to rub and circle her clit.

"Oh, fuck me," she moans.

Her pussy rewards me with wet sucking noises as the sound of the water lapping in the distance fades.

"Lorenzo." Her voice trembles, and I know she's close because her legs begin to quiver. But I'm not done with her. Not yet. I'm nothing if not a cruel man, letting her close to the edge, only to deny her—much like I'm doing to myself. I pull out of her and step back.

"You better not—" she begins, but I cut her off by angling her back and crushing my lips to hers, irritated by this ever-demanding mouth of hers.

She groans as I spin her to face me, pinning her

back against the glass as I undo the binding on her wrists. The moment I do, her sharp, manicured nails pierce my shoulders, and I pick her up by the ass. Her legs naturally wrap around my waist, and one of her high heels, which she's had on this whole time, falls to the ground as I walk her over to the sunbed. I impale her with my cock as I press her into the cushion.

I slam into her as the last of my control snaps, forcing guttural screams to rip out of her, satisfied that I'm marking her with my bruising grip.

Her nails dig into my back, clinging for dear life, as I fuck her into oblivion, my cock making its way home every time.

Home.

I jerk into her, biting into her neck as I come. The moment my teeth sink into her flesh, she curses and cries out, her pussy milking my cock and her legs trembling around my waist as she rides her own high.

I'm breathing heavily as I realize we've slowed into a steady rhythm as our hips meet.

I'm royally fucked because I don't know how I'll ever be able to let her go after this.

She's like my perfect personal sex toy.

But beyond that, there's something I don't want to acknowledge in any way. That brief flashing sense of *home.*

26

LORENZO

Lily's drawing circles over my chest with her fingertips as we stare at the ceiling. I have her pressed against me, the sheets stained from my wound, but she seems unbothered by it. I almost expect her to snap back to reality and reprimand me for the mess.

I purposely ignore thoughts of my mission and the bloody trail I'll be cutting through of those who dared to jeopardize her safety. Right now, she's safe in my arms, soothing something within me.

"Does this tattoo signify anything special?" she asks. I glance down at the one she's skimming with her fingers. Each of my tattoos has a meaning or reason behind it. I find it ironic that the one she's asking about is the most significant one on my arm.

The angel with the bow.

I've never told anyone what that tattoo represents,

and silence fills the air as I ponder how, or if, I should explain it. I don't want my demons or burdens weighing on Lily. Not because she's fragile but because she's empathetic. I don't want her ever thinking I'm anything but strong and stoic.

"I got this tattoo for my sister when I was sixteen." The weight of the words out loud piles in my lower stomach. I try not to think about her often, and I mention her out loud even more rarely. But ever since Lily Taylor came into my life, the memory of her haunts me.

"Sister? You have siblings?" she asks, popping up onto her elbows so she can look at me.

Even with the heaviness the reminder of my younger sister causes, my lip twitches from Lily's open shock. I trace the lock of hair that frames her face. "Despite what you might think of me, I wasn't raised in a cave by wolves. I had a family, too."

Her eyebrows dip. "*Had*?"

Giving her this information does very little to threaten me in any way, and yet, I'm surprised by my hesitation to tell her the truth; that constant ingrained guilt around that day reappearing.

"Lorenzo?" Lily pushes as her hand comes to stop mine from tracing her hair, as if that's what's distracting me. But then she draws it to her cheek, to cup her face, as if giving me her warmth and strength.

She's stronger than she realizes, with fire dancing behind her eyes, and I hope, if nothing else, that even after we part ways, I can help free her from her bonds. Though the thought of never seeing her again makes me feel... Well, it just makes me feel.

"I have a younger brother who may or may not still live in London. God knows where he is now. And I *had* a younger sister." The way her face twists in pain makes me uncomfortable. No one looked at me like that when the incident happened. There wasn't sympathy, only resentment and blame. I almost want to laugh that the type of support and caring I was looking for all those years ago is being offered to me now. Too bad I killed that boy inside me long ago.

"What happened?" she asks gently.

So much.

That day changed everything.

I'm resistant to opening up about it after so many years of suppressing it. But it's the way Lily gazes at me with silent expectation that no matter how long it takes, she'll wait to hear it that has me deciding to tell her.

"My brother and I were put in charge of looking after my younger sister, Milia, one day. She was the apple of my father's eye. At the time, my brother and I were being trained to serve the Armani household when we came of age." I can tell from the way her eyebrows dip that the concept of being trained from a young age to be a killer might seem cruel to some, but I'd be lying if I didn't confess that it came naturally to me. It was those skills that eventually led me to be Luca's bodyguard and second in charge.

"My father had business to deal with while we were staying in a small coastal town in Italy." I remember it vividly, how one second she was there, and the next she was gone. I don't even know how to put that into words. I couldn't even on the day when they found her body at the bottom of the cliff.

But for Lily, I want to try. I don't know why it's important that she knows, but in some sick and twisted way, Lily reminds me of Milia. I can't recall what her voice or laugh sounded like, but I'll never forget her scream.

Milia and Lily share the same bright energy that naturally draws people in. It's probably why she infuriates me so much when she hides inside herself to make herself smaller in order to fit other people's expectations.

"What happened, Lorenzo?" Lily prods gently, and it draws me back into the room. I hadn't even realized I'd gone into distant memories. Their relevance isn't something that should still hinder me today, but alas, here we are.

I stroke her cheek. "We were chasing her, playing a silly game she used to enjoy, but when she got too close to the cliff edge, part of it gave way, and she slipped. I didn't make it in time."

Lily sucks in a harsh breath, and tears spring to her eyes. It surprises even me how she can be so moved by my story. A story that is mine, but was so long ago, I've cut all ties with any emotional response to it.

"My father hated my brother and me after that. It broke apart what was left of my family. My mother had died two years before that, and Milia had become his everything after her passing. After the incident, he couldn't even look at us. He'd often beat us to the point where I didn't think he'd stop. On the nights he drank, it became worse."

I watch her carefully, waiting for any kind of response, because I'm certain she's used to dealing with a similar monster. The difference between then and now is that I'm no longer scared to face it. If anything, I welcome it to bare its ugly fangs at me. But not at Lily. I need to know if her father has given in to his vices as violently as mine did.

When she says nothing, simply feeding me a silent comfort I don't think I deserve, I embrace it. Grateful that, in this small moment of time, someone cares for the boy I'd been. But I won't stop prodding her to tell me about what her father is like when he drinks. For now, though, I continue with my story.

"It's actually Luca I have to be grateful to. I planned on taking my younger brother from my father, but he wouldn't follow. I knew there'd be consequences if we left the family, but I didn't care. I just wanted to make sure he made it out alive. My brother, Dante, is… smart-lipped. Never knew when to keep his mouth shut. One day, my father was beating him so badly I thought he might actually kill him. I was locked in another room, and no matter how much I tried to break down the door, I couldn't. And then I heard Luca's voice."

I smirk, thinking back to the time. I'd hated the Armani family and the subservient relationship we had with them. I'd seen how my father fawned at Luca's father's feet, responding to his every call. By extension, it meant he also revered Luca, even when he was only a teenager.

"Luca was younger than me by a few years, but wielded the power of the next Mafia heir already. He was only there on holidays because by then his father had relocated to Manhattan, while my father conducted business on behalf of his second-in-charge in Italy.

"Luca stopped the beating and told my father if he ever laid a hand on either of his sons again, he'd make sure he felt it tenfold. In a split second, the dynamics had changed. My father, who used to be strong and respected, was now a shell of a man, projecting his grief onto the remaining family he had, worth no more than the last name he carried.

"It wasn't long after that, I helped Luca in a situation and took a bullet for him. He hired me to be his personal bodyguard, and soon after, I became his most trusted confidant. So, when you say I'm a dog chasing their master, you're seeing the reverence and loyalty I have for Luca because I'm certain had he not intervened that day, I would've lost another sibling."

Tears trail down her cheeks, and I wonder if I should be moved by them. I'm so unaffected by the truths of my past that it makes me realize how much of my humanity I've lost over the years. And how undeserving I am of a woman such as Lily to cry over someone like me.

"There was an exhibition we visited that holiday with Milia, and she was drawn to all the little angels." I think back to the day, again, the memory so hazy, but I recall her giggling as she pointed, finding hilarity in them being naked or covered only by a cloth. "She was obsessed with all things angels after that, particularly cherubs. Now that I think back on it, I find it ironic that she would join them only weeks later." I go silent as I let that sink in. "So, when I was sixteen, I got this tattoo to remind me of her." Strange since I've done everything to try and forget her since.

Lily continues stroking my jaw, and the twisted pain in her expression makes me more uncomfortable amidst the resurfacing ghosts that haunt me.

I'm grateful when she shifts the conversation, as if understanding every intricate shift in my mood. "What about your brother?"

I stare back up at the ceiling. Maybe not that topic. It's been years since I saw him last, and it ended with us exchanging blows, until I was the one wise enough to walk away. Then the little fucker has the audacity to turn away from everything he's worked so hard for, and our last phone call didn't end so well either. So, I offer her a cozier story.

"He was studying in London to become a surgeon, but still calls Italy home. Not sure if that's still where he is or if he's still in school. I haven't seen him for years. I made a promise that while I bloodied my hands working with the Armanis, my brother would be a better person for it."

Silence.

"Do you miss him?" she asks gently.

"No," I admit. Family is a weakness, and I want him to have a better life than we did, opportunities to make a positive difference in the world.

"Since you asked me about my tattoo, I get to ask you a question now. How did you get that scar between your shoulder blades?"

She looks up, but her gaze immediately diverts as she slumps back into the mattress. "I told you, just being a kid."

Just like that, the icy wall returns.

My phone begins vibrating, and I snap to attention, answering it.

"We've got him," Sky sing-songs, and I can't help the grin that curls my lips.

Good, because that fucker is about to pay for ever pointing a gun in Lily Taylor's direction.

27

LORENZO

"I ain't telling you shit!" The man spits blood on my shoes. It's a normal Friday night for me. I offer a curt nod, acknowledging how difficult he's chosen to make this for himself, before punching him in the face. He drops to his knees, barely able to focus on any one thing as blood begins to ooze from his ear.

We've dragged him into Luca's bar and down to the fighting ring. I'm only ever down here for two reasons: one, when we're hosting our weekly fight night, which is when we earn most of our money, or two, when I'm torturing assholes like this.

I grab him by the hair, pulling him to stand before driving my knee into his stomach and letting him drop to his back in the center of the ring. Blood splatters on the ground around him. Izak watches from where he sits in a chair with a laptop on his lap. I can see his gaze switch curiously between the man's slow execution and the computer where he's busily typing away.

Often, we tie our "guests" up before torturing them, but I had to get this foreign mix of rage, despair, and fear out of my system. All of these complicated and debilitating emotions that rose the moment this fucker pointed a gun in Lily's direction need to be exorcised somehow.

I no longer suspect they were aiming for Ara that day in Italy. She hasn't once been approached since. Tonight, they came for Lily.

"What do you want with Arabella Armani and Lily Taylor?" I ask again. The man groans, and so I give him a hand up as I grab him by the collar and fling him across the ring. He bounces back from the ropes awkwardly. At this point, I don't care how many of his ribs I've broken. He won't make it out of here alive for trying to harm Lily.

I take two steps toward him, crouching over his crumpled body. "I do give you credit for lasting this long, but tell me, does your loyalty matter when you're going to die anyway? Wouldn't you rather it be quick?" I ask as I pull out my gun and place it down between us.

The man coughs, blood splattering the ground. His hand twitches, as if wanting to reach for the gun. Hmmm, maybe I broke his back.

"This is getting messy," Izak calls out behind me.

"It will only get messier when there's still so much

blood to extract," I say as I pull out my knife. "Shall we begin with one of the ears?" I grab his ear and bring the knife to it.

"Wait! Wait!" The man harshly breathes in and out. "Wait," he whimpers. "Please." There's nothing more empowering than the moment a man realizes I've become his grim reaper.

I've only been working on him for fifteen minutes, but to his credit, he's lasted ten more than I thought he might.

The hound whistles in the background. "I have his wife and kids' names here, based in—"

"Wait!" the man wails, suddenly coming to life. "I'll tell you. Please. Just... not my family."

The easiest ones to extract information from are those who have something to protect. Especially family. Maybe it's a last-ditch effort of courage or to offer some semblance of being a good person, praying to whatever maker they believe is out there. I believe in survival of the fittest and nothing past that.

"You seem to be begging a lot and not offering a lot of information," I say. "Who are you working for, and why are you following Arabella Armani and Lily Taylor?"

The man physically shakes as he grows paler. I imagine he's experiencing hot and cold flashes as his body begins to work against him.

"We aren't interested in Arabella Armani," the man begins. "We didn't know Lily Taylor was your girl."

Suddenly, it feels like a veil is being lifted. "That wasn't what we were told. We were told to kill on sight. It should've been an easy hit when she was in Italy. We didn't know we were in Armani territory."

They're not after Ara. They're after Lily.

"Then you're idiots," I say, grabbing him by the hair and yanking his head up as I bring the knife to his cheek. "Tell me why."

It's easy to surmise her father's done some shady deal with the wrong people, but I need to know who they are before I charge in and wipe them out.

"Her dad owes my boss money. That's all I know. When the money didn't show up on the due date, our boss decided to send him a clear message."

I press the edge of the blade into his cheek. He screams as he tries to buck with very little success.

"You're a coward. You should've gone for Henrith instead."

"She was the easiest member of the family to target," he grits.

It makes sense. Ordinarily, she would've been an easy mark had I not been there that day at the villa. It's the same tactic Luca would've used.

"Who's your boss?" I flip the knife in my hand, and his gaze follows every rotation of the blade as I catch it and repeat the action. My hands are coated in blood, but it feels good to get dirty after so many weeks of seemingly ordinary day-to-day routines.

I'm not cut out for it. *This* is what I'm good at.

Especially if it will protect Lily.

"Nicholas Wayne!" the man shouts.

I frown and look over my shoulder at the hound, who casually shrugs. Who the fuck is Nicholas Wayne?

The man finds a strength he didn't have before, slicing his own throat along the blade of my knife when it lands back in my hand. I close my eyes as blood sprays my face and favorite suit.

I tsk under my breath. "Well, now you just made it messy." The man gurgles and squirms, and I watch the life fade from his eyes.

"I've never heard of him," Izak says as he types away at his laptop, but I already know he's on it. He's second only to Tyson in the enjoyment of the hunt.

"Pass me that towel, would you?" I point to the one beside him. He doesn't even look up as he throws it in my direction. I snatch it from the air, then wipe my face as I bring my phone to my ear.

Luca answers on the third ring. "What did you get from him?"

"It's as I suspected. I don't think it's you or Ara they were after. Henrith Taylor made a deal with Nicholas Wayne to get him out of some financial hardship. Lily seems to be the message they're trying to send to Henrith."

"Who the fuck is Nicholas Wayne?" Luca questions, and I silently agree with him. "Find out everything you can about him."

"Already on it." It's a relief that the Armanis aren't

the target; however, this also means our tactics must change. And that unsettling thought makes me hold my breath for how Luca plans to proceed. The only reason I'm protecting Lily is because his wife demanded it of him under the pretense that we'd involved her by association. Without that, how far is Luca willing to go to keep his wife happy?

For once, I'm grateful for Ara's meddling, and that's a poisonous thought because I shouldn't be prioritizing anything or anyone over Luca's orders, but I hope Ara will push for Lily's continued protection, even when she discovers she doesn't need it herself.

"I want to know everything about this Nicholas person. Either way, there are consequences for conducting business in my city and shooting up my home. They will be made an example of."

"Yes, sir."

"With that said, I want you to meet with Henrith Taylor. Advise him his daughter's life is at risk, and that for the right price, we're willing to take away his problems."

My mouth goes dry. "You want me to use her as a bargaining chip, sir?" Every word tastes like ash as I say it. Izak looks up from his laptop, but I turn my back to him, unsure what my expression is giving away right now.

"Is that a problem, Lorenzo?" Luca's voice cuts lethally through the phone.

I hesitate, thinking of Lily and how she'd react if

she were to find out. I'd be no better than her father, using her for strategic gain. I almost feel resentful toward Luca. The moment that hits me, I pull the brakes on any type of strangled emotion rolling through me.

No.

Luca's word is law.

"No, sir." I can barely swallow. "I do, however, think Ara will have concerns if she discovers we're using her friend as a bargaining tool."

"Ara won't know about any of this. If I didn't know any better, Lorenzo, I'd say you're getting soft on Lily."

I close my eyes, cursing silently. Using Ara as an excuse feels almost like a desperate attempt to... to what? Protect Lily? Defy my boss?

"Nothing to worry about, sir. I'll update you once I've had the meeting."

"Good. I'll be wrapping things up here and returning to New York soon." The phone cuts out, and I hold it so tightly I'm certain it'll crack into a million pieces in my hands.

Since when have I ever had a conscience before?

28

LILY

Sky's leg dangles over the sofa while he whistles an irritating tune. I was fortunate enough to find my favorite iced tea in the fridge, until I realized Lorenzo must've been stocking it in the off chance I'd be here. As I forage through the pantry and fridge, I notice all of my favorite foods.

I look at the spectacular state of Lorenzo's house, still in disbelief that such a brute calls this his home, when I contemplated once he might've lived in a cave. I'm smiling into my tea as I think about the ongoing joke.

Hot flashes rush over my skin as I think back to only hours ago; his lips on mine, the way he devoured me and left me sore and bruised. I'll have marks for days, and yet... I welcome it to happen again.

My life is a chaotic mix of events—the shooting, Lorenzo and me, how my father will respond—yet, I choose to focus on the excited flutters in my stomach opposed to the harsh reality of tomorrow.

I don't enjoy violence or intimidation; ordinarily, I'm scared of it. But I know Lorenzo will never hurt me, which makes it that much more peculiar to discover I *like* pain from a man who's ten years my senior, no less.

The moment Lorenzo and Sky switched places, I decided to explore his home. I want to know more about the man who is slowly opening up to me, and I feel guilty for not doing the same for lying about the scar between my shoulders. But that opens up a whole lot of baggage I don't want to drag anyone else into. *Especially* Lorenzo.

I peek into his office. It matches the rest of the home. Dark woods, deep greens, and browns. I lean back into the hallway, looking over my shoulder, but when I see Sky is distracted, messing around on his phone, I slip inside. I'm certain Lorenzo would kick his ass if he knew Sky's attention wasn't one hundred percent on me, but I'm grateful for the tiny bit of freedom.

My hand grazes over the emerald couch situated next to a side table. Everything about this home screams bachelor pad. And evil spy. Even his wardrobe consists of identical suits. I find myself nibbling at my bottom lip, almost amazed that I get to see this domestic side of him. I wonder how often he actually stays here. He certainly hasn't since he's been with me, but the place is still in an immaculate state.

The light from the living room and kitchen stretches in a stripe across the room, almost like a spotlight on his wooden desk. I peruse some of the titles in his floor-to-ceiling bookshelves spanning one wall, surprised to find a lot of classics. Some in other languages, mostly Italian.

I look back over my shoulder at the door, half expecting Sky to be standing there, but when he's not, I round the desk.

I'm so curious about Lorenzo and his world. What does a man like him do in his spare time? His desk doesn't have much on it—a laptop, a pen, and a piece of paper with a few numbers scribbled on it. Stealing one more glimpse at the door, I open the top drawer, then look down.

Inside the desk is a gun and knife. My breath hitches the moment I spot the weapons, but they don't affect me in the same way they might've months ago. Somehow, I've become almost used to the dangers of his world.

However, it's not the weapons that catch my curiosity but the corner of a partially burned photo. When I pull it out, my eyes widen, connecting the dots as to who's in the picture. I can tell by his eyes. The tall, lanky one who looks like he's only just hit puberty has the same dark-brown eyes as Lorenzo. But it's his scowling expression that gives him away.

I'm smiling because it doesn't surprise me that Lorenzo's expression seemed just as sour even then. He stands behind a slightly shorter boy, that I assume is his younger brother. He has slightly longer hair than Lorenzo, but they have the same eyes, and he's missing one tooth at the front.

My heart stops when I see the little girl, her long, brown hair pulled back into two pigtails. *Milia.*

"You're not very stealthy," Sky says, leaning against the doorframe. I jump, cursing as my heart pounds in my chest.

"I was just…"

"Snooping?" he teases, flashing a beautiful smile that runs a shiver down my spine.

"No." I grab the pen and piece of paper. "Just looking for something to write on."

As I walk past him, he raises an eyebrow and follows me into the kitchen. He then retakes his position on the couch and proceeds to pull out his phone.

I casually lean over the counter, holding the cup of iced tea, irritated that I was caught red-handed. "Shouldn't you be standing guard by a door or something?"

"I should be asking the same thing." The voice comes from the door leading to the garage. I startle, but Sky doesn't even flinch as he casually looks over his shoulder, his hair falling over his forehead and giving him a boyish look.

"Relax, I already knew you were here. Don't get your panties in a twist," Sky says, unconcerned.

"Where's your mask?" the newcomer growls. Ara

stands behind the man, who if memory serves correctly is named Tony.

"Lorenzo told me to remove it so the little lady didn't get scared," he replies, and I can tell Tony isn't impressed.

"Are you okay?" Ara demands as she walks past him, and Sky straightens the moment he spots her, as if standing to attention for their queen.

She looks me over, and I'm genuinely stunned when she brings me in for a hug.

"I'm okay, but Lorenzo got shot in the arm," I tell her.

"You look... surprisingly calm about the situation," Ara notes as she pulls away.

"I mean, I don't know if calm is the right word for it, but maybe desensitized?"

She raises an eyebrow and looks at the tea I'm holding.

"Oh, let me pour you one," I offer, grabbing another glass, acutely aware of Ara watching my every move.

Tony and Sky begin whispering amongst themselves, and Ara looks over her shoulder, as if to check they're not within hearing range.

"Did you two have sex?" she whispers.

The glass slips out of my hand, and I barely catch it in time before it crashes to the counter. When I look up at her, she's smirking.

I look at the others, but they're too preoccupied. I

can feel the heat rising to my cheeks as I turn toward the fridge. "Just a little bit of flirting," I lie.

"The type of flirting that gets you pregnant?" she asks with her hand on her stomach.

I bite my bottom lip, trying not to laugh. Okay, maybe I really am too calm about this situation. "Maybe a little. Are you upset with me?" I hand her the glass.

"Not upset. I just hope you know what you're getting yourself into."

"Just a little bit of fun." I take a sip of my iced tea. *Fun that leaves me battered and bruised... in the best way.* For months, they've been telling me I need to find some fun. I certainly didn't expect to find it in a killer, but here we are. "I'm okay, Ara. I promise."

She slowly takes a sip of her tea, her eyebrows furrowing. "You got shot at tonight."

The truth floats in the air, and yet, all I can find myself saying is, "Yep."

She goes to speak and then closes her mouth again, as if surprised at my response. "Who is this new Lily?"

I shrug with a laugh. "I just... I don't know what to think anymore. The first time at the villa terrified me, and I know I should probably feel a certain way about it right now, but I'm just being reminded that I only have one life. I'm sure not many people have that wake-up call because of something like this, but it's just shifted something within me."

"Or some six-foot-two brute has rattled a screw

loose," she jokes. Heat scorches my cheeks, and I can't help but laugh as well. "Just as long as you don't expect anything serious with Lorenzo. He's... very dedicated to his job."

"You're telling me. I'm surprised he lets me go to the bathroom without him."

She rolls her eyes. "I can understand his overprotective tendencies. He wouldn't leave my side after Luca gave him the order."

A slight pang of sadness hits me, reminding me that this is, after all, a job to Lorenzo. He's protecting me just like he'd been assigned to do for Ara.

"Well, I'm sure this will all be dealt with soon. Any update from Luca?" I ask, pushing that unsettling feeling away.

I feel like I'm in some weird calm before the storm. I thought I'd be more reactive in this situation, but I must be so exhausted from all the bullshit that went down tonight that I can't even muster up the energy to be scared.

"Luca says he'll return to New York soon. Apparently, they have the name of a suspect. Now that they have a lead, it won't take them too long to get this sorted," she says confidently.

"That's good. Good." Meaning that my time with Lorenzo soon will be coming to an end. I should be glad to hear that I'm no longer in the line of fire because of my association with the Armanis, and yet, it feels bittersweet now that Lorenzo and I are finally on good terms.

"Did I hear you went on a date?" Ara asks curiously as my phone buzzes in my pocket.

I roll my eyes. "Courtesy of my father. I'm just hoping the guy doesn't mention how Lorenzo plunged a fork into his hand after storming the restaurant."

Ara's jaw tightens. "He did *what*? Are you okay?"

I wave it off as I unlock my phone to read the message. "No, Lorenzo's a psycho." Yet a small flood of warmth and comfort runs through me, knowing that he came for me when no one else had.

That comfort quickly freezes over at the simple text I receive from my father.

You're expected to return home tomorrow night.

FUCK.

The storm has finally shown itself, and now it's up to me to make sure I'm ready for its impact.

29

LILY

"I would like to speak with my daughter alone," my father says, his eyes turning into narrow slits as he looks down on Lorenzo. I cringe at his scathing expression yet find myself standing in front of Lorenzo, almost as if shielding him. He might not be the greatest man with regard to his career choice, and he may not have much of a moral compass, but there's a sincerity to Lorenzo that deserves to be protected. Because despite those things, he's the person who's encouraged my freedom the most, and in a way that those who are already in my corner couldn't.

My father doesn't miss the movement, and it only causes his face to twist further in disdain.

"Come this way, Lorenzo. I'd love to show you my roses," my mother says enthusiastically as she offers to lead him away.

My brother raises his eyebrows and pockets his

hands as he precedes them out of the room. Lorenzo is reluctant to leave my side, and I offer him a small smile to let him know I'll be okay and that I understand and appreciate his concern. I know this relationship is fake. That we're not really together, and it's all a facade, but the longer it goes on, the more I'm starting to believe it. And the more I'm wanting to. It's becoming dangerous that I can't imagine my days without him.

We even decided to stay at his house, and for the first time in years, I took a "sick day," choosing to be railed within an inch of my life all over his house, instead of going into work.

"We won't be too long," I promise him.

I've thought about how this conversation might go; how I'll advocate to be liberated from my family's expectations. Even if I can't have Lorenzo after all of this, I won't let my father choose who I can and can't date.

"I'd like to have a word with you myself afterward, Henrith," Lorenzo says, and my stomach drops, my courage faltering. The thought of these two men sharing the same room alone terrifies me.

My father says nothing in response, just turns and walks into the family room. The wooden floor is covered with a plush white rug in the center. Floor-to-ceiling windows reveal the afternoon sun, and a long couch and two armchairs surround a beautifully carved table.

"Close the doors behind you," my father instructs. I

do as he says, nervous when I look at the empty glass in his hand. He walks over to the half-empty bottle on the sideboard and fills his glass.

"You've humiliated this family. Are you aware of that?" he says with contempt. "Tell me how one simple date with a longtime family friend went so horribly wrong that he now wants nothing to do with me?" His eyes flash with anger as he takes a harsh swallow.

"Father, you need to let me choose who I date and marry. This pressure you're putting on me lately is too much," I reply, stepping into my power. It's time I stood up to my father, for better or for worse. I've held on to this family for so long, and what have they done for me? Nothing.

I love my mother—would do anything for her— but the sad reality has been sinking in for a while now, that if she's not willing to help herself, what can I do? If anything, I'm only turning into her. Denying the truth of what's in front of me. Continuously breathing in the toxicity, and allowing my father to control me like some puppet.

It still terrifies me that he could cut me from the family, but I can't live like this anymore. I've crumbled down to nothing, having nothing else to give. I'll try to do everything I can to remain by her side, but I just *can't* roll over, allow him to steal my choices and dictate my life anymore. This constant abuse and control will never end.

My father is eerily quiet as he shakes his head manically, then refills his glass. My strength slowly starts to drain because I know nothing good comes when he's drinking this much. But I think of Lorenzo, the courage and strength he would command in a situation like this.

"Do you have any idea what you've cost this family? Who raised you to be so selfish?"

My brow furrows as he verbally assaults me with all of his hatred. I always wanted to convince myself that somewhere deep down, my father cared about me, but as I see him now, the same way I've seen him my whole life—with a bottle in his hand—I realize he's not much of a man or father at all. He might be able to function around others, careful to never reveal his true colors to them, but for someone like me, who's been conditioned to answer his every command and whim, only poison remains. Unfortunately, my father is no longer capable of love—if he ever was.

That saddens me for my mother, considering how she must feel in this loveless marriage.

But for once, I want to put myself first, acknowledging that at no point has this ever been okay.

"Come here," my father demands, pointing to the spot in front of him.

My chest rises as I'm emboldened to say the one word I haven't been daring enough to use until I met Lorenzo. "No."

The glass halts at my father's lips, and his scathing glare cuts to me. A chill runs through me, and my body freezes in place. I try to shake myself, to remind myself that I need to stand up to this man. There's no going back now. No matter how scared I am of being discarded, I might have to leave behind my mother because of it but I can't let that guilt rule me anymore. If only she'd listen to me. If only she'd follow me. But I can no longer allow this man terrorize me as he does her.

I'm the child, am I not? I can't keep treating her like she isn't an adult who can make her own choices. It's her decision to stay, but it doesn't take the hurt away as I not only let go of my father but also parts of her, knowing that after tonight, things will never be the same.

My father points toward the door. "What, you think because you bring in a caveman that you're tough now?" He takes a step toward me. "Did you really think I'd ever allow you to parade around with someone like him?" he seethes in my face, spittle flying. My jaw grinds as I fight against a lifetime of conditioning to remain quiet and take it.

"Who I do or don't choose has nothing to do with you," I say, rolling back my shoulders. "The choice is mine, as is the choice for me to leave."

A dark bubble of laughter rises from him. "You think you can just leave this family?" He gulps down his drink, and my face twists in disgust, for the first time showing him what I really think of this unmasked version of him.

Repulsive.

Abusive.

Demeaning.

Cruel.

A sad man.

A pathetic man.

Rage rolls through him, as if he can hear all of these unsaid things. He grabs my elbow and shakes me.

"You stupid, ungrateful girl. Do you know how much trouble we're in because you won't simply do as you're told?"

Trouble?

I try to tear my arm out of his grip. "Let me go," I grit. "You don't get to treat me like this anymore!" I yank myself free, realizing for the first time that I might be stronger than him.

I'm not that scared little girl anymore.

"You think you're not my daughter anymore?" He steps back into my space. I push him away, and with twice as much force, his open palm strikes me across the face, and I fall to the floor. I'm so stunned and disoriented, it takes me a moment to realize he just struck me.

I'm forced back into memories of being a small child, being beaten or forced to watch my mother step in in my place.

Scissors being thrown at me and slicing down my back one night he went berserk. My mother pulled me into another room, and we hid as she whispered to me that it would be okay. My brother was at a friend's that night, but it didn't excuse him from the many episodes my father often had. And the next day, pretending like nothing had ever happened.

He comes for me again, but this time I kick at his stomach, daring to push the monster away. He's in a fit of rage as I stand, wobbling slightly as I check my ear. When I pull my shaking hand back, it's smeared with blood.

For the first time, it's not fear that makes me tremble but anger. He's nothing but a violent, angry man, a victim to his own demons and hatred that's rotted him from the inside out.

A deep-rooted pain bubbles from my core to the surface, in mourning for the father I wanted him to be and the potential I hoped he was capable of. Because this is all that's left of him. And if it costs me the rest of my family to dig this toxicity out of my life, I'm finally willing to do it, no matter how terrifying.

His shouting comes in waves as he picks up the bottle by the neck and turns it upside down. The liquid pours onto the floor as he storms toward me, and that adrenaline quickly mixes with fear.

A fear that maybe this time he won't stop.

My back hits the wall, and an avalanche of cold

dread rushes over me, freezing me in place. I see the maddening hate, the desperation, the rage in his eyes.

The absence of a father, I always hoped he'd grow into, but never could.

I dodge the bottle as it swings toward my face, clipping my shoulder instead. Glass explodes beside me as I stumble to the side.

The doors burst open, and it's like everything slows down as Lorenzo sweeps across the room in two long strides. The moment I see him, relief washes through me, until I see the murderous intent in those eyes that I've become accustomed to crinkling in the corners when he smiles. Now another monster has come into the arena, and I realize with startling clarity how small my father is compared to him.

Terror wraps around my neck like a noose, and I know without a doubt, he's about to kill my father.

"Who let you in, you—" My father falls to the floor after the first punch, but Lorenzo grabs him by the shirt and punches him again and again, blood splattering the white plush carpet.

"Lorenzo!" I scream, grabbing for his elbow, but his strength is too much for me to hold him back.

My mother gasps from the doorway, where she gapes in horror at the scene. My brother stands beside her, staring, his eyes going wide as he takes it all in. How could they possibly attempt to intervene with a beast and his prey?

Or maybe they don't want to. The dark thought cuts into my worry and fear.

This can't be the way.

"Lorenzo! You're going to kill him!" I scream, grabbing for him again. "Please, don't do this!" I beg as the wild mixture of emotions—grief, mourning, courage—tumultuously roll through my stomach. I push down the bile that wants to rise, fighting against the one man in this room who is truly willing to defend me. But right now, he's willing to take too much away, and I can feel it fracturing us, breaking apart whatever we've built during our time together into a million pieces alongside my heart.

If I don't stop this now, there's no coming back from it.

Lorenzo tries to shake me off, but I hold firm. He doesn't even hear me right now; his movements are more like a wild animal than the man I love.

The man I love.

The startling truth of that statement burns at my insides, and I become more desperate to stop him.

For my family.

For me.

For *us*.

I tug at him, praying I can calm the raging storm that's his unleashed wrath. "Please!" I sob as I get a glimpse of my father, who is a bloody mess against the once-white carpet, gurgling, trying to breathe. "Please!" I say through tears. "He's my *dad!*" My voice breaks.

The glint of Lorenzo's gun catches my eye, and without thought, I steal it from his pocket and point it at his head.

Lorenzo's fist freezes in the air as my father hangs from his shirt, bunched in Lorenzo's other hand. Blood mars my father's face and Lorenzo's fists. Slowly, animalistically, Lorenzo looks over his shoulder, and it's the first time I've seen the killer beneath directed at me. He's more beast than man right now. My hands begin to shake as adrenaline courses through my veins.

But I know he's still in there somewhere.

"Don't make me do this," I say, almost pleading for him to give me another choice. *Don't make me do this.*

"He *hit* you," Lorenzo growls with a sneer that makes him look even more the predator. The gun trembles in my hand as I'm made aware of the pounding on my face from where my father struck me. Tears spill over my cheeks, making it hard to see Lorenzo anymore.

"It's okay," I find myself saying, even when I know it's not.

"It's *okay?*" he scoffs. "Over my dead body."

"Please!" I say before he lands another hit. "Lorenzo, please. He's my family. *Please.*"

Time feels like it stops as we stare into one another's eyes, a wordless conversation passing between us. Just raw, vulnerable emotion. And I pray and beg him to do as I ask... just this once.

I don't even know why I'm begging for my father's

life when he's done nothing but hurt me. I was ready to leave him, not *kill* him. It's all happening far too quickly to process.

Lorenzo shoves my father to the floor. "He doesn't deserve mercy," he spits at my father, who's barely moving but still breathing. Lorenzo grabs my hand and pulls the gun away, relief washing through me.

My brother holds my mother's shoulders as he moves them to the side of the door, giving us a wide berth.

I made the decision to leave my father and his antics behind, but stepping out of that room with Lorenzo doesn't feel right. But I know if I don't leave with him, he won't leave at all. I can feel the roiling rage beneath the surface, and it terrifies me.

I'm not scared of *him,* but of how he loses himself to his own demon.

I feel like a traitor as I leave my father gurgling on the floor behind us. Regret and guilt flood me as I hear my mother cry out my father's name as she runs into the room, and it pains me to know that even when his monster is on full display, she'll run to his side. Or perhaps she's too scared not to when the job hasn't been finished. Did she linger at the door, in shock like me, because she was too scared to interfere with her chance at a way out? At a different life? Does my mother actually love my father?

I was certain my father wouldn't stop this time, and as I stare at the back of Lorenzo's wide shoulders, I can't help but think what I might've done had he not stepped in.

Would I have run away or fought?

Either way, I'd be at peace because it was my choice.

Right now, though, I'm feeling anything but peaceful.

30

LORENZO

I t's not right. Walking away. That man should be dead, and I'm more than happy to serve his punishment. My hands grip the steering wheel so tightly I'm certain I'm about to break it. The only reason I'm driving this car in the opposite direction from him is because she came with me.

Tonight doesn't feel like a victory. Seeing her holding a gun to me, fear in her eyes, and tears streaking down her cheeks, I realized to her I appeared no better than the violent man her father is.

It changes nothing, however.

I asked her time and time again if he'd ever hit her. There's no fucking way I will live in a world where someone hurts her, even if that person is her father. *Especially* if that person is her father.

The palpable tension rolls through the car until we return to my home on the water. The half-moon hangs in the night sky, along with the lights of the city reflecting on the water, but the evening is far from majestic. It takes every ounce of my willpower to get out of the car and walk inside with her.

Lily follows me silently, and I hate the barrier that's now between us. I already know how much she's pulled back from me, and maybe that's because of the decision I've already made. There is no way Henrith Taylor will live until tomorrow. I'll make fucking sure of it.

I beeline for the freezer to grab a bag of peas. I wrap it in a tea towel, and then I face her, getting my first real look at her since leaving her parents' house.

She's a wild mess, her hair in matted chunks. There's a small cut on her shoulder from where the glass broke beside her. And then there's that giant red handprint stained on her beautiful face.

Something felt off the moment we left her in that room alone with Henrith. Call it instinct, but I had the need to check up on her, and I'm so fucking glad I did. I might've looked like a madman as I left her mother and brother in the garden and ran back inside, but had I not, what else would have happened? *What if I hadn't made it in time?*

"Lorenzo." Lily's voice breaks through my thoughts, and I realize the bag of peas has broken open from how tightly I was squeezing it, and they are spilling onto the floor.

I turn to the freezer for a new bag, but she catches

both of my hands and brings them to her face. It's as if she knows this is the only way I'll stop and look at her, and it brings me to a standstill.

"Thank you for protecting me," she says, and I'm taken off guard by her sincerity. She shouldn't be thanking me. I think she's showing me kindness in an attempt to talk me off the ledge. Or maybe she understands the intent I have to kill her father. "Promise me you won't hurt him again."

Anger bubbles from my stomach, not at her but at her unrealistic request. "He *hurt* you."

I step back, the divide between us becoming wider when all I want to do is hold her. Whether she likes this or not, that man doesn't deserve to fucking breathe for another day. "He's a coward for striking you. How long has this been going on for?"

Her brow furrows, and her expression distorts. Evidently, she's not satisfied with my answer, but she gently puts her hand on my chest and pushes me toward the sofa and then into a seated position, where she then sits herself on my lap. I need it more than I realize as I wrap my arms around her waist.

Fuck, do I need her.

I need her to be safe—no matter what.

She's acting contradictory to what I thought she might. I expected her to hate me, seethe with vile words. Not even want to look at me, let alone let me touch her.

It does nothing to shake the knowledge of what I must do.

"He's been like this for as long as I can remember," she quietly admits, lowering the bag of peas and staring down at it. I'm quick to take the bag from her and gently hold it to her face, and she hisses at its cool touch. I fucking hate the fact that I wasn't there to prevent this. She should never have worn his mark like this. I'd take a million hits to ensure she never had to endure this one, or all the ones before it.

"I'm sorry, love," I say, the pain striking me as deeply as if I had laid a hand on her myself.

"Lorenzo, you have nothing to apologize for. But please, promise me you won't come into contact with my father again?" she asks gently. It's not fair how she uses her soft tone against me. Who am I to deny her, when I've already tried for so long?

"Sorry, love, but I don't operate that way. I protect those I love."

It takes me a moment to realize what I've just said. This is what I've been fighting from the moment I first laid eyes on Lily.

Her mouth opens and then closes.

"I don't expect you to say it back," I say flatly, almost willing her not to. I can only be so selfish. Now that I know it myself, it makes everything painfully clear, and I hate knowing that I'll betray her in the next breath. I want to kiss her, make love to her, mark her as mine all over again. I don't have that right, however, not with what I'm about to do. "What happened?"

Mixed emotions seem to roll through her, then she breaks into a small smile that shatters me into a million pieces. Seeing the real Lily beneath—vulnerable and exposed—I can see how much she's been keeping it together. It's a privilege that she's showing me the ugliest version of herself, and it's something I'll never take for granted.

"He wasn't happy about us or how the date went with Riley. I don't think he was told about the fork in the hand, but he knows there is no going forward for us. He told me I was selfish and had no idea what kind of trouble we were in." Her brow wrinkles in confusion. "I don't know what kind of trouble he meant, but to be honest, I don't care anymore. I stayed for so long, scared of what would happen to my mother if I left. I've begged her so many times to leave him, but my mother..." She trails off, and I understand what goes unsaid, so I bring it to life for her.

"She chooses to stay in the monster's home."

Lily's blue eyes slice to mine. Understanding connects us. We've both lived under a roof with a violent parent controlled by his bottle of poison. I brush her hair from her shoulder. "You might think you're a coward, Lily Taylor, but you're not. I was trained to be a killer, and even I didn't have the balls to kill my own father until I was ready to face the consequences."

Lily gasps. "You killed your own father?"

"Yes, and I'd do it again. For my brother. For me. *For you.*"

"I don't want you to kill my father. Please, Lorenzo."

I offer a small apologetic smile. "I can't make that promise." I feel the distance grow between us. "The only one I can make to you is that if any person intends to harm you, then I will dispose of them. I will not live in a world where I can't protect you. Whether you hate me for it or not."

"Lorenzo, please." Her voice cracks, and tears spill over her cheeks. She cups my cheek almost pleadingly.

I'm tempted to tell her the truth—that she's been the target all along—but it remains as a lump in my throat. Making her hate him even more doesn't help the situation, and if anything, I fear it'll only hurt her more.

Either way, I'll ensure she remains protected.

I do everything I can to refrain from touching her, from claiming her in the way I want to, and taking away all of her worries.

I love Lily without a doubt, but it doesn't take away from the fact that I'm poison to her life. I've known this fact about myself from the day I let my sister die. I have nothing good to offer her, except for executing one of the demons that haunt her—knowing she'll hate me for it.

When she doesn't get the answer and promise she wants, she folds further into herself.

"I keep wondering if my father ever really cared for me at all," she says in bewilderment, and a new wave of hurt twists her expression.

"All I know is a man who loves his vices too much can rarely make room for others in his heart," I say as I bundle her up in my arms. "I will always keep you safe." I kiss her temple, embracing the lingering smell of her floral perfume one last time before I put her to bed and watch her fall asleep. Then, I'll become the monster of the night she tried so hard to make me promise I wouldn't be.

31

LORENZO

It's three in the morning, and she's finally asleep. Watching her from the edge of the bed, I stroke her hair, like I've done for the last hour, to try to soothe her. She's exhausted, with dark circles under her eyes. I wish her innocence wasn't just a front, but she's been fighting battles no child should have to endure, and I'm proud of her for finally taking a stand last night.

The rest I'll take care of.

I peel myself away from her side of the bed; each step becomes heavier, as I know without a doubt my next action will destroy anything we've built.

Sky stares at me through his mask from his spot on the sofa, where only hours ago I cradled Lily in my lap.

"Didn't take you as the kind to sing lullabies," he says by way of greeting, forever the fucking smartass. He pisses me off, but he's my favorite of the hounds because he reminds me of my brother. A twisted comfort, indeed.

"Watch over her while I'm gone." I shrug on my long black coat since my suit jacket is completely soiled with her father's blood.

Sky whistles behind me, following me through the house like a pest. "Are you going to tell me what you're up to?"

My silence is answer enough, and he comes to a stop at the door to the garage, leaning against it as he crosses his arms. He looks menacing, his gun glinting from underneath his leather jacket.

"Remove your mask so you don't scare her if she wakes," I order as I walk toward my favorite Lamborghini, the one with no registration plate.

He shakes his head but does as he's told. "You've changed, Lorenzo. I don't know if the boss will be too impressed by you going on solo missions."

I start the engine, ignoring him. I, of all people, don't need to be reminded of my boss's expectations. But I couldn't stop myself even if I tried. Luca Armani's safety has always been my number one priority, and I'm kidding myself by using the short time I have left as Lily's bodyguard as an excuse to take out Henrith Taylor when my boss specifically requested I strike up a deal with him instead. It became impossible the moment my suspicions about him hurting her were confirmed. The only reason I didn't finish the job then and there was so she didn't have to witness it.

It didn't take me long to find out that Henrith Taylor didn't go to any private hospital but was instead treated in his home. It's stupidity, really, whether dictated by him or his wife, because breaking into their estate is far too easy.

I kill the engine, contact Izak, who's talented with all things security, then simply climb over the fence and drop onto their front lawn. Henrith had evidently become paranoid over the last few months, having installed new security cameras, most likely scared of someone coming for his head instead of his daughter's.

I slip through the back door and then silently drift through the mansion. I think about what Lily might've been like as a child, and how her ray of sunshine still survived the depths of this vile home. She was always so reluctant to come back here. I understand the sentiment and find it harder to separate my own memories of my father from what she might feel toward hers.

I finally locate Henrith, and the first thing I notice is the IV drip attached to his arm. His face is swollen and has stitches. I come to a stop beside the bed, looming over him.

It takes me back to the night I stood over my own father, a bottle still in his hand from trying to attack my brother. I told Lily he'd stopped after Luca told him to never raise a hand against us again. I lied to make it cozier for her ears, but the truth of the matter was, my father only lasted another week before falling prey to his own vice and violent rage once again. It was the

reason why I decided to kill him sooner than I anticipated. He didn't just stop because someone told him it
was bad. Men like that never change. Her father would
never change.

I knew the moment I killed my father that I'd have
to step into his role. I didn't want to be the same as
him, living amongst the shadows, even when I knew it
was the most natural calling for me. I thought if I gave
it longer, I could provide more opportunities for my
brother.

But I realized no amount of time would change
that. If I wanted it to happen, I had to make it happen
myself.

And I was willing to do the same for Lily.

Henrith's eyelids open groggily, and those blue eyes
that look too similar to Lily's find me in the dark, as if
he already knew I would be there, waiting. Instead of
beaming with light and kindness like Lily's, his are
only filled with hatred.

"I'm surprised you're not screaming for help," I say
with a cold calm.

"Would it make a difference?" he croaks. "You're
one of Nicholas's men, aren't you?"

Being labeled as anything but one of Armani's men
revolts me, but I don't correct his presumptions.

He shakes his head slowly. "My stupid son messed
it all up."

It comes as no surprise that even on his deathbed,

he's willing to throw his son under the bus in hopes it might save his own sorry ass.

"It's a lot of money you owe," I say, taking a stab. I don't know the precise amount, but if it's enough to put a hit out on his daughter's life, we're talking millions.

"Just give us another month. I'll give you double."

That cruel tendril of anger unfurls in my stomach. He still thinks this is all about him and his money when it has everything to do with his daughter. I couldn't give a shit about what he owes, but I remind myself I have to be patient just a little longer.

It kills me every second he still breathes, but I have that need to be loyal to Luca. He might have my head for this, but if I can provide him with any information, it might be enough of a trade-off. Not that I care about my own ass, but if I can extend security for Lily until those who are still pursuing her are truly gone, I'll spare a few more minutes to listen to this old piece of shit.

"What did your son do?" I ask, flipping the vial in my pocket between my fingers. Focusing on it is the only thing keeping me calm.

Henrith scoffs, which turns into a coughing fit. "I had the money and told him to meet your men that night. Instead, he gambled it away like a fucking moron."

I don't let my expression shift, but I think back on the few encounters I've had with Vince. The night at Dmitri's, him having no money to spend and asking me to spot him. I'd flagged it then, but for him to be so stupid as to gamble all of that money...

"Tell me, Henrith, how much is it you suspect you owe us now?"

Henrith weakly shakes his head. "Twenty million."

Enough to keep the business afloat, but I wonder how much of that Vince gambled and how much he put into his side of the business to look superior to his father. That doesn't entirely sound like an uncalculated move. Unless, of course, he was trying to take his own father out.

Only a moron would think he'd walk out of that unscathed. As a family, he's collateral damage himself.

I remove the vial and a syringe from my pocket. I wanted to make this bloody, brutalize him in a way that he deserves. But unlike my father, who was expected to meet a miserable death, Henrith will be put into an expensive casket, revered and mourned by those who don't truly know him. But at the very least, I do this for *her*.

The grim reaper of her father.

When Henrith notices the vial, he tries to laugh but ends up in a coughing fit. "You think my daughter will accept you as some kind of hero after this?"

I raise the vial, extracting its contents with the syringe. "No, I know she'll hate me because, for whatever reason, she still has love for you. But I'm happy to kill a love when it does not serve her, including her love for me. You will never hurt her again."

Henrith's smile twists cruelly. "She was an obedient daughter until you poisoned her mind."

"Your error was ever thinking she was just a pawn for you to use," I say calmly as I push the contents of the syringe into the IV.

His eyes go wide as he stares at it, and the cowardice and reality of his actions come to the forefront.

"It's only fitting that you're killed with a poison, taking you from the inside out. After all, that's what you've been doing for all of these years with the drinking, isn't it?"

I remove the syringe and stand over him with total ease as the poison does its job. "I'll see you in hell, Henrith."

I watch him gasp his final breaths, and for the first time in a long time, I take true satisfaction in a murder unlike when I killed my father, when I was fueled with so much uncertainty of what was to come.

This time, I know exactly what to expect.

I did this to keep her safe.

Even if I'm ruining her peace, when I want to be it instead.

32

LILY

My eyes feel heavy. I groan in complaint, the side of my face pounding as I look at the empty space beside me in Lorenzo's bed. I don't know what time it is, but I know it took me what felt like forever to finally fall asleep.

I embraced Lorenzo, running his hand over my hair last night, as if gently petting me to sleep. His absence deepens the pit in my stomach. There were so many things I wanted to say to him last night, a wild confession brewing within me. The truth of the matter is, I felt relief when he burst into the family room before being scared by his unhinged rage.

As Lorenzo pried further into my childhood last night, I wanted to combat him, so used to pushing away anyone who looked further into my family dynamics. From a young age, I understood that what happened in my home wasn't normal. That my friends' families didn't harbor such ugly secrets. I was trained and conditioned by my mother to never discuss it, and advised by my father that if I were to tell anyone or try to leave, I'd be cast out from the family with no future in sight. A threat that no longer has a hold over me like it once had.

But up until now, I always smiled and pretended everything was okay. At times, I even convinced myself it was. Especially when he finally let me move out for college. He let me keep my apartment, and with some convincing from my mother, I was permitted to open and run the flower shop. I thought he was seeing me as a grown woman, slowly releasing a shackle. But the only one convincing me of that freedom was myself.

I thought no one understood, but Lorenzo does. However, we still had very different upbringings. Part of that is what makes me admire his strength to step into action, though perhaps not the bloody part. But I also understand that those murderous hands are the same ones that protect me and brush my hair gently when I try to fall asleep at night.

I don't yet know what I'll do about my father. I've finally gained the courage to escape the toxic cycle, but his outburst last night only confirms that he's still very much the same man he was when I lived there.

I sit up on the side of the bed, my toes curling at the coolness of the wooden floors.

I should feel liberated today, and yet, my mind is still drifting back and forth. *How will my father respond?*

Will he ruin me or my shop? Take my apartment away from me? Take it out on my mother?

But there's a small voice inside me, telling me, for once, it's going to be okay.

Maybe that has to do with Lorenzo's confession last night. My heart flutters at the way he expressed he'd protect me no matter what. *That he loves me.*

I wanted to tell him the same, but could immediately sense the wall he put between us. I was also shocked, unsure how I felt about his level of violence. I don't understand the full scope of what being with Lorenzo looks like.

But without a doubt, I know I love him.

My face throbs.

My father did this.

I push to my feet, yet again finding the courage to face him. I'll try to convince my mother one more time to leave him, and if she chooses not to, then I have to finally accept that that's her choice—and I have to make my own. It feels ridiculous how closely I guarded this ugly secret, and now that I've exposed it for what it is, I feel liberated. It's not over, but baby steps.

My phone buzzes on the nightstand, my brother's name appearing on the screen. It's six in the morning, so I've had a few hours of sleep at least. I take a deep breath and answer it, taking the yellow silk robe that's hanging inside the wardrobe. Half of my clothes have since been moved from my apartment to Lorenzo's place. I prepare myself, whether for Vince's scolding or encouragement.

"Dad's dead."

My body goes stiff.

Dad's dead.

Dead.

"Lily?"

"I'm here. I— I—"

"You need to come home," he says. "Do you need me to pick you up?"

A dark laugh creeps from me, and it's so unhinged, I begin weeping instead as my heart shatters into two. Oh God, he didn't listen to me. Lorenzo went behind my back, and I know deep within my heart that my father is dead because of the only man I've ever loved.

I thought last night he understood that we'd created a pocket of peace and a safe space where I could decide how I'd pave my next step forward with his support, but instead he... betrayed me.

"I can manage." I clear my throat. "I'll see you soon."

I hang up the phone, my hand dropping to my side as I numbly walk toward the bedroom door. When I open it, he's there, almost as if waiting, sitting on the floor, back against the wall, his head hanging between his shoulders.

I stand at the door, facing the man I genuinely thought I loved only moments ago, but when he raises his head to meet my eyes, I see the answer before asking the question.

"Did you kill my father?" I ask with an eerie calm that terrifies me. Because only I can hear the breaking of my heart inside.

"Yes," he replies clinically.

I slowly nod, finally acknowledging the decision he's made. I might've hated my father, but it didn't mean I necessarily wanted him dead. *Did I?*

Lorenzo didn't give me time to fight this, to make decisions of my own. He took that away from me, even when I asked him not to. "I specifically told you not to kill my father. You're fucked-up, you know that? You'd rather choose murder over us?"

His betrayal hurts, cuts deeper than any knife. Another boundary broken, another request ignored. Lorenzo will never hear me, and a knot of shock and pain twists in my stomach as it slowly sinks in that my father is dead.

"I choose your safety over us," he says without remorse.

"Oh, you're so fucking high and mighty, aren't you?" I scream, hating that superior air he holds around himself like fucking armor. My fists tremble as tears tumble down my face. This is so fucked-up; I'm mourning him more than my father's death.

"Don't hate me for having the courage to do something you could never have done."

My eyebrows practically hit my hairline, and I

storm forward. "Oh, so you think because you murdered my father, you're in the right now?"

He stands, matching my pose. "I know you'll hate me forever, and I've come to terms with that. I'm not going to fight you."

I scoff. "Are you out of your fucking mind? You sweep into my life for a hot minute and think you know me, know my wounds, know my family. You fucking know nothing!" I shriek, everything falling apart around me.

He's the first person I let in, even when I knew I shouldn't.

The first person I've laughed so freely around.

The first person who made me feel *safe*.

And I hate the fact that none of these things change, even now.

"You betrayed me." My voice trembles.

"Yes. Whether you think I know you or not, Lily, I've only ever done these things for you."

I laugh, crazed, sleep-deprived, and so sick of giving people the benefit of the doubt. I shove at him, and he does nothing. I shove again, looking for some kind of fight instead of him just rolling over and taking it. "Stop treating me like some fragile thing! Fight back!" I yell. He's always told me what's on his mind. Only ever fought with me during our turbulent time together, and now he's rolling over and taking my every scathing word. "I hate you so much!"

I shove again, and he still says nothing. I'm so mad.

He took away my answers, took away my resolve, took away my *choice* to deal with my father myself.

I'm so sick of fighting, of crying, of running. All of these emotions that he brought to the surface have nowhere to go. Now I have no choice but to confront them. Knowing that I'll step back into my childhood home, haunted by memories I've tried to forget, with the knowledge that the man I thought I loved entered it like a wraith to hurt my family.

And how I still hate myself for defending my father even after all he's done.

I take a step back, awkwardly rolling my ankle. His hand shoots out to steady me, and I slap it away. "Don't touch me!" The hatred that spills from my lips is vile. "Ever again! You say I'm the coward, but you're no better. You told me that you love me only to hurt me within the next breath! Go back to your master, Lorenzo. Go get your praise for what a good job you've done. I don't need your services anymore."

His jaw tightens, but he remains still.

For once, I just want to stand on my own two feet.

I go to the wardrobe, snagging the first dress I spot. I look like shit, and the bruise on my face is darkening, but it's as good as it gets right now.

Let this ugly family secret be exposed. Let the truth of that haunted fucking house come to life.

He watches me as I pluck up the keys to his favorite Lamborghini, storm out to the garage, start the car, then pull out of his driveway, making sure to scrape the side of the vehicle along the metal gates as I leave.

I slam on the gas, and the moment I look through the rearview mirror, I scream, "Of fucking course!"

Sky trails me on his motorcycle. The thought of slamming on the brakes and watching him barrel over the back of the car comes to mind, and it terrifies me.

I don't want to become a vile, hateful thing, the same as my father.

But there's just so much hurt, and I don't even know where to begin to piece myself back together. So, I allow him to follow me, simply grateful that it's anyone but Lorenzo.

Anyone can stand by my side but him.

33

LORENZO

I'm staring at the tracker on my phone. Lily hasn't left her family's estate for the last two days. I'm waiting for Luca to storm into his home office any moment now. If I'm lucky, he'll offer some parting words before putting a bullet in my head. If not, I still stand by my decision.

Although I was the first to call Luca and tell him the news of my killing Henrith Taylor, I'm certain he's been bombarded with the gossip and more official statements about Henrith's alleged alcohol poisoning after stumbling home after having too many drinks and getting into a fight.

Luca most definitely asserted his influence to cover up a job I was meant to be cleaning up for *him*, and I don't even want to think about who or how much he had to pay to create the narrative of the story.

The wooden doors open, and Tony shadows the

extremely pissed-off Luca. I straighten, anticipating I'm about to get my ass handed to me. What I'm not expecting is for Ara to follow in behind him. Her expression is just as unreadable; she's growing further into the mafia boss's wife by the day.

"How could you be so stupid?" Luca begins. "I told you to make an agreement with Henrith Taylor, not fucking kill him."

"Yes, sir." I understand full well I fucked up, but it's a decision I've made without regret. I glance at Ara, who bites at the tip of her nail, clearly agitated. Well, I suppose she now knows about her husband's ulterior motives. I'm sure he endured a scathing lecture about it.

"That's all you have to say for yourself? How can I trust you if you have your own objectives in mind? What the fuck were you thinking?"

"He hit her, sir," I say. At its core, that's my only reason. "I won't lie to you or twist it in any way to save my own ass. The moment he struck her, I lost control."

"But then you went *back*." Luca narrows his gaze on me, standing only a few feet away, hands in pockets. Tony stands behind him, expression indifferent. Although we get along, we both know our actions can lead to deadly consequences, ones that we might have to execute against one another. Ara watches me from the corner of the room, her perfectly manicured nail now tapping on her crossed arms.

"I did. The same night."

"And you still didn't strike up a deal, despite his weakened state?"

I'm unsure how to word it. Everything I've worked hard for in my career is about to be taken away. This is the only life I've lived for over a decade, and now I've jeopardized it. "You put me in charge of protecting Lily Taylor. So, I did. That man was a danger to her, and—"

Luca clicks his tongue disapprovingly. "You said you weren't going to twist it."

I look him dead in those cold blue eyes. "I've served you loyally always and will continue to do so if you give me the chance. However, it would appear that the ray of sunshine has become something more to me than a target, sir."

Luca's gaze narrows. "Then you can't be trusted at all."

"Luca," Ara warns.

He faces her. "I permit you in these meetings, dear, but if one of my men is compromised, then they have to be made an example of."

She hauntingly laughs. "Compromised? He's in love, you fucking idiot."

Luca's eyebrows furrow.

Ara then faces me. "And I, for one, am grateful. Coming in here, I thought we were going to kill you. I didn't know that Luca had ulterior motives in this mission. If I had known, I wouldn't have allowed it. But I certainly didn't know that Henrith *hit* her." She then looks at Luca. "Did you not allow me to have my revenge to protect me? Give your men some slack."

Luca scoffs. "Slack? This is how we run things here."

"And what if a man had struck me, Luca?" She pins him with a glare.

"He would never have the chance," Luca growls. I never thought it would be Ara coming to my defense, and I'm not entirely sure I'm worthy of it. Perhaps it's because she's the only woman in the room, and that makes her a better mediator.

Luca scowls at me. "You compromised the identity of one of the hounds."

"I thought it would scare her having a man wearing a mask in her home while I investigated matters for the other part of the job."

Luca's eyes bulge in disbelief. "What the fuck happened to you while I was gone? You're my best, and you've turned into..." He starts clicking his fingers. "What's that term they use in those books? A cinnamon roll?"

Silence fills the air. I don't need to point out to him that, of all people, he's become the exact same fucking thing since rolling over for Ara.

I didn't understand their relationship before, and I still don't entirely understand it now. But I respect that love comes in different forms.

"I'd like to speak to Lorenzo alone," Ara boldly says, ignoring his previous statement with an eyeroll.

"You want me to remove myself from my own meeting?" Luca asks lethally.

"Luca, stop pissing on your belongings when you know he'll still take a bullet for you, and give me a moment alone with him."

Tony and I share a glance. Having Ara around definitely adds a bit of amusement. At first, I saw Ara as someone who was trying to undermine her very powerful husband, but the longer she's been with us, the more apparent it becomes that she's just as ruthless as Luca. He couldn't have found himself a better partner.

Luca walks over to her and grabs her chin, his other hand immediately dropping to her stomach. "Your sharp tongue always seems to get you into trouble, my little viper. You've made a naughty habit of undermining me in front of my men."

She reveals a cruel smile. "Don't let the door hit you on the way out, dear. Next time you try to use one of my friends for your benefit, let me assure you I'll be doing more than undermining you. I'll be putting you in an early grave."

He flashes a wicked grin, and I look away as Luca leans in and kisses her passionately. I know this isn't the last of our conversation, but not having a bullet in my head is promising.

Tony follows Luca, throwing a quick glance and a nod my way. I do the same, respectfully. Tony is one of the few men under Luca's employ who has a family of his own. I always thought having a family was a burden; it's only recently that I've begun to realize it's nice to have someone to go home to.

Ara comes to stand in front of me, and her open palm hits the side of my face. It's barely enough to make my head move, but it makes her point. I grind my jaw, readjusting it and trying to usher away its sting. "That's for using Lily in the first place."

I don't remind her that it was on her husband's orders.

"How many times has her father hit her?" Ara asks carefully, her gaze narrowing.

Although Ara might be one of her closest friends, there's clearly a wall between them, and Lily's secrets will die with me unless she's willing to voice them herself. "If I might be so bold, Mrs. Armani, I think you should ask her yourself." Ara's eyebrows jump, and I continue to carefully explain. "Her father has favored a bottle in his hand for as long as she can remember. I think right now, she doesn't need me exposing her secrets. I think she needs a friend."

Ara seems even more surprised as she looks me up and down, her hand coming to her stomach. "You really love her, don't you? I didn't think you'd have it in you."

My gaze drops to the floor because there's something loaded in Ara's sincerity. It's uncomfortable having a woman provide an opportunity for us to articulate or express ourselves differently after being only us men for so long.

"She's one of the kindest people I've met. Sometimes even someone like me can't defend against that," I say honestly.

"I'm sure you despised it at the start," she says with a small smile.

"More than you'd ever know."

She's still smiling as she takes a seat on the sofa, rubbing her stomach adoringly. "I understand it well. I thought it was all an act when I first met her, until I realized that's just who she is as a person. It's strange to be blinded by that light when you've never been raised with it. It's a strength in itself, but her downside is she's loyal to a fault, even to those who don't deserve it."

I sigh, realizing perhaps Ara and I have more in common than I ever knew.

"If she could ever feel something for a monster like me, she certainly has plenty of room in her heart. If I'm being honest, I find that although I stand by my decision of preventing her father from ever being able to hurt her again, I also can't stand the idea of anyone other than me being by her side. It makes me dislike her big heart."

"I won't argue that you're not my first choice for her," Ara says honestly. "But I've made plenty of my own mistakes. Where Luca and I are cut from the same cloth, you and Lily are on either sides of a coin. You need to make peace with this and also somehow make my husband happy with the outcome."

"Shouldn't you be warning me away?"

She shrugs. "I would if I thought it was the best thing for her, but only she can decide that. As long as you respect her decision, no matter what she decides," Ara warns with an edge to her tone. "I don't want her unguarded until this is dealt with, whether she's involved because of us or not. She's family to me, and I choose to look after family." She sears me with another pointed look.

It hits me then, the realization that Ara, for all her faults, has my back. I dip my head respectfully and quietly say, "Don't ever tell the boss this, but I've come to enjoy how you raise hell for him."

Her grin splits her face as I offer her a hand to help her stand up. "It can be our secret," she replies with a wink.

34

LILY

So many people come to offer their condolences. I stand by my mother's side as she quietly thanks each and every one of them. For the last week, she's faded in and out of a numb type of mourning. Sometimes, when I go to knock on her bedroom door, I open it to reveal her asleep in her bed. Other times, she walks around the house and through her garden as if nothing had happened at all.

I've stayed at our family estate since my father's death, sleeping in my childhood room. Although the monster himself is gone, the haunting memories remain.

My brother has remained at the estate as well, but he often doesn't come home until late into the night, sometimes even in the early hours of the morning.

I suppose we're all mourning differently.

However, I'm less focused on the man in the casket than I am on my mother.

I look to my left, where Sky stands to the side of the crowd, appearing like an idle bystander. However, I notice his sharp attention every time someone offers me their hand in condolence. He's been watching over me in Lorenzo's stead. I haven't seen or heard from Lorenzo since I left his house the morning after he killed my father.

I spot Ara amongst the crowd of mourners and squeeze my mother's hand before walking toward my friends. With everything that's been happening, I've barely been able to talk with them. Sienna and Romi offer small, sad smiles, and Ara stands a few feet away, as if unsure if she's welcome. She most likely feels somewhat responsible for the incident with my father because she undoubtedly knows it was Lorenzo's doing. I've received countless calls from her, but I haven't answered or returned any of them, just needing time for myself.

Romi pulls me in for a hug first. "I'm sorry."

I'm not.

It's a cold response that I'd never say out loud, but since my father's death, I haven't felt anything for him. I hate to admit it—this part of me that feels such freedom because of it. I've had some time to slowly process that, and although I know it's an ugly truth, it's *my* ugly truth.

"Thank you," I say as Sienna pulls me into a hug.

"Whatever you need, let us know. You know we're always here for you, girl," Sienna says sympathetically.

"I know." I rub her arm and then come face-to-face with Ara, who looks as if she doesn't know what to do or say.

I embrace her, and slowly her arms wrap around me. "I'm sorry I haven't called you back," I whisper. "It's just been a lot."

When I pull back, she offers a small smile and a nod. "Let's make some time this week. I want you to depend on me."

I look past the crowd and see a sizable man standing on the hilltop, peering down on us. I know without a doubt it's Lorenzo, watching from a distance.

My stomach curls with yearning, hate, and pain. Because through it all—with all the uncertainty of what's to come—my mind continues to circle back to him. Whether I treated him unfairly, whether I was in the right, whether I still care, when logically I should know better.

Ara follows my gaze, and when she looks back at me, it's with sympathy.

I'm sick of seeing that pitying expression as everyone tells me how much of a "good man" my father was, although this time, it's for an entirely different reason.

I go through the motions, following my mother and supporting her as best I can all the way until we're home and I'm tucking her into bed.

"Let me know when you're ready to talk, Mom," I say, kissing her forehead. I've seen her mentally and physically beaten so many times that the habitual desire to protect her remains. Now I'm certain that if I simply give it more time, I can convince her to choose a better path—to finally focus on herself. We're just not there yet. Where my shackles have freed me to a degree, hers seem to have turned her into an empty shell, and I hope the spark that was once inside of her returns soon.

I close the door behind me as I leave her bedroom and then walk down the stairs. I'm about to step outside into my mother's garden when I notice the light coming from the family room. I haven't been in there since Lorenzo gave my father that bloody beating.

The doors are already open, and when I curiously peek inside, I spot my brother taking a sip of his drink as he looks over some paperwork, his knee bouncing. We haven't had much time to talk, as I've been catering to my mother's needs and he's dealt with the companies, public affairs, and statements.

Despite Lorenzo beating the shit out of my father, my mother and brother never blamed him for his death. My father took a bad beating with a few stitches to the face, and they didn't seem upset by articles announcing he'd gotten into some drunken fight. The articles never mentioned Lorenzo, which I imagine might've been Luca's doing. And it was the doctor who confirmed it was alcohol poisoning that killed him in his sleep.

A glaring truth that they couldn't argue, even though, for once, it wasn't because of his alcohol consumption.

"Vince, are you okay?" I ask, and his leg comes to an immediate stop as he looks up.

"Yeah." He clears his voice. "I just—" He looks at the paper and puts it down, but I know him better than that. I especially know when he's trying to hide something. "I found something in Dad's office. I don't think you're going to like it."

How many more secrets are there to unearth in this home? I step forward, no longer scared of the truth. I told Vince I thought our father was in some financial hardship, and he said he'd look into it. Hopefully, this might give us a lead. He hands me the paper, and my stomach twists into knots as I read the agreement.

"This can't be serious," I say in disbelief, staring at my father's signature and a signature belonging to Mr. Timber. The agreement states that on the announcement of my engagement to Riley, and subsequent marriage, he'd offer my father a substantial loan of twenty million.

My brother's expression is grim. No wonder my father pressured me into the date with Riley. But to sell me off as a bargaining chip like this... I shouldn't be surprised, but it doesn't dull the sting.

"He never even viewed me as a daughter," I state

miserably as I sit beside my brother. I'd been clinging to some type of hope, anything that showed he might've still had a sliver of goodness remaining within his poisoned soul. But if he did, none of it was spared for me.

Vince offers me his glass. I take it and look into the depths of its amber coloring. "It's ironic, isn't it? This was what took him away, and yet, here we are, still drinking it."

My brother doesn't say anything to that, simply takes it back from me and swallows another harsh sip. It's not until it's empty that he wipes his lips and says, "We're nothing like him."

It's the first time I've heard a bitter edge in Vince's tone when speaking about our father. I suppose we all had a strangled relationship with him, but Vince always acted so aloof and indifferent that I thought he wasn't impacted by the same shackles I was.

"What ended up happening on that date with Riley Timber?" Vince asks curiously. Whatever my expression, the moment he looks into my eyes, he holds his hands up defensively. "Whoa, I'm not the enemy. It was just a question, Lily."

I shake my head, feeling like I'm going crazy. He's right; he's not my father. But I can't help feeling bitter toward him after his advice from that night. It felt like even Vince betrayed me.

"We just had different outlooks on life." My eyebrows furrow as I think back to that night. Of course, I leave out the fact that Lorenzo plunged a fork into his hand. "That night, when I called you, you told me I should go, even when I told you I didn't want to. Why?"

Although my brother didn't fall victim to my dad in the same way my mother and I did, I always believed he was on my side. But he betrayed me, and I found comfort in what felt like the only person on my side: a killer. Thinking of Lorenzo still hurts, like a vise around my chest, but he keeps appearing in my mind, every waking hour, and even the few hours I seem to get any sleep, Lorenzo Moretti haunts my dreams.

Vince rolls the empty glass between his hands. "I didn't think it was that big of a deal."

My mouth drops open. "Vince, it wasn't my *choice*. That was the problem."

"I know. I know. I just... Maybe he was trying to help as best as he could?"

I point to the agreement. "By selling me off?" I immediately shrink back into myself, staring at the doors, making sure no one else heard, as he brings his finger to his lips.

I put the paper down on the table in front of us. So many fucking secrets.

"He wasn't a good man. I can't believe he'd go to such lengths either," he admits, disheartened and staring at the piece of paper between us.

"Why would he need a loan for twenty million dollars?" I question.

Vince bites the inside of his cheek, and I immediately realize he knows something that I don't. "We're in a lot of debt, Lils. The companies have been struggling for a few years now." He rubs his eyes and hangs his head in his hands.

I feel the air rush out of my lungs. I've never cared to involve myself in my father's business, but to realize he'd use me as some bargaining tool, all because of his own downfalls?

"He was probably trying to get the money so we weren't at risk of losing everything," he continues.

"What do you mean? Can't we use money from the businesses or try to sell or—"

"Don't you think I've already tried those things?" he says defensively, then flinches under his own raised voice. His hand slides to mine. "I'm sorry. It's been a hard few days. I'm looking into it. I'm just worried, that's all. Do you have any money saved up?"

I look at him quizzically. Sure, I've saved a large amount of the monthly allowance I was given since I didn't need it. I depended on the earnings from my shop. Yet I'm resistant to mention it since that has always been my backup plan. Something doesn't feel right about this entire situation.

"It's a mess. I don't know what else to do," he says, shoving his hands through his hair. "Can't you ask your boyfriend for a loan or something?"

"He's *not* my boyfriend, or did you miss the part where he beat the shit out of our father?"

Vince's knee starts bouncing. "Yeah, well, he was just protecting you, right? He has more courage than I ever did. If anything, I'm envious of him. I wish I were the one who'd beaten the shit out of the old man."

"*Vince,*" I whisper-shout, shocked by his confession. The bouncing of his leg stops, and he looks at me, as if remembering where he is.

"I'm sorry. I just... He wasn't a good man, was he? And now I have to clean up this fucking mess. What if they take the house? What if they put Mom on the streets?"

I grab his forearm. "Look, we'll figure this out, okay? Don't you have any money? Maybe if we tell Mom about this, she—"

"We're not telling Mom about this. Look at her. She's hardly spoken or eaten in a week. We have to fix this." He looks to me then, almost pleading, "We have to fix this family."

Fix this family.

Something I've yearned for, for so many years, and now that it's here, it feels almost too good to be true. Maybe I hadn't realized that I'd long given up on it. Then again, I did finally decide I was ready to cut ties with my father. But now that he's gone, shouldn't I give my everything for my mother and brother at the very least?

"I'll give you some money. It's only a few million. Can you get the rest to cover it? Maybe we can sell some of Dad's car collection?"

Vince shakes his head approvingly. "We'll make this work, Lils. We'll create a new chapter for all of us."

A new chapter.

I've prayed to hear those words for as long as I can remember, yet as of late, that new chapter had very little to do with my family and more to do with a man I put all my trust in, only to be betrayed. Maybe a reminder that blood runs thicker than water.

I push away the thought of telling my brother about recent events and confiding in him about the attempts on my life. It would only stress him out further, and right now, I want to believe we can fix this problem, especially for our mother's sake.

Because if I can't trust my brother, then who can I trust?

35

———

LILY

The vibration from my phone ringing on my bedside table wakes me. I stare at the ceiling of my old childhood bedroom. Not much has changed over the years, except it all feels a little smaller.

I groan as I look at my phone. Four missed calls from Sienna, and it's only seven in the morning. That can't be good. She's never awake this early.

I call her back, noticing the cool drift of air seeping in from the window. My eyebrows furrow as I walk over to close it. I'm certain it was closed last night.

"Oh, thank God, Lily. It's bad!" Sienna says in a rush. "It's Romi. I need you here. It's an emergency."

My heart stops. "Is she okay?"

Please, don't be so cruel as to take one of my best friends. Is this a punishment for not feeling guilt over my father's death?

"It's her roommate. She's dead," Sienna tells me.

Everything stops.

"What?"

"Every morning they walked together after yoga, but yesterday…"

"Romi came to my father's funeral instead," I finish for her, because she still seems to tiptoe around the subject.

"She won't tell me what happened, but she's pretty shaken up." She says the last part quietly.

Something lodges in my throat. I didn't know the woman well, but she and Romi had been roommates and friends for almost two years.

"Why didn't Romi call us?" I ask, wishing she had been more inclined to depend on us. I'm already in action, quickly throwing on a pair of jeans and a top.

"She's just… vacant," Sienna says. "Should I call Ara as well?"

"Maybe not yet. She had a big launch today for a new app, and Romi doesn't do well with being smothered. I'll be there shortly," I promise.

When we were ten, one of Romi's dogs passed away. It was so devastating that she didn't eat or drink for days.

I quickly walk down the hallway, open the door to my mother's room, peek in, and find her sound asleep.

My heart feels divided. I've been holed up here for a week, hovering to make sure she's okay, but to have Romi now going through the same grief…

What the fuck is happening right now?

Is fate so cruel?

I'm hurrying down the stairs and almost run into Bentley.

"I'm sorry, Miss Taylor. Is everything okay?"

"Sorry, Bentley. I'll be gone for the day. Please call me if anything happens with my mother," I say, grabbing my coat and whipping it over my shoulders.

"Do you require me to call the driver?" he asks, flustered by my pace.

I pause, thoughtfully. "No, Bentley. I think I'll drive myself."

He doesn't say anything, only tilts his head slightly in approval as I make my way to the garage. I look through the fine collection of vintage cars. It was always a hobby of my father's. I'd never shown much interest in it, but it was absolutely forbidden that we ever drive one. I look at the array of eight cars, biting at the edge of my nail as I make a quick decision. His old Mustang. The one he loved the most.

I rev the engine, feeling oddly empowered at the way it growls beneath me. It feels like a great "fuck you" to my father, but if he was willing to sell me off before this car, then I think this is a fair trade-off. Bit by bit, I feel his hold slipping from me. Especially as the loose gravel kicks up when I round the corner too fast outside of the gates. My heart pounds with adrenaline, and I *like* it.

I'm not surprised when Sky begins to trail me on

his motorbike. Unlike when the hound gives me space when I'm at the house by remaining on the outside of the property, he's right up my ass anywhere else I go.

I park outside of Romi's apartment, which is located on the outskirts of Manhattan in a slightly quieter part of town. If anything, it's a little run-down, but she always expressed that it was within her room-mate's budget, and she liked the edginess of it—it apparently gave her inspiration.

When I step out of the car, I'm surprised when Sky removes his helmet, revealing his beautiful features as he gets off the bike.

I point to him. "You're not welcome."

"Sorry, miss, but those aren't my orders. I can give you space when you're sweetly tucked up in bed, but anywhere else, I follow."

"Why are you all so infuriating?" I grumble, irritated but beelining for the entrance so I don't waste any more time.

"Comes with the territory, I think. And if Lorenzo found out I wasn't one step behind you at any point, he'd have me neutered."

I pause in the middle of the staircase and look down at him. I'm inclined to ask about the missing brute, but I won't fool myself into believing he's doing this because he cares. So, I settle on, "You're really annoying, do you know that?"

He chuckles. "I've been told it's part of my charm."

I flick my hair over my shoulder as I continue up

the stairs. "You're to remain outside, and I mean that. If not, I'll pull your own gun on you." I refuse to let anyone in Romi's space, except those who can help her. I want to protect her at all costs.

He chuckles behind me. "Wow, you really have grown a pair since hanging around with Lorenzo, haven't you? It looks good on you."

I ignore the strange compliment, refusing to acknowledge anything that ties Lorenzo and me together.

I knock on the door twice, and Sienna opens it, looking worse for wear. She pulls me in for a hug, and I'm stunned. "I'm sorry, I know with your dad's funeral and—"

"Where is she?" I ask, stepping into the apartment and going to close the door. But it's abruptly stopped. When I look back, Sky has his foot in the door.

"Who is this?" Sienna asks, looking between us.

"It's a long story." I pin him with an intense glare that promises imminent death.

"Door stays open this much," he states as he steps away and sits across the hallway. I throw my hands up in the air. *Whatever.*

When I turn, I brace myself. The place is a mess. Beautiful paintings that once hung on walls have been shredded and broken over furniture. It looks like it's been ransacked. Her roommate's door is closed. The small circular staircase that leads to the attic seems as if a barrel of black paint has been thrown down it.

Fuck. If this is what the living room looks like, I don't even want to go upstairs and see the state of Romi's studio. I follow Sienna into Romi's bedroom, and my heart breaks the moment I see her, sitting in the middle of the bed, holding Borris, the little terrier. Romi's staring at the ground, her room a chaotic mess, matching the rest of the apartment.

"Romi, I'm here," I say in my most soothing tone. Romi, who's usually so full of life, has black paint splattered through her red hair and is still wearing the funeral clothes from yesterday.

A pang of guilt floods me; instead of her usual routine, she was supporting me. I push away that unreasonable blame. Right now, I just need to be here for my friend.

"Romi," I repeat as I come to crouch in front of her and grab her hand. She doesn't see me or hear me. Fuck. This is bad.

"I tried," Sienna says from behind me. "I didn't know what to do." Her expression looks hopeless and bleak.

"We need to get her in the shower first," I say, already in action. The black paint matts her vibrant red hair. Fuck, she might have to cut it. "Romi, I need you to work with us."

It's hard seeing her like this, and I can't help but reflect on myself as I stare at her. This shell-shocked version was me only months ago when everything happened in Italy. Romi is one of the strongest, most animated people I know, and yet, seeing that even she can be rattled like this, that her natural instinct is to go within herself, somehow tragically makes me feel more human.

"Hey, little guy," I say to Borris as I try to peel him from her grip, but it only tightens. "Romi," I say again, and bring my hand to cup her cheek. This time she blinks, and her face ever so slowly tilts toward me. "Romi, let's put you in the shower for a little bit, okay? We're not going anywhere. Borris needs to eat."

She blinks twice and then nods, as if understanding, but still doesn't hand over the dog. Instead, she uncurls her legs and walks to the kitchen. She's robotic in movement as she opens the cabinet and pulls out wet food, then slaps it on an open pizza box on the floor and empties its contents.

Slowly, she puts him down and watches as he eats.

Sienna and I share a worried look. It's ironic that here, despite the circumstances, I feel alive and needed. Whereas in my own time of mourning with my family, I just feel empty. I don't feel any sadness for my father's passing. Yet for my best friend, my heart breaks as her world crumbles around her. Because I understand what that feels like, and I know we both still have a long way to go. After all, we're only human, and there's only so much someone can take until they either snap or shut down. I just never thought I'd see the upbeat Romi go through it.

———

AROUND DUSK, I receive a phone call from my brother. For the most part, Sienna and I have cleaned up the apartment around Romi, who's now in track suit pants and a black hoodie. We couldn't scrub all of the paint out, but that's the least of our worries as we tuck her into bed and she finally falls asleep, Borris still tightly clutched to her chest.

"Hey, where are you?" my brother asks.

I step into the hallway. "I'm at Romi's. Her room-mate passed away yesterday, and she's not doing so well."

"Oh, shit, that's bad. I'm so sorry, Lils," he says, and I take the time to have another peek outside the front door, where Sky is still sitting, looking bored out of his mind. Jesus, do they not even go to the bathroom? I feel bad as I go to the kitchen and rummage through the cupboards, where I find a few snack packs. I fling them out the door, and he seems startled but catches all three of them with abnormal reflexes. His eyebrows furrow as he stares at the treats.

"I need you to come back home and watch over Mom while I go out for a bit," Vince says.

I lean against the counter, peering into Romi's room. "I don't know if I'm comfortable leaving her like this."

"Lils, I need you here. I'm trying to figure out this loan stuff, and we really need you. I'm worried about

Mom. One moment she's acting normal, and the next she's walking around like a wraith. I don't want to leave her."

"Well, maybe you should stop leaving every night if you're so worried," I bite back, surprised by my own harshness. I close my eyes and remind myself I'm being unreasonable.

"Lily, it's fine. I can take it from here," Sienna says from Romi's doorway. "She's asleep now. I won't go anywhere. Your family needs you."

All the fight in me slowly recedes. I feel like I'm just going from one fire to another.

I'd transferred my savings to my brother, and he promised he'd make quick work of having it sorted. More than likely, that's what he's doing tonight.

I sigh, exhausted. "I'll be home shortly."

"Okay, I'm heading out now, then. I'll see you later tonight," he says and then hangs up.

"I'm sorry. I'll check in later, okay? Call me if you need anything," I say to Sienna.

Sienna looks tired, her usual perky self nowhere in sight. I pull her in for a hug. "I'm so grateful to have you as a friend." Others might think Sienna is vain and shallow, but she's none of those things. She's only ever been supportive of all of our endeavors, and when we need her most, she's always there.

"Right back at you, girl. It's a shit time, but we'll all make it through this." She presses a kiss to my cheek and then nods toward the door. "We need to have a discussion about you going from chastity belt to rolling through handsome men," she says, aiming for a light-hearted tone. "Is everything okay at home?"

I have no doubt she's probably clued in to the fact that there's more going on than what I'm letting on, but I appreciate her not asking any more questions than necessary. "It will be."

"What happened to Lorenzo?" she asks gently. My body immediately erupts into goose bumps at the mere mention of his name. I hated the idea of a fake relationship, of lying to my friends, but I hadn't real-ized along the way how convincing we'd been. Hell, I'd even convinced myself.

"We broke up. Call me if you need anything," I say with a small smile that doesn't reach my eyes, not leaving any more room for discussion regarding Lorenzo. It was all a lie. Every part of it. Because if I don't believe that, then what can I believe in? I can't love the man who killed my father. Can I?

This is all types of fucked-up.

Sky rises to his feet and follows me, not mentioning how long he sat in the hallway waiting.

I fish for the car keys in my handbag, then freeze the moment I look up at my father's Mustang.

Lorenzo is leaning against it, his hands in his pockets, but the second our eyes meet, he has the audacity to begin to walk away.

I'm storming across the road before I have the better sense to stop myself. "Why are you here?" I demand all the pent-up fury and mixed emotions coming to the surface. If it were anyone else, I would remind myself that all of these complicated emotions aren't all his fault. Yet he's the only person who deserves their scorn, to feel the wrath tenfold, because he's the person who hurt me the most.

I want to push him farther away because I hate this pining for him, not trusting myself when he's near. My heart betrays me. It's complicated, and it's messy, and it doesn't make any fucking sense.

He stops and then turns slowly, reluctant to face me. His gaze moves everywhere but to me, but then his dark-brown eyes finally meet mine. It looks like he hasn't slept in days. *Good.*

I hope his guilt is eating him alive.

"I noticed your tracking device went to an abnormal location, so I wanted to see with my own eyes you were safe."

My eyes bulge. "You're still tracking me?"

He shrugs. "Just because I'm not by your side doesn't mean I've stopped prioritizing your safety."

I scoff. "You lost that privilege when you killed my fucking father," I seethe. "Any update on your boss cleaning up his mess, so I can finally be free of this bodyguard bullshit?"

"What do you want from me?" Lorenzo says far too calmly. "It seems like you're angry with the whole fucking world, and I'm the only person you can take it out on. And although I welcome that poison tongue of yours, sweetheart, you'd better start doing some self-reflecting before you implode. You can't keep taking on everyone's problems. There's only so much I can do to help."

"*Help*?" The word comes out as a squeak. "I've never asked for your help. Never even wanted it in the first place."

He nods slowly, and for a split second, I see the shift in his expression, the pain and sorrow. My heart twists painfully as he then looks over my shoulder at Sky, and I feel the moment his walls go back up. "I just wanted to make sure you're okay," Lorenzo says, quieter this time, before walking away.

"So, you're just going to leave?" I demand, my fingers curling into my hands. I hate him so much, and watching him get into his car, as if I'm still nothing but a mission, abolishes my fake calm.

"Fucking asshole," I grit out as I get into my own car and slam the door. I want to scream, cry, and break his perfect fucking nose.

I hit the gas before he has the chance to drive away, flipping him off as I speed past. Sky immediately tails me.

It's all I can think about as I drive home, tears streaming down my face, the windows down as I welcome the cold slap of fresh air. The lights of the city glow in the distance—a city I used to love because I once felt like I could lose myself amongst the chaos and noise. However, lately, I feel like there are only a few faces I want to see. That it's too loud, too imposing, too shallow a city. Or maybe that's the life I built on top of it.

Before I know it, I'm stopped outside the front gates of my family estate, thinking about the time when Lorenzo parked in the very same spot, only to break in moments later to introduce himself to my parents for dinner. Absolutely ridiculous.

My hands curl around the steering wheel of the Mustang as that feeling of being trapped begins to creep in again, the frightful truth that I no longer have my father to blame for it.

The gates slowly open, and I just stare at the long, winding driveway, resistant to going down it once again.

Sky pulls up beside me, flipping up the visor to his helmet. I glare at him and ask, "What now?"

He raises a brow. "Do you want to know where your brother goes most nights? Or more specifically, where he is tonight?"

I don't like his insinuation that there's more behind this than I realize. Yet, deep down, I know he's offering me the answers I need.

"Why are you offering me this? Won't you get into trouble?" I ask, curiously.

He shrugs. "A part of my annoying charm is also meddling. Don't get this twisted. I'm doing this for my own sake, in hopes I get discharged from playing babysitter."

"I never asked that of you." I'm so sick of being handled like a fragile parcel, yet at heart I am grateful to have him here, so why is it so fucking hard for me to say thank you? When did I turn into this type of person?

"Yeah, but since you've forsaken Lorenzo, I'll get my ass handed to me if I leave my post. Whether you like it or not, he's still a fucking archangel to you; even more than you realize. I think he's a love-struck fool."

I swallow at his last statement and look up to the open gates welcoming me into a home that has been far from warm for as long as I can remember.

Maybe I really have lost it, but I'm tired of leaving my fate in other people's hands. I've let it go on for too long.

I face him again. "Where is he?"

His smile widens. "First of all, you'll need to wear something better than that," he says before closing the visor on his helmet. "I'm thinking something red and short."

"I think you want a punch to the face," I reply blandly, and I'm filled with encouragement as he laughs.

"I can see what Lorenzo saw in you. You might fit in after all," he says before revving his motorcycle and leading me down the driveway to the home I'm ready to see go up in flames.

36

LORENZO

I was meant to only check on her for a moment, but I couldn't make myself leave, not until she came out, and her gaze alone cut me down to size. When I arrived, Sky summarized through text what had happened with her friend Romi. Call me a selfish bastard, but the only one I care about is Lily.

She's always doing this, running to help everyone else before herself. She's been doing it all week, pretending to be the face of calm. If anything, she's been more rigid than the way she acted before I met her, only a crack away from falling into a thousand pieces.

I want her to break, to let it all out, if only to help hasten her ability to rebuild herself. I know she'll do it without me, yet I selfishly wish I could remain by her side, even if silently.

All I can do is have her back, to protect her from afar, even when she doesn't want my help.

It was only a matter of time until her brother showed his true colors, but I never thought he'd be stupid enough to walk into Luca Armani's Balmere Club. Then again, the idiot clearly hasn't pieced together that Luca and I are connected.

It benefits me, however, saving me the effort of paying him a personal visit—he's practically walked straight onto my doorstep.

I've been watching his movements for the past week as he jumps from club to club, accumulating more debt. He's desperate, and I have no doubt that Vince is well aware of the money Henrith owed, but now I know he has a hand in it too.

The bouncer steps to the side as I enter Balmere. Luca isn't here tonight, which means Vince lacks the good sense or connections to ask for a deal with Luca Armani. No, it means he's just here to outright gamble.

I ignore the naked dancers in cages, heading straight to the tables, avoiding the group of men who watch the women with interest, ready to make a purchase.

If Vince were a smarter man, he'd wait until tomorrow night, when big bets are made downstairs in the fighting ring. It's taken me a week too long to get to this point, to have all the information I need regarding the details of the private deal Henrith tried to conduct to save his own ass. Luca wants this dealt with; he wants the Taylor business, and I'm about to make it happen. This way will also ensure Lily no longer has a target on her back.

Since the death of Henrith, Nicholas Wayne hasn't made a move. Still, since their last assassin was returned to them in tiny pieces, I'm sure they've realized they're in over their heads and learning the hard way of whose territory they've stepped into and how insignificant their organization is compared to ours.

"Black," Vince says to the dealer as he shoves half of his chips in. Sweat beads on his forehead as his leg bounces. When the dealer spots me, he stops, and the onlookers knowingly split to the side to let me through as I come to stand behind Vince.

"Why'd you stop?" he asks in anticipation before noticing that everyone else is looking over his shoulder. Slowly, he does the same.

"Oh, Lorenz—"

I grab the back of his neck and slam his head into the table. A woman screams but is quickly pulled away as everyone but the dealer and one of the regulars remain seated at the table.

"Fuck!" Vince screams as I bring him back up by the scruff of his neck and drag him up to a stand. "I think you broke my nose."

"You're lucky it's not your legs or neck. We're overdue for a little chat." I shove him toward the two bouncers who wait behind me. They catch him and drag him along as I lead them to a private booth where Luca often conducts his business.

"What the fuck, man? I thought we were friends," he says nervously as he glances between the two men. "You came in right before I was going to win."

"Don't you think you've lost enough this week?" I ask, pacing back and forth, not at all inclined to take a seat across from a man like this. He might be Lily's brother, but I despise him, knowing the crushing disappointment she'd feel if she knew about his lies.

A gambler.

An addict.

Scum.

My gaze slices to him, and he pales, the pieces slowly clicking together as his jaw tightens. "You're not just in real estate, are you?"

I shoot him a cruel smile. "No, I'm not."

"If this is about the money I owe you, I'm making it back. I'll have it in a few days."

"You know your father said a similar thing right before I killed him," I tell him matter-of-factly, and watch as Vince's expression twists, but I see it in there, the thing he's been trying to hide the most. The truth of what he can't let slip from beneath the mask. "You two are more alike than you care to admit. I'm not the man you owe money to, but you certainly drew them to our territory, which is a problem. So let's just say I'm a man who... holds personal grudges." I remove my knife from my pocket, wanting nothing more than to carve his flesh for everything he's put Lily through, whether his stupid ass is aware of it or not.

"Look, man, I don't want to fight you," he says, raising his hands and trying to lean back as far away as he can from the edge of my blade.

"It wouldn't be much of a fight." One of the bouncers laughs, but at my glare, he clears his throat and stoically stands in silence once again.

"I hold a grudge because you thought you were a clever man when you are not. You thought your spoiled little ass would dance in a playground where you don't even understand the rules.

"Your father borrowed money from Nicholas Wayne, and when he was able to finally repay it with interest, you fucked it all up. You invested half into your company so you wouldn't go under, and the other half you gambled away in hopes of earning it back, plus some, to impress your father. When things didn't go to plan, you thought that was okay, didn't you? Because you thought they'd go for his head, not yours, and it would solve all your problems. You'd finally be free of him."

"What the fuck?" Lily's voice carries over the music and snaps me out of my vengeful daze. I lower the knife from her brother's throat. "Taking my father wasn't enough for you?" she demands, a vision of red as she shoves past people to walk up the stairs. The bouncers step in her way until they notice the hound behind her, masked, hands casually placed in his pockets.

That little meddlesome shit.

"Lily! Your boyfriend's crazy!" Vince yells as he tries to crawl over the chair. But I palm his shoulder, slamming him back down. Okay, his having a bleeding, broken nose right now is not a good look.

"Boss?" one of the bouncers asks.

"Don't you dare throw me out or, so help me, Lorenzo Moretti, I will hunt you down and put a bullet in your brain myself."

My cock twitches, and I look away, ashamed at how proud I am of her but also tangled with the anguish of seeing her again. I thought if I remained watching her from the shadows after today, it'd be enough.

But having her in front of me, her chest rising and falling, yet again in pain because of me? It's enough to make any man want to drop to their knees and beg for forgiveness. I despise that she holds this kind of control over me, despite being the one to give her the collar and leash.

"Lily, he's the asshole who killed our dad!" Vince begins, and I scoff at his theatrics. Slimy little asshole.

"Don't pretend like you're not happy about that. Isn't that what you wanted all along?" I cock my head to the side. I don't like the attention we're drawing. If it were just Vince, I couldn't give a shit about what type of display I make out of him, but having any type of crowd while Lily looks like that infuriates me.

"What are you talking about?" Lily asks me, angrily. She's no longer the woman who immediately has tears spring to her eyes; all that softness has been extinguished, and I'm proud but sorry to see it all the same. Only a few months in this world, and it's already hardened her so much.

She now only has anger to hold on to.

I raise my chin to the bouncers in a gesture for them to clear the room. They immediately spring into action, the floor staff following their silent order as the entire club is closed and everyone is shoved out. I'm going to pay for this later. Luca is not going to be happy, but at this point, I'm already past damnation for this woman.

"He's a liar, Lils. You don't know this man," Vince exclaims, and goes to stand, but I force my hand on his shoulder again, shoving him back into place.

"Quit shoving him," Lily says, coming to stand in front of her brother. I can't help but find her cute.

Despite my yearning for her earlier today, she's in a place now where we conduct business, and I refuse to let on that she's my weakness in front of the few remaining staff.

"Be careful, sweetheart, or you might be punished next," I warn her.

"Don't play your games with me right now," she bites back.

I look at the knife in my hand. "I stopped playing games with you a long time ago, Lily."

The steel of the blade glints in the flashing lights. I pocket it, knowing that despite whatever threats I'll make toward Vince, I won't do anything in front of her. I lost it when it came to her father, but I know she holds love for her brother. And I can't take a second family member from her. It turns out even a man like me has his limits when it comes to the woman he loves.

"Maybe you should be honest with her for once," I encourage Vince. "Either you tell her or I will."

Her gaze narrows on me, a wild storm swirling within those magnificent blue eyes. I've struggled falling asleep every single night, replaying and savoring the hours I've watched her from a distance.

I tell my boss I do it for him, but it'll go to the grave with me that I've done all of this for *her*.

"Vince, what's he talking about?" Lily demands, her gaze finally breaking from mine as she pins it on him. He bites his bottom lip, his gaze skittering around the floor.

"I made a mistake," he confesses.

Her shoulders sag ever so slightly, as if bracing herself for the blow that's about to come.

She deserves the truth, but I hate being the one to bring her the messenger. If I had it my own way, I would've buried this secret and simply made sure this debt was paid and that her brother did nothing to put her in harm's way again.

I'm uncomfortable with my newfound conscience,

brought out by this one tiny woman who can so easily bring me to my knees.

37

LILY

"I made a mistake." The moment those words fall out of my brother's mouth, I know I'm defeated.

I'm exhausted.

Exhausted from being lied to.

Exhausted from trying to keep this family together.

Exhausted from putting everyone else first.

"What did you do, Vince?" I ask carefully. I shake my head when he can't even meet my gaze. I can't believe this. Actually, yes, I can.

I scan the club. I've never been here, but it reeks of ill dealings and money as I stare at the gambling tables. My eyebrows furrow.

"What did you do with my money, Vince?" I ask, and when I focus back on him, he still won't raise his head to look at me. Slowly, I realize I've been conned by my own brother. I scoff in disbelief, finding it almost laughable.

"I'd say half of it is currently sitting on the roulette table where he bet it on black," Lorenzo says. I face him, that buildup of rage and hate, yearning and love coming to the surface. All the things I feel for this man, and yet, it's not his betrayal that hurts me the most right now. It's the fact that I have to hold myself back from running into his arms. It doesn't make any fucking sense.

This gravitational pull toward him never has.

But I know it's the one place I can fall apart and know I'll still be safe.

"If my brother won't answer me, then I demand you do." I level Lorenzo with a glare. "Does my brother owe you money? Is that it?"

Lorenzo is watching me carefully, as if I'm the predator in the room. It's his silence that grates on me most.

"Say something," I grit out. "Someone needs to give me the truth."

"Will you trust what comes out of my mouth?" Lorenzo asks carefully.

"Yes," I reply. Because I do. I don't know how or why, and it goes against all logic, but I do trust him.

"You can't believe him, Lils. He's a liar!" Vince yells from over my shoulder, and I whip my head toward him.

"Is that my money on the table?" I demand of him.

He curls into himself, becoming something I've never seen in my brother before. A coward.

"Your father's business was going under," Lorenzo starts, and takes a few steps back to lean against the railing. I can't help but notice the space he's creating between us, as if trying to make this more of a business transaction. Maybe our time spent together really was only in my head. "He made a deal with a man called Nicholas Wayne. He borrowed some money, and when it was time to pay it back with interest, he thought he could depend on his son to hand over the cash. Instead, Vince used it to save his own ass and gambled the rest away.

"He most likely thought they'd come for your father's head, and it'd eradicate the issues he's been dealing with being under your father's thumb with his expectations and demands."

I look back over my shoulder at my brother, who's still staring at the floor, and I know every word is the truth.

"What he probably didn't realize was that it wasn't your father they came for. It was *you*."

Vince and I both gape at him.

"No," Vince is quick to say. "I would never put my sister in danger. I might not be a good person, but I'd never hurt her."

Lorenzo's lips stretch into a cruel smile filled with disdain. "The thing is, in this world, you don't get to choose who dies when you're the one dealt a beggar's hand."

I begin to piece parts together. "It was never Ara they were after in Italy, was it?"

His brown eyes soak me in, and he simply nods confirmation. I release a breath. "Oh God." My hand falls to my stomach. They were after me this whole time. I mocked Lorenzo for being so on guard that it was a stretch they'd be after me, but they were. "Who are these people? How much do we owe them? When will they come next?"

Lorenzo straightens to his full height. "They won't come anywhere near you. My boss is generously willing to make an offer to get you out. In return, you'll sign over your family's companies but still manage them on the front end."

Vince scoffs. "I'm not giving you shit."

Lorenzo raises an eyebrow. "Oh, so you're certain with all the debt you have, that you can not only pay them with interest but all the others you owe, in enough time to ensure your sister's safety?"

My brother flinches with the realization of how royally fucked he is.

Lorenzo sounds so clinical, so cold, just like when we first began. A lump lodges in my throat as I say, "How convenient an opportunity for you and your boss to gain in this situation. Didn't you say, after all, when your boss makes a profit, so do you?"

"When Ara asked me to watch you, my boss definitely seized an opportunity. Ara, however, had nothing to do with this. She was wholeheartedly concerned for your safety."

I scoff, surprised he's even defending her. "And you?"

He pins me with a glare, promising punishments and sweet nothings. My core floods with warmth, and I hate how my body betrays me. How much it yearns to be with this man who's done nothing but flip my world upside down since he came into it. Then again, pieces were moving against me long before his intervention.

"If my brother signs everything over, and you get what you want, then what, you pay them off? Do I not even get a say in this when it's my family's fight? *My* fight," I correct, because at this point it has nothing to do with the money or danger that lurks around the corner. I just need to know, no matter what, that there was some truth to the time we spent together.

I don't know why, but it feels like the last piece that will keep me intact or break me apart. Through the pain, I'm just so *angry*.

Lorenzo's expression softens. "I have only ever been fighting on your behalf."

"But you want my father's business. Was any of what you said about protecting me the truth?" My voice grows smaller. Because I trusted him, and I'm confused by the fact that I still do. But what I've come to learn is that everyone is only here for themselves.

"Yes. Every word," he says on a breath, his fists

clenched at his sides, and I want to laugh like a madwoman at the man who is still willing to restrain himself, all for his master.

"It's a shame you're in your own shackles, huh?" I bite out.

"From what I can see, sweetheart, you haven't stepped too far out of yours either. A cage is still a cage, whether it's of someone else's making or your own now."

His words are a slap in the face, but one thing I've always been able to depend on with this man is that he's not one to mince words, and he'll bite back tenfold when I shove him.

"So, Vince will sign over the companies, and you'll save our asses. Then we have nothing more to do with you or those other people, correct?" I clarify, wanting to be anywhere but in a room with him.

"Lils, we can't just sign over everything we've worked so hard to build!" Vince argues, and I snap at him.

"Why? You've already gambled it away. And did you forget that they've tried to kill me *twice*? Am I really that fucking replaceable to you?" He falls silent, and I can see the reality of his actions only just setting in. "Then, after I'm gone, if they still don't have their money, they come after you or Mom. Is that what you want?"

"Of course not," he quietly says.

"Then clean up your shit. Once this is dealt with,

you're going to rehab." When he goes to speak, I put my finger up. "I don't give a fuck what anyone thinks about you or the family name. I'm sick of hiding all these secrets. You owe me this at the very least. This isn't a negotiation."

I toss my hair over my shoulder, a mix of being furious and empowered. I take the few steps down the stairs, my heels clicking against the floorboards. Sky watches me and raises a hand, as if to high-five me. I can feel the penetrating glare of Lorenzo, so I purposely make a point to slap his palm with mine.

Fuck this boys' club that decided to put my life on the line.

Fuck all of these secrets and their restraints.

"So, where will it be now, miss?" the hound asks, walking behind me. "Told you the red dress would be a nice touch."

My lips tilt ever slightly, but I refrain from giving in to the smile. "One more night at the estate, then it's time to close one more door," I say, finally feeling like I can take action since I have all the pieces.

I'm uneasy about what will happen next, but at least I feel like I can finally move forward on my terms.

38

LORENZO

Lily rolls over in her sleep. Every night she's stayed in this house, she's slept restlessly. Having Sky follow her day in and day out has never been enough for me to feel she's safe. She'd hate me if she knew I snuck in every night, but it hasn't kept me away.

Watching her sleep is the only peace I seem to find nowadays. She's no more than a few feet away from me, and yet, she couldn't feel more distant.

I'm proud of her for today, for everything she's broken down around her, and for what she's become. I always knew she had it in her, and it's only expected that her scathing tongue be directed toward me.

Looking out the window, I can see the sun has started rising. I don't know how much longer I'll permit myself to do this. Once I close the deal on the Taylors' behalf, I'll have no excuse to do this. But I can't possibly see how I'll stay away. I stand, move to the bed, then crouch beside it, studying the features of her delicate face.

I pick up a strand of her hair between my fingers, watching her.

This is my peace.

There's no denying that she's become my undoing.

Like every other night, I want her to wake, to see her brilliant blue eyes come to life and look at me with adoration like she had only weeks ago.

I made my choice and would never take it back. Standing, I check my phone. Two missed calls from Luca. I told him I'd return to him after the contract was signed, but I came here first.

I've been raised as a person to take, especially on behalf of Luca's whims and wishes. Yet, the only thing that I've ever selfishly wanted, I no longer have the right to touch. And here I am, like a starved man, adoring her, knowing that I can't bring her the same peace she brings me.

I don't know when this unruly obsession took over my life, but it's certainly destroying it.

My routine.

My work.

Me.

I open the window ever so slightly, letting the fresh breeze sweep through the room, then I slip out through the door.

By the time I reach the gates and climb over them,

Sky is sitting on his motorcycle, arms folded in front of him, waiting for me expectantly. "Every morning, I catch you like this. You know they call this stalking, right?"

"Shut the fuck up," I reply. "You're lucky I don't beat you into a bloody pulp after the stunt you pulled."

He ignores my threat.

"What are you going to do when Luca doesn't want us to protect her anymore?" he calls out as I walk to my car.

It goes without saying that once that happens, she won't have anything else to be scared of. The problem will be gone. A problem I would've disposed of, whether or not her brother signed over the companies.

I drive toward the Armani estate. Even with the knowledge that it's not the Bratva retaliating for killing one of their members, Luca has kept himself and Ara in the family compound, opposed to their own home, until the situation is completely handled.

It feels almost nostalgic driving through the gates and walking down halls that have felt like home to me. Even when I had my own place to return to, I often didn't.

I've always lived to serve, still do.

Yet, it feels different now.

I'm different, and part of me wishes I'd never been exposed to the sunshine that is Lily Taylor, because perhaps I wouldn't be questioning my loyalty to Luca and the Armani family.

When I walk into Luca's office, he's sitting behind his desk.

He doesn't even look up as he says, "Are you wanting me to put a bullet in your head, Lorenzo?"

When I don't reply and simply slide the signed contracts in front of him, he continues. "You were supposed to come to me straight away."

"I have no excuse."

He arches an eyebrow. "At the very least, will you tell me where you were? Does it have to do with a certain little blonde friend of Ara's?"

When I don't reply, he shakes his head and grabs the papers. "I've been warned by my wife not to interfere with you and her friend. It was actually more of a threat since she said she won't have sex with me if I force you to never see Lily again."

His blue eyes are lethal, and I have no doubt he wants to kill me simply for the fact that he got threatened with no sex. "I apologize for the complications this has brought to your marriage."

He shakes his head. "Despite your messy interference, we've obtained what we wanted, and now you simply have one more task to finish it. I want this Nicholas Wayne to know exactly what happens when people trespass in my territory. I want them to pay. You deal with them here, and I'll have the remains of their little nest flushed out in Italy."

"Yes, sir."

"This has, however, made me acutely aware of the

fact that I need to replace Ivan's position in Italy. Everything's been working well there, but there's still plenty to be gained and reinstated. Once this is dealt with, you'll relocate to Italy, running affairs on my behalf."

Everything stops.

Relocated?

"Sir?"

He looks up from the papers then. "One might consider this a promotion, Lorenzo. Is it not to your liking?"

I shake my head. "I have always made it clear my post is to be beside you, to protect you. It's why I've always done this."

He shrugs. "You've disobeyed me, Lorenzo, more than once. I trust you, but I can't help but notice your distraction. I'll appoint someone else here to manage your position. I mean it when I say this is an honor. I want you to grow our business. Don't you think a fresh start might be good for you?"

I keep my face expressionless as mixed emotions pass through me, something I've never had to deal with before.

"You're excused," he says.

My hands ball into fists, but I remove myself before I say or do something I'll regret.

Technically, it is an honor to be the head of the Italian arm of the business, but not being by his side makes me uncomfortable.

Not being here where Lily is also makes me feel a particular way.

I have no right to her, and yet, the thought of leaving, of the true end to whatever was growing between us... makes me hate Luca when the only one I should hate is myself.

I chose this, so why the fuck do I hate every single day without her scathing words, laughter, or gentle touch?

I thought I'd come to terms with my decision, but the reality of being moved to a different post, in a completely different country, rattles me in a way I never thought possible.

39

LILY

My eyes flutter, a fresh, cool breeze forcing me to snuggle deeper under my blankets. It took me what felt like hours to fall asleep last night, as I stared at the ceiling, processing everything I learned. I can't even cry anymore. I'm just so tired of people lying and betraying me. It's left a bitter numbness in its wake.

It was definitely the nudge I needed to finally take my life into my own hands, regardless of what happens to others. I love my family, but it doesn't mean I'm only here to serve them.

My feet hit the floor, and I grab my phone, opening the most recent text message from Sienna.

Romi still isn't herself, but apparently she's functioning. And so will I today. I'll go to the flower shop for the first time since my father died. I expect it to be a mess. The fresh flowers I had on display have most likely wilted and need to be thrown out, but I want to put a bouquet together for Romi.

I walk to the window to close it, and find a single lily carefully placed there. I pick it up, rolling it around in my fingers, wondering how it got there. I don't have to question it too much because I *know* Lorenzo was the one who left it there.

There's been a bittersweet exhaustion through all of this that, despite everything, he's still all around me. I don't know if that's because the hatred got sucked out of me or that I know he's still the one person I can depend on to help get me out of this situation that never had anything to do with him from the beginning.

A low, muffled sound comes from my mother's room down the hall. Panic rocks me. What if someone's come for her? What if I'm no longer the target?

I run to her room, collecting a vase from the hall table between our bedroom doors as the only weapon I can find, and fling open her door, raising the vase above my head, my heart racing.

My mother screams, then I scream as I see naked flesh. "Oh, eww. Eww." Two bodies are tangled in the sheets, and I look away, disgusted. "Eww, no. Yuck."

"Lily!" my mother shouts as I slam the door behind me and slowly step away. What the fuck did I just walk in on? I carefully place the vase down, even though the water and flowers remain to be picked up, and then descend the stairs, as if trying to run away from the visual.

I take each step in disbelief, recalling what I just saw.

Mom and Bentley?

"What the fuck?" I say, blinking and shaking my head.

"Lily!" my mother calls over the railing, looking down on me. Bentley is only wearing boxers as he comes to stand behind her.

"Nope." I put my hand up. "I've had my fill of everyone's secrets. I'm done." I throw my hands in the air. "I'm done," I say again, like a crazy person.

I walk to the kitchen and grab my favorite iced tea before pouring it into a tumbler.

My mother calls for me again, but I ignore her, making my way out the back door and into the gardens, losing myself amongst the flowers she worked so hard to maintain all of these years, despite my father threatening to burn them down.

"Lily?" my mother says cautiously from behind me. I turn in the direction of the sun, surprised that all I feel is a little grossed out at catching my mother having sex. I'm not even mad. I don't blame her. My father was a horrible man. But that's something no child wants to see.

"This whole week you've kept to yourself and barely spoken after Dad's funeral, but you've made time to..." I can't even finish the sentence.

She looks ashamed, and I hate that I've made her feel that way.

"I'm the worst mother. I'm sorry you found out the way you did, and right after your father—"

"I don't give a shit about Father," I finally say out loud, and it startles her.

"Don't say that," she says quietly, but it lacks any real forcefulness, and I realize with startling clarity that she was even more conditioned than I to come to his defense. I couldn't even comprehend how jarring my father's death might've been for her. I thought her silence might've been due to her mourning the man she loved, but perhaps it was shock from the freedom she's now been bestowed. Sometimes, it's too scary to believe the cage door is open.

"I just needed time to myself to process. I've always told you and your brother not to worry about me," she says. And it's exactly because of that that I always had.

"Has this just started with Bentley or...?" Her expression is enough of an answer. Right, so it was an affair. "Did Dad know?"

She rolls her eyes. "As if your father paid enough attention to me to even care."

I place my hands on my hips. "Yep, then we're still talking about the same man."

"Let's sit down and talk, shall we?" she says, looking at me as if I might run away at any moment. I sigh, taking a seat beside her, because in truth, I want to have a conversation with her as well. I just wasn't expecting to have it in such an unorthodox way.

My mother stares at me, and the heaviness of all

the things unsaid for so many years begins to settle into place. It's always acted as a barrier between us, except I'm not scared of it anymore.

"I hated him," I confess. "I never understood why you stayed."

She half smiles, then releases it, as if realizing for the first time that she doesn't have to pretend that everything's okay.

"He was a good man once," she says wistfully. "At one point, I thought I was doing the right thing by staying, so you children wouldn't feel his wrath as it became worse. I told myself at times that it wouldn't happen again. Then I came to terms that his outbursts only happened now and then."

"By outbursts, you mean *abuse*, Mom. He was an abusive drunk."

The way she's looking at me, it's as if I've slapped her in the face. Her mouth opens and closes, like she's unable to find a response. Perhaps a week ago, I might've been gentler with my words, sympathetic almost, but it's time we took accountability for the blatant truths.

"I was scared the night your boyfriend hit him." I don't bother to correct her about Lorenzo and me no longer being together, because were we ever? "But I'd be lying if the thought of finally being free didn't go through my head," she admits.

My stomach drops as I acknowledge the same type of sadistic guilt I hear in her voice.

"Why didn't you ever leave him?" I repeat. "And don't say it was for us kids, because we both left this house a long time ago. Why did you choose to stay with him for all these years?"

I don't know why it's so important for me to know, because in my heart of hearts, I stayed, not yet ready to let go of the idea of the father he could've been, but mostly because I was too frightened to let my mother go.

It was only a few weeks ago that I pulled her aside in these very same gardens when Lorenzo ambushed our family dinner, asking her if she was okay—if my father had stopped. She denied knowing what I was talking about, as if I were the one going mad.

My mother sighs and wrings her hands. "I'm not brave like you, sweetheart. I was scared of what would happen if I ever did. I've only ever known this life. I was scared he'd not only take it all away but ruin any chance I had of a future, even if smaller in comparison to all of these things."

My mother is materialistic to a degree; I suppose we all are. It's part of the reason why I thought she might've stayed, but I realize now her fear ran deeper than mine.

"I only ever let myself steal moments of happiness with Bentley over the years. I even considered running away with Bentley once. He promised he had enough money set aside so we could run away and have a simple life." She laughs to herself. "At the time, I thought it was such a pipe dream, and I made him promise to look the other way when your father became... *unpredictable*. Ironically, now that the house is mine, I'm not so sure I want to live in it anymore. Maybe I want that simple life now."

She stares at me, as if expecting guidance. I thought she was so devastated by the loss of my father, but this whole time, much like myself, she's been battling with how to free herself from his ghostly clutches.

"We could sell the house," I suggest.

"You and your brother wouldn't mind?" she asks, sounding surprised.

I scoff. "I'd much rather see this house burn to the ground than you be left in it for another day. I just want you to be happy, Mom. I think it's time we looked for our own happiness. Don't you?"

Her shoulders shift, the noticeable tension she'd walked out with slowly receding. As I look at her, I see the woman who raised me years ago. The woman who used to play with me and my brother in the backyard as children, chasing us as if there were no worries in the world, until we realized the only concerns we had were the ones within the walls of our home.

If Bentley can encourage a rosy-cheeked version of my mother to rise to the surface once again, then they have my blessing.

"Are you happy, Lily? Is the flower shop really what brings you joy? I always thought the reason you opened it was for me, not because you actually wanted it yourself."

My eyebrows shoot up. I'm surprised she's so bold to say it finally. I lean back, weights evaporating layer by layer and freeing me.

"I did open it for you. I loved spending time with you in the garden. Even when I went to college, I knew I didn't want to go into the corporate world like Vince and Dad. But then I made it my own. It wasn't just for you. It was for me too."

"And now?" she carefully asks.

Isn't that the question?

I can be anyone and go anywhere.

This city that I once loved so much seems so small, or maybe I no longer want to be hidden amongst the masses and the chaos.

"I don't know, but I'm working on it," I admit.

The years of suppression and fear have been liberated from my mother in the matter of a week, but there are glimmers of the old her. The one that inspired me as a child. The one who laughed freely and danced on occasion.

The one who was radiant and smiled, not because society and my father told her to, but because she had something to look forward to.

With that knowledge, a certain peace finally begins to settle within me, and for the first time in a long time, I feel like I can breathe.

40

LILY

It's the first day I've been back to the shop, and I've been dreading it. Except when I open the door, it appears to have been perfectly managed in my absence. I flick the light on, shocked that the plants haven't wilted.

Only half of them remain, which means someone's been throwing them out. I look out the window, where Sky stands, casually smoking a cigarette. I don't even have it in me to reprimand him because having him loitering there like that is bad for business.

When I come to a stop at the front counter, my heart drops as I notice a cup of my favorite iced tea, condensation dripping down the side, indicating it hasn't been there that long.

I gnaw at my bottom lip, knowing who's been maintaining the shop and left this tea.

Beside it is a small red box from Cartier. I place my

handbag to the side and open the box, revealing a pair of pink pearl earrings. No name. No card.

My stomach flutters because, in truth, they're beautiful, but it's not the present itself that has my emotions twisting. It's knowing that he's still all around me, even when I cursed and shoved at him. He's still here, as imposing as he was when I first asked him to stop shadowing me. Except now, as much as I hold on to the hate I have for him, I miss him.

Amidst everything, he's still the one person I want to curl into just for a moment of peace.

I'm not the same woman I was six months ago, and as crazy as these few months have been, I'm grateful for that, and a huge part of that transformation is credited to the man I've forsaken.

The front bell jingles, and I snap the box shut. My heart races with anticipation, but I'm somewhat disappointed when I turn and find Ara standing there. Not because I don't want to see her, but because I was expecting, almost hoping, for the giver of this present.

"Hey!" I hide the box behind my back. "Sorry, I haven't stopped by. It's been busy."

"I'm sorry too. I've been busy, as well, but I needed to come see you to apologize." It's strange to see this woman, who struggles to make time for herself, let alone others, show up in my shop, wanting to apologize. Especially when this situation wasn't her fault.

"You don't have to apologize, Ara." I place the box on the counter. "I know what your husband asked

Lorenzo to do," I say, addressing the elephant in the room.

"My husband is an asshole. I just wish I'd known sooner. I don't want you to think I've taken advantage of you in any of this. And if you do, I don't blame you. I just want you to know, whatever you need, simply let me know what it is, and I'll make it happen. I want to make it up to you."

I'm listening as I glance around the shop, my oasis that kept me busy and passionate for years. It feels so small, almost nostalgic now. As Ara apologizes, I can't help but notice the change in me. I've always admired Ara for her bluntness and ability to command a room.

Perhaps I was envious even. I don't feel that any longer, understanding we're still both just women in a man's world. The difference is, I no longer feel weak because of it.

"If I'm being honest, Ara, I don't really care about my father's businesses. And as for my brother, he's lucky I still care about him at all." I do love my brother, but I won't tolerate his bullshit anymore either. I let that slide for too long with my father, and I will *never* make that mistake again. Not for any man. Not for anyone. "In a way, I guess your husband is actually getting me out of a pickle, you know, with someone trying to kill me and all."

Her brow wrinkles slightly, as if she's confused by my casual response. Silence fills the air, and her hand comes to rest on her stomach. I offer her the stool behind the counter, but she smiles and politely refuses.

"You've changed."

"I have," I admit. It's strange to have it recognized by someone other than myself. Once, I might've sought that outside validation, and yet, I don't feel the need anymore. "I've changed a lot."

Ara smiles, deciding to take the seat as she looks at her watch. I know she's a busy woman, and I can tell by the way Tony peers inside that he realizes they're going to be longer than expected. His face drops as he looks at Sky, who is clearly antagonizing him about something.

I walk around the counter and bring some flowers from the back room to the front. Not one thing is out of place. It's as if the shop wasn't even closed for a day.

Ara seems curious about the red box on the counter, but doesn't ask about it. "Apparently, Romi left the house today for the first time."

"Good. I've been worried about her." Still am, because I know she hasn't been the same since her roommate's death. "I wanted to come in and do a bouquet for her." Not that flowers ever replace those who have been lost, but it's always been the place I've been able to express my condolences.

"I've been worried about her too," Ara says quietly, tapping a manicured nail on the edge of the counter, seeming impatient. She's not a woman who often stops, but when she speaks next, I realize it's more to do with the question on her mind.

"Have you spoken to Lorenzo?"

I'm sure she has some insight as to how our conversation went last night.

"Besides last night, telling my brother to sign the contract, and that I basically hated his guts... nope."

Ara slowly nods, her hand rubbing her stomach. A small part of me wonders what it's like to be pregnant, to be married, and start a family. Although I now know that Ara and Luca were far from a fairy-tale romance, I can't help but be slightly envious.

"How did you know Luca was the one for you?" I ask curiously as I begin to put purple and black flowers together. "Knowing who he is and what he does for a living, why did you decide to remain with him?"

She studies me for a few moments, and I know that's when Ara has been caught off guard by a question. She's not someone who is often vulnerable either.

"Sometimes, I don't think we get a choice in how we feel. I'd cut so many people out of my life, and I was even willing to die for my revenge. You have it twisted if you thought I was anything good when Luca and I met. I was fueled by so much hatred that, honestly, he was the first person, in his own sickening way, to remind me of what love was. It was a small step toward the growth I had to make, but I decided to follow where it led me. He infuriates me. We fight just as much as we make up, but I know he's my person. I just *know*.

"There's something attractive about knowing the man you choose is literally willing to take a bullet and die for you. Devotion like that is not something that should be overlooked."

My hand pauses as I go to clip the stem of a black rose.

Devotion.

A man willing to die for you.

He's my person.

All of these I can attribute to someone who, although he isn't here with me, seems to have marked every corner of my life with his overbearing presence.

When I look up at Ara, I know she's been intentional with every word.

She slides off the stool, holding her belly. "I wanted to drop by and let you know Lorenzo is dealing with Nicholas Wayne tomorrow, so you won't have to worry about being a target any longer. Luca has also offered Lorenzo a job in Italy. He'll be due to fly out in a few weeks when he takes over."

My heart stops.

He's leaving?

I should be elated, yet an immediate panic consumes me. I should be grateful I'll never see him again. But my heart and logic express different things.

He can't leave me.

He can't leave me?

What the fuck am I thinking?

"Why are you telling me this?" I ask, hating how small my voice comes out.

I do miss him.

And I hate that type of power he has over me.

It doesn't make sense to love the man who killed my father and used my family for a business deal to please his boss, so he could what... get a promotion?

Then I begin running the list of all the sweet gestures he's made.

Regardless, it's simply how I feel when I'm with him.

I hate him now for the suffering he's caused me, and it's fucked-up that I still yearn for him.

"I wanted to make sure you knew so you could make a choice," she says.

"I've already made my choice."

She nods agreeably. "Yes, but I wonder how authentic that choice is. Is it the one you've made for yourself or the one you think you should make? I know he hurt you, Lily, but he's also done everything for you. I'm overstepping, but he's risked everything for you."

I scoff. "He hasn't risked anything for me."

Ara looks at me pointedly when she adds, "He could've been killed for prioritizing you over Luca's demands. On numerous occasions, actually." My eyebrows furrow because Lorenzo never told me about any of this.

"Didn't you warn me away from Lorenzo? More than once?" I remind her.

She looks over her shoulder at me with a half-smile as she reaches the door. "Who said I'm not still doing that? But I also think it's important you make this decision for yourself, not for anyone else. *You.* I'm here for you no matter what you decide. I just wanted you to know that the fucker's miserable, and it hasn't been easy on him either."

A heavy weight settles in my chest. This whole time, I've been protecting myself, as I felt like everyone I loved was betraying me. And Lorenzo *did* betray me. I let too many people do that—even my family. The difference, however, is that Lorenzo never walked out on me. And he'd always done what he thought was best for my protection. Something shifts within me, causing confusing feelings to bubble up. I can't make an exception for him. I mean, he literally killed my father.

A father you don't miss.

I try to cling to that thought. Because what kind of person does that make me if I stand by him after all he's done?

Or maybe I'm using this as an excuse because I haven't fully accepted the fact that I've fallen in love with a killer. And I can't move forward without either fully embracing that part of him or denying it.

"The earrings are beautiful, by the way," Ara comments, bringing me back to the room.

"When did you look at them?" I ask, shocked by the open box on the counter.

The jingle of the bell chimes as she opens the door, but right before she leaves, I call out for her. She pauses, watching me expectantly. "How do you forgive the man who killed your father?"

She offers a small smile. "I'm the wrong person to ask. I put a bullet through the man's brains who murdered my mother, remember?" she replies, and a shudder runs through me, goose bumps rising on my flesh.

Much like Lorenzo, this is a part of who Ara is. But I so easily accept it about her. I'm shocked but also immediately accepting as she opens up this cold and cruel tendril of her past.

"I loved my mother. And the man I love was willing to give me her killer's head on a silver platter. At his own expense, he showed me he was fighting in my corner. Lorenzo is dangerous, Lily, but he would go to great lengths to set the world on fire for you, if you only asked him."

She's quiet for a moment, then continues, "Had I known about your father and his... vices, I would've killed him myself." It feels strange that others now know his true nature, yet unlike before, I have no urge to defend him. She casually shrugs. "That's how I love. Only you can decide if you feel like it's right or wrong."

My jaw tightens as I'm once again in awe of her. I don't condone violence, but she lives fiercely and passionately. She knows who she is, unapologetically. So why can I embrace this part of her but not the same in Lorenzo?

His hurt is different.

Because I love him.

I internally sigh with the bombardment of the very narrative I've been trying to run away from.

I might not be as ruthless as Ara, but it doesn't mean I can't be a part of their world.

After all, my choices and life are of my own making, and when I think about where I want to be or who I want to be with... my heart screams only one name.

It's fucked-up.

Maybe the craziest choice I've ever made.

There's no guarantee it was ever requited. Maybe his gifts and lingering presence are only part of a twisted game.

But in my heart, I doubt that.

It's time I stopped blaming Lorenzo for ignoring my wishes and thanked him for listening to the small part of me that was crying for help.

I swallow hard, acknowledging that major difference.

Instead of defending the dead man who only ever wanted to keep me caged and hurt me, I should thank the man who did everything he could to free and protect me.

Whether he'll accept me or not.

41

LORENZO

Lily has become my obsession, and I'm checking my phone every few minutes, updating myself on her location. Since the moment I realized she was on her way here, I've been standing at the end of the driveway, waiting for her.

I just finished bagging the twenty million to hand over to Nicholas Wayne, who accepted the invitation personally to receive it. I had the intention to stop by her shop to check on her from a distance, but it appears she's made my work easier for me.

She pulls into the driveway in the Mustang she's recently taken a liking to. It's so opposite to the pink floral dress she wears, but it suits her. The moment she steps out of the car, relief washes through me. There's always a heavy feeling in my gut when she's not within reach. I trust the hound to keep her safe, but I also believe no one is better at the task than myself.

Sky pulls up on his motorcycle shortly behind her, and that light-hearted thought quickly evaporates into irritation. I walk down the driveway, speaking to him before addressing her.

"Leave," I growl.

"You told me to never leave her side and to protect her with my life. I'm just doing what you—"

"*Leave*," I reiterate, sick of this little punk's antics. My gaze slices to Lily, whose mouth is slightly parted.

The hound grumbles under his breath but does as he's told, jumping back onto his motorcycle.

"You're a bossy asshole, you know that?" Is the first thing that comes out of her mouth.

I look down on the little Goody Two-shoes who folds her arms over her chest. Swear words have slowly trickled into her vocabulary, and I can't help but feel smug that it's most likely from my influence. "I distinctly remember a time when you quite liked being told what to do."

A flush of red streaks her cheeks. "I also remember how that pushed me away. You doing what you want with no regard for how I feel."

A breeze sweeps between us, and I notice the goose bumps that immediately erupt over her skin. I want to invite her inside, offer her comfort, since lately I've only seemed to give her pain.

"You know where I stand, sweetheart. As long as you're safe, I don't care how much you hate me. I'll die like that."

The movement in her throat as she swallows gives her nervousness away, and my gaze softens.

How I love this woman.

Her kindness, her softness.

All of the things I can never manage to be are what I admire about her the most.

"Sounds like a lonely death."

"One I've always imagined for myself."

And that's the truth. I never imagined wanting a family of my own, a person to turn to in confidence, or ever needing any kind of comfort. But this woman weaved herself into my heart so effortlessly, it's terrifying to imagine if she ever gave me a chance, what else she might be capable of. One thing's for certain— I'd never let her go.

I might not be capable of being a Prince Charming, but I'll certainly flip the world upside down to give her everything she could ever want, if only to have her look at me in the way she once did, with that benevolent smile pointed in my direction.

She seems unsure as to what to do with her hands. She goes to speak, but then her mouth closes again.

I attempt to say something, but then for the first time ever in my life, I'm not sure what to say.

I want to say the right thing.

Do the right thing.

But it always feels so out of my reach when it comes to this woman.

She feels out of my grasp.

"I'm coming with you tomorrow to deal with Nicholas. This is my family drama. I want to see it through to the end," she finally says defiantly, as if trying to push away the tension that ripples between us.

I hold back a laugh. "You're not coming with me, sweetheart. Who told you about the exchange anyway?" There's no fucking way I'm putting her in harm's way. Even with every precaution that we have, I'm not taking her anywhere near the people who have been trying to kill her.

"Why? Doubting your skills to keep me safe?"

"Watch it," I growl, because if there's one thing I pride myself on, it's keeping this woman safe. If only she had better sense to watch what she says, then she might not get herself into so much trouble.

She casually shrugs. "I have my sources. And it wasn't a request, or are you yet again going to ignore my wishes?"

I lick my lips. This little brat. "That would involve you sitting in a car with me, and last I checked, you can't even stand being in the same hemisphere as me."

"Yet, here we are," she sasses back, begging to be punished.

"Yet, here we are."

Another awkward tendril of tension mixes in the air.

"Were you going to speak to me before going to Italy?" she asks in a rushed breath.

How the fuck does she know about that?

Not even the little dipshit hound would know about that yet. And then it dawns on me. Ara would be the only other person to know.

"It would've been the easiest way," I admit, and her face twists furiously, but I finish before she can spew bloody murder. "However, I haven't yet accepted."

"Oh."

More silence, then, "But you will, won't you?"

Most in my position would jump at an opportunity like that. Hell, it's not like Luca exactly asked, though; it was an order. But there's one thing that keeps me here. It has no logic. No profit. Not even comfort, knowing that part of me wants to stay in the same city as this hellfire of a woman who can't stand me. I simply need to know she's close by and safe.

"Why do you care?" I ask.

She scoffs. "Well, sorry, I thought I deserved a better explanation than that, but if I don't even get that, then I guess that's all I have to say." She turns and opens the car door, but I slam it behind her, locking her between the car and my chest.

I breathe down her neck as I say, "We're not done here. Stop running away, Sunshine."

Her breath is shaky as she looks away, the tinted reflection of the window showing me her every expression.

"What would you have me say?" I ask her honestly. What does she want to hear? For some reason, I always seem to say and do the wrong thing. "I'll always work like this, doing or saying things that displease you when I think it'll protect you. This won't change about me, Lily. I kill for a living. I bring down empires for my own gain. And I certainly don't *share*." The thought of her being with any other man... That'll happen over my dead fucking body. Just the thought makes me livid, and it's the part I struggle to let go of most. It's one of the many reasons I can't imagine myself not being in her life, let alone the same city as her. "I haven't accepted the job because..." It's on the tip of my tongue. I mentally prepare myself for when she'll push me away again. I take one more inhale of her floral scent. "I can't seem to stay away from you."

She lets out a shaky breath, but I continue. "I will never be the man you imagined for yourself, but I'm obsessed, Sunshine, and I don't know how to fix myself. I haven't accepted Luca's offer because of *you*. You've become my undoing, and you can't even stand me. I can have anything in the world, and thought I had everything I needed. But it's nothing without you."

She goes to turn, but I hold her in place, too scared to face her directly. Too fearful of how she'll look at me with disgust. How confusing it is for someone like me to fall to my knees like this when I've dealt with monstrosities.

"I don't know how to forgive you," she confesses quietly.

"I don't regret killing your father. I'd do it again

with the same outcome. Your safety is my first priority."

"And what's your second priority, Lorenzo?"

My eyebrows furrow, and I give her enough space to turn and face me. Her brilliant blue eyes stare up into mine. I can't be so conceited as to think that she'll forgive me, but I'm willing to beg for it.

My second priority? I've never had one past Luca. But the way she's looking at me, she's searching for something, and that heavy weight of not offering the right answer burns at me. But I'll still only give her my truth.

"Your happiness. How can I do that from Italy? How can I have any right when I've made you loathe me so much?" I say earnestly, and I'm surprised when my own voice gives out.

Her eyes soften as her hand gently presses against my chest. My body burns, yearning for her touch. "Do you respect me, Lorenzo?"

My eyebrows dip. "Of course." What kind of question is that?

"Then you will let me join you tomorrow to close this chapter of my family's mess." She raises her finger to my lips before I can adamantly refuse. "If you respect me, you let me in on the decisions. Only I can tell you how to protect me and make me happy. Do you understand? You don't have to make all the decisions, Lorenzo. I'm a part of them, too. I'm not a little doll to be looked after. You need to trust that I can look after myself as well."

"Maybe in your world, but in mine—" Her finger presses harder against my lips, keeping my mouth shut.

"You really like the sound of your own voice, don't you? Listen to what I'm saying. I don't want us to be in separate worlds anymore. I want us to make decisions together, but I need you to meet me halfway. I might not have been raised in a brutal world like you, and if I'm honest, I'm still scared of it, but I want to be with you, Lorenzo. The only way I can do that is if you work with me, instead of bubble wrapping me. If you truly think I'm strong, then let me express it, instead of over-shadowing it."

A mixture of hope and vulnerability swirls in my chest. A distinct proposition. One that I want to grasp onto so quickly, if only to hold her once more. But I'll never agree to this woman half-heartedly. "You're asking me to go against everything I know. I'm here to protect you, to provide everything you ever need. You can't ask me to put you in harm's way."

"And you were willing to do all of those things, even if I still hated you. If you're willing to accept that, won't you consider my offer of a partnership, of love instead of walking down this lonely, dark path? You're not putting me in harm's way. I'm choosing this for myself. I can't forgive you if you don't see or hear my demands, Lorenzo. This is my fight, so let me be a part of it. Let me close this chapter for myself so I can start anew."

I immediately want to argue, but the words fall short on my lips, hindered by the way she earnestly stares at me. She's the strongest woman I've ever fucking met, and I'm so proud of her for standing her ground. But, fuck me, she couldn't make it any more challenging. Yet I cling to the ray of hope like a starved man.

"You can forgive me?" I ask, confirming if I heard her correctly. "Any sane woman would run the other way. Lily, I'm not good for you. You couldn't possibly be suggesting you want to give this a go?" Despite my yearning, I naturally betray myself, still offering her an out because I know it'll be my damnation.

I'll never let her go, even when I know I'm not the best choice for her. Even when I know my hands are bloody and tainted and shouldn't touch something as precious as a woman like this. Even when it terrifies me that the last person I had love for fell off a cliff edge at the age of five. What if I can't protect Lily forever either? What if I only disappoint her and ruin what might've been a normal life for her?

Her hands pull me in by the shirt, and her lips crash against mine, the gentle caress of a woman I've been pushing away for years, ever since the very first time she kissed me.

I consume her, my body crushing her against the

car as I cup her jaw and take as much as she's willing to give me. Fuck, I'm a starved man.

My cock strains against my pants, begging to feel her, if only once more.

She pulls away momentarily, and her rejection causes a cold sweat to run over me, because right now I want to beg her for a second chance. I've never been hopeful. Everything I've done has always been calculated, but for the first time in my life, I'm willing to selfishly get my hopes up, to try to imagine a life where she's in it instead of shunning me.

"Maybe I'm not a sane woman. It doesn't make sense to me either, but I know I want to be with you, Lorenzo. But you have to promise me—" Her voice breaks. "I can't step into this if you plan to cage me and treat me like some gentle thing. Just in the same way, I won't pretend like you're a man who doesn't have blood on his hands."

She stares at me, begging, and I see her. All of her. The unsaid words and the way they make me feel like I've failed her. Did she think I was just like her father? A man with no control over his violent tendencies? To some degree, that might be true, but if she says she's willing to accept that part of me, then can't I change my ideal for her even a fraction?

"I don't want you to get hurt." That's the truth. But I also selfishly want her. "Tomorrow, you do everything I say. That's not up for discussion."

She lets out a shaky breath as any type of control

we might've had snaps, and she jumps into my waiting arms, her legs immediately wrapping around my hips. I kiss her, milking the little moans that escape her, and devour every fucking one. I never want to lose her trust again.

For her, I need to become a better man. I don't know how much I can grow, but I'm willing to dedicate my life to making myself worthy of her. To make sure she's protected. To make sure she's happy. To always ensure that she's mine.

42

LILY

We don't even make it to the bedroom. He props me against the kitchen counter as I undo his belt and zipper, and he's pushing my dress over my hips. How I've missed his touch, and the desperation shows as I bite and tug at his lip.

I've missed him more than words can express, even when I tried to deny my feelings and depend on logic. A man like Lorenzo Moretti should not be the man of my dreams, but I've never experienced a connection— more like an obsession—that's felt so right and fueled me to be better in unconventional ways.

"Fuck, I need a condom," Lorenzo hisses, but I grab his cock and line him up with my throbbing pussy. It's begging for him to break me in two.

"I'm on birth control," I pant, desperately trying to

push myself down on his cock. *Fuck, I forgot how big he is.*

He grabs my hips, impaling me. I cry out, my nails running down his back as I adjust to his size, but he's unrelenting as he pounds into me like a madman. My back grinds against the kitchen counter. Something smashes, but neither of us looks toward it. I cling to him, something inside of me coming to its finality.

I love Lorenzo.

Deeply.

Madly.

Even when it doesn't make sense, I still want to make him mine.

He continues thrusting into me, and I lift my legs higher for a better angle, until he flips me over, my toes barely touching the floor, and then he's fucking me from behind. His hand threads through my hair and yanks, jarring my neck, and I thrive off of it.

"You've driven me absolutely fucking insane these past few months," he growls, slamming his frustration into me. I meet his pace, letting all the anger, pain, and frustration out on his cock.

"Yeah, well, you're kind of an asshole," I bite back through panting breaths.

His lips find the nape of my neck. His other hand wraps around the front of my throat, and a comforting warmth trickles through me as he slowly squeezes.

Home.

Safe.

A security I've been praying for, for as long as I can remember.

It doesn't make sense that it comes in the shape of a man cutting off my air supply, but I also know he's the only one who will give me his last breath in exchange.

A life and promise he can live up to.

"You're so fucking perfect," he praises, and that warmth continues to trickle as I wrap my hand around the back of his neck and pull him back to kiss my neck.

"You talk too much," I berate with a smile, knowing that he'll punish me for it.

It's twisted, endearing, and palpable.

But this is the love my body screams for.

Being dominated as long as he promises that outside the bedroom, I'm his equal in every way.

He increases the pressure of his grip on my throat, and my legs begin to tremble as a quick burst of fear passes through me. I'm held in place, forced to take his enormity, and I hang on his permission for my next breath. Hopefully, not until I come.

The climb begins, ripping out of me in sharp tugs. The moment he jerks into me, I scream out his name as he releases his grip around my throat, and I follow on a wave of pure bliss that breaks me into a million pieces—always disrupting my world and ruining anything that ever made sense.

Reforming into the hands of the man I can't be without.

He slowly rocks back and forth as he kisses down

my nape and wraps an arm around my stomach to pull me farther into him, possessively. I focus on his every breath, a slow settling of ease running through me, that I'm covered in all of his overbearing presence. And for the first time in a long time, I'm at peace.

Feeling that I'm exactly where I'm meant to be.

His.

Home.

Safe.

43

LORENZO

It's painstakingly obvious how in over their heads
Nicholas Wayne and his group are as they pull
up in their cars.

They're stupid enough to bring almost the entirety
of their numbers.

Nicholas himself is here, which makes the head
easy to remove.

They even agreed on our location.

"Fucking idiots," I mumble under my breath as I
stand at the side of my car, waiting for them to step out
of their parked vehicles. I'm surrounded by the
hounds, identities concealed by their helmets as they
wait patiently on their motorcycles as instructed. We
know better than to underestimate any type of enemy,
but I know a group of idiots when I see one.

I look over my shoulder, and although I can't see

her, I know Lily is sitting inside the car, watching. I don't like having her here. It puts me on edge. But if agreeing to this offered me an opportunity to be with her, then I was done with denying myself.

I'm already a miserable asshole, but even I was getting sick of my own mopey ass. I can't stay away. Even if I was convincing myself it was just because of a job. Leaving her side... The thought still feels unimaginable.

"Well, well, no one is more shocked about how we got in this situation than me," Nicholas says as he steps out of the car. I know it's Nicholas because we've already created a profile for him. He's new to the game. Arrogant and naive. "I assumed Luca Armani would be here to handle his affairs himself."

I make a point to hold up the bag of money. "My boss doesn't do delivery jobs."

The man chuckles, clearly amused. "I'd be offended, but we outnumber you."

I arch an eyebrow. Wow, this guy really is an idiot. "I don't take kindly to threats. Do you want your money or not? With this, you cease any communication or business with the Taylor family, including attempting to kill the heiress, Lily Taylor. And let me make this very clear. You are not to step on Armani territory again. There will be immediate retaliation."

The man sucks in a breath and sarcastically wiggles his fingers, as if spooked. "Considering you killed three of my men already, I think it's fair to say we don't play nice."

An understatement.

I walk forward, dependent on the hounds covering my back. If Wayne decides this is going to be a shoot-out, then I'm the first target. If that's to happen, I've notified the driver to immediately drive off with Lily. My only comfort is knowing that the car is bulletproof.

His second, a bulky guy who clearly enjoys the weights, matches my steps. When we come face-to-face, he holds out his hand expectantly, and I drop the bag between us. *Fucker.* He smirks as he bends over and picks it up, unzipping and checking the contents.

"Are we good?" I ask rhetorically, because we are anything but.

"This looks about right." He nods his head. I wonder if the fucker has ever seen this much cash in his life. He certainly seems surprised by its weight as he walks back toward his boss.

I retrace my steps, coming to stand beside the car again, arms folded over my chest.

Nicholas peers into the bag, a smile stretching his face. "Tell your boss it's a pleasure doing business with him. It's a nice story to have in the back pocket, you know?"

"What story is that?" I'm not someone who cares much for elaboration, because I don't give a flying fuck what he thinks. But I do use it as an excuse to fill in time as I count in my head.

"That the Armanis are so accommodating to hand over cash."

"If you want facts in your story, then know not one dime of that is from the Armanis; it's mine. Let's just say I have a personal gripe against those involved with trying to hurt my woman."

Nicholas's eyebrows furrow. "Well—"

BOOM!

An explosion of beautiful orange erupts, and I fight my natural instinct to look away from the scorching heat as fierce flames devour the five cars. Men scream, and shrapnel scatters into the wind. Beads of sweat break out immediately on my forehead as I watch with satisfaction as the cockroaches are exterminated. The flames flicker off the hounds' visors as we watch in spectacular delight as one problem comes to an end.

No man gets away with threatening Luca Armani or the things he cares about.

And certainly no man is going to live to tell the tale of ever attempting to harm *my* woman.

The back door of the car opens, and I step back, not giving enough space for Lily to open it enough to get out. I said she could come, but I'm not a fucking saint.

"What the fuck, Lorenzo?" she says, shocked.

A wicked smile stretches my lips. "You've become quite adept at cursing lately."

"Was that real cash?"

I shrug. "Money is only a tool. It's irrelevant when

compared to keeping you safe, my love." I look down at her, those beautiful blue eyes streaking with colors from the flames. "Are you scared of me? Because this, I very much enjoy doing."

"Handing out punishments?" She rolls her eyes. "Not so much of a surprise."

My smile widens, and I can tell she's trying not to smile herself as she still pretends to be mad. "I just hope you didn't miscount."

"No one else is coming for you, my love."

"So, I'm only stuck managing you now, huh? Maybe I drew the short stick." She finally smiles, and it's as brilliant as it is devastating.

I scowl at the hounds—shitty if any of them saw how beautiful her smile is. "Clean this up. I'll report to Luca."

"Yes, sir," the hounds reply in unison as I slip into the back of the car. The moment I close the door, I scoop Lily into my arms and place her on my lap.

"For someone who isn't very romantic, you sure do enjoy grand gestures." Lily pokes at my chest. "Will you always be surprising me like this?"

"I hope so," I admit, because I believe I'm the furthest thing from surprising; rather, I've always been routine-driven. Predictable. However, with Lily, it's all new, uncomfortable territory.

The moment she offered to give me a second chance, I decided on two things. One, I'd do anything to make her happy. Two, she was and will always be *mine*.

No room for negotiation or doubt. I'd bruise, brand, and mark her in every way, including a more traditional route.

I fish through my pocket until my fingers brush against the smooth metal.

I bring her hand to my lips and kiss her knuckles gently. Her expression softens as she watches me, but the moment I begin to slide the ring on her finger, she stiffens, and her hand yanks back.

"What the fuck are you doing?"

I stare at her, bewildered, as the driver starts the car and pulls away. "Isn't it obvious? You'll be my wife."

"Wh-what? Wait. What? No, Lorenzo. No, we need more time. You didn't even propose," she says, stumbling over her words, and I can't help but smile, still acutely aware that although my beautiful woman has grown so much, there's still that shy, flustered part of her deep within. A side of her I'll only allow myself to see. I'll gouge any fucker's eyes out if they even catch a glimpse.

"I didn't see it as a question, so why would I propose it?"

Her eyes bulge. "You can't just shove a ring on it, Lorenzo. This needs careful thought, planning, and agreement. What if we get sick of each other? What if I don't want marriage?"

My eyebrows drop. The busy questions that

explode her mind are overwhelming even to me, when I thought all of this was quite simple.

"I want all of those things. I want you in every way. As a wife. Mother of my children, if children are what you want. Hell, I'll even deliver the flowers from your shop to your customers. Do you *not* want these things?" I thought Lily would, in many ways, be a woman who wanted a traditional lifestyle, and I'm willing to make it happen as best as I can in every way.

She stares at me, dumbfounded.

"It's rather simple, Lily. The moment you decided to choose me was your agreement. There is no getting out of us unless it ends with me in the ground. And let me assure you, even if you attempt to move on to another man, I'll haunt that motherfucker from my grave."

Her mouth is still gaping. "You can't be this intense all the time," she says, staring at the ring. "When did you even get that? I was literally with you all night."

"It's my mother's."

Her hand goes to her heart. "Lorenzo. This is important."

"*You* are important."

She lets out a shaky breath. "I want to say yes, but there's still so much we need to figure out, and—"

I slowly fold my fingers in with hers. "You have a beautiful, busy mind, my love. But I'm in this. I'm not letting you go. So, whether you decide to wear this ring now or later, it doesn't change our future in the slightest."

She still stares at me, disbelieving. "You're telling me if I refuse to wear this now, you're okay with that?"

"No."

"Lorenzo, you're being unreasonable," she says, shaking her head, but when she looks at me, the corner of her mouth tics. "Don't stare at me with those puppy-dog eyes. How about I wear it on a necklace? I'm not saying yes or no right now. I just—we need time."

I frown. It really is as simple as yes or no. Not that no is an option.

Her hands cup either side of my face. "Lorenzo, we have all the time in the world now. You don't need to rush this. I'm already yours."

Something in my chest shifts, and I know I've lost this battle for now.

I know without a doubt Lily Taylor will be my wife.

She'll be my obsession until I die.

But if she wants to play this game until I drag her down the aisle myself, then so be it.

"Do you promise to deliver flowers from my shop in Italy?" she asks.

My eyebrows furrow. "You want to come to Italy with me?"

She casually shrugs. "I think it's time we both have a fresh start." Her lips brush against mine, and that soft, gentle kiss of hers spreads a peace and contentment through me that I've become entirely addicted to.

I want to pull her back and question her decision, but I've learned to stop doing that. Once she's made her mind up about something, she no longer wavers on it or asks for others' opinions.

Home.

Lily Taylor tastes, smells, and feels like *home.*

44

LORENZO

Luca sits behind his desk, watching me carefully.

A few days ago, I planned on giving him a different answer.

To tell him I couldn't leave Manhattan, all for a woman who didn't even want to talk to me at the time. Now, having her in my bed, in my house, fills me with male pride. But that doesn't mean the business stops.

In fact, Lily choosing to come with me, to have a fresh start herself, has in every aspect been favorable for me, because denying Luca and his demands is unheard of.

"And Lily will go with you?" He frowns. "I'm not sure if my wife will be pleased by this."

"Lily advised me Ara had wished her luck and said, and I quote 'if you're happy, then I'm happy,'" I reply.

Luca squints at me, as if I've grown a second head.

"I never understood that saying. The only thing that makes Ara happy is me."

"Of course, sir," I agree, knowing better than to not.

Luca stands and takes two glasses from the cart beside his wooden desk. "It'll be different not having you around here," he says as he pours two glasses and offers me one. "But you're the only one I trust enough to conduct business on my behalf." He raises his glass, and I tap mine against his.

"It has been my honor serving you, and I look forward to bringing you immeasurable profit. Though I can't deny that I have my doubts as to how things will be run here without me."

Luca kicks up a devilish smirk, then takes a sip. I don't like that smile at all, but I follow his action, taking a mouthful of the smooth whiskey.

"About that. I found your replacement; someone who is competent and has a thirst for blood."

My eyebrows furrow. "I thought you wanted someone to stick to the shadows while doing your work."

He shrugs. "I appreciate a sharp mind and profitable advice. Though he's younger and still needs to be trained. So, until he's ready, Tony will take your place."

"And who is this replacement?" I ask, a sickening taste follows the victory swallow.

"He's standing behind you," Luca says with a wicked grin.

I slowly look over my shoulder, having not heard or felt anyone creep up, and every fiber of my being freezes.

"No."

"It's been a while, big brother," Dante says with his hands casually stuffed in his pockets, an arrogant, virulent smile spreading across his lips.

"Over my dead body," I bite as I storm toward him.

"I'm sure that can be arranged," he says rather smugly.

"No, you promised me you'd finish your schooling to be a surgeon." I tower over him.

"He's advised he needed to take a permanent break," Luca says from behind. "I didn't take you for the coddling type, Lorenzo."

I pin him with a glare. Because, despite my loyalty to Luca, he knows that it was born out of loyalty for my younger brother and the desire to offer him a better future. "I promised to bloody my hands, knowing it would fund yours to be better, to do better. To save lives instead of take them. You promised me you'd take this seriously."

Dante raises a brow. "I have. I'm at the top of my class, and I already have offers from some of the top hospitals. What can I say? I'm an opportunist like my big brother, and I like to see who the highest bidder is."

"Out of the question."

My brother takes another step forward, coming to my side as he clasps his hand on my shoulder.

"You never asked what I wanted. You just charged on with your life instead, thinking you painted the perfect one for me. But you and I aren't so different, Lorenzo. I've had quite a few years to work up the appetite of wanting to shed some blood. Finally, I can do it while being paid."

I grab his forearm, no longer caring if I might offend Luca. "I forbid you."

Dante smiles, but it doesn't reach his eyes. Much like it hasn't since our childhood, but this man is far from the boy I left in Italy to pursue his new life and studies. He yanks his arm out of my grip, surprising me with his strength.

"Congratulations on the promotion, brother. I heard you're also loved up. I hope she's a sweet little thing."

My gaze narrows on him, and every hackle in my body rises as I turn and size him up. "Stay away from Lily."

He laughs then, actually wiping a tear from his eye. "I have no interest in your affairs, brother. I simply wish you the best. Now, if you'll excuse me, I think this is a job interview."

I turn back to Luca, who isn't interested in our strangled family dynamics. I know better than to confront Luca head-on, because he does what he wants, when he wants, and years of loyalty don't simply cease.

"The Morettis were raised to serve the Armanis,"

Luca states matter-of-factly, then looks up from his desk. "That did not stop at you, Lorenzo. If your brother willingly chooses to be here, then so be it."

My jaw tics. I know full well Luca would've been the one to put all of this into motion. But I also know him better than anyone else. He's sharp, and besides the incident when he was courting his wife, his instincts have never failed him.

"You may leave us now," Luca says, and my brother looks over his shoulder once more, giving me a small wave with a shit-eating grin.

Fuck.

It's an honor conducting all of Luca's business in Italy, replacing his former second and advisor. But acid churns in my stomach, not at all agreeable with this change.

Because my brother is the devil in disguise.

And placing a wild card like him beside Luca might certainly set Manhattan alight.

45

LILY

Music echoes throughout Lorenzo's house, and I'm not sure if it was a bright idea putting Sky in charge of it. In fact, I don't recall him being invited, let alone being given that task. The way Lorenzo's left eye is twitching, I'm assuming not.

"Are you ready for the big move?" Sienna asks with a bright smile. Her fiancé, Michael, stands beside her. It's the first time I've seen him since the engagement party, as he's been so busy pursuing gigs in his acting career.

I can't help but notice the tension between them. The way Sienna is acting, though, it would appear all is fine and well, but his body language is saying he would rather be anywhere but here.

"I'm so proud of you," she says, grabbing my arm

and squeezing it. "I'll have to visit once you're all settled in."

"I'd love that." I smile and look back up at Lorenzo, who hasn't taken his eyes off me, except when any male comes into my vicinity.

I have a feeling this overbearingness isn't going to stop, even when he's no longer tasked as my body-guard. In truth, not much has changed in that at all. If anything, he's even more demanding now. Then we argue. Then we make up. I really enjoy the making-up part. Surprisingly, none of it is exhausting. If anything, the brattier I become, the greater the punishment.

A warmth floods my core with tiny flutters as I question how easy it would be to sneak out of our own going-away party. The only reason he agreed to it was because I batted my eyelashes a little longer than usual.

"To think I wasn't invited to my own brother's going-away party," a man announces from behind us. We turn in his direction, and I can immediately see the resemblance. I look up at Lorenzo and know it's the truth because an obvious loathing stirs within his gaze.

That's not good.

"I don't recall sending you an invitation," Lorenzo grits.

"Since when were you so cold toward me, brother?" he says with a smile that doesn't reach his eyes. Imme-diately, I know that these two are very different. Where Lorenzo is cold and indifferent, his brother holds a natural charisma and warmth. But there's something off about it.

My hand goes straight to the ring that hangs on the necklace by my throat, and his brother's gaze dips to it. His expression doesn't change, but an immediate chill runs over me.

Maybe months ago, I might've hidden behind Lorenzo, but I realize as much as I'm dependent on his strength, he can learn to depend on mine as well.

"It's lovely to meet you. I'm Lily Taylor," I say, stepping forward and welcoming him with open arms.

"So, you're the soon-to-be sister-in-law. It's lovely to put a face to the name," he replies, opening his arms. A guttural sound escapes Lorenzo, who still stands behind me, and he pulls me into his chest before any kind of hugging can be conducted.

I try not to roll my eyes, all too used to his overbearing ways and still continuing to ignore them.

Dante looks around the place with appreciation. "It's a nice place here. Maybe I should manage it for you while you're gone."

"You're not staying here," Lorenzo growls.

Tension crackles through the air, and I grab Ara's attention from across the room, pleading for her to save us from whatever the fuck is going down right now. I don't know what the issue is between these brothers, but maybe if Luca stands on the edges of their invisible arena, they might not be so tempted to beat the shit out of one another.

"Maybe he could stay with Romi," Sienna suggests, breaking the silence. Lorenzo and I turn in unison to face her. "I mean, having someone in the apartment with her might be a good thing since she hardly leaves it. I mean, it can't hurt to try, right? I'm worried about her," she confesses quietly.

"That's not a good idea," Lorenzo says flatly.

Dante strokes his chin thoughtfully. "Is this Romi chick hot?"

"No," Lorenzo says, and Sienna takes a sharp inhale. His eyebrows dip before he quickly says. "No, not as in she's not attractive, as in, he's not staying there."

"So, you find her attractive?" I can't help but poke.

"What? No. You're the only woman—" I start laughing, unable to keep a straight face. He grabs the bridge of his nose. "You need to stop teasing me like that." He leans in and whispers into my ear, "I will make you black and blue tonight for that."

A slow trickle of warmth floods my core, and suddenly the room feels hot.

"Damn, woman, watch where you're going," Dante curses as Romi barges past him with a bottle of vodka in her hands.

"Watch it, asshole." She brings the bottle to her lips. Her short black hair looks messy. Her usual vibrant red was cut and dyed since she had matted it with black paint. She ignores us, walking by as if we don't even exist, and my heart crumbles.

Sienna is quick to say, "Sorry about her. She's recently had a loss. I'm going to go check on her." Sienna looks to her fiancé, who nods agreeably and takes a step back.

"I'll go after her," Dante says. "Maybe a conversation with a stranger might help. By the looks of it, whoever that is, you're helicoptering her like crazy, and she wants nothing to do with you, unless you're waiting at the bottom of that bottle of vodka."

"Ouch," Sienna replies, as if she's been burned.

"Am I wrong? Did she want to be here?" he asks, then follows after Romi through the back door toward the dock.

That all-too-familiar guilt floods me. Although I've become better at prioritizing my own needs, Romi is one of few I can give to endlessly because I know she'd do the same for me.

"Are you sure it's okay that I leave?" I ask Sienna. My timing to move overseas couldn't be any worse.

"Of course it is," Sienna assures me, and loops her elbow around Michael's, whose smile seems forced.

They're definitely not okay.

"You have to live your life, Lily. I'm glad you're doing this for you, but you have to look after her." She points at Lorenzo.

"With my life," he swears.

She laughs. "You're always so serious."

If only she knew. I notice her glass is empty, and I offer to take it.

"Let me grab you another one. I'm out as well," I say, grabbing it and taking way too much satisfaction in Lorenzo's helpless expression when I leave him. I walk into the kitchen, pull the bottle of bubbly from the fridge, and refill the two glasses.

I take the time to admire the water glinting in the moonlight and scan the area for Romi. I'm worried about leaving her here while she's—

I immediately divert my gaze the moment I see flesh on flesh near the shore.

Oh fuck. What the fuck?

That didn't take long at all. I bite my bottom lip. That's not good. If Lorenzo finds out his brother is hooking up with one of my friends, I'm certain he'll blow a gasket. Romi has always been the free-loving type. But, damn, did they sit down and decide just to start making out or what?

"Is everything okay?" Lorenzo asks over my shoulder.

"Everything's fine," I squeak with a tight smile, turning so fast I almost spill the two glasses.

I try my hardest to block his view because I know if he sees what's going on outside, it will only make whatever the situation is between him and his brother worse. And I don't want that for Lorenzo. From what I've gathered, his brother is his only family left, and I hope, over time, I can help him fix that relationship. Then again, I now know better than anyone that some families can't be fixed.

But I want to at least try for him, and will patiently wait for him to open up to me, starting with why his brother is even here in Manhattan when he last told me he was studying in London.

Besides all of that, I want this going-away party to go off without a hitch; a final hoorah with the people I love as they send us off for a new start, one we both deserve.

"Can you take this to Sienna?" I ask sweetly.

"Where will you be going?" He frowns, and I give him a slow smile as I stretch onto my tiptoes.

"I thought you promised me a certain punishment. Maybe we can meet in the bedroom, in say, two minutes," I say, nipping at his ear.

A guttural noise escapes him as he's quick to reply, "Make it one minute." He grabs the drinks out of my hand, and I can't help but laugh as I watch him leave the kitchen. I take a moment to admire those who have come to wish us good luck, and another piece of me feels relieved, ready to say goodbye to this city.

Ready to start my new life and a new chapter.

That niggling sense of guilt is still there, though. For leaving my mother to sell the house and find a new one. For my brother starting his rehabilitation to recover from gambling. For Romi in her mourning. And maybe for Sienna and her relationship.

With all of that, I choose to prioritize myself and Lorenzo.

I'm trying to hide the smile as he scans the room,

his gaze landing back on me with an impatient jerk of his head toward the bedroom.

I don't think I'll ever get sick of having this man jump when I tell him to, and to have him come running and asking, "How high?" To be in his arms every night and protected—no matter what comes our way.

Danger.

Pleasure.

Marriage.

I wouldn't want to stake this unruly obsession on anyone but Lorenzo Moretti.

THANK YOU FOR READING LORENZO AND LILY'S STORY, IF YOU LOVE IT I WOULD APPRECIATE IF YOU LEFT A REVIEW.

ALSO BY KIA CARRINGTON-RUSSELL

Insidious Obsession, Insidious Obsession Book 1

Fractured Obsession, Insidious Obsession Book 2

Unruly Obsession, Insidious Obsession Book 3

Carnal Obsession, Insidious Obsession Book 4

Captured Obsession, Insidious Obsession Book 5

Beautiful Things Obey, Beautiful Things Obey Book 1

Lethal Vows, Lethal Vows Book 1

Virtuous Vows, Lethal Vows Book 2

Cunning Vows, Lethal Vows Book 3

Deranged Vows, Lethal Vows Book 4

Misguided Vows, Lethal Vows Book 5

Vengeful Lies, Vengeful Lies Book 1

Promiscuous Lies, Vengeful Lies Book 2

Addicted Lies, Vengeful Lies Book 3

Conflicted Lies, Vengeful Lies Book 4

Mischievous Lies, Vengeful Lies Book 5

Mine for the Night, New York Nights Book 1

Us for the Night, New York Nights Book 2

Stranded for the Night, New York Nights 3

Token Huntress, Token Huntress Book 1

Token Vampire, Token Huntress Book 2

Token Wolf, Token Huntress Book 3

Token Phantom, Token Huntress Book 4

Token Darkness, Token Huntress Book 5

Token Kingdom, Token Huntress Book 6

The Shadow Minds Journal

ABOUT THE AUTHOR

Australian Author, Kia Carrington-Russell is known for her recognizable style of kick-butt heroines, enemies to lovers, fast paced action and romance that dances from light to dark. Including multiples genres such as Dark Romance, Contemporary Romance and Fantasy Romance. Obsessed with all things coffee, food and travel, Kia is always seeking out her next international adventure.

Now back in her home country of Australia, she takes her Cavoodle, Sia along morning walks on beautiful coastline beaches, building worlds in the sea breezes and contemplating which deliciously haunting story to write next.

Connect with me: kiacarrington-russell.com

www.ingramcontent.com/pod-product-compliance
Lightning Source LLC
Chambersburg PA
CBHW050958180726
48291CB00006B/1881